the angry millionaire

by Selwyn Jepson

POPULAR LIBRARY • NEW YORK

POPULAR LIBRARY EDITION

Copyright © 1968 by Selwyn Jepson

Library of Congress Catalog Card Number: 68-28231
Published by arrangement with Harper & Row, Publishers, Incorporated

A JOAN KAHN-HARPER NOVEL OF SUSPENSE

"IT'S BEAUTIFUL"

1

The girl with fat legs looked over his shoulder at the map. It was pinned on top of several others because this was the only solid wall amid the glass. She said, "Where's that, Mr. Addis?"

"Nuristan."

"You say it like a girl's name. . . . Mine's Marlene."

"Yes?"

"As if you cared."

He knew he was mean, the sort who wouldn't care enough to ask a girl her name unless her legs would bear looking at. He knew the name of the *other* girl, who brought his memoranda, papers, and so on from the main research division and sometimes collected the occasional fruits of his slow work on them, for Mr. Anderson's use—if inconceivably he could find one.

Perhaps, the trouble was less his cynicism, and of course the low state of his morale, than the brutal demand of these minimal skirts. They put such an onus on what they showed.

"Nuristan," she repeated; her voice was pleasant, musical, or—meanness again—the word itself would give any voice its chance.

"Yes."

"But that's India," she said, still staring at the big map.

"North India. Nuristan is part of Afghanistan, its eastern province."

"I thought your work was Africa."

So. But not his infatuation.

"A hundred mountains, valleys between so deep the sun never reaches them. Forests, rocks, rivers and more rocks, no roads, scarcely any people in five thousand square miles. You use mules, I suppose, or perhaps it's safer on foot."

"You don't know for sure?"

"Not till I get there."

"Don't say they're *sending* you all that way!"

"No."

"That's right, you're a desk man—a boffin, kind of. You

5

mean it's for your holidays?" she asked incredulously. "Just for two weeks?"

"No," he said again and dragged his dreaming eyes from the map. He kept them off Marlene's legs while he sat at the desk to give her the report he had spent half a month preparing. Its final sentence proclaimed its fatuity: *But these conclusions must be considered in the context of an imminent military coup, in the event of which the country's economic structure will automatically and immediately cease to be viable.*

Viable. One of the new words without which a present-day economist would find survival difficult. But the sense of the paragraph was honest enough. Somawi's democratic leaders had filled their bellies to bursting with the loot of foreign aid; the generals would take over as surely as the sun would rise. They'd done it with most of the others.

He shut his eyes while the girl with fat legs went away. He opened them for comfort and reassurance in the direction of the right-hand wall and the young woman visible through its floor-to-ceiling sheet of glass. There was nothing wrong with *her* legs, or indeed any part of her. Even her giant spectacles, so often a gimmick, were acceptable as part of her devastating effect on you. She would certainly rate as beautiful in most opinions, perhaps even in those of her own sex. To him, in his low state of morale, she was utterly ravishing.

And as inaccessible as Nuristan. In the eleven and a half weeks, nine o'clock to five-thirty, five days a week, he had spent in this neon-lit air-conditioned pit, this basement computer room under half a million tons of steel and concrete, she hadn't shown by so much as a lifted eyebrow corner that she knew he was there, dying of mental and spiritual suffocation within twelve feet of her.

"MISS V. NORTON" said the name plaque on the corner of her desk, a gray steel functional twin of the one they had chained him to, and that was about the limit of his knowledge of her as a person.

His idea of her job as chief computer programmer was vague, but she seemed wholly dedicated to it. He guessed she was about his own age, twenty-six or maybe a year older. She had a cool, impersonal voice, but since he had exchanged nothing in the way of conversation with her but six or seven "good mornings" spaced over nearly three months, he wasn't an authority on it—or her.

Naturally he was beginning to dislike her.

6

What, when you came to the point, *had* he asked of her? Just an occasional glance to meet his, perhaps the hint of a smile to let him know she didn't mind if he had made her the symbol of happiness and freedom he could no longer expect or even hope for? But as if—to quote Marlene—she cared. It was just as well. One push of that kind might have destroyed his shaky resolution, sent him running to the elevators and the great doors of Number One City Wall and out into the street and away, never to return.

The risk was remote that she might suddenly become aware of his existence, but to be on the safe side he turned his ill favor to the other equally unresponsive object with which he shared this tomb: the computer. It bulked hugely, five great steel cabinets in a semicircle around the control console, watched over in shifts by three anonymous men in white coats. From time to time V. Norton or one of her dull-faced assistants carried propitiatory offerings to it, in the form of punch cards coded for processing from the mass of material sent down by the various divisions and departments of Hammond and Morgan and its subsidiaries.

The monster sucked them into its maw, flashed its banks of circuit check lights in symmetrical patterns to indicate its infallibility, and at the same time rolled and squinted its tape reels in mock surprise at the problems its priestesses prayed it to solve.

Sometimes he sneered with it. What had gone so wrong with Hammond and Morgan, whose human brainwork had brought it successfully through the ups and downs of three hundred years of the world's financial history, that it now had to rely on electronics to do its thinking?

The hell with it, another bloody depressing day only half done. Masochistically he took another look at V. Norton— to think that he'd once cared to know what the "V" stood for.

She began to frown. He couldn't remember having seen this before. It made her, if slightly and briefly, human. Then, stranger still, she turned her head to return his glance as though at last, by way of her unconscious, his interest in her had gotten through. Because the frown stayed on her smooth forehead he thought this must be the reason for it. He felt silly. He averted his eyes and finished the paragraph he had begun on the subject of Tanzania's breath-taking decision to expand next year's grapefruit crop by eleven per cent.

He sensed rather than heard the opening of the glass door.

7

The store-dummy designer who had put V. Norton together must be the best in the business.

Standing a yard from him she still wasn't quite real. The hand she stretched out to him with a sheet of foolscap in its fingers was perhaps made of flesh and blood, but that didn't require it to be warm to the touch.

"These figures, Mr. Addis, one lines eight and nine in respect of Ghana's alfalfa output—"

"What's the matter with them?" He didn't mean to be irritable with her, cause though he imagined he had. "How did you get hold of this?"

"In the usual way," she said coldly. "It came down from research for inclusion in an interim scanning of African economic development in time for the investment committee to put before the Full Board meeting on Thursday next. Should it happen to ask for it."

It seemed nutty to send the fruits of his labor all the way up to the eighth floor in order to reach the next-door glass box, but that would be organization; like putting him down here on his own, eight floors plus two basements below the research division to which he was supposed to belong.

She was telling him sternly that if he wanted to know what was wrong with the figures he would notice that those relative to the year sixty-five appeared to be identical with those of sixty-six, to three places of decimals.

"We reject the coincidence, Mr. Addis, as being twelve million to one against its occurrence."

"We," a married couple or lovers, she and her computer.

"Thank you," he said, "I'll check the figures."

If only, like anyone else, she'd simply pointed out that in carelessness and inattention he'd put down the same figure for both years, he might have uttered a cry of happy relief in finding she was like anyone else. He didn't know what had triggered the impulse to ask her to have lunch with him. It may have been a sudden last upsurge of hope for that symbol.

"Lunch with you?" There was no surprise, and no emphasis that he could detect on the "you." She peered at him, perhaps tempted to put on her spectacles.

"Well, I don't know how you feel about this but we're buried down here, buried alive together . . ."

John's speech tailed off into a mutter as a coldness enveloped him as of the north face of a high mountain in winter.

8

Myopic violet-blue eyes examined him with the analytical stare of a lepidopterist engaged with a moth on a pin.

"I don't expect, Mr. Addis, that you took a job with a Merchant Banker"—she used noticeable capitals—"by accident. Which means that money is important to you. So you mustn't, on impulse, spend it unproductively."

A new way of being told there was nothing doing. He couldn't explain to an icicle about his need to get closer to a hopeless sign of better things to come. But however little he cared for being lectured for his own good he shouldn't discourage her. After all, he only wanted to be near her, not to listen to her.

"Oh, come on now," he said, "just this once."

"I'd expect an economist," she said, "to know that pennies saved are pennies made."

"Good lord, of course I do."

"Or you wouldn't have done the right thing, going where the money is."

"Hammond and Morgan, you mean? Is that why *you* are here? Where the money is?"

She began to recite the glories of Hammond and Morgan rather in the manner of a litany, ending with "It's the third largest Merchant Bank in the world with a turnover of never less than an average million and a half a day. A *day*, Mr. Addis!"

So this icicle was more like an iceberg, with the usual nine-tenths of her invisible in the deeps. Fascinating. He told her he hadn't realized it was such an amount of money, and she said, "Think—if only a tiny half of one per cent sticks to their fingers as it passes through!"

"It's good of you to worry about my finances, but I still don't see how the cost of a lunch would start me off on the road to ruin."

"It isn't only that—" She paused. He didn't finish it for her. She hadn't refused only because he was homely and undersized, but his lowly significance in her scale of values would make time spent with him a waste of it. She'd lunch with a one-legged baboon if the animal looked as if he might take her near a handful of the stuff of her dreams.

Which stuff, he now tentatively suggested to her, was chiefly made in the executive suite. "That's where you should be, not down here in this hole in the ground. But it's a long way up, I suppose. Twenty stories or so."

"There's a fast elevator." She wasn't smiling. "You watch me—if you're still around."

"I'll stick it out somehow."

"But will Hammond and Morgan?"

This aspect of his dilemma hadn't crossed his mind.

"If you'll forgive me saying so," she went on, "I don't think your attitude is one they'll put up with for long."

He shook his head, but he was surprised that she had been as aware of him as this.

"I'm sure my secret is safe with you."

"I don't think it's much of one," she said.

As she turned to leave, his intercom buzzed. He moved the switch and a female voice announced that the director of personnel would like to see Mr. Addis, please, at three-thirty this afternoon.

V. Norton's expression was objective but held a hint of "I told you so."

"You could be right," he said.

"I know the system."

"And the director of personnel?"

She nodded and said a shade too quickly, "I process personnel data from time to time."

He also knew the personnel director; he had seen, or rather been seen by, him once, and wouldn't put it past him to set someone like V. Norton to keeping an eye on a new boy. There was a lot of the schoolmistress about her. Pay attention, Addis, or take a hundred lines!

"He's on the tenth floor," he remarked. "On the way up." He regretted it, a cheap crack. Why be unpleasant to her? None of this was her fault. Even her icebound soul would have come to her by inheritance from some snow-maiden ancestress.

She lingered at the door for a moment, looking at him with baffling intentness. Sorrow or sadism? Take your choice, said the eyes like mountain pools, and be no wiser about me. If, as she believed, he was for the high jump, please God she was right, it was idle to begin thinking now that entombment with her might after all turn out to be quite stimulating in an off-beat kind of way. Was she at last seeing something in him she hadn't expected, as though in spite of the pin the insect still had a wriggle in it?

She startled him by seeming to bear out this theory, saying, "But I'd like to have a drink with you this evening, if you're free."

10

"I shall be nothing else but for a long time, if the personnel director means what you think he means."

"You'll find another job. Not in an office, perhaps. You aren't the type."

It foxed him again how she managed to observe him so accurately without seeming to, and he almost forgot to show pleasure and gratitude about the drinks this evening. He suggested the Old City Bar, which was near the office but not too near. She said yes, that would do nicely, and came back to his desk. She took an indent slip (Form R/321—Files Only) from the stationery rack in front of his blotter.

"I'd almost forgotten," she said. "If you'd be good enough —You're in the research division and registry will treat it as urgent—quicker than if I ask for them." She filled in the indent form with three longish file numbers and turned it toward him to sign. He didn't really need her dazzling, persuasive smile but it was nice to know she could rise to one if only when she wanted something.

He signed "J. Addis (Research Division. Room S-B/A5)," a little puzzled that as chief programmer in the computer department she couldn't ask registry for what she needed without risk of delay in getting it.

She put the indent form in his out tray. If she was in such a hurry for the material why didn't she send it to registry by hand? She had two or three assistants and a typist. Perhaps she was trying to make him feel he wasn't all that useless?

No. He didn't think it was like that.

Another smile for him, perhaps not quite such a knee-shaker, and she returned to her side of the partition where she became absorbed again in programming the wide accountancy sheets that had occupied her attention for the last few days. She was like a child eating a cream cake, fragment by careful fragment to prolong the pleasure. Now and again he had thought he caught sight of a glow in her, secretly burning in the glacial depths. But without a fire's heat, of course.

He checked the carbon of the West African development report and wasn't altogether surprised to find that the sixty-five and sixty-six figures for Ghanaian alfalfa production differed by 4.32 hundred tons.

Beautiful girl, but strange.

11

2

The directorate of peronnel on the tenth floor consisted of the director, his p.a., a deputy director, three personnel officers, four secretaries and a boy.

The director himself could be imagined as crouching in the center of a web from which strands reached out to the nooks and crannies of Number One City Wall, holding and controlling its human components by the power of authority to hire and fire.

But the analogy fell down when you looked at the web's present incumbent. Boyle Glover's arms and legs were as unlike a spider's as you could imagine, being short and plump, and judging by the smooth, shiny skin of his hands, quite hairless; also he exercised his power less with poisoned fangs and silk-spinning tentacles than with the stifling verbiage of quasi-scientific psychology.

He also knew how to soften you up for it with eroding suspense.

His p.a. was a superior maiden in her forties with an acid voice.

"Ah, yes. You're John Addis, for three-thirty. The director will see you in a moment. Take a seat in the waiting room, please."

It was a small room with hard lighting and harder chairs, where you were put to reflect on your inadequacies for the job to which it had pleased great Hammond and Morgan to call you.

However, John's own inadequacies weren't bothering him at the moment and he was able to put his feet up on another chair and slip off into a light doze. This was fortunate, because the moment of waiting became fifty minutes.

The director's office was large, yellowish and windowless but lit with soft daylight neon, its walls hung with charts, penny-plain and twopence colored, and many graphs of assorted kinds.

The director's desk was a huge bare slab of oiled teak that had a companion piece in mid-room, where the apparatus of

12

the Aptitude Tests was set out. There were several easy chairs in black leather, and upright ones at the table. A similar chair was placed, for occasions of this sort, facing the desk squarely but at a respectful distance, so that you should not feel embarrassed by near contact with the arbiter of your fate, and Boyle Glover would at the same time have you in sight. But there were no straps to hold you on it, and in theory there was nothing to stop you from getting up and running like hell for the elevators, the street and freedom, etcetera. . . .

John sat down and said, "Good afternoon, sir."

Mr. Glover did not have to consult his charts to know what he needed to know about Unit S-B/A5/R. In any case, the relevant file open before him contained only three sheets of paper, and thirty seconds would have been long enough to put himself in the picture.

"Ah, yes. John Addis. . . . Now, John, I know you're not afraid to face facts any more than I'm a man to beat about the bush. Also we don't have to remind ourselves of our wise precaution set out in the final paragraph of our Provisional Agreement, the safeguard by which we do not become too deeply committed to one another before it is too late— Please, my dear boy, let me finish—"

"I wasn't going to say anything."

Mr. Glover was too skilled to blink; usually at this point they began to protest, and the File clearly showed Addis, J.'s inclination to be "self-assertive," and his "individualism" also was clearly indicated by the Tests.

However . . .

"So I welcome"—Mr. Glover got going again—"this face-to-face opportunity for you to voice, to voice fearlessly I hope, any criticism you may have of the company's part in this unhappy—"

"I'm sorry if Mr. Anderson doesn't think I'm suitable."

"The chief executive in charge of the research division may or may not have views on such work as a provisional employee may have submitted during probation, but only this directorate can make the decision for permanent engagement. This is done on assessment of the Adaptability and Integration coefficients as observed during the three-month probationary period."

"Ah!" said John, thinking of V. Norton.

"I beg your pardon?"

He shook his head and watched Mr. Glover bring his little hands together with a slap that finally trapped the fly. "I'm

13

sorry, John, very sorry. From now on you may of course use office time for the rest of the week to find other employment."

"Thank you, sir. Can I ask a couple of questions?"

"As many as you like!" Mr. Glover could relax. No sign of that aggressiveness, thank goodness.

"I get a reference to help me find another job?"

Mr. Glover became less noticeably avuncular. He pointed out that a reference based on less than three months *here* wouldn't mean much to a prospective employer, even if it leaned over backward in skating around the facts. Mr. Glover could mix his metaphors with the best of them. "Thank you, Addis, that will be all."

But Addis sat on, remarking conversationally that they were right who said that to get and keep a good job wasn't easy without influence.

Nepotism, Mr. Glover retorted coldly, was impossible in Hammond and Morgan. Only applications resulting from press advertisement of staff vacancies were considered. "Such as yours, Addis. I can assure you that a recommendation from the chairman himself would have availed you nothing."

"You're not a betting man, sir?"

Mr. Glover managed to subdue an uprush of unseemly anger but had to limit himself to a single, sharp "Good afternoon, Addis."

Mr. Glover watched the broad back disappear behind the closing door with considerable relief. His choler subsided gradually, leaving a residue of uneasiness that he couldn't put his finger on. Young whippersnapper! Why hadn't the Aggressive Potential shown itself? He studied the test sheets again. The answer could be in the high figure for Social Manipulation, which would of course lead to catalytic involvement with people and situations. Personality control, always to be read as a contradiction to Aggressives, was also well marked. In which case such a high degree of Withdrawal (through Fantasy) predicated a psychosis verging on the schizoid. But the Analysis offered no suggestion remotely like it, and he had to admit that something was out of whack here.

Damn the fellow! He'd acted as though he was trying to manipulate *him*.

He shut the file and with a red-ink pen drew two parallel lines diagonally across the cover from corner to corner and

14

felt better. To complete his recovery he dialed a number on the house phone.

The sound of her cool voice gave him a boost. She listened to his thanks for a valuable piece of observation. "He would have been quite wrong for us," he told her.

She said she was glad to have helped. "I'm grateful to you for giving me the opportunity. I find personnel work very interesting. I was quite entranced by the picture of it you gave me at lunch the other day."

How easy, then, to invite her to dine with him. She said she would enjoy that very much.

"Why not tonight, then?"

Not tonight. He got another boost from her pretense of being slightly hard to get. But tomorrow, she said, would suit her and she had always wanted to be taken to Angelino's, if she was wasn't being bold and extravagant? He would meet her at Angelino's at eight tomorrow, Thursday.

He put down the receiver and wiped the palms of his hands on his rounded, dark-blue thighs. What should he sweat about? None of his fellow board members was likely to take himself or be taken to Angelino's, and of those the chairman was the only one who really mattered. But H.H. would never allow his public image to rub shoulders with those twenty-four life-sized nude angels molded in such sophisticated positions and high relief, half a dozen to each wall of the main dining room

He unlocked a drawer in his desk where he had been keeping her personnel file, took it out, and after looking at her photograph for a long, yearning moment, turned to her Psychiatric Assessment sheet. . . . Emotional Stability at eighty-four over a hundred was indeed satisfactory employer-wise, but perhaps less so in the romantic field. On the other hand, Ambition Potential was almost as highly marked, suggesting that her emotions might become less stable in the context of a Hammond and Morgan director—albeit nonvoting —than in the case of other men such as a mere computer programmer would normally meet up with.

Which reminded him that their conversation at Angelino's mustn't be allowed to bog down, as it had at that luncheon, in talk about his fellows on the board. She seemed fascinated by company directors the way other girls went gooey-eyed over football players. What, for instance, had Gordon Parthessen got that he hadn't? Control of a few voting shares and chairmanship of the investment advisory committee didn't make him all that superior. If she wanted market tips he was fully able to give her some himself. And other kinds. He was all the company director she needed.

His palms were sticky again.

Coincidentally her Ambition Potential was under discussion again within an hour or so. But this time it was between herself and John Addis, whose job she had helped to lose for him.

She sipped a martini—"as dry as possible please," and what more suitable?—while he had settled for an Amontillado sherry. He had always seen her wearing an aseptic white overall thing, and this green-blue (or blue-green) frock was a nice change. Although it didn't suggest that the flesh it covered was warm, it revealed the fine shape of her breasts and more of her creamy throat and arms than did the overall. In spite of a tendency to shiver when he looked at her, he kept coming back to the fact that she really was beautiful, with much of Renaissance portraiture about her. But not all of it. Unlike their women, V. Norton was neither sensual nor innocent; merely ambitious, as she was saying herself: "I can't remember when I didn't want things I couldn't have. Or how early I found out the only way to get them—how anybody ever does—is with money."

She raised her flawless face and gazed with cold demand into a diamond-studded fairyland waiting for her somewhere beyond the opposite wall of the bar.

He wished he had ordered himself whisky to keep out the winter wind.

"Admitting," he said, "that the world is full of pretty girls with everything it takes, you still shouldn't have any competition."

She accepted the compliment, and unflinchingly the accusation also that she would rely on her looks to make her rich.

"The trouble is," he said persuasively, "there are so few millionaires and how many of them are single? And do those marry except for more money to strengthen their fortifications against the women who are after what they themselves already have?"

"The married ones," she said, "are sometimes easier to get close to than they think."

"Oh, sex." He tried to sound cynical.

16

"Oh, sex isn't as old-fashioned as it's sometimes made out to be, and if a girl brings more than sex . . ."

She was staring into her fairyland again, now as though the wall was opening and revealing a wider vista of it.

"More than?" he asked quietly so as not to disturb her visions. "Such as?"

But she slid away into a generality: "Knowing something about business and money can be an advantage in friendship with a rich man."

He tried jolting her. "Does the tycoon give his mistress grander presents because she can arouse his ardor by chatting him up with the Companies Act?"

She wasn't insulted, so he reminded her of her remark about the fast elevator to the executive suite. It also went one floor higher, to the penthouse. "You had our chairman in mind, perhaps?"

She laughed but without mirth. "You're taking me too seriously."

He drank half his sherry to tide over a pause and said, "But it's an interesting thought, that maybe Bertie *is* a pushover for the right girl with the right curves plus some angles about sinking funds, and the A-share principle of stock control."

"If anyone heard you calling Mr. Herbert Hammond 'Bertie,' " she said, as though she were repeating a blasphemy, "you wouldn't last even to the end of the week."

"But you think he's a pushover?"

"All men are," she said briskly, "up to and including chairmen of merchant banks. Nature and women keep them that way. Besides, he's only forty-three."

"Not forty-two or forty-four?"

"I like to be accurate."

"And well informed." This was the right line. She eyed him severely.

He made his voice crawl with envy. "He must be very very rich."

"He has a fourteen-per cent interest in Hammond and Morgan—the parent company H and M."

"Good gracious!"

Ignoring his unfitness to be instructed in the stratospheric finances of Hammond and Morgan, she nevertheless went ahead and did so with an awe that you might have heard in another girl's description of a Courrèges collection.

None of the other stock-voting members of the H and M board (she named them alphabetically: George Fanshawe, R.

W. Horton, Loanis-Andrews and Gordon Parthessen) held individually—or represented, as in the case of the last two, their wives' holdings—more than did Herbert Hammond with his fourteen shares. Of course, in total, their percentages were more than twice his, but H.H.'s real supremacy rested in his control of the remaining fifty-three per cent of stock under a power of attorney from old Mrs. Acantha Morgan, widow of Arthur, the last Morgan.

"It's a fabulous position to be in," she said in all-but-religious tones. "The board eats out of his hand. 'Yes, H.H., yes, H.H.—just as you say, H.H.' " And as for the three non-stock-owning directors, Boyle Glover, Stanley Ledger and F. F. Clayton, they scarcely dared open their mouths even to that extent.

"No other Hammond left?"

She shook her head. "None that counts. Herbert Hammond's children are still kids. There's a son of John Hammond—the previous chairman—but as everybody knows he's a Good-Time Charley, spends most of his time abroad, and doesn't want to know."

"Well," he said as jealously as he could, "I wish you the best of luck with H.H."

"Thank you, but I shouldn't think of setting my sights so high." Which didn't deny she was setting them elsewhere.

But she seemed to be a little restless with the conversation, as though she might find herself saying more than was wise. So he pursued the jealousy angle as a retreat from curiosity. He said, "I think I don't care for that man Glover. I also think he used you to spy on me."

"What a thing to say!"

"You can't deny it, you know. You must be on very good terms with him."

She arched delicate eyebrows at him. "I didn't know you when he asked me, almost as a duty to the company, for my views. What else could I do but give them?"

"Ah, yes, he's a member of the board. But didn't you say he was nonshareholding? Is he rich enough?"

Ambition had thickened her skin against every insult you could think up. "No," she said, "he isn't."

"Not the chairman, not Glover . . . ?"

"We'll talk about something else."

At least he had got her breathing deeply with wondrous effect on her breasts. Hoping to keep her dreaming he asked

18

softly, "Have you decided on just how much money in the piggy bank would be enough?"

He hadn't realized that specific questions asked of someone in the autohypnosis of fantasy often produced no less specific answers. She took an even deeper and more fascinating breath. "It will have to be a large piggy bank to hold two hundred and thirteen thousand pounds." Her voice sounded rather like that of a telephone answering service. Then she woke up, as though at a broken bra strap, which the effect of her emotion might reasonably have caused.

Wonderingly he thought she must have put her fantasy through the computer, programmed as a rich girl's budget. "Well, that's exact enough." He put on a glum expression, easily done in these days. "It's a lot more than enough to put you beyond the reach of someone from the toiling masses. I hope you won't miss your darling computer."

"That old-fashioned thing."

He was genuinely startled. To speak like that of something pertaining to Hammond and Morgan's streamlined efficiency seemed little short of heresy. He told her so.

"Maybe," she said, "but today's microcircuitry can put that roomful of stuff into a machine the size of a typewriter."

"Microcircuitry?"

"I won't try to explain," she said as to a moron, and looked him over in the objective fashion he was getting used to but which in her infinite superiority made him still more aware of his ordinariness. His suit came off a peg in a multiple tailors, its economy in quality and quantity of stuff made it tight and thin across his shoulders. If they were big shoulders because his chest was wide and deep, these were aspects that gave him satisfactory proportions only so long as he was sitting down, preferably behind a table. But get to his feet, and people, meaning any young and pretty woman, at once noticed his undersized homeliness and lost whatever interest she might have begun to take in him. It meant nothing to her that the knot of his tie tended to creep sideways under his collar because his neck was too muscular as a result of too much boxing, wrestling, judo and similarly strenuous sports by which he had sometimes escaped the awful hard work of equipping himself mentally.

So as usual, even if he had no wish for this particular girl to be interested in him, she wasn't seeing more in him than her eyes told her.

19

"Forgive the outburst just now," he said. "I'm realizing it's going to be hell, with every day like Saturdays and Sundays for me now . . . not being able to be near you . . ." Deception came to him easily, too, it seemed.

But mooning love talk had as little impact as gratuitous insults. She was still eying him, now as though she had pros and cons under analysis. "About this job thing," she said. "You're obviously useless behind a desk."

It was a clue you could follow without having to know the script. "I can't stand being cooped up all day. I shall go steadily crackers."

"I expect you can drive a car?"

He said he could.

Did he know anything about its insides?

He said he could cope with running repairs. "You're saying I should get a job as a truck or taxi driver?"

"If you can forget white-collar status."

"God yes, easily."

"Chauffeur, then. Chauffeur plus. You're educated."

"Chauffeur companion? Look for a nice elderly old dear who'll remember me in her will? I might get my two hundred and thirteen thousand before you do. And bring it to you. Come here, Fido, there's a good dog—drop it now."

"I'm serious, John. I shall need someone like you. I can't drive and don't want to. And there are other things. You'll remind me of everything I loathed in the past, and help me to count my blessings. What are you grinning at?"

He couldn't tell her, but there was irony in his symbol of the future turning on him and making him the symbol of her past.

"Grinning, was I? Relief that there's still a small chance for me. But there's a problem. How long do I have to wait for the job to start?"

But she was telling him about the advantages in having him around. He wouldn't be just a chauffeur. For instance she would need protection from the wrong kind of man on the make for her.

"Chauffeur-companion-bodyguard?"

And it would be respectable, too. "A chauffeur is regarded as part of the furniture," she pointed out.

"And one day I might be promoted *cicisbeo?*"

"What's that?"

"A Renaissance reference—the Venetians invented him to

20

keep society decent but their women happy. He enjoyed considerable social status as well."

"We aren't in Venice in the Middle Ages."

"More's the pity."

"I should still like to have you near me."

Women kept pets. Monkeys even. Beauty and the Beast syndrome. He had a regrettably un-petlike wish to take V. Norton away to an isolated place and show her how perilous the furniture could be. He overcame it and listened to her remote voice telling him that he could count on her for the job but he must be patient. It mightn't be so long.

"Waiting won't be easy, even a day."

He caught another glimpse of that cold but intense glow as she lifted her glass to him. "I'm going to trust you, John, a very great deal."

"You have a plan—" he began, but the glow became instant lightning.

"You will mind your own business," she said. "Now and always."

"I'm sorry, sorry . . ." he mumbled into his glass. "Of course that's the way it shall be."

"But we must be practical. How would it be if you went to work, temporarily, in a garage? You'd earn as much as a junior economist. More perhaps."

"If you say so."

Her eyes were compelling and no doubt meant to weaken his knee joints. "That's settled, then. A garage." She was a girl who liked to get things settled her way and at once. Pity the rich man she finally chose.

An idea came to him. He asked what sort of car would she have when the time came.

"The best of course."

"Rolls or Bentley?"

"Yes."

"A Bentley is a younger kind of car. You'd look absolutely right in it—a beautiful car for a beautiful girl."

"Yes?"

Ambition always hid quick vanity. "What color Bentley?" she asked.

"Oh, gray, I think. A pale gray."

"So a pale-gray Bentley."

"Yes, madam."

The word caused a brief flash of the inner glow. She finished her drink as though to douse it.

He asked, "May I practice bodyguarding by walking you to wherever you take off for home? Please?"

She nodded her gold sculptured head indifferently and he was supinely grateful.

On the way to Moorgate Station his now-established inequality helped him feel better about being the shorter by several inches when they were continuously on their feet side by side like this.

It was as though she sensed this when she said unexpectdly, "But you are very strong, aren't tou?" "But" was the clue. It was comforting to his sore ego that his physique had not gone unnoticed.

She said goodbye at the station barrier but proper to her superiority refrained from thanking him either for the drink or his company, which if he had had any qualms made trailing her through the home-going crowds of commuters easily ethical. He was helped in this by his ordinary appearance to hide him amongst them and by the kind of girl she was, one of those who never looks behind her for any reason whatsoever.

Three-quarters of an hour and twelve stations later, at Sloane Square, plus a five-minute walk in the dusk, he was watching V. Norton enter a small, rather run-down apartment block, Number Six Haycott Close, a short, narrow cul-de-sac off Haycott Avenue.

Through the glass panel of the street door he saw an elderly porter come out of a small lodge in the hallway to hand her an evening newspaper, a few letters and a carton of milk.

She disappeared into the single lift opposite the door. He watched the pointer above it swing slowly to the figure 4 and stop.

He crossed the roadway and stood with his back to the iron railings of a basement area to look up at the face of the building opposite. Lights came on immediately up there in the center of the fourth floor.

So now he knew where she lived, and wished he could feel more pleased with himself for having found out. Or rather that she was the kind of girl you wanted to know where she lived. All he seemed to have left, now that he had spent three-quarters of an hour talking with her, was a moderate curiosity about her as a type of human animal, a predatory, ambitious female at the point of taking off on a hunt she had long been planning. She even had an exact sum of money so clearly in her mind that it must exist in fact.

He leaned against the railings, thought about this, and felt a stronger curiosity. It promised something better than an exploration into the arid wastes of feminine coldheartedness. Not a Nuristan, of course, but at least it was more practical. It should be interesting, too, to see what circumstance would get up to now.

A voice, a woman's close but oddly from below, made him turn suddenly. She stood at an open door in the basement area, a dim white face looking up at him from the murk.

"I'm so sorry, Mr. Borrowdale"—she had a twittering voice—"I didn't hear the bell and anyway I'd quite given you up. I'll be up right away."

Only a fool would intervene in this sort of circumstance, so he muttered, "Um, ah," and waited for her to open the door for Mr. Borrowdale, whoever he might be.

She was a birdlike creature in her forties, gypsy-haired, wearing green stretch pants on spindle legs and a crimson polo-neck jumper on a torso as flat as a board.

She fired words at him like arrows. "Oh, but *you* aren't Mr. Borrowdale! I thought you must be but I *was* looking at you from underneath wasn't I how silly of me. But it's still free. He said the man Borrowdale said he'd come back this afternoon but he didn't so it's his own fault and you can have it if you like it I mean. Oh do please come in. My name's Harrington, widow of course."

Shrewd shoe-button eyes assessed the cost of his mass-produced suit and probably with accuracy how many times his shirt would drip dry before disintegrating.

He opened his mouth to say she was mistaken in thinking he was another room seeker, but stopped himself. This was a circumstance . . .

She was saying she was afraid the room was at the top and four flights up but very nice when you got there. Long jet earrings danced animatedly. "I'll lead the way."

She turned and scuttled down a bare hall to steep stairs carpeted with good if worn red Wilton. He followed her up them. Japanese glass mobiles tinkled from the landing ceiling. "I only have gentlemen," she told him over her shoulder. "Girls are hell. Bring fellas to their rooms they can't control. Typists callin' themselves secretaries, and 'models' as often as not strippers. A young man now, says he's a clerk and works for so-and-so, that's what he is and that's where he works, Mister . . . er . . . ?" They were on the last flight of stairs, narrow and bare.

23

"Addis. John Addis. I'm in a private bank."

"My goodness, Mr. Addis, yes! I'm sure you're doing—going to do very well."

He said he had recently started there but not that it was also where he had more recently finished. On the other hand he wasn't likely to bring girls to his room whom he couldn't control, like V. Norton for instance.

It was a room at the top all right. Any more so and his head would have gone through the tiles. A true attic, with a dormer window in a mansard roof, its furnishings ill-matched but adequate and clean. Satisfactorily there was a pay telephone on the wall by the window. He heard himself say, "I'd like to take it."

Mrs. Harrington blinked her bright black eyes. "Don't you want to know how much it is?"

He said he knew it would be reasonable—she was obviously a reasonable person. She smiled brightly at him and rattled through a list of the amenities, such as use of bath and kitchen on the half-landing below and of course a lovely view from the window.

She showed him the lovely view. It included the uncurtained windows of a room on the fourth floor immediately opposite in which a golden blonde was peeling off a blue-green (or green-blue) frock. Under it she wore a black bra and unexpectedly frilly pants.

Mrs. Harrington laughed apologetically—he saw, didn't he, what she'd meant about strippers? "But you won't mind I'm sure, if *she* doesn't."

He assured her he didn't mind, turned away, and said perhaps because the lady could see clear across the roofs of this side of Haycott Close, she didn't realize *she* could be seen from this particular window. There spoke, said Mrs. Harrington, a true gentleman. She added, still at the window, that the girl had now taken off the bra, "and very nice, too, I say enviously. But I shan't charge you extra."

A weekly rent was fixed, payable monthly in advance. He would move in first thing in the morning. He paid for the four weeks and downstairs again she gave him a key for the street door and another for his room; they parted with mutal satisfaction.

He walked out into the evening, hoping that his curiosity, aided by helpful circumstances, would keep boredom on the run for a while.

Poor Miss V. Norton, unaware of his hot breath at the neck of her mysterious project.

She didn't even know she had taken off her clothes in front of him long before he had become her chauffeur, let alone promoted to *cicisbeo*. He could only regret that it had given him no more than the faintest perceptible pleasure.

3

The legend on the rear wall said "FOUR PERSONS ONLY," which together with the quilted white-leather lining made the point that whereas the larger stainless steel elevators in the main lobby were for the common herd, this elegant box carried only superior creatures like the chairman and perhaps his senior directors on special occasions.

Small red-lit numbers winking above the door told you that the G factor having been successfully smoothed out on take-off, you were now traveling upward at jet speed. It was easy to feel you were hidden in a secret missile fired from somewhere near Room One, as they called the suite containing the private bank. The next moment you were penetrating the lower atmosphere of the group, the subsidiary and dependent companies: Anglo-American Precision; Cawfield Lands; Harbord Associates; Passfield Corporation; Caribbean Ports Development Comapny, and a clutch of smaller outfits such as Maynard Company and Soyson Transport.

Thereafter you were passing through the more rarefied air of Hammond and Morgan's own divisions and departments: research; management; security; legal; accounts and so on.

Finally you reached the stratosphere toward which you had launched yourself by the simple act of pressing the button marked "P," the Penthouse Suite, where the executive and chairman in supreme command dwelt in sublime splendor.

The lift stopped with a scarcely perceptible quiver, the door slid into the wall with a faint hissing, and he was hit by a blast of sunshine from the huge picture windows that formed the opposite wall. It was a very large room indeed, a conference room, as you could tell by the big crescent-shaped walnut table with high-backed white-leather chairs ranged around it, the one at the apogee of its outer curve being three inches larger in all dimensions than the others. This imposing furniture, however, still left half the room available for a walnut desk of noble proportions strategically placed to control the traffic in and out of a white-paneled door in the farthest white-paneled wall. There was still space in front of it for a hundred or so square yards of thick white carpet to protect your shoes from the harsh reality of the floor while you were approaching it.

But there was nothing to save someone like himself from the middle-aged lady who got to her feet behind the desk. She demanded to know, instantly, who he was and what he was doing here. In her severe black dress she looked like a crow in a shining white snowfield.

His reply, that she "must be Miss Maple, good morning," was not the one she wanted. She didn't wait for another and pressed a bell push on the desk as he began to tell her his name was John Addis and he would like, please, to see Mr. Herbert Hammond.

"Your name conveys nothing to me. You haven't an appointment—"

He was moving toward the sacred white door but heard a man's sharp command somewhere behind him: "Hold it, you."

A husky young man in a business suit, with a broken nose, had appeared from nowhere and was advancing on him purposefully. "Harris," said Miss Maple, "this man came up in the director's lift. He is an intruder of some sort."

"I work here." John side-stepped and backed away from Harris's outstretched hands. "I want to see the chairman."

"What department?" Harris arranged himself to pounce.

"Economic Research. I'm—"

"Room number?"

"S hyphen B stroke A five."

"No such room on fourteen."

"I didn't say it was—" John had backed to where the forbidden lift should be.

"You should have done your homework," said Harris confidently. "Research is on fourteen."

The lift door had vanished into the fifty-foot wall-to-ceiling mural depicting Hammond and Morgan's triumphant march through the City of London history, which started off soon after the Great Fire of 1666 and ended at the distant door with the populace on the steps of rebuilt St. Paul's cheering the news of Waterloo, the cost of which had been in part borne profitably by the company.

John made swift tracks for this door, Harris following him even more swiftly, calling back to Miss Maple not to worry. These crazy people got in now and again.

"But never before as far in as this," she complained. "It's security's reponsibility to prevent this kind of thing. It's too bad for you, Harris."

"I know, I know. It was lucky I was around. Come here, *you.*" He gripped John's right upper arm with a muscular left hand and propelled him through the door, kicking it shut behind him.

"Let go of me."

"Says you."

This room, peach-colored instead of white, wasn't so much smaller than the conference chamber and scarcely less sumptuous. The Hammond and Morgan saga continued along the right-hand wall and finally ended thirty feet later in the city's second holocaust, Hitler's blitz of forty-one. Above it rose the new Number One, equipped with wings, a phoenix flapping upward in a cloud of fiery steam.

At four pale-oak desks sat four young women, the nearest of whom rated a padded chair and the key position near the conference room door, suggesting a degree of superiority.

John's sense of outrage at the assaulting hold on his arm did not prevent his noticing also that this nearest girl was a brunette, wore a high-necked dove-gray frock that molded a nice bosom, and was in fact strikingly pretty, with warm, full lips that he couldn't help comparing with V. Norton's as an ultimate in contrast.

Also in her favor: she wasn't seeing this situation at its face value, although like Miss Maple a few moments ago, she sensed its unusualness and got to her feet. This put her attractiveness beyond doubt. He realized that whatever the height of her shoe heels she was three or four inches shorter than himself. All this meant he could *not* allow himself to be stronged-armed before her very eyes.

"I've changed my mind, Mr. Harris," he said, crossed his forearms and caught his own left wrist tightly with his right hand on the assumption that the security man would, and should, make at once for an armlock.

He did so, and was in trouble. As he reached across, gripped and jerked the prisoner's right wrist with his free hand, a prerequisite first move toward the armlock, John followed the pull without resistance and at the same time twisted on his hips in the same direction, causing Harris momentarily to lose balance. To regain it he had to release the prisoner's wrist but, worse, sacrifice the strength of his hold on the right upper arm.

Too late he realized that he had been trapped into a fundamental error and was irretrievably undone. The heels of his captive's hands struck him a solid blow just below his breastbone in the region of the solar plexus. He staggered backward, semiconscious before he tripped over his own feet and unconscious by the time he completed his fall.

Unlike the three subsecretaries, the dove-gray girl made no sound of alarm at this unseemly intrusion of violence into their correct lives. If she took a longer breath than usual it was with an undisclosed emotion.

John read the name board on her desk. "I am sorry about that, Miss Stewart"—there was the initial "R" before it—"but I do have to see Mr. Hammond."

"Yes?" Her brown eyes held his for an appreciable number of seconds, then as he looked down, followed his glance to the peach-colored intercom. He couldn't expect Harris to remain on the floor forever.

"Would it cost you your job, Miss Stewart, to press the top button and say, 'I'm sorry to disturb you, Mr. Hammond, but I have a Mr. John Addis from the research division out here. He hasn't an appointment. I have told him, of course, that you cannot possibly see him.' Would it?"

Harris was beginning to stir.

"Yes," she said. "It would be in character for Miss Maple to arrange for me to be fired out of hand for going over her head after she'd obviously ordered you to be thrown out." Her large eyes went briefly to the defeated security man.

John thought a strange thought out of the blue.

"Do you *like* working under Miss Maple?"

"No," she said, and at once relayed John's message to Mr. Herbert Hammond word for word, and then, "Yes, sir. I'll bring him in to you."

The chairman and managing director of Hammond and Morgan was lying back in a well-worn leather armchair near the big window using a mobile "communication unit" with which he could speak to the outside world by every means from house phone to orbiting satellite. At the moment he was talking to somebody in Valparaiso, apparently to find out—

although an oil merger was briefly mentioned—what the weather was like over there.

He waved a hand to the visitors' chair next to him. John sat down in it and admired the panorama of city spread out below, from Tower Bridge and the Pool to the Houses of Parliament by way of St. Paul's, the Stock Exchange, Mansion House and the Bank of England.

The room was a faithful replica of its eighteenth-century original in the old Number One. Modest in size, with dark paneling under a dull gold ceiling, it had early Georgian furniture, the main piece of beautiful writing table with silver inkstand and silver candlesticks. A mellow Bokhara carpet went well with the two portraits, both by Kneller at his best; John Hammond, the First, ruddy, square-shouldered and smiling, hung above the carved mantel shelf and looked across the room at the first Morgan, pale and stern between twin Chippendale bookcases. Their charter as founders, solemnly sworn and decorated with their beribboned red wax seals, was displayed in a flat mahogany showcase on the wall opposite the window.

Herbert Hammond himself seemed to have been designed for both the elegance of the room and the efficiency of the communications gadget. He was patrician in appearance: tall, distinguished, with brown hair and white, translucent skin. In particular he fulfilled the accepted picture of a successful man whose métier happened, by chance to be business: shrewd brow, strong nose, forceful chin. If his mouth was thin, suggesting parsimony, was that a handicap for such a character? But if it was a limiting characteristic in a really big businessman, Herbert Hammond didn't have to worry about it. The past's momentum was there behind him to take up the slack.

His telephoning came to a murmuring end. He put the receiver in its cradle and raised his eyebrows a quarter of an inch.

"So, John . . . ?"

"It hasn't worked out."

"You have been recognized?"

"No." John added that if he had agreed with anybody at that family conclave it had been with whoever had pointed out that he hadn't put foot in Number One before in his life, except briefly at the new building's inaugural party six years ago. He had been introduced only to the top brass, none of whom he would be likely to run into as a junior researcher.

"And Boyle Glover, who hired and fired me as 'Addis,' wasn't one of them."

"Why did he fire you?"

"He called it inability to integrate or something, but I think there may have been an element of courtship display in it. Destroy another male in the female presence to indicate his suitability under the laws of natural selection."

Cousin Herbert recognized nonsense when he heard it and merely said that Anderson, as director of research, must have found John's work unsatisfactory.

"That would assume he knew I existed."

"You *have* been working?"

"As hard, my dear Bertie, as being buried alive lets one. But the truth is—and you as good as said so at the family talk —I am just not fit to have a nine-to-five job, lacking the virtues of patience and perseverance. And you would have said it louder if, like everybody else, you weren't slightly afraid of Great-Aunt Acantha."

"She won't like this."

John was silent. That was the only blessed thing worrying him too. He was so very fond of her. This plan had been a mistake all along, and if it had perhaps been made worse by starting him too literally at the bottom, the primary fact remained: a mistake.

He realized that Herbert was also silent, but shouldn't be. If Herbert really wanted John Hammond the Seventh to join the firm, he could reach for one of those buttons and rescind Glover's decision in two words. What was he chairman of this great vast business for, if he couldn't shove his oar into what on the surface was a minuscule matter? The "John Addis" pseudonym needn't be endangered if it was still policy to hide his insignificant light under a bushel.

But Herbert was giving an imitation of a man faced with alternative earth-shaking decisions. He frowned. "You set out to show us it was a bad plan before it even got going. The overemphasis. Moving out of White House to some godforsaken bed-sitting room at the wrong end of Fulham and wearing dreadful clothes. That suit—" Herbert nearly shuddered. "You made it as difficult as you could for us and for yourself."

This was injustice but, from Herbert, predictable. John explained that if he wasn't going to give himself away he had to get into a John Addis skin, live on his salary, *be* the man. In fact the family meeting had approved this idea, although now that he came to think of it, perhaps they were merely pleased that he should contribute to the discussion at all.

But Herbert might be partially right about him. Years of dread of the eventual and inevitable day when accident of birth would catch up with him could have bitten deep into him to fester resistances, just as Herbert's own attitude in this affair had been dictated by the fact that he had sons, three or four of them, but all placed several twigs away from the main branch of Hammond and its inheritances.

John tried to feel sorry for him and waited for the judgment: John Addis, worker, had lost out to John Hammond, playboy.

But Herbert hadn't finished stating his position, as though he wanted it on record, which in fact it might be if that communication unit had a tape-machine switch amongst the others. "You shouldn't have overdone it so. Even the poverty-stricken act. Your account at London and Counties Bank—not a check drawn on it in weeks. Excessive, *obsessive* camouflage is worse than none if you carry inconspicuousness to the point of nonentity."

"Nonentity" came out a shade too easily, as though he'd said or thought it before in the same context.

John clamped his jaws together and counted a silent ten while Herbert shook a finger at him. "You have many qualities, but it has been clear for a long time that they were never likely to develop into those necessary to shouldering the responsibilities of a seventh John Hammond in as far as Hammond and Morgan is concerned. I do not think"—he got to it at last and stood up to deliver judgment—"that I should be discharging my duty to the company if I intervened. You will break this awkward news of your failure to Acantha?"

In other words let her shove you back down my throat, because I won't swallow you if I can bloody well help it. Assuming Bertie knew how to talk like that. . . .

"Yes, Bertie, I'll tell her." John also got to his feet, the interview behind him, thank God.

The chairman hated being called Bertie, but John admired the way he hid it, and stood there tall and magnificent in his certitudes, the sun shining on him, chairman and king of Hammond and Morgan, with the great city far below, suitably nowhere but at his feet.

He was welcome to the lot. It wouldn't really bother him when Great-Aunt once again rode roughshod over him in this

31

ambition for her nephew. He could rely on the nephew to let her down again. And again and again.

At the door a thought crossed John's mind.

"Bertie, does the sum of two hundred and thirteen thousand ring a bell with you?"

Herbert Hammond looked neither surprised nor startled. "Not offhand. Should it?"

"If it doesn't, it doesn't. Just one other thing: How many people knew I was down there?"

"Very few indeed."

"Not Glover, obviously, nor your p.a. So who?"

"What's the point of this now? You say nobody has recognized you."

"Say it's for my peace of mind."

An impatient gesture. "Only the board knew, and that means only the shareholding members of it. I think your peace of mind should be intact within such narrow limits of confidential knowledge. Besides," he added, "you have nothing to be ashamed of. It takes all sorts . . ." He waved a soft white hand.

"Thank you, Bertie."

John continued on his way out, passing Miss Maple and several people standing near her desk without really seeing them. But halfway down the long conference room he became aware of someone a few paces behind him. He didn't look back and wasn't going to. The carpet deadened footfall, but he knew it was a man; he was still there while he was crossing the secretariat. John also avoided glancing at Miss Stewart, to whom he owed at least a smile of gratitude, but he didn't wish to make things worse for her than perhaps they already were.

The man was behind him in the elevator down to the sub-basement and had drawn almost level with him by the time he reached his office door. And by then he had seen him as a slender, medium-sized fellow with an intelligent nose. Or sensitive, anyway. John opened the door and stood aside. "After you, sir."

"Randall, Chief of Security." He wore a white executive shirt and his tie had a blue stripe in it, an old Etonian? He reminded John of somebody he knew but couldn't place. He went to his chair and could feel V. Norton watching the proceedings through the glass wall.

Randall sat down across the desk from him and said politely that he was merely checking. He had received a copy of

32

a personnel directorate memorandum to the effect that Mr. Addis's employment by Hammond and Morgan had been terminated. Recently.

"That's right, Mr. Randall. Fired."

The security chief's eyes were of the gimlet kind. It had seemed necessary to him, he explained, to make sure Mr. Addis wasn't perhaps harboring a grudge against the company on account of being fired?

"Not in the least." John allowed a new cheerfulness to take over. "Glad, in fact."

Randall considered this and said he found it a little difficult to believe that Mr. Addis had forced his way into the chairman's presence to express gratitude for having lost his job.

V. Norton's gaze was beginning to feel like a busy ice pick.

"Nevertheless." John shrugged his shoulders.

"Nevertheless?"

"You could say that that was in the main what we talked about. Analyzed to its basics. And I didn't force my way. He could have told Miss Stewart he didn't want to see me."

"What about my man Harris? Wasn't that force?"

"Ask your man Harris whose force. He'll tell you, assuming he's honest and knows any judo."

"He's a Brown Belt."

John didn't mention that Harris should by now have realized he had met up with a Black Belt. Randall said there was something screwy about all this.

You could be sorry for this rather pleasant man. Everybody here had to feel their way through their jobs in fear of offending protocol, the first requirement of an institutional organization. Which was why even the security chief wouldn't check direct with the chairman in something less than an emergency, and presumably this was not one.

"How long have you known Rosemary Stewart?"

John glanced at his wrist watch. "Twenty-eight minutes." So the "R" stood for Rosemary. "Rosemary for remembrance," he added, and then apologetically, "Mr. Randall, everything is really all right."

"I'd like to know more about you."

"So should I," John told him, without meaning to be clever. Randall didn't slam the door but he closed it with a firm decisive snap.

John sighed and stared at his blotter and the next moment was aware of V. Norton standing in front of him. "John! Wake up! That was chief of security." She looked behind

33

her for once, as though afraid he would return. "What did he want?" Her pale cheekbones were touched with pink patches; he had never seen this before.

She repeated her question, What had the man wanted?

"Reassurance."

"About this?" She laid a piece of paper on the blotter, the requisition for the three files he had signed yesterday on her behalf. The numbers were now bracketed with a blue-penciled "N/A" in a large scrawl.

He didn't answer her question but remarked that it looked as though someone else had taken the files out of registry for the moment.

"No!"

"That's what N/A means."

"It means"—the pink was darker—"that he has had them restricted."

"Who's 'he'?"

"You wouldn't understand." She was recovering. "John, you're absolutely sure Captain Randall didn't want to know why you had asked for these files?" Ice-pick eyes probed again. However, it wasn't a lie: Randall had come, he told her, to make sure he wasn't harboring a grudge against the company on account of being fired. If Randall had also wanted to know what secret business he had transacted with the chairman, that was Randall's affair, not his.

The pink was fading from her cheeks but there was enough left to suggest her guard was still down.

"Why should these particular files be given restricted circulation?" He kept his tone to a mild inquisitiveness.

"Because they must almost certainly reveal—" She stopped.

"Yes?"

"Something was swept under the carpet some while ago. I think I know what. The consolidated accounts, computerized, show a discrep—" She stopped again, picked up the indent form, tore it across and dropped it in the wastebasket—*his* wastebasket, he noted, thus continuing to preserve her innocence in the matter.

She told him with a return of her normal tone of detached command that *his* worry was to try for that job in a garage. And *nothing* else. "I hope you've already made a start? You're late enough in this morning."

"I think I can promise to fix it quite soon."

"Good." She went back to her office, collected a pile of

punch cards and took them out to the computer, which removed her eagle eye long enough for him to recover the discarded indent form, fit the pieces together, copy the file numbers onto a slip of paper and throw the bits back in the wastebasket.

He looked up "Registry" in the staff book and dialed its "Inquiries." It took the clerk there only a moment to look up the reference numbers and confirm that the files weren't available. Who had them? Just a minute, sir . . . marked out to the legal division. Date? Yes, here it is . . .

"Isn't two years rather a long time for files to be out?"

"Well, sir, it *is* the legal division, and lawyers take their time. If you should wish to chase them yourself the indent was signed 'P. Taylor' bracket 'Legal.' Room eight-oh-two."

John thanked him, put the slip of paper away in his wallet, and consulted the staff book again. He couldn't find "P. Taylor" but was intrigued to see that Room 802, eighth floor, was occupied by "Storage, Stationery (Legal)."

It was two years ago, of course, and P. Taylor could have left and his room been re-allocated; "Legal" would always be short of space for paper, used or otherwise.

He felt hungrier than he'd been in weeks. It was half-past twelve; he would buy himself a slap-up lunch and do some quiet and if possible orderly thinking. But he hadn't enough money in his pocket, after paying Mrs. Harrington's rent, for any sort of lunch. He couldn't very well get some from his capital account in Room One, where the currency unit started at ten thousand; he would have to call at London and Counties. Damn Bertie and his watchdog's remark, "No checks drawn in weeks." Never mind. . . .

Halfway to the elevator his conscience about Rosemary Stewart held up a restraining hand and he went back to his house phone.

One of the secretaries answered. Miss Stewart wasn't at her desk. Who was calling, please? His "John Addis" was met with a girlish gasp at the other end.

His conscience withdrew its objections for the moment, but it wasn't going to let him forget that he had taken advantage of Miss Stewart's weakness in disliking Miss Maple. He hoped she would guess he had called because he was worried on her behalf, an interim repayment.

4

The cashier had an indoors face and alert eyes older than the rest of him; they were quicker even than Mrs. Harrington's in the craft of assessment. They told him that this was not a typical caller at London and Counties branch, or any other. It was a superior bank.

"Mr. Roberts isn't the manager?" John repeated.

"Our manager is Mr. Soames, and has been for several years." This was likely, of course. Five of those years had passed since John last enetered this railroad terminal of a place, and then only that once because the Hammond trustees had reluctantly allowed him certain limited rights over his own money, causing the then manager, Mr. Roberts, to invite him along to say how d'you do. Since then he had written checks at a distance and cashed them for pocket money wherever he had happened to be.

Naturally the cashier—T. Brinkley, according to the plaque facing you inside his grille—didn't know him and wasn't having any of him. Brinkley regretted that the manager could not see anyone without prior appointment. However, if one could be told in what connection . . . ?

This ubiquitous protection of the upper echelons by the lower was no comfort when you were in a hurry. The man wasn't to blame. Power couldn't survive without mystiques of ritualistic respect for it.

"Only Mr. Soames will do," John said in an attempt to compete.

"I'm very sorry, sir."

John gave up. Hunger wasn't the best of bodily states in which to be persistent. In any case he had lost interest in having a row with Manager Soames.

"Never mind. Just let me know what my credit balance is."

"The name?"

"John Addis."

Brinkley said it would take a few minutes. "We have a large number of customers, you understand."

"I'll wait."

The name, written on a piece of paper, was being passed to

a clerk at the inner counter when John remembered. "No. I mean 'Hammond.' 'John A. Hammond.' "

Brinkley turned to look at him with greater suspicion. " 'Hammond,' Mr. Addis?"

"Yes—I'm sorry." He took a loose check from his wallet, signed it, and slid it across the counter. "Just fill it in for the total amount. I'll pick it up in about an hour. Folding money, of course."

He turned and walked across the half acre of marble to the swing doors and out.

Brinkley released a held breath, took his foot off the knob of the alarm bell and picked up the check by its edges to avoid smearing fingerprints.

In the street again, John realized that his somewhat childish effort to establish a political position by militant demonstration had not only made him hungrier than ever but had frustrated one of his reasons for calling at the bank. He still couldn't pay for more than a cup of coffee.

He sighed at this further instance of predestination usurping free will and decided to have lunch at home. It would mean having to face Great-Aunt Acantha sooner rather than later.

He hailed a cab.

White House stood somewhat grand but welcoming at the top of a semicircle of drive in what was still a wooded area of St. John's Wood. Here Regent's Park had only just relinquished its four hundred and seventy odd acres of city countryside to the northern suburbs. The air was clean for the sun of early summer to shine undiminished on trees and lawns.

Nostalgia filled him as he left the taxi to mount the steps under the portico.

This had been a Hammond home for a hundred and fifty years, and returning to it after weeks of imprisonment he saw it suddenly for what it had always been, the heart and pivot of his life, his starting-off place and the place he came back to. Perhaps Bertie had had something in saying he had overdone it. But it hadn't felt like it at the time. Walking out of this house could have been an act of self-immolating banishment, but the fateful conference of trustees and family had been held in its library and he hadn't wanted to see it again for a very long time. It hadn't been deliberate on their part. Such gatherings had always taken place there since the fourth

37

John Hammond built the "town house"; in any case Acantha, widow of the last Morgan and John's guardian and chief trustee, lived here and for all of twenty years had been the natural hostess for these affairs.

Part of shaking off the dust so thoroughly had been deliberately to leave his key behind. MacGregor's startled pleasure when he answered the bell was good to see.

"Sir John—!" MacGregor would have suffered keen deprivation if he'd been denied the formality of the inherited title to which John would never admit he had any right except by accident of birth. However, he allowed no other member of the household to use it.

He asked MacGregor to pay off the cab. No, there wasn't a bag. "I'm here just for lunch. A last-minute thought and no time to let you know." By now MacGregor had seen the suit and the shirt and was hiding his horror and disapproval as best he could. Luncheon was about to be served in the orangery. "Madam is sitting in the sun there. She finds it beneficial."

The welcome-home feeling grew stronger as he moved into the square pine-walled hallway and increased immeasurably when Great-Aunt proved almost tearfully happy at the sight of him, saying, "Bertie telephoned only half an hour ago. I was so worried."

He kissed her and she held his arm for a moment with gentle fingers. "I'm glad you came at once. I know how upset you are."

"For your sake, Great-Aunt."

"That's what I meant."

The pervasive scent of orange blossom was a world away from the machine-made ozone of the computer room. The sherry was chilled as it should always be. He sat down in a basket chair next to her. "So Bertie didn't waste any time."

"He doesn't in things like this," she said enigmatically.

She rocked herself in a favorite silk-padded chair. Frail, with gleaming silver hair piled high over a small oval face that smiled easily and often, she dressed summer and winter in shades of blue that never failed to match her eyes. Frail as glass, yes, but tough as steel, this was Acantha Morgan; lovable if you could stand up to her, frightening if you couldn't.

"Poor darling," she said.

He eyed her circumspectly. "Don't tell me you *expected* me to fall down on the idea?"

She began to speak and he to doubt his ears.

"Dear boy, for obvious reasons I couldn't let you see my doubts. And in any case they only really came to a head *after* that silly meeting. The trouble was that with your father's will written the way it was, I, and everybody else, looked on your eventual succession as a foregone conclusion. Nobody stopped to look at *you*, except Bertie, perhaps, looking for what he hoped to see. It's easy to tell a child about the shape of things to come because he takes them as a matter of course and one thinks, *that's* settled, quite forgetting that a child doesn't stay a child. He grows up in patterns of his own that don't necessarily fit the circumstances that his birth and family and all that stuff and nonsense have designed for him."

She was practically quoting him, particularly his protests when an earlier get-together of the family had decided that he should read economics at Oxford instead of history or English. His feeble mewings of protest had been ignored as those of someone not yet old enough to know his own mind.

But he loved her too much to say I told you so, and in any case his heart was singing "Freedom's banner streaming o'er us" and that was enough and be thankful.

"Of course Bertie puts it the other way round," she said. "He feels that *he* has failed in this."

"Does he now?"

"He said we must all put on our thinking caps and find another way to get you acclimatized. He's a fool."

"He's certainly wrong there. I never could be."

"He's a fool if he thinks I can't hear him chortling with satisfaction. That son of his—what's his name, Gilbert—is growing up."

"Rupert. As brainy, they say, as his father."

Great-Aunt Acantha said *ha!* and MacGregor came in with a trolley table laid for two with the whitest linen and brightest silver. Caviar for starters by the double tablespoonful. Iranian. None of your common Beluga for Mrs. Acantha Morgan. The vodka ice-cold in Venetian glasses, hot toast and flat pats of frozen butter. MacGregor went away and John was able to get on with making quite sure the banner was kept streaming o'er him.

"Bertie may be a fool in some ways and naturally enough is looking out for his son's interests. But he's right that I'd be useless in Hammond and Morgan."

She disregarded this in favor of her interrupted train of thought.

"Brainy?" She pyramided dark-gray succulence on a corner

of toast. "A man can be brainy without developing—or better still, without being born with—the quality of mind that produces sound judgment about people and the events they cause."

He couldn't but agree with her and wait for her to finish.

"I've often thought," she went on, "that Bertie wouldn't be even moderately successful without the Hammond and Morgan wealth and tradition to push him along. That quarter-mile walk through those ridiculous great salons to get to him in the Founders' Room, with the Pagnetti murals to tell mere people how privileged they are. The whole thing is what you children call a load of old rubbish."

"But it works, Great-Aunt."

"We agree as a sign of your coming of financial age that you should call me Acantha."

"I'm sorry, and I love you under any name. Acantha, I really am profoundly sorry to have let you down."

Her one-track mind led on: "Mere people, mere foolish, dependent people, poor dears, who don't know that it's by my say-so that Bertie controls the majority block of voting stock."

"Fifty-three percent."

"Thirty of which, as you well know, became yours when your father died."

He had hoped she wouldn't remind him. "But the trustees and everybody suggested that the arrangement should continue. Including me."

"I know. But the trustees ceased to exist as from the fourteenth December last. They and everybody, which means Bertie and Gordon Parthessen, can suggest all they like, but legally they've no more say than flies on the ceiling about how your thirty per cent is administered, controlled, voted, or any damn thing, darling boy. Why are you scowling so?"

He said he wasn't and Acantha said she'd invite him to go and look in the mirror behind him, except that'd crack it with an expression like that. . . .

"Let's keep to the point," he said. "I'm best out of it. I haven't a head for business. And whatever you say, we *did* agree we wouldn't interfere with existing arrangements."

"In case we upset Bertie and Gordon Thing and their chorus of yes-men?"

It was odd within a few hours to hear the same view of the board from such dissimilars as Great-Aunt and V. Norton.

40

"But it works," he protested. "It suits everybody and you've gone along with it for years."

"As one gets older one can go along with practically anything. You aren't older yet. You don't have to if you don't like it."

In other words, if he didn't like Bertie and Parthessen running Hammond and Morgan as a private partnership.

Acantha finished off her caviar and drained her vodka.

"Anyway you'll have time now to get down to work with those boxes."

He nodded. But he doubted it. He should have done so months ago. The three large steel deed boxes still lay upstairs in a disused dressing room where they'd been put the day they arrived from the lawyers. He hadn't dared touch them, fetters and bars from the past to hold him back from the future.

MacGregor returned with the serving trolley and the ingredients of *rognons de veau au vin blanc*, which he cooked swiftly in a chafing dish.

When he had gone, Acantha waited until she had sliced a kidney and tasted it critically but with satisfaction before saying, "Let's not talk about business any more. And don't look so glum, dearest boy. I'm nothing like as disappointed as you think."

She said she had been a sentimental old woman clinging to outmoded tradition. Even his father hadn't stopped to question it. "That he was the sixth John Hammond and you the seventh was enough to guarantee the continuity of inheritance. There weren't even any Morgans left, with my Arthur dead, to compete with you. Second cousin Herbert was to be no more than a stopgap, a caretaker, and he wouldn't even have been that if he'd had another name. Your father was worse than me in thinking the world would always be the same—not that that stopped him doubling his fortune by foreseeing that it wouldn't be." She laughed lightly. "I'm sure you're perfectly right. Bertie is doing very well for us. And dear old Gordon Thing, and that means my little sister-in-law."

She was alluding to the fact that Parthessen was Martha Morgan's husband. "Anyway one good thing has certainly come out of all this. You can throw away that appalling suit." And perhaps answer some of the forty-odd invitations to coming-out balls and parties that had accumulated on the desk in the library.

"You never know. The right girl could be accepting the same ones this very minute."

"Not yet, Acantha."

"Oh, you can't be sure."

"I meant about coming home."

Her soft blue eyes rested on his face. "Not yet?"

"I have one or two things to clear up."

"At Number One?"

He nodded.

She looked away, quickly. "You know best, darling. Oh yes, before I forget—before we put business behind us for good and all—about my twenty-three per cent . . ." She hesitated. "It's lumped together with yours."

"But it always has been."

"Only for proxy voting purposes, through Bertie. Not as part of your holding. Don't look so stricken." She was smiling again. "It was always coming to you, but six or seven years ago I decided to deed-gift it to you to avoid the death duties, as everyone was doing. So I did, a bit secretly."

"Great-Aunt—I mean Acantha, for God's sake—"

"Nobody knew and needn't know until I'm dead. It didn't and doesn't affect the company. As your guardian-trustee I could still exercise its vote through Bertie and that's what I've been doing."

"I don't want it!" he said loudly.

"Well, you've got it, dear." She was still smiling but her eyes were eager and watchful. "Anyhow, it won't make the slightest difference to your right to lead your own life. You can give Bertie your proxy just as I used to when a formal voting matter appears on the agenda. But I suggest *not* a carte blanche power of attorney. I withdrew mine some while back in favor of the proxy system. It only means you sign bits of paper occasionally instead of just the one. Where's MacGregor? The sherbet will be running away. Ring the bell, dear."

John remained a little stunned. This wasn't the first time he'd believed that Acantha could make arrangements with the Devil when she felt like it.

After lunch he went up to his own rooms and packed a suitcase with things he thought he might need; these included the suit he had on. To wear now he put on a medium-gray worsted that he had worn often enough to break in. Its creation in Savile Row would perhaps be noticeable to the discerning eye but not obtrusively so. He also changed the drip-dry shirt for something more pleasing without going all the way to silk. Shoes, however, could be handmade and not look it.

He found Fred Ross in his small flat over the garage, once the coach house and stables at the back of the house with its courtyard gates onto Thame Road.

Fred was as thin as a small rail. He was a first-class driver and mechanic, not yet forty, but he had worshiped his father, the fifth John Hammond's coachman, and imitatively behaved as though transport hadn't progressed beyond the horse. He made hissing noises. He also wore a straw in the corner of his mouth, although nobody knew where in a now-strawless city he got it from.

"Well, sir, so you've come for one of 'em, eh? Thought you might. Who'd want to walk when he can ride . . . the Bentley? Lord knows he needs exercise, I've run him round the park a couple of mornings but it scarcely warms him up."

"I did tell Mrs. Morgan she was welcome to use it."

"Sir, it's always the little black Rolls if she goes out at all these days. And about the Daimler, it breaks my heart but I think we should put him down. He's sound enough but he's had his day. Now that MacGregor has the Mini-Cooper for shopping, he just stands there, bone idle through no fault of his own. We'd get fifteen hundred for him from the knackers." He shifted the straw to the other side of his mouth and rubbed the Daimler's radiator. "Poor old boy."

"Put him down, then, Fred."

"Thank you, sir."

While the little man was maneuvering the Bentley out into the courtyard John eyed the three peaked caps hanging on one-time harness pegs at the back of the garage. Two were black, the third was gray, matching the Bentley. Since he didn't propose to bring back the car for a while, Fred wouldn't be driving it, so he took down the cap, buttoned it inside his jacket, and drove the Bentley around to the front door to pick up his suitcase. He put the cap in the glove compartment and went to say goodbye to Acantha and to ask one or two questions.

He tried to make them sound unimportant but he felt he wasn't fooling her.

"The company is doing well?"

"Heavens yes, doesn't it always?"

"No setbacks, big losses in the last year or so?"

43

She was looking closely at him again; she shook her head. "You would know?" he asked.

"The dividends haven't shown it. The balance sheets—" She hesitated. "Arthur always insisted I should take an intelligent interest in that sort of thing and I'm sure I would have noticed. When you say 'big,' how big?"

"A couple of hundred thousand."

"That would make a dent." Looking down, she said he seemed to be taking an interest in spite of his uselessness as a businessman.

"I'd be a clot if I didn't give some thought to where it all came from." He kissed her and went out to the car, thinking that the Hammond and Morgan balance sheets weren't in the simple arithmetic her Arthur had taught her to be intelligent about, forty years ago.

He drove back to the city. His appetite had been pleasantly dealt with, Acantha hadn't made the tearful fuss he had been afraid of, and Freedom's banner was still unfurled. But he did *not* like this twenty-three per cent on top of his thirty, which had been bad enough, and still less Acantha's hint that he should now begin doing his own voting.

Fifty-three per cent? Damn, blast, and to hell!

Acantha, blue-eyed sweet old lady and all, thought nothing of playing tiddlywinks with a person's very soul.

He turned the car through the archway into the quadrangle of London and Counties, and parked it opposite the inner entrance.

Brinkley the cashier had a hunted look and his eyes were older than ever. He made a gesture indicating that John should go to the end of the counter, where he met him, sliding away a portion of the grille and lifting a flap to let him through. Mr. Soames would be grateful for a few moments of Sir John's time. "Mr. Soames is extremely upset."

"You mean he gave you hell for not recognizing a dwarf-like young man in a cheap suit whom you'd never seen before in your life."

Brinkley was shivering. John was aware of anger. He shut his eyes, containing it with effort. He kept them shut while he spoke because he couldn't bear the sight of Brinkley's expression.

"Give Soames my respectful regards and tell him I am taking my money away from this bloody bank—mind you get this word for word—because he broke the first rule of ethics in banker-customer relations by divulging a customer's business to a third party. *My* business."

He heard Brinkley's exclamation of incredulity and opened his eyes. Brinkley had stopped shivering. "Soames did *that?*"

"Herbert Hammond inquired into the state of my account, and Soames told him. He's the man with a hot line to Mammon and a company banking its spare millions here. But in this context he is still no more than a third party. Where's my money?"

"Mr. Soames said—"

"The brute didn't stop your getting it ready?"

"He said he was sure you'd reconsider, but in fact I didn't think you would and it's ready for you in here."

"Good for you."

Brinkley unlocked a small bare office; two large packages and a rectangular envelope were on a table in the center of it. He said the total in the current account had been seventy-eight thousand two hundred and ten pounds. For convenience in carrying he had split the money into two equal lots of thousand-pound packets, thirty-nine in each parcel, but he hadn't closed and sealed them. "You may wish to check the count. The odd two hundred and ten is in the envelope." He straightened his shoulders and added that he would give Mr. Soames the message, and gladly. "I shall be happy to be out of this rat race."

"He can't *fire* you for this, for heaven's sake?"

"We don't do it like that." He explained that managers sent in bi-annual confidential staff reports and there were branches in remote little country towns to which not-quite-suitable cashiers could be banished. Forever.

"If that's the way it is," John said, "I could send in a confidential staff report myself."

Brinkley grinned. "That might fix Soames but it would also fix me, beautifully. Then I should also have offended by making a complaint to a customer. It's good of you, but no. Anyway it will take the children away from the carbon monoxide. I shall get a good price for my house. It's new, we've just moved in, but what the hell? I wouldn't wish him a cerebral thrombosis."

John felt the hidden drive of circumstance again and thought of resisting it, but it was too insistent.

He asked Brinkley how strongly he felt about being a banker, had it been a long-standing choice? After a moment's surprise at the intimacy of the question, Brinkley said he had gone into public banking rather than insurance or a stock-broker's office or something like that because banking would bring him in contact with people, people in general. Also it extended one's capabilities in a technical way too. "I passed the Institute of Bankers examination Part Two, so I can say I have a fair knowledge of company law as well as general finance. Why, Sir John?"

"Never 'Sir' John me, and forget the Hammond part too if you'd like to change horses in midstream and come and work with me. I shall have to stick to 'Addis' for a while."

Brinkley stared, his eyes becoming younger by the moment. "Work with you? In Hammond and Morgan? But they're very choosey. . . ."

"Not as choosey as I am." John took a packet of notes from each package; one he put in his inside pocket, the other he handed to Brinkley. "Advance on salary to be discussed later. I'll let you know when we start. Let's close up these packets. Thirty-eight thousand in each now, right? I have the car at the quadrangle door." He paused. "Do I seem crazy to you?"

Brinkley, staring at the money in his hand, shook his head slowly. "I expect you have a good reason."

John realized that in fact he had: "Three great tin boxes full of Hammond affairs that I want to dump in your lap as soon as possible. Your main job will be to get to know what's in them and hide it from me except when you think I must, as a last resort, be told."

Helped by a uniformed bank guard, they carried the pack-ages to the car and locked them in the trunk. Now and again Brinkley let out a small, crowing chuckle. He said he was composing a short speech to deliver to Mr. Soames and an-other for his wife. Sally wouldn't be as startled as the man-ager. She was psychic. She had been saying for weeks that his career was coming to a turning point whereafter it would be roses all the way.

John wondered if Sally would have said the same for him-self. "When can you start?"

Brinkley was due some leave that he could take any time. Resignation could take effect after that. John said he would be in touch with him during the coming week.

They parted with mutual esteem.

John parked the car at the north entrance of Number One, using a space marked "Directors Only." The commissionaire

46

raised no objection, indeed touched his hat. A Bentley is a Bentley.

5

About to step out of the elevator on the eighth floor John came face to face with a small brown-haired girl about to enter it. Recognition was immediate. Rosemary Stewart looked at him with gold-flecked eyes magnified by moisture.

He backed into the elevator again, and she went past him and buried herself behind a clutch of proper-faced executives, all of them taller than he, so that he couldn't even see her. But an exodus at the fifteenth left only four people and he was able to reach her. "You've been fired?"

"No. But I'm likely to fire myself. It appears that you're some kind of crook."

"That's security's diagnosis?"

At least two of the remaining passengers were paying interested if corner-eyed attention to the conversation. She turned on them.

"All right! Suppose he is a crook," she told them. "I have been warned. It's my lookout if I talk to him."

"Thank you," he said.

"Don't. I'm my own worst enemy."

Between the eighteenth floor and the penthouse they were alone and he tried to comfort her. "I can't tell you how sorry I am."

"The Maple didn't *have* to send me to Captain Randall for a lecture on security. She could have told them Mr. Hammond didn't *have* to see you if he didn't want to. Let Rosemary suffer for her impertinence."

They were out of the elevator, which closed behind them and silently betook itself downward.

"And you don't have to worry about me," she said.

He was as angry as he had been in the matter of Manager Soames. "Bertie, blast him, should have backed you up."

"Bertie-blast-him, as you call our august chairman, is never put in the position of having to concern himself with the troubles of totally unimportant members of the staff."

"Then he ought to be."

47

"You tell him that."

He walked by her side along the wide lushly carpeted corridor that was thick with atmosphere of top brain cells working away behind anonymous sycamore doors.

At the door of the secretariat she held out her hand. "Goodbye, Mr. Addis." Her eyes were still wet with tears of mortification.

He took her hand. "How long have you worked here?"

"Two years and five months. It's one of the best jobs I could ever get, and the Maple must retire one day."

"Then you'd be p.a.?"

She realized he hadn't shaken her hand but simply held it. She withdrew it. "If one day I'm Private Assistant to the Chairman of Hammond and Morgan my father will stop going on at me for letting down the regiment. He has just retired as colonel in the Brigade of Guards, you see."

John opened the door for her.

"Ah, Rosemary, thank God you've got him! The p.a. is livid. . . ." It was the blondest subsecretary. She flicked her intercom. "Miss Stewart has located Mr. Addis, Miss Maple. He is here with her now."

The intercom snapped back that this was very inconvenient. Its circuit closed and everyone watched it as though it was a snake about to strike again. It did so. I had explained to the chairman that Mr. Addis had been given the wrong message and was here in person. Mr. Hammond would, however, stretch a point and see Mr. Addis.

Rosemary Stewart was in worse distress.

"I'd forgotten we were trying to reach you. Now I *am* done for."

"You are *not*," he said, but was more concerned with a bright new thought. He asked how would she—the secretariat —get hold of a particular file when they needed it?

"Requisition it, of course," she said mechanically.

"An ordinary indent?"

"No, one of these." She took a form from a drawer. He saw that unlike the indent used by the proletariat it was headed "From the Desk of the Chairman."

"It's a little involved," he said, "but in the end this could be a good thing for you." He gave her the slip of paper from his wallet. If she would kindly put these file numbers on a requisition with her pretty pink all-electric typewriter, he would come back for it when Mr. Hammond was through with him.

He went into the conference chamber without waiting for her reaction. Miss Maple's disapproving air as he passed her to go into the Founders' Room was as cold as anything V. Norton could have projected. Would it have consoled her to know he was as much in the dark as she was about Bertie's need for further talk with him? Probably not. She was as jealous of her official prerogatives as a wife of her husband's fidelity.

"Ah, John—yes . . ." The pale, noble forehead was puckered. "I'm sorry you should have had to come all this way when a telephone call would have done. A failure in communication into which I shall inquire." And a golden-brown head would roll.

John waited. Bertie explained that he had only wanted him to know that he had decided to break the news to Acantha himself. John realized Bertie didn't know he had just been with Acantha. Bertie was looking wise. "At Acantha's age disappointment must be avoided. But in the meantime you should keep out of her way, don't you think? I'll let you know the moment I can advise you that it would be safe for you to return to the fold."

"That's very good of you."

"My dear fellow, it's the least I can do." He changed the subject but not his expression. "I have been thinking that in consequence of this situation you may feel the logic of a suggestion that you should withdraw entirely from your commitment with Hammond and Morgan. It would make psychological good sense, a load off your mind, a release from guilt, if that's not putting it too strongly."

"Withdraw from my commitment? I've already been slung out of it."

Bertie frowned. God give him patience with the dull-witted.

"Your financial commitment, John. Your thirty per cent of the company's ordinary stock."

"Oh, that."

"That," Bertie echoed—the shortest sentence he had used for some years. But it would have been longer, John felt, or mightn't have been uttered at all, if Acantha had been less secretive about what she'd done with her twenty-three per cent.

Bertie hammered in another nail. "If you look at it objectively you will come to see that there's no true freedom for you otherwise."

Freedom. A clever, powerful word.

"Sell out?"

"It would make you more demonstrably one of the richest young men in the world."

"More demonstrably? In what way?"

"Money—cash. Instead of pieces of paper."

John asked how much money and Bertie shrugged his shoulders. That would have to be gone into.

"At a guess?"

"I don't like to guess in millions," but he was keeping alive the thought of money in vast quantity.

"Have a go."

Bertie manfully ignored the frivolity.

"The market value of the Hammond and Morgan shares was last assessed in eighteen seventy-six," he said. "At that time the book valuation stood at between four and five hundred."

"Each?"

Bertie explained as to a retarded child that that was the customary way of referring to stock prices.

"Gosh," John said, "and since then . . ."

"Currency index has appreciated five- or sixfold, and the company's expansion has been scarcely less."

"Gosh," John said again, and left his mouth open.

"Would Tuesday suit you for lunch, to discuss this in detail?"

"My word, yes, thank you."

"Mention it, would you, to my p.a. as you go out." Dismissal. But John hesitated at the door.

"Isn't there something in the covenant that nobody's allowed to sell except to another member or members of the families?"

"It should be possible"—Bertie's confident casualness was superb—"to arrange matters with the legal status of the covenant in mind."

John gazed at him with admiration. "Oh, good."

Such a powerful, powerful second cousin. He really would have to be, too, when he finally learned what Acantha had done with her twenty-three per cent.

Miss Maple barely glanced at him with a sour expression that made it impossible to give her the chairman's message about a luncheon date.

He was unhappy but not surprised to see that Rosemary Stewart's eyes were as moist if not moister than before. But perhaps in symbolic defiance of oppressive authority, she had typed in the file numbers on the requisiton form. He couldn't believe she had faith in his vague promise that it could be a good thing for her in the end.

"Thank you." He put the indent in his pocket.

"It has to be signed by Miss Maple."

"Or by Mr. Hammond himself, of course. Could you spare me a moment?" He indicated the door to the corridor.

She was near enough to open tears to be glad to escape the interested attention of the other girls. He closed the door and led her a few yards away from it where he could listen in peace to the dictates of circumstance.

"Would you," he asked, "like to take a gamble and work with me?"

"With *you*?"

He thought she was about to fall down, and he put out a hand. But it was unnecessary. She was in command of herself. "In research, Mr. Addis?"

He slid around this by saying it wouldn't be in the research division itself. "A separate project. I badly need a personal assistant."

She looked at him with doubtful but beautiful eyes and repeated "personal assistant" as though tasting the tempting bait.

"This way you don't have to wait," he said, "for Miss Maple to retire. Although of course I'm not Herbert Hammond."

"No," she agreed, "you aren't. You would ask for me to be transferred?"

He shook his head. It would be quicker and easier if she quit her present job through the usual personnel directorate procedures and did not mention, incidentally, what her new one would be or with whom she would be working. "You have to trust me when I say that you'd be concerned in a worthwhile project."

"Hammond and Morgan, apart from Miss Maple, has been good to me in its odd way."

"And to me. You might come to feel that you were repaying it, in an odd way."

"Things like this are always a matter of trust," she said, more perhaps for her own benefit than his.

"Please give it serious thought. Can I call you at your home tomorrow evening?"

"You'll find the number under Colonel J. Z. Stewart."

He thanked her and prepared to leave.

"I've given it serious thought," she said, "I'll take the job."

He turned to face her again.

"That's a quick decision."

"I like quick decisions. Don't you?"

"No."

"But you make them."

God help him, yes.

"You'll know what salary you want and that will be all right with me. However"—he took out the envelope Brinkley had given him, and handed it to her—"you will have preliminary expenses. Clothes and so on."

"Clothes?"

"And accessories." He explained that in any case she would no longer be sitting behind a typewriter but initially her work would entail meeting people in a semisocial way; that it would be obviously unfair and unbusinesslike to ask her to use her private wardrobe.

She looked at the envelope and turned it over in her small hands. "You mean I shall have to dress up?"

"Somewhat. Would it worry you?"

She laughed.

He said, "So that's settled. I'll call you about a starting date." He went along the corridor at a good speed because Miss Stewart's large brown eyes had begun to regard him with a warmth to which it was impractical for him to respond in the corridor of the executive suite. The vibrations might have upset the delicate balance of the busy brain cells at work behind the sycamore doors.

According to the gold-on-walnut inscription in the lobby, the eighth floor was occupied exclusively by the Legal Division. The door marked 802, second along the westward passage, had nothing on it about "Stationery Storage (Legal)," and when he knocked and tried to enter he found it locked.

But another door opened farther down the passage and a voice said, "What can we do for you?"

It was Harris, the security man, who now recognized him.

John strove to keep the pain of surprise from his face. For "Stationery Storage (Legal)" read "Security Section (Cover)," the last place in the building he wanted to be.

He tried a smile as a substitute for taking to his heels. "I'm looking for P. Taylor, who has some files I need. Registry shows them booked out to him."

"Taylor is unavailable."

John felt rising anger at the ubiquitous "unavailable" and

52

he said that didn't matter as long as these files were. He held out the indent. He had signed it in the elevator coming down; the "Hammond" was legible, but the initials were run together so that the J ran into the A and could be read alternatively as H. H.—and would be, in view of the indent's heading. He was also relying on Bertie's signatures' being rarely seen by the lowly.

Harris looked at the requisition, controlled a double take, and glanced up with unaffected curiosity, saying that this, of course, explained a whole lot. It was a matter for the chief. "Out of my league. Like this morning. Black Belt to my Brown?"

John returned the grin. "How were you to know?"

Harris shook his square head. "High finance doesn't often involve physical protest and I don't get much practice anyway."

Requisition in his hand, he went back into the room, an outer officer as John saw when he followed, not having been told to wait. By the same token he crossed to an inner room at Harris's heels. Randall sat there at a cluttered desk.

John felt excessively nervous about the ability of happenstance to come out best again. He seemed to be asking a lot from it this time.

"Chickens, captain"—Harris sounded happy—"chickens we'd thought we'd never see again have come home to roost."

He laid the requisition in front of the chief security officer, who, if he didn't recognize the file numbers as immediately as his subordinate had done, lagged only a moment or so behind. "Fording Lencorp?" he said under his breath and looked up.

"Fording Lencorp, captain. I'm not saying I told you so. I was never more than guessing and you were right to slap me down. But this is it, sir. Someone from outside. It's how they'd go about it."

"Please take a seat, Mr. Addis. What agency are you with?"

It would be as dangerous to invent an agency as to name an existing one—if he could remember one. Harris unwittingly rescued him. "The best private chaps in the business these days are specialists working on their own."

"Who if they need help," John said, "particularly in an internal investigation of this kind, look for it in the security section that generally exists in organizations as big as Hammond and Morgan. And quite unofficially, Captain Randall."

Randall said he could see the necessity for that, but the se-

53

curity section could reasonably expect to be informed of it—unofficially—through normal channels, in this instance the legal division.

John was by now ready for obstacles of this kind, normal reactions, in fact. "Would you? When clearly there's top-brass involvement? Channels leak. You could find yourself up against pressures you couldn't fight simply because you're an integral part of the organization. And I'd be hamstrung before I could begin to move."

Randall nodded slowly. It made sense.

Harris wasn't interested in the niceties of protocol. He had a point to make. "So the chairman has changed his mind. That's all we need."

Randall was seeing the light. "You're assuming, Ted, that he knew about it at the time. He can't have known. A loss of half a million? Somehow it was kept from him."

"All right, captain. Point is, he knows now and here's Mr. Addis."

Randall lost some of his uncertainty. "You're very welcome, Addis. In any case, finance, company law and so on aren't our specialities." He laid a thin hand on the indent form. "We'll help all we can, of course."

What had Randall said? *Half a million?*

"This is the first time," John said, feeling his way as never before, "that an actual figure has been mentioned."

"Four hundred and twenty-six thousand," Harris said. "No more, no less."

"You'll have gathered," Randall remarked, "that Harris has a good memory."

"For this Fording Lencorp caper, I have." Harris was a bird dog, stiff with eagerness.

John hadn't a mathematical brain that could instantaneously see all around a figure, but it was able to tell him quite quickly that half of four hundred and twenty-six was two hundred and thirteen. Remembering where he had heard that figure in the first place, it could mean that V. Norton had modestly decided to sell her silence for only half the take.

And would Bertie have reacted differently to "four hundred and twenty-six thousand"? No. These people were right. Bertie had known nothing of the fraud. Nothing at all.

He said, "I'm very grateful to you for seeing how things are."

Randall said, "Get out these files for Mr. Addis."

While Harris was away Randall explained their original in-

54

terest in them. The circumstances in which they were sent to security had been a little unusual. One of the secretaries had taken an interhouse call from someone, who hadn't given a name, to the effect that some material—the file numbers were stated—was on the way from registry for security safekeeping. The girl had relayed the message to Harris because he was in charge of the strong room. The files had arrived within a few minutes, addressed to P. Taylor.

This being a generic cover name for the security section, Harris assumed that whoever had instructed registry must be fairly high up. Strictly, only deputy heads of divisions and upward were supposed to know and use it. But why had the call asking for security safekeeping been made to a secretary instead of one of the section officers? There was an atmosphere of inconsistency.

"Before putting the files away, Harris referred to me and asked if he should look them over. I saw no objection. He spent two days on them and if I'd listened to him we'd have raised the roof even of the penthouse."

John waited; Randall, thinking of his own position, weighed his words. "As I say, I'm not an expert in this sort of stuff, nor is Harris. But that didn't stop his thinking the files had been rifled before they reached us."

"In what way?"

"Could have been as many as half the papers extracted."

"You followed it up?"

"As far as seemed practical."

Randall had let Harris nose around in the investment division and found the girl who'd telephoned. She was secretary to the advisory committee chairman's p.a., George Rogers. Rogers had instructed her. It was he who had told her to give registry P. Taylor as the addressee. "I actually had a word with Rogers on the security angle and he couldn't have been more sorry."

"You didn't go into it?"

"My terms of reference don't include questioning high-level policy."

"You'd have liked to."

"Let's say Harris would have liked to. He'd have saddled his horse and gone a-hunting if I hadn't locked the door on him."

"So there was a fox?"

"Harris thought there might be two of them. To start with. One died, perhaps the important one clue-wise as to how they'd opened up the hen house." Randall added that in short the files told enough of the story to suggest fraud but not enough to make evidence.

"A waste of time?"

"No. You may be able to get your fingers into a crack somewhere and begin to pull it apart."

There was one particular piece of paper that looked as though it had been missed during the mutilation: a letter from Fording Lencorp's registrar in answer to an investment division letter that was *not* in the files, saying he couldn't confirm a stock transaction because the numbers on the certificates quoted in a letter of such or such date didn't correspond with any in his issue ledgers and perhaps there had been a clerical error in stating the numbers.

"Or perhaps not?"

Randall shrugged his shoulders. It was a case of guess and guess again, but the inference remained: if the numbers were accurate and the registrar disowned them, then the certificates could have been forgeries.

"Anything else you can tell me, to save time?" John asked. Randall thought a moment.

"In Harris's opinion there was a faint smell connected with the original introduction of the business. But I can't to along with him. The people—the firm concerned—was and is completely reputable."

Harris returned with three yellow folders, which together made a solid six inches of paper, and Randall became official.

"Mr. Addis will sign the requisition as having taken delivery. And that's all we have to know."

Harris's face fell. "I was hoping—"

"That's between you and Mr. Addis." Randall tried to sound nonchalant. "If you're not around when I want you, I'll curse you for taking time off for your private affairs and manage with Platt as a stand-in. Mr. Addis, about the dead fox. You'll be fascinated to find that it took its own life while the balance of its mind was disturbed. Good afternoon."

Back in his own room Harris wanted to know, parceling up the files for Mr. Addis's convenience in carrying them, when they could get together. "You can't go on using that glass cage down there. It's as private as a goldfish bowl, and anyway you've been fired from the research division. I suppose you fixed that too?"

"Indirectly. I'd been there long enough and wanted to make a move."

"Of course. The trick is to drop a cover before it's blown." Harris was showing that he was familiar with the arts of the underground. "How about setting up another?"

John said he was giving thought to it, and brought up the point Randall had mentioned, the question of the introduction of the business that had led to the fraud. "So far only suspected," he added to make it clear that all was still surmise.

"Axiom Limited," said Harris, "have a very good name. They'd never knowingly let a crook into the old-boy network through which most of these big deals usually get started."

"What's Axiom's function?"

"I guess you'd call them financial agents. They bring together people who need capital and those who have it."

"And in this instance?"

Harris hesitated. "The captain convinced me there was nothing to it."

"Yes?" John waited.

"One of our directors has a sister married to a then newish member of Axiom's board, a man called Carstairs. Our chap is someone you'll have met, Boyle Glover, personnel." Harris added that this was the sort of thing you expected to find and to regard as natural on the old-boy network. "What else is the network but a backward, forward and sideways interlock of friends and relations. Like you and I, who have the same basic interests, so we tend to exchange information, favors and so on."

"That's true." John decided he mustn't prejudge Boyle Glover's possible involvement merely because he thought of him as a pompous ass doing a job that could be better done with phony frills.

Harris pursued his hint about exchange of information, stumbling a bit because, he said, this was a subject not lightly discussed in Number One. But did this secret inquiry set up by H.H. mean it had dawned on him that the investment committee was no more than a rubber stamp for its chairman's say-so?

"It's chairman being Gordon Parthessen."

Harris didn't say *ssh!* but he looked it. However, he said for God's sake don't hesitate to take advantage of the captain's back-door offer. "I'd like nothing better than to get my teeth into this."

"I think you can be a very great help."

Harris nodded and grinned. "Old H.H. has done the right thing at last."

John stopped off at the ground floor on his way down to the comupter room and put the parcel of files in the Bentley, relocking the door. What with the packages in the boot and files worth a potential half-million, the car was becoming uncomfortably valuable. So he gave the commissionaire a lordly tip and asked him to see that the kids didn't write rude words in the dust on the paintwork.

The commissionaire gave the crashing salute of the soldier he had once been and said that although kids weren't a hazard in these parts, anybody laying as much as a finger on the Bentley would do so at his peril.

6

V. Norton must have been watching for him through the successive glass walls; she was at the door of his office when John reached it and he saw for a second time that the skin of her cheekbones could suggest blood in her veins after all.

"*Where* have you been?"

She was entitled since yesterday evening to use a demanding tone with him and he began to move carefully into the necessary evasions. He reminded her with timid self-justification that she had been anxious he should get that garage job and since Mr. Glover had kindly said he could take time off . . .

She told him to never mind about that. Something was going on that she didn't understand. No less than three times the chairman's Miss Maple had tried to reach him, the last call having been put through to the adjoining office, hers, and what did it all mean?

"Nothing." He went into his office, she following him.

"Nothing? *The chairman* wanting to speak to you?"

Once again he took the shadow of a truth as a shield. "It seems that somebody who imagined they had a pull with him hoped he'd give me a second chance."

She didn't relax but she was a little less worried. "Who?"

"An elderly lady, a family connection."

"Of Herbert Hammond's?"

"No. Mine." This also was true, jesuitically speaking. "Although not in blood."

"So?" V. Norton wanted it all.

"Suppose her influence *could* have meant anything, I didn't want it to. I assumed you meant what you said last night about my being your chauffeur and bodyguard and everything?" He gazed at her with the lovesick expression that seemed to convince her.

"Of course." She lowered her eyes but he couldn't believe she was embarrassed.

Suspicion allayed, she came back to how he'd spent the afternoon. Had he found a job?

If she'd said "garage job" he might have stumbled in the truth game. Yes, he had found a job.

"That's good. Will you have a chance to work on Bentley cars?"

"And better. I have the use of one so you won't have to buy yours until you're good and ready. I wonder what Anderson wants?" He had found a note on his blotter "Call Mr. Anderson, please."

The lovely face was intent. "Use of a Bentley? You can't mean it."

"Nothing to it."

"I may seem dense but it can't be *free* use."

"We'll have to pay running costs, of course."

"It's too good to be true."

"Look, I remembered a chap I've known for years, a chauffeur-mechanic. His people have several cars, this Bentley amongst them. He trusts me." He grinned apologetically. "People do for some reason."

"What's his name, this friend?"

"Fred Ross," he said, with no cause for hesitation.

She had wanted to be convinced, of course, and her critical faculty fell apart. "Could we have the car tonight?"

"Tonight?" He pretended doubt.

"It's important. I'm going out with someone."

She was looking at him with her laboratory expression. He was alive but securely pinned.

"It's Boyle Glover," she said.

"For heaven's sake!"

She snapped back at him that if there was any more tiresome jealousy he could forget the whole thing right now!

"I was only going to say," he stammered, "that you're attractive enough"—he showed boldness—"in your own right

59

for a pot-bellied frog like Glover to want to kiss the ground you walk on."

"Maybe I am, but men like Glover will kiss it more easily if my Bentley's wheels have gone over it first. I understand this power thing. They want to go to bed with me but they'll want to much more if it's going to bed with a Bentley too. Is it a very old one?"

"This year's."

He was afraid she might become suspicious again about this fortuitous car, but she was now seeing it wholly in terms of its tactical value to her. She smiled slowly but not with her eyes. She remembered to pat the faithful slave:

"John, you're doing very well."

She proceeded to give him his orders with all the assurance of a chauffeur-driven Bentley owner of long standing.

"Haycott House. It's Number Six in Haycott Close, a small dead end at the bottom of Haycott Avenue."

"I know it."

"At seven-thirty, then, to pick me up and take me to Jermyn Street."

In her euphoria she hadn't considered a possible danger and it was sensible to reassure her now rather than have it come up later at a wrong moment. "You made the point that nobody notices the chauffeur. I don't think Glover will recognize me in such a different context. Anyway, he'll have his eyes on you exclusively."

"I shall have to make sure of that, shan't I?"

She asked him the Bentley's color and nodded when he told her. Of course it would be gray; fate lay too obedient in her cold hands for it to be any other color. On the other hand, dazzled perhaps by a future more foreseeably glorious than ever, she returned to her own office without having noticed that over the lunch break his suit had ceased to be the blue one he had worn every day since she had first seen him.

All the same he was impressed by the way she continued to behave like a girl who had no other thought in her head but duty to her employers and a determination to do her job with exemplary industry. The day wasn't long enough for it. It was typical that she should take work home with her even when she was planning a life in which she would never do another stroke of it; covertly he watched her square up several of those large account sheets and fold them to fit into a worn black briefcase.

He called Anderson. The director of research had a gritty voice but it was cheerful with approval. "Your paper on Botswana. Good work, Addis. Just what I need. Words of one syllable I can lift whole chunks of for the Investment Committee. They like things simple. Keep it up." He rang off before John could suggest he should have read today's batch of interhouse memoranda before wasting his breath on bouquets.

V. Norton came in again wearing her pale tweed coat and carrying her purse and the briefcase. She said she had decided on a slight change of plan. "It will save me saying it twice if I use your house phone."

She dialed a number. "Miss Norton here, Mr. Glover, please . . . Boyle? This is Victoria Norton. About tonight. Would it be a great inconvenience to you if I collected you say at Claridges? . . . Thank you. At seven-forty-five. I shall have my car so don't bother to bring one. . . ." She laughed dutifully at something he said and cradled the receiver. "So, John, you will call for me ten minutes earlier than I said?"

"Very good, madam." But she was already growing accustomed to his subservience. He offered to escort her again to the station but she shook her head impatiently. She would take a cab. And he should write down her telephone number and keep it with him. In case . . .

He watched her graceful departure through the main room, a girl on her way places.

He had made a little progress himself. He knew now, for instance, what the "V" stood for.

Of all names! Her royal namesake wouldn't have been amused by quite a number of things.

He began sorting through his desk, getting rid of odds and ends of waste, preparing for the final clear-out before his departure. His glance fell on the map of Nuristan. It wasn't the kind that rolled up. But to fold it would be no less significant and he couldn't bring himself to do it. Leave it here for the moment.

He drove westward in the heavy outgoing traffic with Fred's cap on his head to get the feel of chauffeuring. He didn't like to think it made him sit more resignedly in traffic hold-ups but it did give him a slightly objective attitude; a chauffeur does not own the car he drives.

He put the cap back in the glove compartment before he reached the garage he had picked out that morning as being only a five-minute walk from Haycott Close. It had lock-ups, and he now rented one at an extortionate weekly rate. He used it straight-away on account of the Bentley's trunkful of money. He got out the suitcase and the parcel of files and carried them to Haycott Close.

Mrs. Harrington opened the door before he could get out his key. She was in a tizzy, earrings rattling like castanets.

"Mr. Addis! Will you please explain to this man that you really *have* taken the room! I found him another round the corner but he won't even go look at it."

He saw a white, hungry face looming above her head. He put down the suitcase in the hall and kept the parcel under his arm.

Mrs. Harrington shut the door but had her hand on the knob, ready to open it again.

A hollow, worried voice said loudly, "On the contrary, it's *my* room. I'm Frank Borrowdale."

A tiresome, extraneous circumstance John could have done without.

He was a tall man in his thirties with a livid face, lank dark hair that lay in separated corrugations from front to back on a skeletal head. He didn't look seedy, but one day soon he would. Nondescript clothes hung on him from bony shoulders.

"*My* room," he repeated. "I must insist on my prior right to it. I definitely told this lady yesterday morning—"

Mrs. Harrington cut him short. Yes, he'd definitely told her he'd come back in the afternoon to fix it *and he hadn't*.

"It took me longer to arrange—"

She said that was nothing to do with her. Mr. Addis had paid over his money and moved in. She began to open the door. "So it's *out* for you, Mr. Borrowdale."

The man said, "Oh God!" and looked at John. "Can I please come up with you for a moment? It's important and urgent."

"I won't have him in *my* house!"

Only her ill nature prompted John's reaction. "It's all right, Mrs. Harrington. It won't hurt for him to see I really am in possession. Come on up, then."

But as Borrowdale followed him up the stairs, instinct nudged. There were other rooms to rent in this neighborhood. Dozens. What made this one so desirable?

The answer surprised him, ready though he was to be surprised.

The moment Borrowdale came into the attic he began edging toward the window embrasure, covering the maneuver with a barrage of repetition of what he had said down in the hall about his right to the room. It came to a sudden stop like a tap turned off. He stood at the window, motionless, staring out. John moved up to his side.

Whereas Mrs. Harrington had remarked on the view as being very nice too, Borrowdale was silent except for a sound like teeth grating. Victoria Norton wasn't, like yesterday evening, walking about while she undressed. She had already done so and was now seated at her dressing table painting her nails.

John said what he'd said before: obviously the girl didn't realize she could be seen.

Borrowdale gave a final grind to his teeth and unclamped his jaw. "She cares not one damn," he said caustically. "She's a pathological exhibitionist and always has been."

"So you know her?"

"Know her? Oh dear me, yes, the bitch. I'm her husband."

"Yes," said Borrowdale. "She won't divorce me, so I have to divorce her. Because she went off with every cent I had, I can't pay a private eye, so it's a case of do-it-yourself." He pulled John away from the window. "Now do you understand? The street is a dead end, no traffic. She'd spot me and get rid of any man she had with her before they were at the street door of her damned love nest."

"She's that sort?"

"Quick and cunning as a jay bird." Was there a note of pride? John said he'd meant was she the sort to take men home with her? Borrowdale shook his head. Not in the usual sense, but with her looks plus a driving compulsion to better herself, how else was she going to make it?

"It's eighteen months since she walked out. She could have something going by now. I don't know. I only found her again last Monday, saw her in the street, followed her."

He strode up and down. "Vicky is cursed with a belief that she's special. Her old man put it into her head. A sheet-metal worker in Sheffield. Six kids, she the prettiest. Extra education, clothes, treats, the lot, including elocution lessons to ease out the dialect."

He could see now, he ranted on, that even when she chose to become Mrs. Frank Borrowdale, wife of a white-collar boy

63

from the big city, it had just been a first step in a long-term plan that wouldn't always include him.

"I have no more prospect of becoming a millionaire than something out of the woodwork."

He added that he could see her point, but he'd never forgive her for going off with his every last penny by the simple act of writing a check on their joint account. "And by God I'm going to get it back!"

Why wouldn't she divorce him?

"She isn't the cold-fish unromantic she gives out she is. She gets impulses. Being married is an insurance against falling for some bloke who'd be no use in her grand design. And she'll make it. She's too bloody shrewd *and* beautiful not to."

John was embarrassed by pity for the man. He seemed the sort who invariably took hold of the dirty end of the stick without waiting for someone to hand it to him.

But he mustn't have this room.

"Borrowdale, why shouldn't I keep some sort of watch on her? It shouldn't be difficult if the likely times will be at night and first thing in the morning, when I shall be here anyway." And if there was a telephone number he could call should he see signs . . . ?

Borrowdale stared at him. "You'd do that for me? And I'd come right over and burst in on them and that would be that!" He became almost cheerful. He talked some more about what Vicky had done to ruin him and how badly he wanted to be free of her.

Finally he wrote a number on the pad on the small table below the telphone. He explained that he was working as a waiter in a Bloomsbury hotel—the Paradiso—until he could organize himself and go after something better. "And I'll take this number if I may?"

He copied it off the dial into a tattered pocket diary and shook hands warmly. John thought of escorting him down to the front door in case Mrs. Harrington was lying in wait for him with virago scorn and good riddance, but his satisfaction at having found someone else to take on his problem should help him to face her. John recognized this element in Borrowdale's nature because he had plenty of it in his own.

He would have liked to find somebody, for instance, to relieve him of the burden of being John Addis Hammond.

He unpacked the suitcase and put his things away in the chest of drawers and wardrobe; the top of the latter provided a token place of safety, within the hollow formed by the molding, for the Lencorp files.

7

Victoria's mauve evening frock in dull, heavy satin looked expensively simple. A three-quarter cloak of the same material hung open from her shoulders to show enough of her for John to judge its considerable effectiveness. Presumably the back was cut as low if not lower than the front, if that were possible. As a rule he noticed women's clothes, but he didn't have to know much about them to see that such an outfit could have cost the earth from a Paris couturier or next to nothing if run up by a little woman around the corner.

And if she wore no jewelry who could say she hadn't a phobia about diamonds with mauve? Or in that case why not amethysts, unless, as would be reasonable, hers were too big for dining in public?

But one aspect of her investment in herself had cost money, the pervasive scent that began to fill the Bentley as soon as he handed her into the rear seat. Whose money you couldn't, of course, know. But she had still to choose to wear it on an occasion like this, which seemed to indicate a considerable erotic perception. Husband Frank's reading of her seemed to be accurate.

Boyle Glover wouldn't stand a chance. She'd knock his eye out.

And so she did, presenting herself to him as a living color print of an adman's glossiest fantasy of gracious living. Drawn up at the door of the internationally famous hotel was one of the world's finest motor cars containing a lovely woman, dolled up by at least a Balmain and as bright as any Christmas tree in a brand-new Bentley's interior lighting.

Glover did not quite stumble with surprise, and he quickened his pace to cover the two yards separating him from these goodies. If he didn't see the imposing top-hatted and attentive doorman, he certainly wasn't aware of the short, gray figure of the chauffeur who was also there to make sure that he should enter the car without mishap and sink his chubby bottom into the seat at the lady's side.

65

The doorman saluted, the chauffeur took his place again behind the wheel, and the car slid silkily into the Brook Street traffic stream.

"Angelino's?" Victoria asked.

"Angelino's." Glover spoke on an exhaling lungful of held breath.

"Angelino's, please, Johnson."

The "Johnson" on the spur of the moment was suitable and clever. If she caught herself calling him "John" when they weren't alone she would have time to add the "son."

Glover had recovered from the initial shock of realizing he might have bitten off more than he could chew unless he went at it carefully bite by bite.

He said, "Victoria, you have a great gift for the unexpected."

"Are you trying to say," Victoria inquired with unwonted gentleness—unwonted as John knew her—"that you've never come across anyone before who has a job like everybody else because she can't bear an idle life?"

"Yes, of course, but—" Glover decided to give himself a little time before the next mouthful.

The interior lights were still on because she hadn't ordered them to be switched off and John assumed she not only wished Glover to be fully aware that he was in touching distance of a gorgeous status symbol but also that he should be seen to be.

The whole performance seemed as crude as all get-out, but Glover appeared to be having no trouble suspending disbelief.

The doorman at Angelino's, dressed as an Italian *carabinière*, was at hand to avert disaster during the transit overland from car to restaurant door ten feet away, but before leaving the car they had a short discussion about when it should return. Glover thought not before midnight at earliest —it was a wonderful dance band—but Victoria felt that perhaps Johnson should telephone the restaurant reception desk around, say, ten o'clock just to check their plans.

"Very good, madam." Johnson made no attempt to disguise his voice beyond a hint of cockney such as any Londoner could manage. As he went into the routine of supervising the *carabinière's* duties with regard to the Bentley's door handle, Glover looked straight at him but did not recognize him from Adam.

John locked the car in the garage again and bought cold

meats, salads, bread, butter and beer at a delicatessen on the way to his room at Mrs. Harrington's.

Before starting supper he got down the parcel of files and arranged the first one so that he could look through it while he ate.

Within minutes he began to realize an economist's limitations when faced with what seemed an average sort of commercial situation.

He ploughed doggedly on, and after half an hour's solid reading, began to see a hazy picture of intitial events that had occurred some three years before.

A Dr. Charles Bowen, Ph.D., D.Sc., etcetera, a scientist on the payroll of Fording Machine Tools, a subsidiary of Fording Lencorp, had invented an automatic tool of surpassing economy in manufacture and operation that used the new principle of ESMS—electronic separation of metallic substances.

Skipping through a hundred-page specification of technical data you could safely conclude, since the doctor's application of ESMS would enable heavy engineering to cut through six-inch steel plate as though it were butter at a third the cost of any similar tool, that Fording Lencorp had been on to a good thing.

It followed naturally enough that having taken out world provisional patents on it they should go foraging in the city for capital with which to develop and produce their wonder tool. It was also in the natural order of things that Hammond and Morgan should be approached to this end; they were there to do this kind of business. The preliminary introductions and negotiations had been effected by a firm specializing in such service, Axiom Limited.

John was ready to believe that somewhere in this area of the story was hidden the trap that the fox had set and that Dr. Bowen's version of ESMS was the bait in it. The fact that at first sniffing the trap couldn't be spotted was to be expected, and John couldn't criticize himself for not being sharper than Hammond and Morgan experts, who apparently had failed to do so at the time. In fact, he couldn't see that they had had any reason to imagine it was a trap. They had a wealth of detail on which to check. Patents, specifications, blueprints, figures—it seemed as comprehensive as anyone could ask. Then the legal division, accounts department, and outside group of experts in mechanical engineering design, as the second of the three files testified, had in their various fields examined and passed the project as worthy of the investment committee's serious attention.

This began to show in the last of the four sections of the second file, when the other side's negotiator emerged as a director of Fording Lencorp, his signature on letters an undecipherable scrawl, but translated below in the clear print of an electric typewriter was the name Samuel Wetherfield.

On the Hammond and Morgan side, however, since the letters were carbon copies, they weren't signed but had been written by the Secretary to the Committee on its behalf, which was probably inevitable and typical of any departmentalized organization in which individual responsibility decreased in ratio to its corporate increase.

By now it was ten o'clock. Reluctant to interrupt his researches, John hoped that the message for him at Angelino's would be to tell him they were staying on for a while.

But no. Miss Norton required her car at ten-thirty.

He stole another few minutes with the third file and came on a four-page official-looking report on pale-blue foolscap headed: "Samuel Wetherfield, dec'd.," and its subtitle was unequivocal: "Résumé of Inquiry into circumstances surrounding the death of Wetherfield, Samuel. Including transcript of Coroner's Proceedings."

Samuel Wetherfield . . . a director of Fording Lencorp . . . Randall's fox whose death had stopped Harris the huntsman in his tracks?

It took him an effort of will to put the files back of the wardrobe.

He pulled Fred's cap down over his eyebrows and drove fast, his mind full of what he had been reading. As he had expected, the key question it raised was the investment committee's degree of responsibility. He remembered committees at Oxford. In one or two the chairman had been elected for the easy reason that he had seemed prepared to do all the work, ready to make decisions and take action without waiting for the committee's endorsement, knowing that it would back him up, and gladly. His skill, of course, was in his ability to present a fait accompli and at the same time indicate that he couldn't have done a thing except by his good fortune in having such a tip-top group of men to inspire him. His greater skill lay in his capacity to goof and get away with it. On these occasions the committee, in a cleft stick, would take the coward's way out of it, remembering past successes to which it

68

had contributed nothing except complaisance, and accept the chairman's assurance that there were plenty more of those to come.

John wasn't sure who were members of the Hammond and Morgan investment committee—Colonel Gregory, Richard Horton perhaps, and two or three others, but Gordon Parthessen was its chairman. Dear old Gordon, who wasn't particularly old, and seemed too big, too heavy-faced and fisheyed, to merit such a cozy word as "dear."

John had always avoided him, not in particular but in general as being a Hammond and Morgan executive and therefore an enemy of freedom. In fact, he had only once met him to talk to for a few minutes two or three years ago at an Acantha cocktail party he'd accidentally stepped into.

He knew more by inference than direct information, again mostly through Acantha, that dear old Gordon, apart from his function as Bertie's right-hand man, was favorably looked upon by the "city" as a money-market expert and, as far as Hammond and Morgan was concerned, its main contact man who, as a good mixer, was all that Bertie was not.

It was typical of circumstance that Gordon Parthessen should be on the minds of Victoria and Boyle Glover when they got into the car at Angelino's.

They didn't mention him by name, an anonymity that would have continued longer if John hadn't remembered a drive with Acantha across Hampstead Heath last summer. She had remarked casually on passing a house isolated in walled grounds at the heath's highest point, that it was "dear old Gordon's" splendiferous new place. His reaction at the time had been negative but now, nearly a year later, it was positive and brightly tinged with anticipation.

Victoria said, "Johnson, we're going on somewhere. Boyle, tell him, please, how to get there."

Boyle Glover issued instructions to the back of Johnson's neck. "Hampstead Heath, the upper road. About a quarter of a mile this side of the Bull and Bush. Cornaway House. You'll know it by a high stone wall before you see the entrance gates. And, Johnson, let's have these lights out, eh?"

John waited for Victoria to authorize this, took her silence for consent, and switched them off.

Glover's voice lacked its usual plummy self-confidence but wasn't noticeably uncertain; you could imagine that he had a problem but not an unwelcome one. As a man needing to establish a prior claim to a woman and not much time for it before it might be threatened, he wanted at least semidarkness in order to hold her hand and perhaps to kiss her for the first time if she'd let him.

Victoria's position, however, was as crystal, and in strength, rock crystal at that. She was quietly working away behind a cool façade that Glover's hottest kisses wouldn't raise a tenth in temperature.

"Boyle, I think I'm putting you in a false position."

"Good heavens, child, in what way?"

"Well, you said you'd refused his invitation weeks ago. I oughtn't to have done this to you. It's very wrong of me."

"But, Vicky, dear, it's perfectly all right."

"I could be the cause of his having every reason to be offended with you."

He protested that that was impossible. "With *me*, close to him as I am? Besides, I had the best excuse in the world. I told him that I had someone with me he simply must meet. That I was crazy about her."

"You're very sweet," she said in the low, throaty voice. By now he'd probably gotten hold of her hand and was wishing the Bentley had a division to prevent the chauffeur's sharing the intimate moments of the passengers.

It was also apt to this fruitful day that John should find himself drinking excellent dry champagne and eating, perhaps incongruously, cold ham in a place where he might continue to pursue his objective: the servants' hall of Gordon Parthessen's house on Hampstead Heath.

There were nearly a dozen people at the big table; guests' chauffeurs and household servants taking a breather from their party duties. The faint beat of a small orchestra in the ballroom made a background to the gossip around the table.

He listened to it, marveling again at their total identification with the people they served. He spoke less than he was spoken to, but he interested them as a new face in the wide yet interdependent society to which their employers belonged, a new face representing a new face, in fact. The steward or butler who had opened the door to Victoria was sitting opposite him and a maid who had seen her at close quarters in the powder room vouched for the young lady's stunning good looks. "My, but she's got everything, that one. But did you see the fella she brought with her?"

Someone remarked that certain kinds of gentlemen in commerce seemed to have social advantages that you wouldn't notice just to look at them.

The powder room maid had a view on this. "All the same a lady can be seen with any gentleman, irrespective, if she's a lady *born*."

John realized that they were waiting for him to substantiate his employer's right to breathe the rarefied air in which she had arrived under doubtful auspices. None of the staff seemed to know Glover by name, and John assumed that he was not a frequent visitor. But his greater concern was in Victoria's failure to have provided him with a story which her chauffeur might use against inevitable inquisitiveness. This was the first flaw he had met in her planning. The table did not stop eating or drinking but its expectancy deepened. He went easy on the cockney accent:

"Our acquaintance with the gentleman is only recent"— the plural pronoun was below-stairs custom—"but he seems a nice enough gentleman considering—" a qualifier to add to "irrespective." "As for a lady born, I'd take the late dowager duchess's opinion before anyone's and what's good enough for her in that way is good enough for anybody."

"But too good for some?" asked a man at the other end of the table, and John saw a thin, dark face leaning forward to look at him. The ripple of laughter helped to carry the conversation past the moment when somebody might have asked him which dowager duchess.

"We like it down here in the south," he went on, munching ham. "We're independent now and can live where we like. Although I daresay the villa will see something of us once it's put in order." He added that he didn't suppose his lady was exactly *against* Edwardian art nouveau, although it could be somewhat overwhelming in the sun and heat and all. But of course Monte Carlo wasn't what it used to be. Personally he'd sell out before the place became quite impossible for decent people.

This seemed to satisfy the table, but now and again the lean face turned in his direction as though the man's curiosity wasn't wholly appeased. But John was careful not to talk any more and presently slipped away. He went out to the gravel space where the guests' cars were parked, the Bentley being the farthest from the house. He got into the back seat.

Close by, a large lily pool glimmered against a curtain of black trees touched here and there with vivid green where the lights from the house caught them. Every window was a beacon, music and voices vibrating from them into the stillness of the garden.

He was grateful for the peace, a moment to be quiet after a crowded day so greatly in contrast with the empty ones of the last weeks. He stretched out his legs, relaxed his back and shoulders in the soft upholstery.

Victoria's perfume mingled with the scents of the garden and gave them no quarter. Pity it did nothing for him. But it would be doing what it was designed to do for those involved in her strategems in the house—a fine neo-Georgian house, a mansion indeed, set in several acres of grounds and gardens in a large patch of countryside scarcely seven miles from Charing Cross. It made White House an urban cottage.

Drifting half-consciously into his thoughts was something that Acantha had added to her comment about "Gordon's splendiferous new place." "He has done well with my little Martha's six per cent."

John had only a dim memory of Martha, and he couldn't guess how smart she would be in dealing with an occupational hazard like Victoria, who might be able to hide her purposes from most men most of the time but not from their wives any of the time. Victoria, in fact, could run up against an obstacle here.

However, he learned in the next few minutes that in this instance she might not. A voice said, "You left us before the cigars. Thought I'd bring one out to you. I'm Tankerton." The face at the car's open window was the lean dark one from the other end of the servants' table. "I'm Mr. Parthessen's gentleman's gentleman, although of course I'm something more than that, naturally."

The cigar was large, and assuming it was from Mr. Parthessen's private stock, would be the best. John said thank you and got out of the car, aware of the man's extra three inches, and explained that Madam wouldn't like the smell of cigars in the car, she being what they called delicately nurtured.

"And I expect, of course, you're something more than her chauffeur, eh?" Tankerton chuckled in a jolly way that didn't go with his gravedigger's face. So it made it easy, he said, to ask for a little chat about matters of mutual interest.

"Let's be considerate of your lady's aversion to cigar smoke and take a little stroll."

The valet struck a match. "I have taken the liberty of piercing the cigar."

"Thank you, Mr. Tankerton."

"Sid Tankerton."

"Johnson—people call me John."

"It's nice and private in the Dutch garden. This way, John. So it looks as though we'll be working together—from different ends, as it were, but toward the same one." He repeated the fat chuckle.

"Sid, you'll excuse me if I say you seem to be talking riddles."

"But an easy one to guess, eh, John? It must have happened before."

John thought he could guess but the sooner the plain words the better. "If it's something to do with madam—"

"*And* with my Mr. P. You've hit it in one. To start off let me mention that our wife is in Canada." A stone bench was luminous in the gloom of the garden. They sat down.

"Yes," Tankerton went on, "Mrs. P. has been three thousand miles from home these last two months, and what's more, as we understand from her recent letter, she has no immediate intention of returning."

John said personally he never liked being in a household with a rocky marriage.

"On the other hand," said the gentleman's gentleman, "in *ours* we wouldn't call our soul our own. She watched us like a hawk in case we closed in on some passing dish that'd caught our fancy."

"Sid, I hope sincerely no one is thinking of *us* in a vulgar way."

This was hurriedly denied.

"Well, nobody better had, Sid, because we are prepared to bounce all lechers off the nearest wall. Whoever they may be. See, Sid?"

Sid said he saw, of course he saw. But it wasn't at all like that in this instance. No one could accuse Mr. Parthessen of being anything but a gentleman. A gentleman to his fingertips.

John said again that he sincerely hoped so. On the other hand Sid would agree that even gentlemen to their fingertips were sometimes blind to the social distinctions between one bed and another.

"Yes, Sid, it's beds we're talking about, so let's not kid ourselves." He added, to soften the impeachment, that perhaps in fact there weren't so many such distinctions as females liked to think.

Tankerton was silent for a moment. "I got off on the

wrong foot with you. She is a proper lady. All I can say. I've never seen us take such a shine to one so bloody immediate, and I am here to tell you she is looking as though she likes it."

John asked, and where was the gentleman we came here with while we were looking like we liked it?

"Him?" said Tankerton. "Such as him come two a penny. He is in our firm, you see. If we tell him to roll over and die for his country, that's what he does." Mr. Glover, in short, having been given the nod, had gone to the bar and was staying there.

"Our firm?" John prompted.

"Hammond and Morgan. Rings a bell?"

John agreed that it did.

"So maybe your lady would appreciate a word in her pretty ear from you, to the effect that we're in a position to be very generous. In the most gentlemanly way, of course."

John became silent. It would be poor tactics to fight any harder for Victoria's virtue with someone who was being something more than his gentleman's gentleman; in this instance his ponce, who as such was busily spelling out the score.

"Cigar all right, John?"

"Thank you, Sid, very good indeed."

"I don't suppose you've had time to make many friends. I hope you'll look on us here at Cornaway House as a friendly lot, for that's what we are."

"I will, Sid, and grateful." This seemed an opportunity to collect a quid pro quo. "Talking of friends, I'd half-expected tonight to run into a chap I used to know who drove for a business friend of your Mr. Parthessen, I believe."

"What name?"

"Billy Landon or Lawler. Something like that. A biggish chap."

"I meant the business friend."

"Oh, him. Let me think. . . . Waterhead, a Mr. Waterhead?"

"Wetherfield?"

"Could be. It was some while ago. Wetherfield. It sounds right."

"Remember his first name?"

"You've got me there."

"Samuel?"

"Could be. Not that I ever heard Billy mention it."

"No more than an acquaintance. I'm sorry, Johnny, but I'm pretty sure I heard he died a couple of years back."

"Oh, well. Not much chance of finding Billy in that case. That's our life, eh? Cars that pass in the night."

John laughed at his own bad joke and, having established that Parthessen had had personal contact with Samuel Wetherfield, wanted to drop the subject. But Tankerton wouldn't let him.

"Come to think of it I don't remember that Mr. Wetherfield even had a car, let alone a man to drive it."

"Then it's not the same chap."

"But his brother, that's Mr. Owen Wetherfield, would be able to tell you for sure, or maybe Billy Lawler drove for *him?*"

"Ah," John said, "that's an idea. He wouldn't mind if I gave Mr. Owen a call and asked? He'll be in the telephone book?"

Tankerton shook his head regretfully, or so it seemed in the semidarkness. Mr. Owen Wetherfield lived in Switzerland. Which in the context was another word for the moon.

"Oh, well, that's it."

But Tankerton still hadn't done with it. "Yes, the brother came to see us after the tragedy."

"A tragedy was it? Unexpected?"

"Drowned himself. An interesting case, too. One of those where the coroner hasn't a body to hold an inquest over, only circumstantial evidence in lieu of. Indisputable it has to be, of course."

"I didn't know that ever happened." John's neck hairs crawled slightly with a warning signal. Tankerton *might* only be engaging himself in morbid gossip, but there could be something behind it.

Guilt?

But guilt was in the air and you had to suspect your own eagerness to spot it. Yet if this valet who was more than a valet had been involved in Parthessen's criminal dealings with the brothers Wetherfield, the very mention of the name would set alarm bells ringing. Was that it?

But leave it, leave it. . . .

"For me, Sid, they can keep their dead bodies and inquests and what not. I'm for life and living. Like my Miss Norton. She knows how."

"That makes good hearing, Johnny. And don't forget what

I said. Generous to a fault"—the man's voice had no jollity in the misty dark—"but mean as hell when we're crossed. That's how we are, John."

"Yes, Sid?" It was John's turn to see, and he saw that a gentleman's gentleman on the ponce would also have to be the gentleman's bully boy.

At a few minutes past one, the host himself brought Miss Norton out to her car at the porch steps. The party was still going strong.

Parthessen was saying, "My dear, you really mustn't worry about him."

"You're terribly kind, but I feel awful, leaving him like this. He did bring me to your delicious party."

"I promise you he will be perfectly all right. We'll give him a bed for the night. It's much better this way."

Parthessen, a huge figure against the lighted hall, held the car door open for her. She arranged herself on the rear seat, folding her mauve cloak around her.

"I'll telephone you at nine-thirty," he said, "the day after tomorrow. That's Saturday. It would give me great pleasure to drive you out into the country for lunch somewhere."

"Thank you, but . . ." She hesitated just long enough—"Yes, I'd like that. Good night. Home, Johnson, please."

John started the motor and drove off, reflecting that while Victoria had beauty and cunning for weapons, dear old Gordon wasn't unarmed. The physical size of him, his wealth, his obvious experience with women, the hypnosis of his eyes and voice of powerful charm, would call for everything she had to hold her own with him, let alone get the better of him.

Gordon Parthessen had known perfectly well, for instance, that her objection to leaving Glover behind was lip service to convention, that she had wanted to be separated from him and by no one but Gordon Parthessen.

In short, she hadn't won the first round and maybe not even drawn it.

This now seemed to occur to her. The silence was broken a moment after he drove through the Cornaway gates.

"Stop!" she said sharply. "Stop at once!"

He swung in to the side of the road and braked. "What is it?"

"I can't leave Boyle there."

76

8

John pointed out that it would be a little difficult to do anything else but leave Boyle Glover behind. "It was all settled. Parthessen setttled it."

"I can't help that. I just mustn't leave him there. That's definite."

"You mean he'll tell Parthessen who you are?"

"He mayn't want to, but Mr. Parthessen is more important to him than he led me to think."

"And Parthessen will remind himself that the brass doesn't roll in the hay with the payroll."

"Don't be flippant!"

"Sorry. But I agree Glover is a Parthessen creature. His valet is another, a jackal to reconnoiter the area of a proposed kill." He told her briefly about Tankerton's inquisitiveness and the cover-story trouble. She asked with sharp suspicion why he had picked on the north as her place of origin.

"Because it's geographically and socially distant from the south."

She accepted it, and said she saw nothing unusual in the valet's interest in her. A man in Gordon Parthessen's position naturally had a protective screen around him.

"Parthessen won't let Glover go if he wants to pump him about you."

"Perhaps, but that wouldn't be his chief reason. He's kept him there as a beginning to breaking it up between us."

"You don't say."

"Gordon is very interested."

"The hell he is—" John remembered to be jealous.

"Now stop it!"

"But assuming you can get him to relinquish Glover he will still have all tomorrow to cross-question him about you, before your Saturday date."

"Not if I get him back now and have the rest of tonight to work on him. He won't tell Parthessen a thing about me. And this isn't an occasion for you to bother me with another scene. Anyway you've no worry. He's too drunk," she pointed out with chilling practicality. "So do as I tell you. Go back."

"What are you proposing to tell Parthessen?"

"Nothing. You'll deal with it. You must get Boyle away without involving me directly. What about the valet? You've made friends with him. Use your head. And don't argue with me. You're wasting *time*."

"Where was Glover when you last saw him?"

"Half-asleep in an armchair in the room they're using as a bar, a library they'd call it."

She took for granted that he was ready to stick his neck out for her, merely saying "you'll manage it."

He drove back to the house, passed behind the parked cars and stopped in a dark place on the narrow roadway that led to the service entrance. He walked the rest of the way to it and went in. He found a maid in the servants' hall who was willing to look for Sid Tankerton. John sat down at the table and waited for a long three minutes before the valet arrived. He raised a black, quizzical eyebrow.

"Forgotten our gloves or something?"

"Not gloves—Glover. We have changed our impulsive mind about deserting him. We are sorry for him. We're thinking of his embarrassment in the morning."

"Whereas I imagine *we* are thinking of your lady's embarrassment tonight."

'*We* understand that he could move under his own steam if he knew we were waiting for him. Perhaps he could leave this way, by the service door?"

Sid considered. "With a hand under his elbow maybe."

"We'd be grateful, Sid, if it was your hand."

The hand did a neat vanishing trick with the folding money John slipped into it.

And there was no need, was there, for Sid to mention our attack of conscience? "We shouldn't care for Mr. P. to read more into it than simple consideration on our part."

Sid agreed there was no need. When the party broke up— might be a couple of hours yet—and Mr. Glover wasn't around, it would be assumed that he had been given a lift home by another guest. So if John would wait at the north corner of the back terrace, to the right of the service door, "I will bring him out by the library French window. He's sitting right by it."

"Thank you, Sid."

"I'm sure you'd do the same for me in similar circumstances."

"Of course, Sid."

But it took Tankerton longer than John expected to fetch out Boyle Glover, and when at last he delivered him, semimobile, at the north corner of the terrace he left quickly like a man who had let good nature take precedence over common sense. John supported the mumbling, teetering man through the darkness to the car.

Victoria had moved to the front seat so that Glover could have the rear one to himself. He needed all of it for his sprawling legs and arms. He was only vaguely aware that he had been restored to favor and was asleep and snoring before they were out of the gates again.

"That was very efficient," she said. "I hope you can be as much so in getting hold of this car for the weekend."

"Weekend?" he asked. Hadn't Parthessen said "lunch"? And also indicated that he would supply transport?

Victoria was explicit. "It won't be the first lunch in the country that turned into a couple of days." And Gordon Parthessen would appreciate the discretion in using her car instead of his.

"His wife is abroad," John thought she ought to know.

"And likely to stay there indefinitely." So they hadn't spent all their time on sweet nothings.

"As long as you aren't confusing his need for caution as a rich man pursued by women with his greater caution as a guilty one."

He heard her sharp intake of breath. She would have liked to ignore the fuse he had lit but it fizzed and had a hot smell. She used misunderstanding to extinguish it.

"Why should a sophisticated man like Gordon feel guilty about cheating on a wife who has deserted him?"

John could have allowed the fuse to burn on and explode the bomb by telling her in words of one syllable what *he* meant by guilty. But he resisted the impulse. Not yet, not while she so valuably believed that she alone knew Parthessen's secret.

But although he kept his eyes on the road and did not dare look at her because the slightest hint from him might reach the antennae of her suspicion, conscience pricked him. A change in her mood gave him an opportunity to ease it.

She put her hand lightly on his thigh and said she was truly very, very grateful to him. And how was he proposing to get Boyle up to her flat, which was on the fourth floor, without the man's waking up the whole building?

79

John said he thought Glover would realize he was doing a Casanova and sober up sufficiently to creep about like one even if he ultimately found he couldn't act like one. "I'm trying my best not to be jealous."

Her hand tightened. "All this will be worth it—for us both, John."

"I sincerely hope so. Glover doesn't really worry me. This Parthessen, though. He's something else. I don't like the look of him. He has to be more than just clever to have climbed to where he is."

"Does it take more than clever to find himself a rich woman to marry?"

"A starter, no more. After that he's on the road to power, and ruthless to get it, if he's that sort of man. And he is. There isn't a soul at Number One who doesn't know it."

"I can handle him." She took her hand away from his thigh. But remembering she still needed his help, forced a lightness into her tone. "Stop worrying about me. Just concentrate on getting Boyle up to my flat so that not a soul in the world knows he's there and I'll love you forever."

"Night porter?"

"There isn't one."

Five minutes later they were in a deserted Haycott Close. The lobby of Number 6 was dark.

Victoria took keys from her purse and went ahead to unlock the outer door.

Glover was sound asleep. John used a fireman's lift to carry him to the elevator, thankful not to have had to con the man into being quiet. He kept him like that, over his shoulder, all the way up rather than repeat the exertion of lifting him again.

The building remained wrapped in its convenient sleep.

9

Victoria's bed was large and unexpectedly frivolous, with a headboard draped in white muslin tied about with large mauve satin bows, and had an eiderdown with a similar cover. Dressing table and stool were decorated with flounces in the same motif, whereas the window curtains, which Victoria closed for once, continued it in reverse, muslin white bows on mauve satin.

Boyle Glover's complexion didn't clash with her bedroom's color scheme but his porcine features, the eyes asleep and half hidden in rolls of fat, looked quite horrible on the lace-edged pillow.

Victoria's clinical attitude toward this time-honored recipe for making sure of a man's loyalty remained impressively unwavering throughout their joint process of undressing him. Neither doubt nor distaste were in her.

She thanked him at the end of it, but without suggesting that his help in the preliminaries was not within the normal duties of someone who was more than her chauffeur. She gave him her keys, telling him to lock the street door on his way out and return them to her at the office in the morning.

He went down in the lift, locked the street door after him and drove the Bentley to the garage. Victoria's windows, living-room and bedroom, were dark by the time he reached his room. He took off his clothes and slid into the small bed, tired and anxious for sleep.

But the longest day of his life refused to let it come, parading a jumble of memories. One of them was particularly obstinate, perhaps because unlike the others it bothered his conscience: Frank Borrowdale.

At the time, to suit his own book, it had been easy to agree to watch for evidence for Borrowdale's badly needed divorce. But now that it had become suddenly available, with the man's number on the pad by the telephone and the keys of his wife's flat lying there between the hairbrushes, it wasn't so easy to ignore the moral responsibility involved.

Were his own needs greater in justice and virtue than those of a wronged and cheated husband? This brought him to an effort to define his own needs.

Staring up at the attic's invisible ceiling in the lonely darkness, he tried to analyze and understand them. They were elusive and confused and seemed to be greater than he had ever had to grapple with. Trying to deal with them was leading him into dark corners of doubtful morality. . . .

Oh, the hell with it, and also with Victoria's present adultery. In any case she was planning to repeat it with a more vulnerable co-respondent than a mere Boyle Glover, and there would be time and to spare to fulfill what was a minor obligation compared with the others that were plaguing John Hammond the Seventh. Yes, that was at the root of it. His bloody genes.

In the meantime, circumstance was busily throwing him into still deeper water. If he had been asleep or merely lying there with his eyes closed, he wouldn't have seen the faint patch of diffused light that suddenly broke the darkness of the ceiling where it sloped inward above the door.

Then the thought came that the origin of the light might be in Victoria's flat, that it was penetrating the dormer window's thin curtains. He got out of bed in a subconscious movement more alien to thought than action. He went to embrasure and pulled aside the curtain.

The window across the way was like a bright television screen, but silent, as though a technical fault had cut off the sound.

Victoria again was all but naked in a filmy nightgown that gave her insecure coverage in her agitated movements. Her mime was of desperate alarm caused by something that had happened or was still happening in the unlit bedroom off screen to the right.

She went twice toward its door and each time backed away. Now she stood in mid-stage, forcing herself to think more calmly. She must summon help. Decision made, she walked quickly to the telephone on the small bureau. But as her hand went out to the receiver, she let it drop to her side in despair. Clearly she knew whom she wanted to call but not the number.

A good actress. But this was not acting.

John went to the chest of drawers and groped for his lighter amongst the things he had emptied from his pockets, and by its small flame found the necessary coin for his pay telephone and managed to dial her number without fumbling.

He stood with the receiver to his ear and watched her startled reaction to the first ring of the bell. He saw her summon all her will power to answer it and for a long moment while her hand hovered over the receiver he was afraid she might be too scared to take it up. The insistence of the continuous ringing turned the scales for her.

To preserve the secret of his nearness he began to speak the moment the receiver reached her ear. "This is John, worrying about you. I'm thinking that a drunk can wake up violent and abusive. I should be there, if you—"

82

Her frightened whisper broke in.

"Oh, John, *John* . . ."

He could now ask what was wrong. Her harsh, dry swallow was louder than her barely audible words. "He . . . he isn't breathing."

Unconsciously prepared for it, the shock still hit him like a blow. She spoke his name again with intolerable anxiety.

"I'm here . . ."

"I've just realized I don't know where you live. A long way? Can you come . . . quickly?"

"You're sure that he—?"

"Yes, yes!"

"I'll come. Sit down and do nothing, except take a drink. Brandy if you have it. A stiff one."

He rang off, his racing thoughts incapable for the moment of anything more useful than a repetitive jingle, "Well, well, dead in her bed, Boyle Glover's dead in her bed, dead in her bed."

10

The next moment John decided flatly that Glover couldn't be dead, must *not* be dead. Wasn't there a simple explanation—that Victoria, for instance, had suddenly realized when she began actually to get into that bed that what had been an objective intention was about to become an unpalatable fact?

Revulsion could have contributed to her panic, when at the same moment Glover's drunken stupor had given way to normal sleep. He had abruptly stopped snoring, and she had assumed that he had stopped breathing.

It was so obvious, so why tell yourself that the kind of girl she was could hang on to an objective intention longer than most and be more able than most to get into bed with a drunken man she scarcely knew and stay in it?

Dressed and ready to go to her, he put the keys in his pocket and took another look out of the window.

She was sitting at the bureau, her back to the bedroom, her chin in her cupped hands. She was still in robeless half-nakedness.

She must be wrong. Glover couldn't be dead, couldn't be dead. . . .

But John was still very frightened when he tapped softly on the door of her flat before turning the key and opening it. He crossed a small pale-blue foyer to the living room. She hadn't moved nor did she do so while he went to the window, lowered the blind and pulled the side cord to flatten the slats. There were curtains, too, which he closed.

Continuing to the bedroom, he pushed open the door and felt for the switch.

Glover lay on his back, sightless eyes staring at the ceiling, and there was no doubt whatever.

John stood motionless, "heart attack" leaping to his mind. Behind the presence of death was the path to it: overweight, a sedentary job, the strains of ambition, tonight's exhaustions from spells on Angelino's dance floor in order to hold a beautiful woman in his arms, the excitement of her challenge to his manhood. Add alcohol in quantity and top off with frustration when Parthessen showed clear signs of wanting her.

He turned from the door to great surprise and a violent physical contact. The beautiful woman poor Glover had lost was clinging to him in a state of more passion and nakedness than would have been possible at Angelino's or anywhere except in deepest privacy such as Glover in dying had ironically provided.

Her lips were touching his ear. "John, oh, John. Thank God for you!"

Was this the ice maiden?

"John, *take him away!*" Her mouth closed on his as though to draw his consent before it could dare deny her.

A remarkable moment. But in spite of its unsettling effect on him he was able to wonder whether this sexuality was in reflex to her fear or a larger bribe, a bigger promise than merely stroking his thigh. A sick thought: would she have kept it now if the bed had been unoccupied?

It helped him to loosen her arms and put her firmly from him.

He saw a doubt in her eyes, as though she was afraid she had lost her power over him.

"I need you, John."

"You'll freeze like that."

She realized her state of undress and made a movement of her hands to hide herself. But her doubt passed: he hadn't rejected her. She dropped her hands. Let him continue to see and want her.

He went along with it as usual and she got to work on him again. He had successfully brought Boyle up here, it should be just as easy to take him down—down to the car and put him in the trunk, take him somewhere, anywhere no one could see, and dump him. "John, you will? For God's sake, say you will."

"It looks as though I shall have to, doesn't it? But not the elevator again. The stairs. And you leading the way as before."

"No!"

He looked at her blankly. She was moving her head from side to side in refusal. "No! I can't involve myself!"

"You haven't had that drink? I could do with one too."

She stared at him and made her limbs move. The simple act of fetching glasses and a bottle from a sideboard seemed to ease her tension a little. She put the things on the table with a clatter and he half-filled the glasses. Not restorative brandy but homely gin; however, it might bring courage they both needed.

"We haven't much time," he said but sat down in one of the easy chairs and gulped at his drink.

"Not 'we.' "

He took no notice. "Not in the trunk of the car."

"You haven't the key to it?"

He shook his head. He couldn't explain that it already held something. At another time he might have laughed at another sick notion: would she have come to a settlement with her ambition for what was in the trunk?

"How then?" she asked.

"Stop hovering and sit down."

She sat down but on the arm of his chair, which wasn't what he meant.

"Patrol cars." He began to speak his calmer thoughts. "Even in this so-called swinging city their inquisitiveness increases as the traffic thins. It's going to be bloody difficult."

"Don't fail me. Concentrate. What are you going to do— every step of the way—*what?*"

"Well, for one thing, if I'm to meet anyone on the way out I'd prefer to be seen carrying a clothed drunk rather than a nude one."

"It was difficult enough undressing him when he—"

"And much more so to dress him now. It will take the two of us again."

She cried, "Oh no!" in horror.

"There is too much 'no' from you. You talk about me not failing you. You're failing yourself."

It steadied her a little. "If I must help you dress him—"

"You must. Where does he—did he live?"

She didn't know. But perhaps his wallet would show?

Married? She didn't think so. It hadn't come up in conversation. On the whole she'd had the impression of a professional bachelor. She was beginning to gain strength from the mixture of gin and rational talk. She repeated that his wallet should be full of information.

"I don't propose to touch it. Or anything more of him than is absolutely necessary."

"Fingerprints? But, John, it's natural death. Probably heart? There won't be a—won't be an investigation?"

He finished his drink. "Come on, then. And when we've dressed him again, you dress yourself. The mauve satin." He got up.

She slid off the chair arm and sat on the floor, looking up at him in horror. "Mauve satin? What on earth for?"

A plan was forming, but there wasn't time to talk about it.

"First we put his clothes on him." He dragged her to her feet and pulled her toward the bedroom, she protesting that she wouldn't and *couldn't* have any part in it. It would be the end of her. She jerked herself free and backed away from him.

"Johnny, you must be strong and brave for both of us!"

He told her brutally that this was her flat, her bed, and her decision to bring Glover back to it.

"I wish to God I hadn't!"

"But you did. Have you forgotten why?"

She stood straighter. "That's also why you must get rid of it. You understand, Johnny? Must!"

"I hate being called Johnny and I absolutely refuse to go one step further without your cooperation. All the way."

She clenched her hands into fists and glared at him while he explained the alternative. "I walk out of here and you call the police, tell them, Oh dear, my friend has had a coronary—what shall I do, what shall I do?"

"Impossible!"

"You wouldn't be the first girl they'd rescued from that sort of problem, with know-how and cups of hot, sweet tea."

"It would be in the papers, dreadful scandal!"

"You'd live it down."

"But Mr. Parthessen—"

"Ah!" It was the best of all moments to test her resolution "You—wouldn't live it down with *him*."

Her self-confidence rose to it.

"I want him!" She must have heard the determination in her voice and was afraid of its effect. She came up to him and linked her hands behind his neck. "But I don't *want* him in the way. One day, I may want you, dear John." She took her hands away and smiled mockingly. "Strong mind, strong body," she added. "You win, sadist. I'll cooperate. Do whatever you say. But I shall have to have another drink."

She became as good as gold, meaning as insensitive as he could ask, throughout the unpleasant business of getting the husk of what had been Boyle Glover into his clothes. She contained her impatience while he double-checked details such as knotting tie and shoe laces as the wearer would have fastened them. She balked only at being left alone while she dressed, so he stayed in the bedroom. He insisted that she should put on a careful make-up.

"No one is going to see me close to."

"We hope not. But please do it."

She came to him to zip up the frock and stood with pretense of passivity while he inspected her. He couldn't have picked on a better tonic for her. She looked scarcely less wonderful than when she had set out for Angelino's and knew it.

"Well?"

"You'll do."

She lifted her chin at him with something of her old dominance. "Understatement doesn't suit you."

"I beg madam's pardon. We now go through his pockets."

"What for? You said you wouldn't touch anything."

"He could have a diary with an entry about tonight, or your telephone number or something."

It was a valid precaution and she was so far recovered from her collapse that she did the actual taking things from Glover's pockets and shared his search of the wallet and diary she found. There was no reference anywhere to Victoria Norton.

John nearly had a coronary himself, carrying Glover down the stairs and into the car. And it all but finished Victoria when she realized she had to sit at the back with the body and do what she could to prevent its looking like one. Somebody had to, and she couldn't have driven the Bentley.

11

The journey back to Hampstead was the continuation of the nightmare, and when they arrived within a quarter of a mile of Cornaway House John realized that the worst was to come. How to turn into the gates and drive toward the house at a time when the party was beginning to break up, and not to meet cars leaving—cars that were now emerging with full headlights because of the darkness of the grounds?

He drew up at the side of the road and sat undecided for a long minute. There was at least two hundred yards of drive before the turn-off he had noticed earlier, during which the risk of more outcoming cars would be considerable. It was a temptation to wait until the last guest had left. But wait where? Or drive around for an hour? Both alternatives would bring the danger of police-car attention. Also there was the condition called *rigor mortis,* the specifics of which he was totally ignorant of. Finally there was Victoria, sitting helplessly within inches of a dead man while someone whom she regarded as her inferior in mental capacity took the responsibility for plan and action.

Not surprisingly she asked what he was waiting for. "Don't tell me we've come as far as this for you to get cold feet!" It sounded gritty in her throat, as though the tension was strangling her.

So he set his teeth, knowing that it was a case of now or never, and drove on and through the gates, alert for the first warning flicker of headlights from the direction of the house. He would have liked to feel his way without lights at all but had to compromise with parking lights for fear of missing the turn-off.

Luck held. He saw the opening just in time, swung off into it, and dropped speed to creep along a track through the woods toward what he was expecting to see: a glitter of glass heralding greenhouses, sheds and other necessities of a large garden. He stopped short of an open space that would be large enough to turn the car in, switched off the ignition and sidelights, and brought welcome silence and near-darkness in which to prepare for the last move.

Victoria's anxiety had eased a little as she sensed his relief, and she now gave him credit for greater boldness than he possessed. "Are you going to put him back in the library?"

"I'm crazy, but not that much, or rather don't have to be. Tankerton went back to the service door after he'd delivered him to me *without waiting to see me hand him into the car.*"

"So he could have just wandered off anywhere. John, why couldn't you have told me that before?" She was angry with him but saw the point: no one could say for certain that Glover had gone home with her. Now she could easily explain her part in it, merely had to say that Glover had been drunker than she'd thought so she'd changed her mind yet again. "I wouldn't have him in the car with me in that state."

"Or he refused to come with you because he remembered which side of his bread was buttered? Didn't want *him* to think he was trying to hang on after he'd been told to give up the goodie?"

He didn't have to name "him" nor what the goodie was that Glover wouldn't wish to be thought he was hanging on to.

"I prefer," she said, "the first explanation."

Of course she did.

He left the wheel, telling her if she felt safer, to leave the car for the shelter of the trees until he returned.

He dragged Glover out of the back seat and for the last time hoisted him over his shoulder. Starlight and the occasional shafts of light from departing cars helped him find the way to the lake. There was a path around it, and he came finally to the stone seat in the Dutch garden.

This was the sort of place where a man might sit down to sober up before going back to the party, a place to be alone to reflect on the harshness of a dependency that had forced him to give up the most promising bit of stuff he had found in years.

He draped one of the flaccid arms over the back of the seat to hold the body on it.

On his return to the car an abrupt nausea seized him. He had to stop and cling to a tree. He was sick, briefly, and felt better although his knee and ankle joints seemed dangerously slack.

Victoria's reaction took a different form. She came out of the shadows, settled herself in the front seat and became garrulous, not waiting for him to ease the door shut before she began to relive the worst car trip . . . my heart was in my

89

mouth . . . those awful moments when you were carrying him . . . any second someone might have crossed the end of the street. "And then when you insisted on having the light on inside and I—"

He shut her up sharply and she choked harshly on a flood of words cut off.

Fifteen yards from the drive he had to stop for an outgoing car to pass before slipping the Bentley into its wake and so, thank God, away from the place.

Victoria began to talk again but now of the present and less hysterically. A call box . . . she would watch out and tell him the moment she saw one . . .

"What for?"

"To telephone, of course."

Whom, in heaven's name, did she want to telephone?

"For you to telephone. Don't you remember? It's been long enough already."

"What has?" He was tired, tired of thinking.

"Since the valet handed Boyle over to you. Don't be so dim." she said angrily. "You have to call him and say thanks all the same but Mr. Glover was too far gone for Miss Norton to have anything to do with him, and he'll say that's funny because he isn't around anywhere. And then you clinch it. You say he must be because the last you saw of him he was weaving off into the garden saying he wanted fresh air. That will get me out of this mess once and for all!"

"Or once and for all drop you right into it."

"What do you mean?"

"That Tankerton would immediately ask himself *why* I had gone to all the trouble of calling."

"But it would be a message from me. You could say I realized I had placed him in an awkward position with his master over it."

"So I could. And even then how long would it stand up after someone finds Glover stone cold dead on a garden bench? Not five seconds. Tankerton would say, 'Ah, so *that's* why she had Johnson call me, to plant the idea that she had left him behind when in fact she *did* take him away as she came back to do. But then when he died on her she brought him straight back and landed *us* with the unpleasantness.'"

"Oh," she said, positiveness gone out of her. "You think that's how he'd reason?"

"And so would Parthessen, and that would put you well and truly at the wrong end of a barge pole he wouldn't touch you with. Or have you at last come to see that's the best possible place for you?"

"No!"

"All right. Then you must take a chance that even without your planting a get-out story they won't ever reason that way."

"I see. Yes." She seemed convinced. He certainly was.

She became suddenly drowsy, an honest reaction to the strains of the last hour. Her head drooped toward his shoulder, where it came to rest.

But ladies don't sleep on their chauffeurs. Not in Bentleys. So he took off Fred's cap and let it drop on the floor rather than disturb her by leaning forward to put it in the compartment.

Her hair was soft and fragrant against his cheek, a tender moment he would have enjoyed if she'd been practically any other girl showing trust and gratitude in such a fashion.

Trust and gratitude? But would he have raised a finger for her if it hadn't suited him?

The sour taste of this thought saw him through the next tender moment when he stopped the car in Haycott Close. She raised her head and shivered, and said, "Come up with me, I can't be alone."

"You'll be all right."

She caught his hand. "I shan't be able to sleep. My heart's still bumping. Feel it."

"Give yourself another gin and you'll be asleep in no time."

"Alone in that bed? I shall imagine him still there! Please, Johnny. Isn't it what you want?"

He remembered his devotion.

"God, yes, but—" He also remembered that an hour or so earlier she had planned to take Boyle Glover in her arms to consolidate *his* loyalty.

"Did you say 'but'?"

"It's a false situation."

She thrust his hand from her. *"False?"*

"You know what I mean. We've both been through it tonight."

"You'll never have another chance!"

"I'd risk that rather than spoil something beautiful just because it's therapeutically convenient." An inspired escape. He hadn't finished admiring it before she all but flounced out of the car, saying, "Save me from sentimentalists." She slammed the heavy coach-built door with a thunk that echoed loudly in

91

the confined space of the Close. He hoped the furious neighbors would note that such selfishness showed she had nothing to hide.

As he walked back from putting the car away, he thought over the events of the night with a hot wave of retrospective fear at the risks he had taken. The truth was, he'd had luck, all the luck in the world.

He took off his shoes in the hall before climbing to the attic and undressed by the light of the shaded bedside lamp. Before turning it out, he wound his watch. Twenty-four minutes past two.

There was no interval at all between that moment and finding himself in the middle of the room, now full of sunlight, on his way to answer the telephone.

He became half-awake with the thought that Victoria was calling him, then remembered how he had avoided giving her the number. His second thought suggested that it could be someone wanting a previous tenant. His third brought him fully awake: Frank Borrowdale, of whom he had a clear picture writing down the number from the dial yesterday evening.

A few seconds to prepare for the high, rapid voice but not for what it said.

"Addis. She *has* started, something!"

John gripped the receiver, controlling shock. "Such as?"

"Taking men home with her. One there now."

Taking men home with her.

"Hold it a moment—" John tried to arrange his mind. "I'll have a look." He had to go through the motions. He let the receiver dangle on its cord and went to the window. He returned and found the earpiece talking to itself.

"Addis, are you there, *Addis?*"

"Her curtains are closed."

"I could have told you that. But it proves it, if nothing else does."

"What else does?"

"Evidence of my own eyes. And the chauffeur's. Now in a minute there'll be yours!"

"Chauffeur" was not a word that John was pleased to hear in this context. Its synonym was "disaster." Borrowdale was triumphant. They had her cold, just as he'd prophesied. "Addis, you take the elevator up to the fourth, bang on her door and walk in on them."

"Oh no, Addis doesn't."

"But, old man—"

"If we had an arrangement it was I should be at my window while you did the bursting in."

"All right," said Borrowdale reluctantly. "I'll need three or four minutes to get there, but don't leave the window. If the bastard does happen to leave before I get to them at least you'll know him again and that will tie in with the chauffeur's evidence."

John said, please take it easy. "I'm still half-asleep. What is all this about a chauffeur?"

Borrowdale explained impatiently how some nights when he couldn't sleep he came over and wandered around, mostly the other side of Haycott Avenue, where Vicky couldn't catch sight of him. Last night he had struck lucky. She had arrived in a chauffeur-driven Bentley. "In her glad rags and with a man in a tuxedo who was so well oiled that she had to get his chauffeur to help her get him in and up to her flat! And nobody says it was an innocent last drink for the road as late as that."

"How late?"

"A bit past one o'clock. We're wasting time. The moment she opens the door to me I'll make for the windows and get the curtains pulled back so that you can see her and the man. . . ."

How was he so sure the man was still there?

Borrowdale was positive of it. The chauffeur had taken his master up to the flat and come out alone and driven off. It stood to reason his master was making a night of it—when he'd recovered sufficiently with black coffee and so on. "Vicky's bloody obstinate when she's made up her mind." He broke off to say that after the burst-in he'd come straight down again and be at his front door to meet him and compare notes at once. "What with you, me, and the chauffeur, she's cooked."

John said he couldn't keep watch and dress and be downstairs all at the same time. And the less Borrowdale risked another tangle with Mrs. Harrington the better. There was a coffee bar in King's Road, first one on the right after turning left out of the avenue. They would meet there. He rang off before Borrowdale could object.

He dressed without going near the window. It wouldn't help an investigation into fraudulent conversion of Hammond and Morgan money to watch a husband confront his wife and

93

a lover who wasn't there over an adultery that hadn't happened. As for Victoria, she would have a second reason for being grateful to him for refusing to spend the rest of the night with her.

It was remarkable how the luck had held.

Predictably Borrowdale was staring haggardly into his coffee cup saying, "A most God-awful mistake . . . she laughed at me. You saw that? Once she was over the shock of seeing me, she had it all her own way, said I was dreaming, that the same old jealousy had affected my mind. You should have heard her!"

"Better luck next time," John said hypocritically. He didn't like Frank Borrowdale, and much as it would have suited him to blame Victoria as an ambitious climber over broken hearts, it wasn't easy. The nicest girl might break Borrowdale's heart and be justified.

The fellow was perking up now, and talking about who'd have the last laugh. "I didn't let on to her about the chauffeur." He drained his cup. "Even if his employer sent him away and made his own way home when he was good and ready, the chauffeur's evidence will be enough for the judge. A lawyer will know how to build it up."

"The chap will have to be found first. A needle in a haystack."

Borrowdale began to enjoy the last laugh. No problem there.

John suddenly saw why. "Of course . . ."

Plenty of time while the chauffeur was helping his master up to the flat. Plenty of time to cross the road and take the Bentley's license number.

Yes, they had all the luck in the world, except that all the while they were enjoying it Victoria's husband had been robbing them of it by not being able to sleep. Luck? The worst kind, the false kind.

But this was ingratitude for the little that remained, and in any case you made your own luck. Everybody said so.

And Borrowdale was saying that if he wasn't back at his bloody Hotel Paradiso by nine he'd be thrown out on his neck. *Paradiso.* You should see the kitchens!

John paid for the coffee. "I'll walk to the bus stop with you."

Borrowdale looked at the clock behind the counter. "Christ, I ought to take a cab, me a lousy waiter worrying about a waiter's lousy job." He went out and moved along the curb, looking up and down the street for a vacant taxi.

Make your own luck, John told himself, following him and praying for inspiration.

A thought came . . . try it:

"Why a waiter?"

"Who'd give me a decent job in the state I'm in?"

"What would you try for if you weren't in a state?"

"Industrial research. I have a degree—London School of Economics."

John said what a coincidence—economics was his subject, too. Borrowdale commented that the Harrington creature had put on the dog, telling him Mr. Addis was a banker.

"I work for a bank. Banks use economists." He added that it was also a coincidence in another way, since it so happened that he knew of a temporary research job to which it might be possible to steer a fellow economist.

Borrowdale shook his head emphatically. It was good of Addis, but any job that needed concentration was out. These days, even as a waiter, he had to write down an order if it meant fetching more than two dishes at a time.

John said, "This is something I know you can do. Your effort last night and again this morning shows it. But first we are going to have another cup of coffee and some bacon sandwiches." He took Borrowdale firmly by the elbow, pointed him back in the direction of the coffee bar and began walking. And talking. "It isn't likely to involve much head work, simply a matter of taking notes about a situation as you go along on the basis of a verbal report to us when you get back." He opened the coffee bar door for Borrowdale to go in.

"Back?" he asked as John pulled up a stool for him. "Back from where?"

"Switzerland. The man is in Switzerland. Two bacon sandwiches, please, miss."

What did you say?

"We need to have a report on the man."

"I heard that part of it. But you said Switzerland."

"That's right. This afternoon, for a few days. There's some urgency."

"This—but I—"

"Why not?"

"It's a credit-rating inquiry?"

"You could say it's that."

95

"There are agencies that specialize."

"Not for this one. Too delicate. You know how it is."

Borrowdale asked with suspicion how came it that a bank empowered a junior to go around handing out jobs? John kept his fingers crossed and said that ordinarily it didn't, of course. "It simply happens that the—er—customer is my pigeon and I'm responsible. You have a passport?"

Borrowdale said yes he had a passport, and come to look at it, the way things were with him he'd be glad to take this on —a gleam showed in his eye—but he wasn't in any shape, clotheswise. . . . This suit, for instance, was his best; he had another, but it was in a worse mess.

John waved his hand. There would be ample expenses to cover that sort of thing.

"Ah," said Borrowdale, the gleam brighter still; then it vanished. "But my divorce! I have to find a lawyer, fix an appointment—one can't just walk in on these fellows. What a damn shame. I'm sorry, old boy." You could feel his expectancy as clearly as his voice revealed it. John obliged it.

"I suppose you wouldn't let me handle the preliminary steps—set it up for you against your return?"

"You'd do that? But you've already done a lot for me."

"And for myself," John was grateful to be able to say. Making your own luck could be hard on the conscience.

"You find that chauffeur," said Borrowdale, "and it's in the bag. Whereabouts in Switzerland?"

This was a faculty for escaping the issue that John, an expert, could envy.

"And who's the man your people want the dirt on?"

John finished a mouthful of bacon sandwich.

"His name is Owen Wetherfield. If you'll stay here, I'll slip back and check the address. Also you'll need the advance for expenses." He could have put his hand in his pocket there and then, but even a wishful thinker of Borrowdale's competence might have become suspicious.

He returned fast to Mrs. Harrington's. For the first time the house was full of life: voices, doors opening and shutting, two young men running down the stairs on their way out to work. They looked as though they'd slept well, undisturbed by nocturnal comings and goings.

He took down the Lencorp files. The blue-colored paper of the Samuel Wetherfield inquest made it easy to turn to, and the information he needed was where he looked for it, at the beginning of the elder brother's evidence: "Owen James

Wetherfield, only surviving relative, domiciled in Switzerland. Address: La Rouette, Chexbres, Canton de Vaud, Switzerland."

The files back again on the wardrobe, John thought to take a look across at the flat to see how Victoria had survived her husband's unannounced and inopportune reappearance in her life.

She also had neither failed to realize that luck had worn thin nor hesitated, like himself, to begin at once to make her own.

She was packing.

On her rumpled bed were two large open suitcases, and a small wardrobe trunk stood between clothes closet and dressing table. By the look of it she didn't propose to leave so much as a handkerchief behind. He hoped she'd remember to keep out something to wear for the journey to wherever she was going. She wouldn't get far as she was, not without being arrested; topless wasn't the half of it.

He went to the telephone and called her, and once again saw her doubt the wisdom of answering. She was right to think twice about it. Borrowdale could be renewing his attack by telephone. But it rang on and she had to risk it.

"John here," he said, a repetition of his call to her last night. "I'm just checking to find out if you are all right?"

"No, I'm *not!* I'm leaving this place. Now!" Her pause was infinitesimal. She couldn't tell him she was married, that her husband was pursuing her for a divorce she didn't want to give him. But her quick wits found another reason for flight.

"This flat is *haunted!*"

"Haunted?"

"Have you *no* imagination? My nerve has gone! I can't stand another minute here!"

"I should have stayed."

"Your regrets aren't going to help me now." Which neatly made it all his fault. "I can't take any more!" Her voice was distraught, but he could see only composure and command in the poise of her lovely body.

He said she couldn't just walk out like that. Where would she go?

"A hotel, anywhere, so long as I'm settled in with a substitute telephone number I can give Gordon Parthessen before nine tomorrow or he'll start trying to get me at this one."

"A hotel is no sort of background for you." Now it was for him to think fast.

She said it would have to be a hotel and a first-class one, which would cost her the earth but it was all or nothing now. "I'll see you in the office?"

He said he supposed so, although it was his last day and no work to do.

"There'll be your last salary check."

This was interesting and to be encouraged. "I'd forgotten."

"You *are* impractical."

"You're welcome to it if it would help. And something from my savings, perhaps?"

"You mean that?"

"Of course." He seized the opening. "I'm thinking a hotel would be wrong for your image as a rich girl from the north. You should have a swank apartment."

"I know I should, and it's also impractical to talk about miracles. Goodbye."

"I think I know of a place in Mayfair."

"My dear fool, flats in Mayfair come dearer than any in the world."

"I wouldn't have started this if I didn't think I could work it. I came up with a Bentley, didn't I?"

A moment's pause, then her voice was honey-sweet in his ear. "A fantasy, John? But I'll allow you to believe it until, say, noon? Will that do?"

He saw her put back the receiver and stand for a moment in thought, as though examining all that had been said. She nodded to herself, satisfied with it, and resumed her packing. She unlocked the top drawer of the bureau and took out the black briefcase she had brought home from the office yesterday. She carrried it into the bedroom and put it in one of the suitcases.

Perhaps it was the way she held it, or simply his own association processes, but he wondered if the thing contained routine homework. Those large sheets had looked like accounts of some sort—the consolidated accounts? The ones that revealed the discrepancy?

He was stupid not to have thought of this before.

Meanwhile, her husband was waiting in the coffee shop.

John found him full of optimism and bacon sandwiches, a piece of greasy paper by his plate. He gave it to John. "You'll need this for the lawyer."

"Ah, yes—" as offhand as John could make it—"the car number."

"The magic wand— What's so funny?"

"I was seeing the chauffeur's face." John looked at himself in the mirror behind the counter. "Quite a shock for him."

"Serve him right, lending a hand to adultery." Righteousness didn't become Mr. Borrowdale.

John looked at the number again. Why try to force your luck when you had only to sit still and leave it to circumstance?

Seven digits in the Bentley's registration number . . . Borrowdale, more right than he knew when he'd said his concentration wasn't what it once was, had written down a K that should have been an X, and a 3 for an 8.

All this panic for nothing. But if he hadn't needed, after all, to save himself, he had saved Victoria from the distraction of having to run away from her husband at the same time that she pursued Parthessen, which John was determined she should continue to do. She would push the man into a corner where he might begin to make mistakes.

And Borrowdale in Switzerland nosing around Samuel Wetherfield's brother might even turn up something of peripheral use.

In fact, the only debit against the panic was its enlarged effect on him due to the nightmare of last night.

He used the pay telephone at the end of the counter to call Swissair to book a seat for Mr. Frank Borrowdale on the 3:15 Geneva flight.

Borrowdale's eyes were frankly avid at the sight and feel of the generous expenses money. Divorcing Vicky had taken second place in his immediate future, which was Switzerland with money to spend.

John arranged with him that should he want to get in touch, he should call the Harrington attic number either before 8:30 A.M. or after 11 P.M. But there was no urgency about this assignment. "Report on return" was the essence of it. Antipathy increased with the minutes you spent with the man. John saw the back of him with relief.

The next getting-rid-of concerned the packages in the Bentley's trunk, but it was still too early, not yet nine, to start on it. He decided to go back to the attic to put in another half hour on the files, particularly the inquest report.

He took a sharp look around the corner of Haycott Close before sidling into it and up to the Harrington door. But, as he saw when he reached the attic window, if Victoria had finished packing, she was still only in the bra-and-panties stage of getting ready for the street.

His visual, if one-sided, intimacy with her was beginning to take on a kind of cozy domesticity.

12

CORONER: Thank you, sir. Mr. Owen Wetherfield, aged forty-eight, naturalized Swiss subject of British birth, domiciled at La Rouette, Chexbres, Switzerland. Occupation: "retired." . . . I'll now ask you to look at this letter—the clerk will hand it to you. Please take it from the envelope. Do you confirm the handwriting?

O. W.: Yes. It is my brother Samuel's.

CORONER: It is addressed to you at Chexbres and begins "Dear Owen." When did you receive it?

O. W.: By the first post on September seventeenth.

CORONER: Would you look at the postmark.

O. W. [reads]: "Penzance, postmarked four-thirty P.M., the fourteenth of September."

CORONER: So it was in the mail for three days, a normal period, I should say, for a letter going to the continent. However, by the time it reached you, when you at once, and very properly, informed the Swiss police, who immediately telephoned our chief constable, there was little the authorities here at Penzance could do about it. The wind, gentlemen of the jury, as you will hear, was strong from the northeast on the night of the fourteenth and continued so into the late morning of the fifteenth. In the opinion of the lifeboat coxswain and others, including myself, if I may say so, who are acquainted with conditions at Porth Cove, it is certain that the small dinghy would have been driven many miles into the Atlantic even if its occupant had changed his mind and tried to return to shore. But I am anticipating. Let us consider the letter first [reads]:

"Dear Owen. Sorry about this. I shall have done it in the tidiest fashion I could arrange—to borrow a dinghy from the beach at Porth Cove—you remember that summer?—and row out to the horizon. (If the wind holds I shall have an easy row.) There is enough left in the cash box for you to pay the dinghy's owner for the loss of it.

As to the loss of me, no one will regret it except your dear self, and for this grief I am truly sorry. I won't bother you with the reasons. They will be trivial to other people, but seen through my black cloud they are convincing enough for me. Would the head shrinkers have rid me of it as you said they could if I would go to them? Too late to find out. But I know I shall have left it behind forever once I reach the sea's end. Again, how sorry I am for the trouble this will cause you, but you are the only person who will understand—your affectionate brother, Sam."

So there it is. He says that you will understand. Do you, sir?

O. W.: Only that this tragedy is the logical outcome of the intermittent fits of depression he suffered from all his life and refused to consult a doctor about.

CORONER: You were close to him?

O. W.: He was fifteen years my junior and inclined to be solitary. But I suppose I knew him as well as anybody could.

CORONER: When was the last occasion on which you saw him?

O. W.: Very nearly five years ago.

CORONER: What do you know of his affairs, business and otherwise?

O. W.: Nothing, I am afraid.

CORONER: You cannot help me?

O. W. [*with a gesture of regret*]: No, sir.

CORONER: The police report suggests something of a mystery man. But that is the effect of being what you yourself called him, a solitary fellow. Police evidence that you will hear, gentlemen, is likely to bring us to the same conclusion. But before we come to that, perhaps, Mr. Wetherfield, you can confirm now, rather than on a re-call to the stand, that you have no idea of your brother's address prior to his tenancy of a small furnished house in Tunbridge Wells—The Laurels, Bickley Road?

O. W.: None, sir.

CORONER: That was only three months ago. Also the City of London Police have been unable to determine the exact nature of the business he conducted from 208 Ledden Street. And less than four months there. Somewhat of a mystery man—but nothing necessarily sinister in that, although we do have this rather complete destruction of

101

all papers and documents that might have shed light. Can you, Mr. Wetherfield, account for that?

o. w.: I can only say that he was a very tidy sort of man. Also the way he chose to end his life surely showed his anxiety not to cause trouble for those who would have to cope with it.

CORONER: You must leave the deductions to me, sir.

o. w.: I beg your pardon.

CORONER: Whereas his privacy and tidiness have actually led to confusion, uncertainty and ignorance. These tiresome fellows who mistakenly believe—I beg *your* pardon, sir. We must respect your grief.

John paused in his reading. The police, the coroner and his jury, the brother and all in the court were in no doubt in the first place that Sam was dead, and in the second that he was one of those individuals, by no means rare, who, departing this life in madness by their own hands, try to do so with the least embarrassment for those they leave behind but succeed in their exaggeration only in adding to the chaos.

In Sam's case, however, the chief embarrassment did not trouble them, because no one knew it, no one mentioned it: what might he have done with the large amount of other people's money that had come into his possession so shortly before he set out for the sea's end?

Was it lying in a bank account, the record burned with his other papers? Or had he converted it to cash and taken it with him to the sea's end as a symbol for the world's love of Mammon?

Possible answers. But the whole first premise in this thing was that Sam had come into possession of it with help from someone inside Hammond and Morgan. Would that someone have let Sam's craziness go so far?

Not bloody likely, as the saying went.

John straightened the files and reconstituted the parcel in which he had carried them here. A glance across the road told him it was safe for him to sally forth for the day. Mrs. Borrowdale, bag and baggage, had gone.

13

"You'd like to open an account, Mr. Hammond? We are at your service." Mr. Brown, the manager, pink-skinned, white-haired in spite of youth, and clearly destined to become somebody's favorite uncle, shook his hand, put him in a chair by the desk in the ten-by-ten office and seated himself, asking, "And who recommended us to you?"

John replied that perhaps foolish idiosyncrasy had had something to do with it. He had been attracted more by the physical aspects of this branch than by St. Justin's total reserves, the vastness of which he took for granted. This must surely be the smallest of the great bank's hundreds of branches up and down the country?

Mr. Brown beamed, he sincerely hoped that it was so, and personally understood Mr. Hammond's idiosyncrasy.

"Yes, in the heart of Mayfair but no more than a single door, a six-foot counter, one cashier, two girls and me."

"And the lilac on that modest table where the customers write their checks."

"And their paying-in slips," Mr. Brown added urbanely. "But you should see our early daffodils. People stand at the door to look in at them."

John had done exactly that a few weeks ago. "And here I am."

The manager was further pleased. "Spring comes to Brook Street on that little table." He sighed. He was sorry it had to come to an end.

"Spring?"

Mr. Brown shook his head. He was referring to this branch. "Profit is all, Mr. Hammond."

"This— You're *closing* the branch?"

Mr. Brown shrugged his shoulders. "Not I, Mr. Hammond. It's a head-office decision. Small premises mean small accounts, and these days it's only the small people who object to being overawed by big battalions." He explained that the bank didn't own this property and, although it was now on the market, didn't propose either to buy it or negotiate a new lease with whoever did buy it.

"I'm sorry if you'd set your heart. However, we shall be moving into that new building on the corner of Davies Street. Head office points out that it's only a stone's throw from here and our customers won't mind."

"This one would. You say this house is for sale?"

"Georgian at its best, in my opinion. Yes, as far as I know. It's disposal is in the hands of Trueliff and Binns. You perhaps work for a property company?" Mr. Brown took a sheet of paper, saying he hoped Mr. Hammond still wished to open an account. It might be several weeks or even months before the ax fell. "We aren't at all grand here. You can start it with a few pounds."

John sighed and confessed that there were seventy-odd thousand of them outside in the car. "I can't very well cart them about indefinitely."

Mr. Brown put down his pen carefully. "Not very well, no."

"It's all right. I didn't get it with a gun."

"Good heavens, of course not," said Mr. Brown a little too quickly.

"I am afraid there is more."

"More?"

"Securities I should like to lodge with you."

"I am sure we can accommodate you. The certificates and so on—have you them with you too?"

"There wasn't room."

"Rather bulky?"

John nodded. "My late trustees rather spread the capital around."

"Can you tell me what the total might be?"

John said he couldn't, not wouldn't. But he had arranged to go into the arithmetic of it in the coming week or so. Mr. Brown asked, he didn't wish to press him, but it would help in a possible administrative difficulty, to have a rough idea.

John shifted in the chair.

"It's a terrible lot."

"Six figures?"

"Seven."

"A million?"

"Several."

Mr. Brown suddenly cleared his throat. " 'Hammond' . . . Hammond and Morgan . . . one of those?" And when John admitted it, feeling not for the first time that he came from a race apart, Mr. Brown said, "Oh, dearie me. . . ."

Before John could warm to the sympathetic comment, the bank manager explained that this presented difficulties vis-à-vis head office. "We aren't geared here for business of this size. They'll expect me to explain that you'd be able to cash your personal checks here and so on while the main account is handled by one of our larger—" Mr. Brown stopped and nodded. "Exactly. If I talked like that you would walk out as easily as you walked in, and keep your money in a sock or something, thank you very much."

"So you sensibly accepted my point of view and agreed without waiting for head-office approval."

Mr. Brown laughed. "Yes. And if I am promoted to a branch in the Derbyshire hills, Thursdays only, ten A.M. to noon, with reduced pension rights, so be it."

John's thoughts had not been idle.

"In that case, what was that name—Trueliff and Binns?"

"Hanover Square, Number Twelve. The idea being?"

"Buying the house would be the first step toward buying the branch?"

Mr. Brown laughed again. "I don't believe that we sell our branches."

"Oh, we'd change the name, of course. You'd stay on?"

Mr. Brown scarcely hesitated. "I've often dreamed I'd like to be a private banker."

"There's more to be said for it than I realized myself. . . . Could we get the money out of the car? Do you think Trueliff and Binns have furnished apartments on their books?"

Mr. Brown said he shouldn't be surprised, which perhaps together with his ability to laugh stated his philosophy in a nutshell.

Before transferring the parcels from the Bentley to Mr. Brown's strong room, John took a further thousand-pound packet from each because, in the fluid state of his present operations, cash was proving a handy catalyst.

He finally reached the office at eleven-thirty and Victoria glanced at the clock. "You've failed, haven't you?"

He put one set of keys in front of her and kept the other in his pocket. She read the label on the key ring and said incredulously, "Grosvenor Towers?"

He told her that he had been able to take it for her for three months and to pay the rent in advance. "You'll look wonderful in it. All gold and white and crystal chandeliers.

It's rather big, but service is included, also a gardener for the roof garden."

She recovered quickly from her pleased astonishment. "So you meant it, about your savings."

"There's some over." He put a sheaf of notes beside the keys. She touched it and looked up at him with an expression he hadn't imagined possible on her beautiful face. It went in a flash, and he thought perhaps he *had* imagined it. "You'll get it all back," she said in a businesslike voice and went on to the Glover business. It was too early for the newspapers, of course, but there was nothing on the radio yet. She had a small transistor set in a half-open drawer.

"He has to be found first," he said, "which depends on the chance of someone going near the bench. In the meantime you act and *feel* innocent."

"But I am."

"Not of knowledge."

"That's difficult."

"So is everyhing likely to be." He was thinking of her ambition, and she understood him.

She put the keys in her purse and asked for the apartment's telephone number so that she could call Gordon Parthessen and forestall his ringing her old number.

John's reply was to produce half a dozen sheets of writing paper and envelopes he had filched from a writing-table drawer. She approved both his foresight and the quality of the handmade paper. "Yes. Much better to *write*. You can leave the letter with reception in the main hall. He'll get it this afternoon."

He argued with her about the first sentence she wrote: *If you still want me to take you to lunch.* The word "still," she retorted, meant if he still found her attractive and wanted to see her again. But she gave in and wrote the note the way he suggested. However, as she put it in an envelope and sealed it, she turned steely eyes on him and said she was obliged, of course, for his advice, but he mustn't think he had any more right than before to tell her what or what not to do.

"I understand that, absolutely."

"Good."

"But I still don't think you should stretch the lunch date into a weekend."

"I thought I was making it clear," she said icily, "that you don't own me just because you've paid for a penthouse for a few weeks. Can't you see that it's no more than an investment?"

"I only want to protect it by pointing out that the Parthessen kind of market you're trying to tap doesn't buy a cheap product."

She laughed. "How I despise you, John Addis. But don't worry. I know my price. And how to sell."

He hoped so. He put on a hurt expression suitable to her unkindness to him, took the Parthessen letter and went out to the car, parked in its now usual slot by the north door. He drove around to the main entrance, putting on Fred's cap before he got there.

The clerk at the reception desk, appreciating the chauffeur and the solid quality of the envelope, pressed a bell for a messenger boy: Mr. Parthessen should have it straightaway.

"Thank you, sir." John touched Fred's cap and turned, and there was Bertie two yards from him.

Bertie: tall, distinguished, flanked by two aides who bustled discreetly to draw the privileged bystanders' attention to the important personage; Bertie looked through him without a flicker of recognition.

Why should there be? Could the chairman of a multi-million-pound company be expected to recognize a face under a chauffeur's cap in a place as crowded as this?

Of course not. Then why this sudden anger simmering as he shared the hush of the people near him, watching the great man step into the private elevator and the door close silkily behind him.

Why? Injured self-esteem? His own self-importance slighted?

John decided, yes, probably, to a degree. But the thing that really fazed him was the dishonesty of the performance, its unreality. Its *silliness*.

He drove back to the north entrance, put away the cap, took the Lencorp files from behind the seat and went to look for Harris.

Harris all but embraced him. "Get me out of this madhouse, for God's sake." The matter? A director of the company had chosen Friday to have himself an attack of amnesia and disappear. "And that rates a weekend stand-by call for the whole section, not just to find the man but help public relations protect the good name of Hammond and Morgan, if you follow me."

John said he thought he did. Harris explained that in this

107

instance there was more than the usual flapping in the dove-cote.

"I didn't know the man was so important. I hope we find him or more likely he'll find himself in the next few hours. Three months' sick leave or shelved with full pension. End of story or bang goes my weekend."

"One of your directors?"

"Glover, the personnel—" Harris paused. "Ah," he said softly. "Maybe *not* the end of the story?"

"It's much too early," John assured him, to know. "In any case this doesn't have to have any connection at all. Can you and I get together?"

Harris glanced at the parcel under John's arm and spoke on the intercom to someone called Platt, saying he wouldn't be available for the rest of the day, and switched off the pro-testing noises that followed.

In the corridor he asked how John was making out so far.

"Nothing but gaps, and I agree that the letter about a mix-up in share-certificate numbers is significant. The other document that caught my mind is the inquest on Samuel Wetherfield. I'd like you to read it again."

Harris said of course, but in the meantime what about a base, somewhere to sit down and not be disturbed?

John had had the same thought. He had noticed a suite of unoccupied offices on the floor below. Harris knew about it. "Seven-oh-nine? The new people aren't due to move in for a couple of weeks." What the management division didn't know wouldn't hurt it, besides which an item in his security equip-ment was a master key.

So they descended one floor and Harris led the way to door 709, on which a man in white coat and apron was gold-leafing an inscription. He had completed the word "Conway" and four letters of the penciled outline of "Plastics."

"Excuse me," Harris said, and unlocked the door. They went in and he closed it, remarking that at this rate of diversi-fication the board would have to build on another dozen stories. "But three more staffers for the security section—not on your life! Try to remember to use the ash trays."

Sumptuous was the only description for the suite of six rooms. Eight-foot desks, wall-to-wall green carpet through-out, darker-green leather chairs, cream paint and a pervading smell of multiple newness.

John untied the parcel on the desk in the room designated "Managing Director" and said this didn't look like a place to

108

manufacture plastics in. Harris blessed his soul for such ignorance, this was to be the Conway Plastics head office; the plant was a hundred and something miles away in the country.

"Why?"

"Why what?"

"Are they separated by a hundred and something miles?"

"Don't say this is the first time you've seen the inside of a big organization?"

John laughed at the very idea. "But I can't get over the fact that this fabulous Number One is just a collection of H.Q.'s and all the real work being done somewhere else."

"North, east, south and west. But they keep our service divisions in bread and butter."

"Why?"

Harris looked at him again.

"Your trouble is an investigative mind. I know what it feels like. It's forever asking questions. But it isn't our business how Hammond and Morgan choose to waste money, only how they get it stolen from them." On the general question, however, of why everybody had to have a city office, one word answered it. Status. "The top brass sit in offices like this and know that they've got it made, and more, that they can be seen to have. What's success if visitors can't wade ankle-deep through all-over carpet?"

John apologized for asking silly questions. Back to their muttons.

Since Samuel Wetherfield had gone to the sea's end, he wasn't around now to name, or be made somehow to name, the crooked ears in Hammond and Morgan that had listened to his fraudulent plan; the files needed a fine-tooth comb through them to find other sources for this information.

"Yes," Harris agreed, "but first this Glover thing. You could be right, Axiom's respectability notwithstanding. I wonder if the captain is having second thoughts about it? Shall we raise it with him? Suggest it mayn't be loss of memory but that Glover introduced Sam Wetherfield, *knowing* he was bent? And now, suddenly, there's your investigation and he takes off for South America or somewhere?"

"How would he hear about it?" John probed.

"A leak from our top brass. They're shockingly lacking in security."

That top brass knew John Addis was investigating anything

was another false premise, and anyway Glover hadn't run away—he was dead of a coronary.

"Let's not involve Captain Randall at the moment."

"Okay by me." Harris opened up the files. "Now this inquest. You think there's something I missed?"

John said he wouldn't put ideas into his head before he had read the report again and, to avoid disturbing him, used the telephone in an adjoining room to call Rosemary Stewart to ask her if she could come in for an hour this afternoon. She sounded pleased and eager but suitably formal.

"Of course, Mr. Addis. Room Seven-oh-nine, at three."

He went back to Harris and lay restfully in one of the overstuffed armchairs while the other man frowned his way through the report. Body and mind clamored for sleep. Too much had happened to him too quickly for his powers of adjustment.

Harris stirred, coughed, lit a cigarette and said, "Are you thinking that if brother Owen Wetherfield's picture of Samuel was true, the fellow was too raving mad to steal a cent, let alone half a million?" He frowned again. "What in fact had the coroner to work with? A single letter confirming Owen's view of Samuel's mental instability, no evidence that it was Samuel's handwriting, and a missing dinghy that anybody could have towed a mile offshore and taken the stopper out of."

"Bung, like in a barrel."

"Bung, stopper. I'm left with a feeling I'd like to know more about Samuel Wetherfield."

John said he felt exactly the same way and would Harris care to go down to Tunbridge Wells this afternoon?

"Meaning he may still be alive?"

"I don't know."

"No more does anyone. But he mayn't be dead."

"He mayn't be dead."

"Whichever way it is, one thing's sure: he didn't go back to Tunbridge Wells."

"But his neighbors in Bickley Road aren't likely to have left it."

Harris saw the point. It was still a logical place to begin asking questions, even if only about Samuel's mental state.

"And what he looked like physically," John suggested.

"A description?" Harris was puzzled. "You can't judge a man's sanity by his looks." But Tunbridge Wells it should be.

John went down to the computer room to check on Victo-

110

ria's morale. Waiting for news of Glover's being found could have started her thinking, as he himself had been thinking, that if she and her chauffeur could break ordinances by failing to notify the police of a sudden death and by moving a corpse without doctor's or coroner's certificate in order to escape the scandal of a dead man in her bed, so could Parthessen and his valet in order to avoid the inconvenience of having it turn up on their garden bench.

But Victoria had left the office fifteen minutes ago, saying she wouldn't be in until Monday. "Some urgent family thing," said one of her assistants.

He shut himself in his one-time office and called the Grosvenor Towers flat. She was there, settling in. She was ecstatic. The place belonged to dreams. This was the way she should and would live.

"Yes," he said. "There's no news yet."

"Who's worrying about that? I'm not."

She responded with a light laugh to his guess as to how Parthessen might have dealt with the situation. So what if he had? It would put her in a still stronger position with him.

John asked how she worked that out.

"Because he will know that I know that our mutual friend was at the party, and that I didn't take him home from it. I shall make that quite clear to him at the very first opportunity."

"Other people at the party saw the man there."

"I don't believe they knew who he was. He wasn't introduced to anybody and I didn't see anyone talking to him. He was just drinking and grouching by himself at the bar."

He asked why she hadn't mentioned this earlier.

"Was it significant earlier? And before I forget it again, do you realize that after today I shan't know how to get in touch with you if I need you urgently?"

"I shall call you every morning whatever time you say. For instructions." But this was not enough for her. He felt it was safe, now that she had left the area, to give her his number at Mrs. Harrington's. She made a note of it and asked for "the garage number," too. When he demurred, saying he mightn't be there, she was alarmed.

"You must hang on to that job. It means the use of the car."

"You'll have the car any time you want it, day or night."

"The lunch trip tomorrow? And probably over the weekend."

"Of course," he said after a pause, jealousy overcome.

"Very well. But give me the garage number just the same."

"If you're so exercised about being able to reach me, there are at least three spare bedrooms in that apartment."

Her reply was probably meant to stagger him. "I am having enough trouble with myself over that aspect of you, John dear, without adding too much propinquity."

He hadn't an adequate reaction ready, but she didn't wait for one, urging him instead to devise a less intimate form of communication than nudging him with an elbow.

Cornered but not entirely confused, he said maybe he could ask his Uncle Mac to take messages, and he gave her the number at White House. "He's butler there." He didn't have to say in whose household. As for "Uncle Mac," what else had MacGregor been to him but a Dutch uncle? Who else, for instance, would have told him in a more avuncular fashion, if tinged with Calvinistic warnings, about those pleasant facts of life that Victoria herself claimed to be bothered by at the moment?

He had now to warn MacGregor of possible calls for "John Addis"; he could do this by telephone but he also realized he should see Acantha again without delay.

It was twelve-thirty. Luncheon with her two days running? She would suspect that he wanted something. Well, so he did. He hoped she would want it, too.

John's difficulty was how to trespass, however diffidently, into the relationships of the elder generation. Acantha might think that dear old Gordon was the best thing that had ever happened to Martha, and for all he knew she might have engineered the marriage to Parthessen as a haven of security for the poor, defenseless little creature—a born orphan, if you could have such a thing—and would rush to salvage it at the first hint that there was a rift in it that might widen.

But he had to chance this. His opportunity came when they were near the end of the *sole bonne femme*. Acantha was on to the problem of Selkon Manor, whether John should let the Delawares have it for another three years or end the arrangement because he might be needing the house himself. "After all, you may be settling down in the next few months to the kind of life that the manor is so right for."

A discussion about marrying one of the young women to be discovered through the deb system wasn't on his agenda just now, and he side-stepped it by saying that whoever lived

112

at Selkon, it would need to be rewired; the smell of hot rubber whenever you turned on a switch suggested that another architectural gem in our national heritage was about to go up in flames.

"It needs," he added, proud of the improvisation, "at least ten thirteen-amp ring circuits put in, as they did at Cornaway House." It was a safe assumption; electricians today installed nothing else. "That part of it must have cost a fortune there, but Martha, getting richer by the minute, wouldn't have minded."

"If Gordon bothered to mention it to her. Another half-glass, please."

He poured the Moselle. "I don't suppose she has a practical mind."

"Martha's mind is a mystery to me. Sometimes it doesn't exist, at others it, or something, shows signs of breaking down altogether under the strain."

"Is that why she's still away? To avoid the strain?"

"What strain?"

"You said it."

"Did I?" Acantha dabbed her lips with her napkin and looked at him over its white shield. "How did you know she was away at all, let alone still?"

He tried to look surprised. "Who doesn't know it?"

"Lots of us know she went to stay with friends in Canada and isn't hurrying home, but you, dear boy, do not in the ordinary course of events take the slightest interest in family comings and goings, and therefore," she continued relentlessly, "this isn't an ordinary course of events. *What do you want?*"

Fast as he would have liked to move, haste at this speed was more than he was ready for. He pretended not to hear the question.

"So the Parthessen idyll is collapsing?"

Acantha said sadly that idyll had never been the word. Gordon hadn't been faithful to Martha, either in intention or fact, for years. "She puts up with it, but now and again she has to get away where she can't see it. But, as you say, this time . . ."

Easier to reverse the tides than to change Acantha's train of thought. Her eyes bored into his. What was behind this gossipy stuff that was so totally out of character?

All right.

"Does Martha still hold her A-shares in her own name?"

Acantha was surprised but not beyond calling a spade a spade. "You mean has he taken them from her?"

"Has he?"

"No. It occurred to me that he might try to, so I took precautions just before he married her."

She let silence tantalize him, again a weapon to make him do the talking. She might be a saint, but occasional truck with the Devil had taught her the sweetness of power.

"So you took precautions?"

"I made her give me an option to buy her stock."

"Option . . . to buy. What happened?"

"Nothing. Why should it?"

"You let it run out?"

"Of course not. It couldn't," she added.

"Why couldn't it?"

"There was no time limit on my right to exercise it."

"You—you, Acantha—"

"Cheating the orphan? Better me than him, I thought."

In John's pleased view, however, she had thought right, and all those years ago had unknowingly leaped today's hurdle for him.

"But, of course," she went on, "my option didn't affect her right to give him her power of attorney over the use of the stock, its voting rights particularly."

"Which would automatically cease if you exercised your option," he said, stating the obvious.

He found himself looking at Acantha, looking her in the eye, which was steady and comprehending.

"The king is dead, long live the king," she said almost inaudibly. She could have asked, since twenty-four hours ago at this very table he had affirmed his unfitness and unwillingness even to touch the scepter, let alone take it up, what had happened to change his mind in so short a time.

But she did not. She smiled her benediction and became businesslike. She would write at once to Martha to say that she proposed to exercise the option. "It will be just the smack in the eye for Gordon that she needs to give him at this moment. I shall use your money, of course. In fact, I'll make over the option to you and it will be your purchase."

"I don't want—"

"We had that out yesterday," she said sharply, but he was able to get his own back: instead of her writing to Martha, it would suit him better if she went over and dealt with the thing on the spot.

"It would suit *you* better?" she repeated with asperity. "What about me?"

"Martha's six per cent must be out of his control by Thursday noon of this coming week. Jet flight would get you to Montreal in a few hours, say tomorrow or Sunday." He occupied himself with breaking off and buttering a piece of roll.

She addressed the top of his head. "In other words, you are so set on breaking Gordon Parthessen at once if not sooner that it's the hell with everything and everybody?"

"It comes to that."

"May I ask, then, what has happened or is happening to make you feel so strongly? What this crisis is?"

"No, Acantha. I'm afraid you may not."

Her hand came into view, holding out her glass again. "You can order me around all you have to, dear boy, but you can't stop my getting faintly sloshed when I feel like it."

He noticed the "have to." It suggested recognition that he was only doing his duty in all this. His heart sank a little at the thought and rose not a millimeter when MacGregor came in to say that Mr. Herbert Hammond's personal assistant was on the telphone asking if Sir John was available to speak to Mr. Hammond on a matter of importance; indeed, the personal assistant seemed to consider it fortunate that she had found Sir John at home. "I assumed, therefore, Sir John, that you would have no objection to speaking."

"I'll take the call here," John said. "Mrs. Morgan would also like to have a word with Mr. Hammond."

MacGregor brought the extension instrument to the table and went away to put the call through to it. Acantha inquired what word was she supposed to like to have with Bertie?

"At a guess, he is calling to make sure I've accepted an invitation to lunch with him so that we can talk about my selling out. I shall have to accept. But I'm also thinking this is a nice chance for you to tell him that the effort to get me into Hammond and Morgan from the bottom having failed, an attempt should now be made to get me in from the top."

"Yes?"

"He will ask how, and you will say why shouldn't I be elected to the board."

"He'll think I'm out of my mind."

"You mean it has never occurred to you?"

She was silent, then said Bertie would scoff, promise to think it over, and spend the next five years finding excellent reasons for not doing anything about it.

He nodded. "Except that he'll be keener than ever to buy me out now."

"You want that?"

"That he should be keen to, yes."

"He doesn't realize . . ."

"No, he doesn't realize that my thirty per cent has become fifty-three per cent, and I don't want him to, yet."

"Plus Martha's six. Which, of course, I don't mention either. You don't *need* it, of course. You have control without it."

"I need it."

"Yes." She couldn't bring herself to ask why he needed it, but there was relish in her blue eyes.

John grinned at her, took up the receiver and at the back of his throat asked Miss Maple to put Mr. Herbert Hammond on the line. Acantha did ask why the funny voice.

"She knows me as John Addis."

"Poor deceived creature, but of course so's everybody down there with that silly 'Addis' business. And you want to keep it up?"

He said, for the moment, yes, he would keep it up.

"I'll talk to Bertie when you've finished."

He spoke with Bertie and handed her the telephone.

After a word with MacGregor on how to deal with possible calls from a Miss Norton he drove back to the city with a feeling of something accomplished, something done that should have made him easier in mind but didn't. Bertie hadn't wanted merely to confirm the lunch date; he had asked for it to be changed and brought forward to dinner tonight. Why?

Agreed, Bertie was stupid, and clairvoyance was at its best amongst peasants. Had he sensed danger lurking in the anthill under him, his very inertness increasing his perception?

Or was the perception Parthessen's, guilt a more active stimulus than sloth?

14

John awoke with a jumping heart to stare upward at a pale object suspended over him; it became a face framed in brown hair, its tilted angle making the eyes expressionless. But he could assume that Rosemary Stewart was now seeing her new

116

employer as one of those unable to attempt his afternoon's labor without a period of postprandial sleep. How unjust.

He went to sit at the desk and make a start on being a boss. She followed him, took the chair opposite him and produced a notebook from her purse. He noticed how perfectly the cream sharkskin suit brought out the color of her hair.

Before he could begin, "Well now, Miss Stewart . . ." she said she didn't want to sail under false colors; she knew absolutely nothing whatever about plastic except that you mustn't put a pan straight from the stove on it.

He remembered the inscription on the door and told her hastily that technical knowledge was immaterial in this instance.

"You're saying that research in any field entails application of the same general basic principles, once the particular vocabulary is agreed and mastered. These are systematic approach, clarity of communication, coordination of results and logical conclusions—a fixed pattern of procedure."

"Dear me, yes, I suppose so."

Reproof was in her eyes but without chill. She was trying, she said, to demonstrate her efficiency. He sighed.

"In this job you may find you're better off without it."

She frowned with a dimpled crease between her nice eyebrows. How could one survive in the business world without efficiency? What else was there? she asked.

While John was looking for an answer that hadn't the word "charm" in it, the door opened and a man walked in. He stopped short at seeing them.

"I beg your pardon. I didn't know anybody was here."

The tone implied, however, that it was a forgivable intrusion. "I'm Philip Conway. We're moving into these offices at the beginning of the month and I dropped in to see how things looked."

"I'm John Addis, an intruder." John stood up. "This is Miss Stewart, a new colleague." Destiny moving again? "We're on the research side. Economics."

"I thought all that was over and done with." Conway looked puzzled. He was fair, slim and young-looking. Also, he wore a pale tweed suit, which gave him an amateur air as a businessman.

John explained that he wasn't researching Conway Plastics. He was only in this office because space was short. "We'll clear out at once." But he sat down again because Conway was saying that as founder, chairman and managing director

117

of Conway Plastics, enjoying the knowledge that his troubles were behind him, he was all the more sensitive to the slightest sign of a hold-up in the deal.

He looked at Rosemary's notebook and smiled. "But I should have realized there'd be a great deal more paper around and that you'd be doing it elsewhere—if Hammond and Morgan had found a last-minute snag."

"So you're happy about the deal?" John asked.

Conway was a little puzzled. Of course I am." He sat down in an armchair. "An odd question, Mr. Addis."

"I apologize for it. I shouldn't have asked it."

"The deal is completed except for formal ratification by your board come Thursday next," Conway said defensively.

Rosemary gave a small cough, and nodded. John assumed that she had typed the agenda.

"My trouble," John said, getting ready to trample on Philip Conway's most delicate and private feelings, "is that of a non-conforming economist asking himself why a man should have to sacrifice his autonomy and independence simply because he wants to expand his business."

Conway stared at him. "Forgive me, but that's a little naïve. Life isn't like that. Nor these particular circumstances."

"Believe me, I know nothing about the deal, only that it may be one-sided."

Conway shrugged his shoulders. "A man needing money to fulfill export orders from foreigners nobody seems to have done business with before must expect to sacrifice the luxury of being entirely his own master."

"I feel he shouldn't have to," said John. "Maybe I'm being obstinate or dim or both."

Conway stretched out his legs, showing feet shod in uncity-like Hush Puppies. "It's one of the inescapable facts that when the big banks and insurance companies turn down a man wanting a long-term loan of three hundred thousand, he has to go to the merchant bankers, starting with a short list of the larger ones in order of preference."

John asked what had governed his order of preference.

"Reputations."

"For what?"

"Living and letting live."

"For grabbing less than the others?" "Grabbing" hung in the air. "Where did Hammond and Morgan come on your list?"

"Fourth. The first three would have played, but their in-

118

vestment capital is fully committed." Conway seemed glad now to talk. "I'm not complaining, and as I say, I expected to lose my autonomy. Your people are taking up an issue of three hundred thousand Conway ordinary stock in exchange for their investment. And my board is to be reconstructed to include two of your directors."

John thought about this for a moment and asked if the directors had been named.

"Loanis-Andrews and Parthessen."

John said yes, Parthessen, and might he continue to ask questions? "What stake in Conway Plastics does the stock issue bring with it?"

"Twenty-five per cent."

"Will your efficiency be increased by Hammond and Morgan representation on your board and by moving your administration into the city?"

"It was a simple choice: expand now or lose our momentum. And our new market."

John said, please, about efficiency? Conway admitted that it would not be improved, might even decline unless he watched it carefully. Which, of course, he was going to do. He looked around the grand room, gloomily.

John went gently but relentlessly on, asking how much would Conway have saved if he could have had a straightforward, no-strings loan at say seven and one-half per cent. "No stock issue, no reconstruction, no move to the city?"

"Six per cent." The answer came promptly, as though he had mulled over this crucial piece of arithmetic. "Apart from profits." He looked down at his Hush Puppies.

"Have you estimated . . . ?"

"Leaving aside these export contracts, I've one or two new things, products that show how young this polymer chemistry really is. . . . Luck, hard work, normal development—the profits could be bloody millions, and they know it. Why else should they bother?" he asked himself explosively.

"Suppose the three hundred thousand isn't enough?"

"It's got to be." The silence spoke of imponderables, and Hammond and Morgan waiting for a bigger bite of the apple.

"A bad deal," John said. "But a provisional contract can be scrapped by mutual agreement of the parties to it. So can a signed and sealed one, I should imagine."

"What are you talking about? I don't want it scrapped!"

"Not for another, fairer one?"

"If pigs could fly!"

119

"You never know."

Conway stood up, staring at John in perplexity. "Look," he said, "you wouldn't be talking this wild nonsense just for the fun of it. Something's going on I should know about."

John too stood up and then sat down again. He had let his thoughts take over his tongue. "I'm sorry, Mr. Conway. I had no intention of prying, of upsetting you. Economics are hell—get one theorizing."

Conway got up and went to the door. "I hope to God that's all it is. If this deal goes sour I've had it." He closed the door a shade emphatically.

Rosemary Stewart, perforce silent during the conversation, spoke as though under pressure.

"Theorizing, Mr. Addis?"

He nodded, but more to his thoughts than to her.

"Wasn't it—a little unkind?" she asked.

"I was trying to do two things at once." He left his chair and made a detour around the room, arranging his mind.

"Was dangling a carrot at the poor man one of them?" she asked.

"You didn't take your eyes off him."

"I was sorry for him."

"Good. That's part of your job."

"Being sorry for Mr. Conway?"

"And the others," he said. "That talk with Conway would have been easier for him if it had been with you rather than me. Freer. It would have gone deeper and quicker. You're a woman, a kind woman."

"Thank you. Would that be research?"

"You helped me—"

"I meant being sorry for the people involved in Hammond and Morgan's take-overs?"

"Broadly speaking. But in detail, finding out if it could be avoided or put right."

She was perplexed. How would it help Hammond and Morgan? "They can't possibly care if someone gets hurt."

"Exactly. That was the other thing I was trying to show."

"This sounds as if it is *against* Hammond and Morgan." She was more puzzled than ever. "What is in the chairman's mind?"

To this he could honestly answer that he wasn't in a position to know.

Could he tell her then—she was sorry but she felt she had

120

to know if she was to take this job—but could he tell her something about his terms of reference?

"Why not?" He wished he felt as casual. Spoken words could never be unsaid, and these would make her a witness to another of his points of no return. There was a frog in his throat.

"In 1663—" he began, and coughed, but the thickness remained—"one day in 1663 two men sat down in a coffee-house on the corner of City Wall and Moorgate and wrote out a hundred-word declaration of intent in creating one of the first merchant banks—" He paused, because she wanted to say something; this time she was welcome.

"That's the framed parchment with the seals, in the Founders' Room, but I can't say I ever counted the words. I remember the first few, though: *We herein state our purpose . . ."*

That she should know and remember them was a significance to release the constriction in his throat, and he was able to continue unhesitatingly: *". . . that by virtuous use of the joint resources of our partnership in the assistance of those craftsmen and tradesmen of honest and industrious habit as may address themselves to us that under God's will we may bring them to prosperity. And we further say and declare that we shall ask no more in recompense for this aid than a fair percentum per annum mutually agreed by all concerned and that this shall cease forthwith upon repayment of the principal which time in each and every instance shall be at the convenience wholly of the borrower."*

She broke a short silence by saying lightly, as though disguising the effect on her of the deeps she had glimpsed, that no one who had taken the trouble to learn a hundred words by heart could be all that against efficiency.

He dared not tell her how long ago he had learned them, a small boy running to keep up with his father who was reciting them over and over as he walked the ancient turf at Selkon. A jingle at the time. What trick of ancestral memory had kept the words fresh and green until he needed them again?

"Certainly," she was saying, "nobody has to listen to Mr. Conway's troubles or those of anyone in the companies Hammond and Morgan have absorbed to know that the declaration lost its meaning a long time ago." She looked very straightly at him. "But now suddenly the chairman wants it spelled out for him. Why, Mr. Addis? He must know perfectly well that Hammond and Morgan don't assist craftsmen

121

and tradesmen of honest and industrious habit etcetera merely by lending money on convenient terms. They have stuck as many thumbs into their pies as there were plums to pull out."

She got up and went to the window, where she stood with her back to him, slapping her thigh gently with the notebook as though to goad herself into comprehension. She returned but did not sit down again.

"I *don't* understand. These men, in their positions, spend their time watching out for straws in the wind. How could I or anybody stop them from seeing more in it than just research—like Mr. Conway just now?"

He said he didn't think that would matter. She was baffled. "Someone *wants* them to think there's going to be a change in Hammond and Morgan policy? A *basic* change?"

"Could be."

"You—I mean the chairman realizes that this could start a panic?"

He shrugged his shoulders, implying that the effects were no concern of his and neither, therefore, of hers.

"So this is why you recruited me? Because I know a bit about what happens at top levels, and who is who and so on?"

He admitted it was one of the reasons.

"Spying is one thing," she said. "Sabotage is something else."

"Dirtier still?"

"Oh yes, very much so." But her eyes were questioning. She asked if he himself believed that this would be good for Hammond and Morgan. "The company has been good to me in its funny way."

"And to me. I believe this will be right for it."

After a pause she said she could accept that. From him.

"I'm glad. But why?"

She hesitated, then told him it was because he had spoken that declaration of intent as though it meant something important and she thought he wouldn't work without a cause that, forgive the squareness, had to be good and not evil. It wouldn't be just for the money. She had learned, from her father perhaps, to despise going after money, which he was always obsessively warning her about. It could totally destroy. As though she were in danger from it. "My boy friend will never make any money, brilliant as he is."

How inevitable that she should have a boy friend. Also she

122

would be faithful to him unto death. "Brilliance," he said, "is sometimes rewarded."

Rosemary Stewart shook her head. "There's a very small market for handmade harpsichords, and a one-man production line is terribly slow anyway. Charles lost his sight in Korea. That's why he won't marry me."

"He will."

"Of course, but thank you for the encouragement. And for the job, Mr. Addis. When do you want me to start?"

"Monday?"

"I shall tell Father that I'm a p.a. at last. Where is your office?"

He looked blank and she caught the expression.

"You *have* an office?"

"Most of my work seems to be done in my head and on other people's telephones." But he agreed that an office was probably necessary. And since she might be shopping in the West End tomorrow morning, he'd be grateful if she could find a moment to call in on a Mr. Brown at 169 Brook Street —he was on the ground floor, managing a bank—and introduce herself to him. Tell him that the deal to buy 169 was going through and would it be possible for her to take a look over the upper floors to find a corner where they could work from and even in. At the same time she should go into the question of a service contract, explaining to Mr. Brown what salary she wanted and so on.

"What I want? What about you? You're paying it."

Maybe, he said, but only she could know her needs in that way.

She shook her head as at a child's innocence. She hoped that Mr. Brown, as his bank manager and business adviser, would turn out to be more sensible. As for office premises, if this operation was halfway successful there would be plenty of space here at Number One, and cheap. "They'll be glad to find tenants."

"God forbid!" he said sharply, startling her. She went a shade hurriedly to the door and was gone.

He called Mr. Brown, warned him of her impending visit and its purposes, and also asked if he would mind going along with the fact that he was calling himself by his middle name, Addis, and concealing the Hammond. Mr. Brown saw it at once; using a pseudonym was a common practice of the rich as a protection against cranks and beggars and so forth.

"Trust me to observe this convention with Miss Stewart. Had you a salary figure in mind for her?"

John said he hadn't but she would know what it should be. "But make sure it is more than she was getting in her last job."

"Certainly, Mr. Addis."

As John put down the receiver, liking Mr. Brown more than ever, the house phone rang and a voice on it announced that it was Platt of security asking if, since Harris, the proper channel, was absent, might he "speak direct to you, Mr. Addis, please, on an aspect of the Boyle Glover case where you could possibly help?"

"Go ahead."

It came to this: an environmental coincidence had placed Mr. Addis in the adjoining office to that of a young woman with whom Mr. Glover might be on friendly terms in an extramural sense. "Did you ever see Mr. Glover in Miss Norton's office, Mr. Addis?"

"Miss Norton being the girl next door?"

"I do beg your pardon. I omitted to state her name." Platt clearly wouldn't bother with a short word where a long would do.

John said he couldn't remember having seen Mr. Glover in Miss Norton's office—assuming that he would recognize Mr. Glover, which was a small trap for Platt, who got out of it apologetically, saying he hadn't the slightest idea what Mr. Addis was working on, but he did happen to know from something Mr. Harris had let drop that Mr. Addis's cover had been established—"very neatly if I may say so"—through the usual personnel procedures. This naturally had brought him in contact with Mr. Glover, so he would know him.

"Of course," John said. "And Miss Norton is a strong lead?"

Yes indeed. First, Miss Norton's personnel file had been found in a most unusual place, a locked drawer in Mr. Glover's desk. Secondly, Miss Norton had left her office unexpectedly quite soon after coming in this morning, something she hadn't done before in the two and a half years of her employment. Nor was she now at home, or at least if she was, she didn't answer the telephone. A man had been sent to check there.

John had taken out a handkerchief to dab his sweating forehead. He asked, did the security section always react as energetically as this?

Platt considered for a moment. Perhaps not, but in this instance a top executive was involved, and also it so happened that a senior member of the board wished urgently to confer with Mr. Glover. He had twice this morning asked that Mr. Glover contact him as soon as possible—a gentleman, confidentially, Mr. Addis, whose "soon as possible" means "if not sooner." "He has also personally instructed me to keep him abreast of the case."

John wiped his forehead again. Parthessen's defense was moving into attack.

"Mr. Platt," he said, "I must ask you to keep this information to yourself."

"*What* did you say?"

"To reveal it might jeopardize my work here. I can't tell you more than that."

"I don't see—"

"Then I suggest you refer to Captain Randall."

"The captain is in the field."

"He'll be back from it. I'm sorry, Mr. Platt. I have to insist you consult him. And of course you won't go further as far as Miss Norton is concerned. *That* would be fatal."

He hung up, hoping he had shaken the man into resisting the pressures of Parthessen's enormous authority. But it was hoping a lot.

And Victoria must be warned at once, even if her break with Haycott Close to escape her husband might also fortuitously keep her ahead of the security section for the next few critical days. She must stay away from the office, of course.

He reached for the telephone.

The instant she heard his voice she said, "Ah, yes, Johnson. I don't think I shall want the car tonight, but call in for further orders around six." She rang off immediately as though not trusting him to remember in time to say, "Very good, madam," for the benefit of someone who was perhaps close enough to hear the small noises escaping from the earpiece.

Someone? The someone to whom she had sent a little note on her new writing paper, telling him of the changed telephone number, and to whom she would open her door with triumph, convinced that the man had hurried to her to make sure that she would keep his secret about Glover's dying in the Cornaway gardens. Apart, of course, from his urge for her desirable body.

She had all the cards. Yes, indeed. But for how long after

125

Parthessen was told that Glover had found her among the employees of the company?

However subtly she set about her blackmail, the man would see its full significance at once. Glover had died, but this woman must have been more than his girl friend in prospect, the computer programmer at Hammond and Morgan. And she might know— How much might she know?

Call her back at once. *Make* her listen.

But he sat with the receiver untouched. How would he prevent her saying something before he could begin, such as, "*Now* what is it? I'm busy."

He could almost hear Parthessen's suspicious question and her protest, "But, Gordon, I promise you Johnson's absolutely loyal to me. In fact, he depends on me to such an extent that he scarcely exists as a person. I can absolutely guarantee him. In love with me? Oh, please, Gordon, *really!*"

Wouldn't Parthessen want to know a bit more about this Johnson who couldn't keep off the telephone, and Victoria, pressed, might easily show her hand: "Johnson, don't forget, Gordon dear, is a witness to what happened last night at the party!"

But even if it didn't get as bad as that, she might discard the "Johnson" fiction and let out his name—the name she knew him by. She had no particular reason to conceal it. But the moment Parthessen heard that "John Addis" was in this thing, the man would know he was up to his ears in something far more dangerous to him than an attempt at blackmail by a young woman on the make like a thousand others in this city.

Parthessen's reaction as far as it affected Victoria would be unpredictable but mightn't preclude violence. But what would be predictable was that all chances of getting solid evidence of the fraud would vanish in highly skilled evasion.

So he must wait until his audience with her at six o'clock and in the meantime make not the slightest move that might jeopardize her seduction of Parthessen.

As he shook his head at the tempting telephone, it began to ring. Harris was calling from Tunbridge Wells. He thought he might have something. The chief witness at the Wetherfield inquest was brother Owen? Right? Owen's age had been mentioned and also the fact that Samuel had been his younger brother? Agreed? Good.

Now, please, would Addis check in the report—top of the second page, as Harris remembered it—where these two

126

points occurred. In case Addis hadn't found them, the files were in the desk, second drawer left.

"I don't have to look. Owen gave his age as forty-eight and a little later said Samuel was fifteen years his junior."

Harris blew out a long breath. "Then there's nothing more for us here. Almost by chance I asked one of the first people I talked with what sort of age was Mr. Samuel Wetherfield who lived for a while at The Laurels? The answer came without hesitation. Around forty-five, fifty. So I tried another neighbor, then a third. I couldn't get any of them to bring it below forty. . . . You knew this might be the answer? *Owen calling himself Samuel, a brother who didn't exist?* Poor old coroner and all the other suckers." Harris said he should be back by six-thirty. "You'll still be there?"

John said he had a date at six but hoped to be back by then or shortly afterward. "But before you ring off . . ." He told him briefly about Platt's discovery of Glover's association with Victoria Norton, "who just *might* be involved in our thing," and his own request for its being kept under the wraps.

Harris knew at once where he was—that snooty computer programmer. "So your cover story down there had a dual purpose?"

John could truthfully admit he hadn't been installed "down there" by accident. Could he have a reinforcing word with Platt? "He's anxious to show he has been busy."

"He would be. The captain isn't back yet? This should have his weight. No? Okay, jiggle the receiver and get me put through to extension eight-one-six. I'll do what I can."

This was a day for sweating. He no sooner thought he had gotten up a couple of steps than he slipped back three. At the time of the fraud, brother "Samuel" either had been long dead or never existed to begin with. *The other partner in it, therefore, was Owen Wetherfield, of La Rouette, Chexbres, Switzerland.*

He could still be at that address.

John stared at his watch for a frozen moment. But he couldn't think of a better alternative. . . .

He spent the next quarter of an hour getting through to Geneva airport with an urgent message for Mr. Frank Borrowdale to be given to him when he came off the 3:15 flight from London—by this time due in a few minutes.

John kept it as short as he could make it. *Mr. Borrowdale*

is to take no action, repeat no action, until he has phoned Mr. Addis at 23:00 hours, as arranged.

It was part of slipping back three steps to be fully aware that he himself had personally and with some ingenuity put the worst kind of cat among the pigeons. Borrowdale nosing around Owen Wetherfield. God, *no!*

Three steps? Nearer five. As he finished speaking to Geneva the house phone rang, and Platt superfluously told him that Harris had spoken to him about the danger of crossing wires, but he was still uneasy. However, he was calling now about something else. "An indent has just come in from the investment division, requisitioning three files we had in safe-keeping that our records show you signed for. You have them, I hope?"

"Did you mention this to Harris?"

"I saw no reason to." Platt was well back in the saddle again.

"Captain Randall isn't back yet?"

"No. But this raises an interhouse procedure. If you wish to keep the files you are required to say so and for what further period."

"All right. I say so and I don't know how much longer."

"You have to tell the indent's signatory. I will send it over for you to pin a chit to it, explaining your requirement for them, and in view of the high-level request, perhaps you should go into details."

John would have laughed if he could have summoned a shred of a sense of humor just then.

"Who is the high-level signatory in the investment division?"

"Secretary to the director's p.a."

"I should have thought you'd need more authority than a secretary's before you recommended release of material lately under security restriction."

Platt was in his element. The files had *originated* with the investment division, and the secretary was acting for Rogers, the p.a. who was acting for the director. "And that's good enough for me."

And good enough, John realized, for Parthessen, wanting to get the files back without sticking out his personal neck.

"I can let you have them," he told Platt with what he hoped was the right kind of vocabulary, "for onward transmission to the requisitioning source at nine o'clock on Monday morning."

128

Platt fought back well. "I should prefer to have them this evening. In fact I should like to send someone for them now."

"I need them over the weekend."

"In that case you must explain—"

"All right. You win. But if you're sending for them, I'm leaving soon."

Soon was a comparative term. He immediately got out the files and left the Conway offices with them, releasing the spring lock of the outer door.

He went down to the fifth floor, where he had noticed in early explorations a door marked "Secretarial Serivces." Beyond it he found what he needed. He placed an order in Harris's name for the files to be photostated and asked that the microfilm be ready for collection at nine o'clock on Monday morning.

He continued on down to ground level and the main hall, where he settled in one of the yellow-leather sofas with an evening paper he had bought at the kiosk.

Platt wouldn't think to look for him here, and it was an excellent place to waylay Randall if—with luck—he returned before John had to leave for his six o'clock appointment.

There was nothing in the paper about Boyle Glover. . . .

At five-forty, just as he was about to leave, Randall came through the main entrance and made for the elevators. John stood up and raised his hand; the captain changed direction and came toward him.

John knew that the body had been found.

Randall looked drawn and anxious. He was glad to sit down for a moment. "Trouble," he said. "It looks as though there may have been something crooked in the Axiom introduction after all. Sudden interest in something Glover thought was long and safely hidden—didn't care to face. Horrible business, all the same. Nothing like this before."

This meant that Randall was assuming it was suicide; it would be interesting to know why. So John said, "Suicide?"

Randall nodded somberly. "Five-and-a-half thousand acres of peace and quiet, a million trees to choose from to lean against while you swallow your little tablets. Always beats me how they manage without water to wash them down, their mouths being dry, the state the wretched creatures must be in. Mine's dry just talking about it."

So was John's, listening to it. "There's no doubt, is there—" he began, and stopped. Five-and-a-half thousand acres? And *tablets?* What in God's name had Parthessen done?

129

"Doubt if it's Glover?" Randall shook his head. "I was with our police friend when the description came in, and it was near enough right for us to drive out to Epping Forest and take a look. The local men were grateful for such quick identification. They get a lot of suicides, you see, the forest being handy for the peace and quiet prerequisite, only a few miles out of town like that. It was worse in the old days, of course. Messier. Everyone had a gun in his bedside table drawer. Now it's barbiturates. No disfiguration." Randall was becoming garrulous from shock and fatigue but John had to force the issue.

"I was going to say, there isn't any doubt he took something? There hasn't been time for an autopsy."

"No doubt at all, I should say. Just how many Soneryls he swallowed will, of course, have to wait on the pathologist. But that doesn't alter the fact that he killed himself, or lessen the problems it sets up. The brass isn't going to like it at all, particularly if it *is* linked to your fraud investigation."

John was beginning to have difficulty in reconciling all this with the indisputable fact that Glover died of a heart attack in Victoria's bed. In the meantime, Randall sighed and stood up and said he'd have to get busy with the telephone, breaking the news to those most concerned. There was quite a list of them.

John walked with him toward the elevators. "Did I hear you put a name to the drug he used?"

"I'm pretty sure it was Soneryl. I recognized it because my wife uses them when she can't sleep. Pink, with an indentation across them, to break into half doses. Just how much he took will be for the pathologist to say."

"So you recognized it?" John was feeling very stupid and no doubt sounding so.

"One tablet left in a corner of an envelope in his pocket," Randall told him. "Come up and share my burden—and a bottle I keep for days like this. I can't have Platt see me alone with it. I'd never live it down."

"Sorry. I have a date I can't get out of"—a poor mumble of an excuse however true it was—"but before you go, something turned up."

He told Randall about Platt's search for Victoria Norton as a possible girl friend who might be a lead to Glover's whereabouts. "I tried to head him off, but it's now more important still that she shouldn't be brought into this except by me."

"You're saying she could know something about the fraud,

even have played a part in it? Yes . . . I see that. On the other hand if we could produce a love affair that had gone wrong, we'd have an external reason for the suicide. The p.r. people would be very happy. The chairman would hand out medals."

"As far as I'm concerned," John said firmly, "I can do without p.r. in my hair at this moment."

"I second that motion. I'll talk to Platt."

"Would it be too much also to ask—" John realized that it might be precisely that—"to ask you to put off your telephoning for a while?"

Randall's "why?" was unequivocal.

"Harris and I are beginning to make headway, and I am seeing the chairman this evening. If it's to be a useful meeting I don't want him distracted by recent news of Glover's death." He avoided the word suicide.

"But it's a clincher," Randall pointed out, "as further evidence, or at least supposition, that there was fraud."

John agreed but said that unfortunately, if surprisingly, the chairman didn't seem like a man able to think on two separate levels at the same time. He would tend to become preoccupied with this tragedy's effect on the company's present interests rather than with the past events that had led to it.

More deceitful double talk. Convincing, even to himself. He would end up forgetting Glover hadn't killed himself and that this meeting with Bertie was on an altogether different subject and that Bertie knew nothing of the fraud.

He decided Randall was mind-weary enough to fall for it if pushed a little. John said, "I'm saying you can't very well give the brass this news and exclude the chairman."

"Not without getting myself fired."

"So that means not telling anybody for a few hours, say until early tomorrow morning, before they see the morning papers."

"You'll cover for me if they ultimately discover I held it up?"

"Of course."

"Okay." Randall turned toward an emptying elevator, the homing workers dividing into two streams as they passed him. John let himself be swept out of the building by them, as glad to be leaving it as they were at the end of their week's labor.

For him steel and concrete were already shuddering. A single pink tablet in a dead man's pocket, ordinarily a simple soporific, was likely to go off, as far as the great company of

Hammond and Morgan were concerned, with the explosive effect of a minor thermonuclear device.

But before that happened Victoria Norton had to be taken off the job she didn't know she was doing for that great company.

It had suddenly become very dangerous for her.

15

John put Fred's cap on an onyx table in the hall and followed Victoria into the white and gold living room.

She wore a white frock and large gold earrings shaped as lovers' knots and she was high on champagne and victory.

"There's still some." She took the bottle from a silver ice bucket on a low table in front of the large white settee. Cigar smoke hazed the crystal chandelier above it and fat cigar stubs lay in an ash tray near two empty champagne glasses.

"Get yourself a glass from that secretaire." She divided the last of the bottle, taking solemn care to share it evenly with him. "Drink to me, drink to me!"

The hitherto secret glow of her obsession had burst into flame, setting her whole being alight. The usually cool and steady eyes were dancing in the warmth of it, and the touches of color that had now and again shown high on her cheeks were spread now over the rest of them. Beauty had come to life.

He said, "You appear to have been kissed by Prince Charming."

"He obviously wanted to, but I didn't let the mood develop." Euphoria hadn't swamped her literal-mindedness. "Two and a half hours with me, a man so busy, so important . . ." Her triumph was overflowing.

"In that case there can't be much you don't know about each other by now."

"Let's say *he* knows as much about me as is good for him to know."

"Including where you work?"

"He already knew that." She dropped onto the sofa, stretching out like a cat after a meal.

John's heart's being in his mouth at this, he had to pause a moment before asking if Parthessen seemed to mind that she was a Hammond and Morgan employee.

"Certainly not. He sees that a girl having money of her own has no excuse to be idle. He's a *modern* man."

"Yes? He doesn't find it odd then that you should be able to run a Bentley?"

"Obviously it's part of having money."

"And naturally that you have a chauffeur to drive it?"

A frown marred her happy expression. "What are you worrying about? You're just Johnson, as far as he's concerned. Nothing more. I saw it. He was here when you called me this afternoon. In fact, he had already accepted all this, and most important, that I work for the company."

"Meaning he had already heard it? From whom?"

"Boyle Glover, of course. Who else?"

"He admitted it?"

" 'Admitted'? Gordon isn't a man who 'admits' anything."

John would bet on that too.

"I realized," she added, "that before Boyle got plastered he could have told him something about me. Gordon would naturally ask who I was." She looked up at him with lazy sensuality. "Dear jealous John. Wouldn't you have done the same if it had been your party and I'd suddenly appeared?"

He nodded. "And with added curiosity if the man who'd brought you to it had been involved with me in an enormous fraud on the company of which I was a director of its investment division."

There was a moment's silence. Then she was on her feet, her extra inches giving power and force to her angry demand that he should explain what he was talking about.

"A fraud that Glover helped to set up with Parthessen and another man. I think Glover's part in it was comparatively small and his share of the take commensurate with it. A greedy man, he could have been dissatisfied. This made him a potential blackmailer of the other two, Parthessen in particular because he was more available and more vulnerable."

"This is the most arrant nonsense! I refuse—"

"You'll listen, Victoria, because you must. I think that when you asked Glover to take you to that party last night, he used the power he had over Parthessen to get himself—and you—invited to it. And to Parthessen this meant that the blackmail he'd been afraid of was taking shape."

"Blackmail! You're out of your mind!"

"And I'm fairly sure he thinks you are in it too."

She exploded with indignation but in the midst of it realized she might reveal things that John Addis couldn't possibly know. She regained her wits.

"This is all guessing and invention!" she accused him. "Frauds, blackmail! Even if I was in a position to blackmail Gordon, would I when there's no *need* to?"

"You may think there isn't at the moment. But if the going gets tough, you might. It would *not* be advisable."

"*You*, John, would be advised to be very careful." This was the Victoria he was accustomed to, cold and full of certitude. "You think you can come in on this with cold improved terms on the basis of a lot of guessing and no evidence whatever. You really *are* a fool."

"I didn't know I was in on it on any terms at all."

She was still recovering. She even smiled at him. " 'Cicisbeo,' wasn't that the word? You know, I shall have lots of time to spare simply because Gordon is a very busy man. So please don't spoil what is a good moment for us both, you and me. There's no blackmail, no need for it. And certainly not from you. You'd be very much alone. Gordon and I are *together*. You must understand that. There's not even a Boyle Glover to worry about. If he did know something—which I can't believe—he's dead, John."

"Yes. The one difficult fact in all this that can't be talked away."

"Difficult?" she retorted. "If you must know I *did* tell Gordon how I came back for Boyle and discovered for myself that he wasn't fit to be near me. Gordon quite understood and was glad I told him. He didn't question it."

"This as when you were discussing Glover's disappearance?"

"We didn't discuss it."

"Because it was a mutually awkward subject."

"How could he tell even *me* that he'd had to smuggle the body away from that bench you put it on, and lose it?"

"But he asked you to keep it under your hat about Glover's being at the party at all?"

"He didn't need to. I let him understand tacitly but clearly that whatever happened I'd never mention it to a soul."

"And he understands that that goes for your chauffeur too?"

"Yes, of course."

"He accepted it?"

"Why not? His own feelings for me tell him that I inspire

134

loyalty. I could see him working it out like that. He's easy to read. Men in love always are. He'll never be able to hide anything from me."

John shook his head. "He has already begun. First of all, Glover has been found in Epping Forest."

Victoria considered this and said it had been a good place to think of. "Clever devil, but I don't expect he meant it to be found quite so soon."

"I'm wondering," he said gently, "if you're ever right about anything. You saw all the things that were in Glover's pockets before we took him back to Cornaway?"

She sat up and stared at him. "*Now* what?"

"Did you see an envelope with a pink tablet in it?"

"Envelope . . . no, there wasn't one. I'm sure."

"There was when the police searched the body in Epping Forest."

"It—then it can't be Boyle."

"Positively identified. The assumption is suicide."

"But it wasn't suicide. . . ." She became less tense. "It was his heart. We both thought so."

"I'm not a doctor and I don't think you are."

"A clever devil," she said again. "He must have had a good reason for the pink tablet."

"Not so clever if the autopsy shows it as the only one."

"What do you mean?"

"I agree he's a clever devil. There'll be enough of the stuff in Glover to have killed him."

She was incredulous. "Even if it made sense it would have been impossible. Boyle had been dead for hours."

"Of course. So it was put in him when he was alive."

She took a moment to realize what he had said.

"No, *no!*"

"I think yes." He would make it clear to her if it meant dotting all the i's and crossing every t. "When we went back to fetch him you stayed in the car while I went looking for Tankerton. How long did you have to wait before I brought Glover out?"

"It seemed an age," she said in a subdued voice, "because I was so anxious about getting him away."

"It took me fifteen seconds to find someone to fetch the valet to the servants' room. He arrived in about a minute and was with me for another minute while I bribed him to help me get Glover to the car, and not to tell Parthessen that you'd changed your mind about leaving him there. Tankerton

135

agreed. He sent me to wait at the corner of the rear terrace because it was near the French window of the room where Glover was sitting. I expected to have to wait two or three minutes. I waited for ten, more than ten."

Couldn't she see what he was seeing? It didn't call for a great deal of imagination. She shook her beautiful head; he crossed a final t.

"Although Tankerton agreed to help, he couldn't *not* tell his master. He must have done so. After that, what took up the rest of ten minutes or more?"

"Boyle may have refused to budge at first."

"When Tankerton told him you had come back for him?"

She shook her head again, watching him narrowly.

He said, "Glover was a dangerous liability to Parthessen, and quite possibly you were in the blackmail project with him. Parthessen sent Glover out to your car with enough barbiturate in him to kill him *while he was with you*."

"No!"

"At best you'd be in bad trouble; at least you'd be thoroughly warned off. But it misfired because apparently you changed your mind *again*: you hadn't in fact taken Glover with you. The result: Glover appeared to have died on a bench in Parthessen's own garden. Parthessen made quite a good job of the cover-up, even to a circumstantial suicide tablet in a pocket before dumping him in Epping Forest. One problem left for him."

"What?" she asked, still watching him carefully.

"*You*, the surviving would-be blackmailer. You had escaped the trouble and the warning. His two and a half hours with you this afternoon could have been well spent looking for another solution."

"This is craziness! Your manic jealousy again! These tablets you keep talking about. Making Boyle take them would have been even more difficult when he was alive!"

"Would it? When he was drunk and someone as persuasive and full of authority as Parthessen said, 'Look at you, you can't go with her in the state you're in, so take these, they'll sober you up'?"

"No!"

"But Glover said yes, and swallowed them down and that was that. Miss Norton can take him away with her now, thank you very much." John added that again neither she nor he had to be a doctor to know that alcohol greatly increased

136

the speed and efficacy of barbiturate. "He was as good as dead from that moment."

She put her hands over her ears. He raised his voice to tell her Gordon Parthessen couldn't have come up here without applying to the porter's desk, otherwise he, John Addis, wouldn't personally have cared to touch the champagne, even to drink her precarious health. "It shouldn't take another two and a half hours to persuade him you don't want to know him any more. If you can do that you're safe. Not otherwise."

She had taken her hands from her ears; pressing on them so hard she had involved the earrings and they had hurt her. She removed them and put them, two golden lovers' knots, beside the empty glasses. He hoped it was a symbolic act.

But it wasn't. She glared at him. If this fantastic story was true, then, thank you! He had given her another high card to play, should it ever be necessary! Otherwise nothing had changed. "Except, John Addis, this is the end of the road for you. I simply will not tolerate you anywhere near me. From this moment. You will work out the amount of your investment as you called it—the rent of this flat, car expenses and the cash you gave me this morning—and put it on a piece of paper on the writing table over there, with an address, please. I will send you a check in settlement within a week or so. You will now go away and stay away. I never want to set eyes on you again!"

The icy blast of her eyes meant him to realize the irrevocable sentence: banishment for life.

But it would be out of character to forgo appeal against it, however feeble.

"What about the car for tomorrow's lunch?"

"I shan't need the car tomorrow or later or ever again."

He stood for a moment, head down as though stunned, then went slowly to the writing table. He took a pen from the jade stand and a sheet of the same writing paper he had brought her for her note to Parthessen. Her voice from the sofa reached him with soul-freezing finality.

"You might try to revenge yourself by going to the police with what you and I did last night. Whether they believed you and it brought me down, they wouldn't let you off either. Nor would Mr. Parthessen. You've explained how ruthless he can be. Keep it in mind."

"I will," he said. "I won't be a worry to you."

Instead of putting down the amount of his investment in

her it seemed only fair to write: *But you should perhaps worry about where you keep that briefcase. He probably won't kill you until he gets his hands on it.*

He left the writing table, and passed the back of the sofa and went into the foyer where he picked up Fred's cap and put it on. He let himself out and continued on down in the elevator and across the elephant-gray Wilton of the lobby to the wide glass doors. He pushed through one of them and out into Grosvenor Square.

Talking had done damned little good. And never would, not with her. But that didn't absolve him. . . .

He waited at the curb for an opening in the traffic in order to cross to the parking meter where he had left the car, but he missed the next opportunity because a neat, dark-faced man in a neat black suit and a bowler hat came up from behind and touched his arm. "Hullo, Johnny, and how's tricks?"

"Sid, I'd say fancy seeing you if I didn't know you knew I'd been up there seeing Madam, and would be coming out any minute."

Tankerton laughed. "You got me there. My gentleman mentioned you'd be this way around sixish. The truth is, I'd like a word with you—private, you understand."

"About tricks?"

"About things going along faster even than usual, although I did say, didn't I, that we go along at a fair rate, once we start?"

"So you did, Sid, and I agree you're going along at a fair rate."

"Like a trip to the continent instead of a mere lunch in the country, eh?"

"Makes me quite dizzy." Which was true. Suddenly dizzy.

So she wouldn't have needed the car anyway.

"What about a snort to settle the nerves?" Tankerton was solicitous. "The Running Man is just around the corner." His hand remained on John's arm; a little extra pressure and he'd be holding him by it. John moved it in order to push back the cuff of his other sleeve to look at his watch.

"I have a date, Sid."

"Let the bird wait for five minutes. Anyway I haven't a lot of time myself, what with having to pack for my Mr. P. if he's to be back here to collect Miss Norton by nine-thirty, ready to go. Come on, Johnny, how about it?"

The valet's hand was on his arm again. Mustn't be too

138

eager, even if this was a chance to see more of how Parthessen's mind was working. "I don't know, Sid. You see"—gratuitously provided with an excuse, John used it—"there's this bird—"

"She'll keep. It's not as though you have to drive our loving couple to the airport. Mr. P. will be using the Rolls for that. And you have a week off, I shouldn't be surprised. The bird will forgive you when she hears that."

"I could do with a whisky, I must say."

"And I say you're a sensible fella, Johnny, like I told Mr. P. 'Sir,' I said, 'Johnny's a man that'll know a good thing when he sees it.'"

"Will I now?" John asked curiously and allowed Tankerton to lead him toward The Running Man. "What is it?"

"Let's get a shot of something inside us first."

"Anybody'd think, Sid, you were going to put me a proposition."

"You're a sharp fella, Johnny."

"And you think I need softening up before I hear it. Does it stink that bad?"

"You hear it before you cast aspersions."

"I'd never do that, not on one coming from a gentleman like yours who can sweet-talk my madam into a naughty week after she's only known him for a few hours. I want to know a bit more about that, too."

"You scratch my back, I'll scratch yours." Tankerton pushed ahead of him through the swing door of the pub.

Ten minutes later, having assured himself that the valet had really caught a cab back to Hampstead to pack for his Mr. P.'s week on the continent with Victoria, John went back into The Running Man and its telephone booth in the rear.

Harris had been expecting him to call. "I thought you might, when the captain told me you had had to leave. You can guess how things are here. You'd think it was the first time someone had cracked up under the all-work-and-no-play system of shortening a businessman's life." Harris was in effect telling him that Randall was keeping quiet about Victoria Norton as a possible factor in Glover's suicide.

Suicide my foot, John reminded himself again, and came to the reason for telephoning.

"Have I a *what?*" Harris seemed shocked. How could anyone imagine that Hammond and Morgan should ever have use for such subversive contraptions.

139

"If you haven't," John said with an edge in his voice, "say so at once and begin thinking where I can get hold of one. It has to be installed and ready to function in a room near Sloane Square by nine-thirty. It's now five past seven."

"There's a law against—"

"There are laws against worse things than invasions of privacy, and I'm thinking of worse, too, than fraud, misappropriation and embezzlement."

Harris was silent for a moment. "What size and shape is the room and its height from the ground?"

John told him.

"Busy street?"

"Haycott Close, exceptionally quiet, a dead end. How long would you need to get hold of the things?"

"As long as it takes me to unlock my cupboard here."

"Unlock it and come and have a drink at The Running Man. It's in Brook Mews behind Grosvenor Square."

"Seven-thirty at my club," Bertie had said, typically shutting his memory against the tradition in which every John Hammond from the Third on down had become a member of the Malvern on attaining his majority—now-the-boy's-a-man-he-must-have-a-man's-club sort of stuff.

So instead of having to be announced John could go through into the lounge to look for Bertie.

He had no intention whatever of sneaking up on him, but in effect that was what he did.

Bertie, in one of three tall-backed, wide-winged leather chairs grouped around a small table, didn't see him in time to interrupt his conversation with someone in the next chair.

". . . better, in that case," Bertie was saying, "if perhaps I left it to you to explain the details of the proposal?"

In some panic, John recognized the voice that replied. "Of course, H.H., if you wish. But whoever handles it, he won't understand a word of it—which should save time."

Bertie looked up and to the cost of his distinguished image, raised his voice to drown Parthessen's.

"*Hullo*, John, how did you get past—but how stupid of me—" He had remembered the tradition. "You know Gordon Parthessen, of course." He added that Gordon had come along to assist in the discussion. "He is fully aware of what is in our minds."

Bertie could speak for himself. However, John said it was very good of Mr. Parthessen. Personally, he needed lots of help. "Economics come in all sorts; mine—as much as the poor old dons could manage to get into me—is more theoretical than practical. What do I know about business procedure and all? Too much arithmetic. Drives me up the wall. Always did." He looked vaguely around but not at Parthessen and prayed there was no recognition in those cod's eyes. He could sense them on him, assessing the opposition to the con job ahead.

But a chauffeur remained, thank God, part of the furniture.

All Mr. Parthessen was seeing was a young man whose hold on a great merchant bank was less than he would apply to the wheel of a fast car or a faster girl's waist. John tucked in his chin and devoted his attention to looking like one of P. G. Wodehouse's completest idiots.

Parthessen consulted his watch and glanced at Bertie, who took the hint. "You won't mind, John, if we go in to dinner fairly soon? Gordon has to catch a plane immediately afterward."

"Eh?" John woke up. "Oh no, of course not. As a matter of fact, I'll have to be on my way too, pretty sharply. New show at the Dip Inn." He polished off the sherry with a shameless gulp.

The hard sell began before he had taken the third spoonful of soup. He listened with apologetic uncertainty to a deluge of figures and put in a wondering question. "How'd you ever arrive at the true value of the stock? H and M seems an awfully complicated business from the glimpses I've had of it."

"An hour or so with a computer," Parthessen said, "equals ten accountants working seven days a week for six months. Wonderful thing, a computer."

Was there a note of bitterness? However, Parthessen had given him an opening through which to insert a delicate probe. "Jolly old computer down there, buzzing away and me in my little glass box. Only one thing I'm going to miss though, and that was the view from it. Gorgeous!" he added with nostalgic enthusiasm. "An absolutely fabulous *bird!*"

This went past Bertie but not Parthessen. "How did you make out?"

"The view was as close as I could get." John let his enthusiasm evaporate.

"She didn't know who you were?"

"How could I tell her? I'd given an undertaking about the 'Addis' thing."

141

Parthessen nodded, jowls quivering. "Now the undertaking has lapsed, you could unmask and try your hand."

John shook his head. "It did cross my mind. But then I thought, how can she suddenly start giving me the time of day after a solid month of barge-pole treatment? I mean, without her seeming the worst sort of gold digger?"

Parthessen laughed. "You don't know 'em, boy, you don't know 'em." The contempt in his voice could have been for John or for the Victoria Nortons of this world, or for both.

"Just the same," John said, "There are other pebbles." He felt rather than saw Parthessen's relief.

Bertie shook his head. "I expect you both know what you're talking about."

"The social advantages, H.H., of having ready money in uncountable quantities," Parthessen told him. "Acantha kept John short, you know, and he hasn't had time to find out what it's like to be otherwise. Anyway, John, we can take it you agree to our plan in principle?" Which was a statement of the equation: money equals blondes.

"I suppose it's all right."

"What can be wrong with it, my dear boy?"

"I meant from your point of view, yours and Bertie's and the rest of the board's. I'm being naïve, I know, but I still don't see where the money's to come from to buy me out."

"That's our worry too"—Parthessen put down his spoon and leaned forward, bulging eyes glistening brighter still— "but with millions waiting for us to tap, it's not one to keep us awake at night."

"Oh?" John was genuinely surprised. "Hammond and Morgan would go public?"

Parthessen all but patted his hand. "Not in the first instance. Later on, perhaps. I know about these things, you see. Let me sort it all out, eh?"

John realized why they called the man "dear old Gordon." That tremendous expanse of face in a great grin of beneficent good humor was staggering in its power to convince you of his trustworthy wisdom and know-how.

Bertie put on his wisest expression and said, "Financial reconstruction had to come, and this is the moment for it."

John asked, it wasn't true, then, that right now investors in general were practically psychotic with nervousness?

"John knows more about current economics than he thinks," Parthessen put in. "You're quite right. They look

142

dead, but they're playing possum, waiting for some new, bright-blue chip to fall on the table."

John nodded and blinked and took another vague glance around. "I thought there was some claret coming."

"It will be here with the chateaubriand," Bertie soothed him.

"John, my boy"—Parthessen wasn't letting up—"you realize of course that your thirty per cent is worth millions."

"I guess it is." John inflated his chest but forbore to mention that fifty-nine percent was worth even more millions.

Parthessen smiled his terrible smile again. "On the other hand, should you wish to leave your capital invested in a good thing, my—our consortium would probably play ball on allotting you shares in the new company. Think about that."

"I will," John said. "Very kind of you, sir."

Such thinking as he'd be allowed to do would have Parthessen's full-time assistance when the time came.

Consortium meant Parthessen and his pals, and Bertie as the permissive authority for the take-over; a holding company formed to buy the Hammond and Morgan ordinary stock as cheaply as they could get it, and cheap it would be. The next step would also be normal procedure: float a public company to acquire the holding company's assets, in other words Hammond and Morgan, for twice or three times what the boys had paid for it, largely on paper in the shape of stock in the public company.

There was a certain fairy-tale magnificence about the scheme. And how often, as in this instance, was so much stock of the victim company held by one single, solitary mug? If, as yet unbeknownst to them, the mug owned not just one-third but two-thirds, all but, it would be a shock when they discovered it, of course, but immaterial to the situation as far as they were concerned. The mug would merely be allotted a larger block of shares in the public company. And welcome. By then they would have made their killing.

What fun!

John kept it going as soon as the steaks had arrived and the claret poured. "Sorry if I seemed to be looking for snags, but what about the old girl's cockeyed notion?"

"Mrs. Morgan?" Parthessen translated.

"She's still fixed on my going into the business. I think she said something to Bertie about a seat on the H and M board for me."

143

"Oh?" Parthessen hadn't heard about this. He glanced at Bertie, who shrugged his shoulders.

"She did say something, but quite honestly, John, I didn't think you'd be interested."

"In any case," John said cheerfully, "I dare say this reconstruction thing would kibosh it?"

Parthessen said he was afraid it would, and John said what a pity, ha ha. "What do I do next?"

"Nothing, really." Parthessen's grin was endemic now. "You merely tell us you agree to our proposal."

"No difficulty there," John assured him, "but what happens to the covenant about only selling or disposing of stock within the family?"

Parthessen waved a soft white hand. "Legally unenforceable. We have taken counsel's opinion. Unenforceable."

"Except, I suppose, if a majority vote of the board wanted to stick to it?" John asked, but with enough uncertainty.

"That's the point. There was a unanimous board decision to break the covenant if it could be done. Sometime last November, I think it was?" He cocked his massive head at Bertie, who at once agreed it had been at the November board meeting.

And that, John worked out, would have been a week or so before the trust had come to an end and he had become arbiter of his own financial destiny. Had they really thought he might try to control it? Probably they hadn't, but wished to be on the safe side. Bertie would have voted on Acantha's proxy, which covered both her own and the John Hammond shares.

He said, "I'm sure it was a good thing—although I know damn-all about the legal aspect, I'm sure you had the best advice."

Parthessen bit juicily into a large forkful of chateaubriand, demolished the rest of it in a matter of minutes, looked at his watch and remarked how sorry he was but he must fly, literally.

"A lot of ground to cover."

"Of course, my dear Gordon." Bertie gave permission he hadn't been asked for.

Parthessen went, grand and confident, to the high mahogany door and was gone. Bertie regained the stature his right-hand man's propinquity had noticeably lessened.

"Well, John?"

"Tremendous fella."

144

"Yes indeed"—Bertie's tone claimed credit for it—"you can safely trust him to do the best for you."

"Acantha—"

"Whom you can safely leave to *me*. In her heart of hearts she knows you'll never make a businessman. And why, for heaven's sake, should you?"

"Never a truer word. But I was thinking more of this consortium thing. Foreigners? She won't like that. Insular. And sentimental."

Bertie agreed it was a pity about the foreigners. "I'll make her understand. It's one world when it comes to finance and money, if in no other sector."

"The gnomes of Zürich and all that?"

"Precisely." Bertie glanced at him, as though faintly surprised—but not worried—that he should know so much as that about it. He beckoned the waiter and asked to see the cheese board. "I can recommend the double Gloucester."

Perhaps he was being too sensitive again to nuances but nobody had yet mentioned Glover's disappearance. True he'd been missing only a day, and this meeting had had another purpose than to gossip.

John felt like trying it for size, however.

"This chap what's-his-name isn't my favorite personnel director, but I hope nothing ropy has happened to him."

"Boyle Glover?" Bertie seemed unconcerned. "Irritating of him. Bad for our image. But the doctors hope it will prove only a temporary loss of memory."

In a nasty way John wondered how Bertie would react when Randall woke him up in the cold gray dawn with the news that the personnel director had lost more than his memory.

Obedient to Bertie's authoritative announcement, he cut himself a wedge of double Gloucester.

16

On the dot of nine-thirty the bell over the attic door rang the prearranged three times and John went down to let in his visitor. Tankerton oozed pleasure at seeing him, as though they hadn't met for months.

"I do hope, Johnny, the bird didn't mind you cutting it short?"

"I remembered what you said." John led the way up the interminable stairs, lit only at the landings.

"I don't expect she believed you had to see a man about a business deal?"

"You know how they are, Sid."

Tankerton's need for secrecy, on which John had played in The Running Man by saying whatever the proposition was, he'd prefer to hear it in a more private place, was real enough. Instead of taking one of the two hard chairs John offered him at the table, he went around the room, lifting the carpet, running his fingers along the wainscoting, looking behind the picture and inspecting the underside of the table and so on, and appeared satisfied.

But his television viewing wasn't up to date. When he finally sat down at the table he placed himself within five feet, just the right distance, from the matchbox that looked like a matchbox and nothing else, lying among odds and ends on the mantel shelf. He grinned confidingly.

"My gentleman said, 'Tankerton,' he said, 'I've no doubt you're right about your friend Johnson, but it could be that he might do things under orders that he wouldn't dream of on his own.' So I'm right."

"But it doesn't look as though he trusted my madam as a gentleman should who's attracted to her to the extent I now agree with you he seems to be, carrying her off all of a sudden like this."

"Love isn't always as blind as they make out."

"Like me not being so blind as to think he'd be offering me money just to take myself off for a few days so she'll be a poor unprotected young lady with no one to lift a finger."

"It's take off and don't come back, Johnny. Not ever."

"*Oh?*"

"That's how it is, Johnny."

"I don't see it, Sid, I really don't. Perhaps I'm being thick, but would you spell it out for me?"

"The point is, Johnny, you go and you stay gone. You forget about last night as though it had never happened. That's what this five hundred is buying."

Tankerton put an elastic-banded bundle of folding money on the table. John looked at it with suitable respect. "Used notes," he commented for the matchbox's tiny electronic ears. "Sid," he added, "all I know about last night is, I drove my

146

madam to your Mr. Parthessen's party. She stayed there a couple of hours and I drove her home just like any other evening. What's to forget about that?"

"You're doing fine, Johnny."

"Of course, there was the chap that was with her, what's-his-name. The one she thought she'd give a lift to and then said he was too sloshed for us to be responsible for. We were both thinking of the upholstery, me in particular was."

"Yes, Johnny? What about him?"

"Well, I sort of gathered from her this evening, before you and I met up, that she'd like to forget him too."

"She tell you why?"

"It seems he has disappeared, for no reason anybody knows. Naturally nobody wants to be mixed up in a scandal, if there is one, that is. And 'nobody' includes my lady. The last thing she or any female of gentle birth would care for is to have to give evidence at an inquest, for instance."

"Who said anything about an inquest?" Tankerton was startled.

"Well, this Glover *has* disappeared and you never know, do you?"

"Suddenly remembered his name, have you?"

"Miss Norton did mention it. It slipped my mind for the moment."

"This five-hundred nicker says it stays slipped, Johnny. What's the matter?"

"It's too much, Sid."

"We're generous, we—"

"I'd say five hundred is an awful lot of dough for keeping quiet about a thing we've all agreed is to no one's interest to get involved in. I think he's paying for something more than that, eh, Mr. Tankerton?"

Mr. Tankerton looked casual and said, well, yes, there was one other little thing.

"Ah, but maybe too big for me to swallow?"

"I don't think so, it being such a small thing—a fancy we have to look over that swank apartment of hers."

"So that's it."

"Yes, Johnny."

"What for?"

"Let's say you can tell one sort of bird from another by her nest. It's natural my gentleman should want to know what kind she is."

"He's seen it for himself."

"But not *all* of it, like what sort of undies she's partial to and so on."

"I don't like you calling her a bird."

"Oh balls, Johnny! Maybe she did come from up north with a bit of loot, but she has been down here in the big city for a couple of years and more, looking for a caper like this one."

"Caper, Sid, *caper?*" John said in a shocked tone.

Sid grinned at him. "I told Mr. P. maybe you didn't know the whole score, and he said, maybe he does, maybe he doesn't, but either way he has to do just what we want."

"I wonder what you're trying to say?"

"Don't play dumb with me, Johnny, for God's sake. This is serious. He can be generous, but like I told you he can be bloody mean too."

"As he was with Mr. Glover?"

"Mr. Glover—" the valet began and stopped.

John waited but nothing followed, so he said, "And suppose I tell you to tell him to stuff it."

The valet looked dangerously at him. "That's a message you won't send."

"No, Sid?"

"Because, you see, that bit about Glover being a risk to the upholstery isn't on the up and up. You know how we know?"

"Tell me, Sid."

"You think, don't you, that after I handed him to you on the terrace I went back into the house without worrying whether you got him safe into the car? Well, you think wrong. I turned around and watched from the corner and I saw you put him on the back seat and drive off just like she wanted it. So when it comes to the inquest, the question of who last saw him alive isn't *our* worry. It's yours."

"So now it's *when* it comes to the inquest?"

"Why can't you keep it plain and simple?" Tankerton was angry. "Here's five hundred for using your bloody head. *Use* it to keep out of trouble."

"Do you think Mr. Parthessen has told Madam all this?"

"Who cares? Maybe he has, or he will if she tries to hold out on him with too much virtue for her own good. But that's their business. So like I said, put it in your pocket and be thankful that's the end of it."

"Except for getting you into the flat?"

"All that means is putting me right with the porter. He knows you. You call him up and tell him I have Madam's

148

permission to spend a few minutes in the penthouse on her behalf and he'll open it up for me."

"When?"

"Right away. Mr. P. is most anxious to know the results of my, um, inspection."

"But it's nearly ten. They're just about boarding the plane."

"He'll telephone."

"Important as that? But who cares . . . okay, Sid, you've sold me." He picked up the wad of notes and stuffed it into his hip pocket. "And I can do better than the hall porter."

He took out the second set of penthouse keys and jangled them. "Keys," he said so that the tape should know what the sound was.

"Now that"—Tankerton grinned darkly and took them—"is what I call cooperation. So it's goodbye, Johnny. A pity we shan't be seeing any more of one another."

"You never know."

"I hope you aren't serious about that?"

John laughed. "You told me he can be very generous or bloody mean?"

"Yes," the valet said, and went.

John listened to the footsteps receding down the bare stairway before he took the matchbox from the mantel shelf and spoke to it softly.

"So far so good—switch off the tape. This went much as I expected, but I didn't foresee the search of Victoria Norton's place, the penthouse at Grosvenor Towers. He is going to look for anything she might have that would incriminate Parthessen. It may be there—a black briefcase containing computer analyses of Hammond and Morgan accounts. If he finds it, you shouldn't have difficulty taking it away from him either in the flat or when he leaves, and also persuading him to wait for me. I'll join you as soon as possible, but I have to be here to take a phone call due any minute now. If I don't turn up, the other thing I want from him is the fullest information he has about Parthessen's continental trip—the places and timetable. Signal you've registered what I have been saying by sounding your horn."

A car horn bleeped twice in the street below. John put the matchbox carefully away in his breast pocket and lay down on the bed with such patience as he could muster.

The call came four minutes later. Frank Borrowdale sounded peevish but as self-confident as ever. "I got your message at the airport," he began at once, "but this is a waste

149

of money, telephoning you"—ignoring whose money it was
—"but it gives me a chance to ask you just what kind of a
fool you think I am."

"What are you trying to say?"

"Simply that any bank anywhere could—"

"Where are you speaking from?"

"What the hell does it matter? I'm trying to tell you that a
bona fide bank wanting to check this man's credit rating—"

"I have to know where you are," John told him.

"Hotel du Lac."

"At Chexbres?"

"Stop changing the subject. I've said before, a *bank* would
only have to pick up a telephone and call its Swiss agents.
They'd say at once, without having to look him up or ask
around, that he's a banker himself, a man of substance, a
solid citizen, owns a mountain with a great stone house on it,
a respected member of the foreign colony—"

"You're talking about Owen Wetherfield?"

"Go on! Tell me there's been a balls-up and you meant
somebody else!"

"This is pointless. I tried to make it clear in my message
there was no longer need for you to go on with this. The job
is being done by other means."

Borrowdale retorted that there'd never been a job to do,
not one that made sense from any angle that he'd been able
to spot as yet. Oh, but in time he would! He'd snoop around
on his own account, get an ear to the ground, find out what
was cooking—the clichés came streaming—and if he didn't
come up with something before the money ran out he'd drop
in on Wetherfield for a little talk. Wetherfield would pay well
for his information. Maybe it fitted in with a racket he already
knew was building up against him.

John sighed. Mistakes you made yourself were the last kind
you could undo by ignoring them.

Borrowdale hadn't finished with him. Borrowdale was also
ready to bet that his offer to help set up a divorce from Vicky
had been part of playing him for a sucker. "But tell me I'm
wrong. Tell me you've seen a lawyer and he's tracing the
car."

"Nobody can. You got the number wrong."

"That's what you say!"

Borrowdale slammed down the reciever in whichever Hotel
du Lac he happened to have chosen among the many there

must inevitably be of that name along the shores of Lake Geneva, not counting the French side of it.

Since the Bentley was parked around the corner in Haycott Avenue and traffic at this hour in the evening was mostly going the other way, he was able to reach Grosvenor Square in under ten minutes. He left the car, holding Fred's cap under his arm, and took up a position several yards from Grosvenor Towers' main entrance, but where the glow from its wide canopy could still shine on him. He had to stand there only a few moments before Harris strolled up.

"How long has he been in there?"

"Seven or eight minutes, not counting the time he'd take going up. You still want to nab him with the stuff on him?"

"Yes—if he finds it. But chiefly I want to talk to him again, and record it."

"I have the equipment with me. You have the matchbox?" Harris added that he would like to move a bit nearer in. These big modern buildings were full of deflecting steel.

"Outside the apartment door be all right?"

Harris said that should do fine. As they moved together toward the frameless glass doors he said, "You got everything you needed for identification purposes onto the tape. And I'd like to say you do a good job—and apparently have been doing it from way back. You kept it very nicely under that chauffeur's cap how you were already on to the Norton woman."

"Yes." John went to the desk, taking off the cap when the porter had seen it. He asked if Miss Norton had left a message for him. "No? Then there'll be something for us in the apartment." He turned away without giving the man a chance to question his right to go up to the penthouse. He made for the elevator with Harris at his side, Harris saying, it would be a privilege if Addis would call him by his first name. "Ted, for Edward. It's a pleasure to work with you."

"And I'm John." He pressed the top button. "In effect, Victoria Norton is working for us."

Harris digested this. "Like going off with Mr. P. all prepared to sacrifice honor and virtue, hers not to reason why?"

"It's not quite like that."

"Nothing else is either," Harris said cryptically, "but I'm catching on fast. You know, John, I thought there was something funny about your setting up shop in the computer room."

151

"Funny, Ted? You don't know the half of it."

The elevator settled to a stop and opened its doors. In front of them the short flight of wide, shallow stairs, covered with the same gray carpet of the ground floor lobby, rose to the gold-leaf door of the penthouse. Harris asked how John proposed to get in.

"Ring the bell."

"He'll not answer it."

"In that case, we'll think of something else." John asked him to stay outside with the tape recorder. "Not too far away, in case he gets tricky."

Ted Harris took out a cigarette pack that looked exactly like a cigarette pack, plugged a monitoring hearing aid into it, returned it to his breast pocket and put the ivory-plastic button in his ear.

John touched the bell push three times, spacing the contacts to correspond with those Tankerton had used to announce himself at Haycott Close.

Nothing happened. He gave it half a minute, repeated the three-buzz pattern, put his mouth close to the panel and said, "It's *me*, Sid."

Tankerton opened the door three inches. "Go away, Johnny, for crissake!"

"I forgot something."

Tankerton tried to shut the door but John leaned hard against it. "Something important."

"Blast you to hell! You took the money and agreed——" But there wasn't much he could do against the pressure on the door. He let him in.

"It's got to be bloody important." Tankerton closed the door quickly and John made for the big living room. "There should be a bottle of whisky in the secretaire . . . ah, you've found it. Good."

It was on the coffee table, a half-full glass beside it, where earlier the celebratory champagne had stood. John also saw the chaos of the valet's search: writing-table drawers pulled out, the secretaire doors standing wide, and through the open door of the main bedroom, gaping closets and clothes scattered on the floor.

He sat down on the white sofa and helped himself to a cigarette from the casket beyond the whisky bottle. He took out the matchbox, shook it gently, but sufficiently to show that he found it empty and done with, and put it in the ash tray to join Parthessen's afternoon cigar stubs.

152

"Got a light, Sid?"

Tankerton, standing over him, ignored the request and demanded that he should say what he had to say and get out.

"Yes, of course." John looked around. "Couldn't you find any? She'd scarcely take the whole lot away with her. Coals to Newcastle. Have you tried the chest of drawers in the small dressing room?"

Tankerton looked startled, and John asked, why the surprise? "In my experience chests of drawers are where they usually keep their undies."

"Johnny, I'm getting very tired of you."

"Beg pardon, Sid." By now Harris would have taken up station. "Sorry to tease you. Undies another time, eh? Now it's a matter of thinking Madam has something on your Mr. P.? And maybe it's backed up in writing, as it were? Letters perhaps? So you're here to relieve her of them. *Me* object? With five hundred good reasons why I shouldn't?"

"Ask your question."

"No hurry. I'll get me a glass and you join me when you're through."

Tankerton stared down at him for a moment with a dark, grim face before turning away and going into the bedroom. John went to the secretaire to fetch a glass, clinked it against another to account for his absense from view, and used the opportunity to slip back to the hall and the front door, turn back the knob of the spring lock, moving the snib into the holding position. He was in the living room again and on the sofa pouring himself a drink in plenty of time for Tankerton's return.

The black briefcase dangled from the man's raised hand, and he was smiling, all suspicious thoughts forgotten. "I should have guessed you were giving me a tip, Johnny. There it was, in the space between the lower drawer and the floor."

John hid his astonishment in his whisky glass but acknowledged to himself that circumstance was taking a hand again.

Tankerton sat himself at the other end of the sofa with the briefcase between his knees and picked up the drink he had put ready against the moment of success. "And now, Johnny, what's your little trouble?"

"That inquest, Sid."

"You should get it into your noggin, old friend, there's nothing for you to worry about, but nothing, old friend."

"I'm not worried about *me*. It's simply that I just can't believe someone someday isn't going to look at it again and say, *Suppose there never was a body?*"

Tankerton laughed and took another large sip. "Read tomorrow's papers."

"Oh, you misunderstand. I'm talking, Sid, about *the other inquest*."

Tankerton put down his glass. "Which one was that?" The careless tone was overdone.

"Why, the inquest you told me about after supper last night. At Penzance, wasn't it? A couple of years ago. The death of Samuel Wetherfield. Remember?"

The man sat very still. "Did I mention Penzance?"

"Didn't you? Well, it would be the county town nearest Porth Cove that would have a coroner."

"Yes?"

"Porth Cove, where you and/or Mr. P., or whoever he nominated for the job, stole a boat as part of arranging a suicide for a chap who didn't exist except on paper— Now, *Sid!* Pulling out a knife in the middle of a friendly talk is no way at all to settle this. I'm surprised at you, I really am!"

It was a short, broad knife. Tankerton held it like a professional, blade upward from a fist grip, and John stared at it with suitable alarm. "Put it away . . . there's no reason . . ."

Tankerton rose slowly and watchfully and John besought him to sit down again. "I didn't mean to upset you, I promise I didn't." He hoped Ted Harris wouldn't take the agonized tone of voice too literally and feel he should do something about it.

So to be on the safe side he said, "That's better," as though the threat had passed, and went quickly on: "Sid, I'm thinking of you, too. I don't want either of us to be accessory after the fact of murder."

"After the fact of what?" The man spaced the question with deliberation.

"Murder, Sid. Murder."

"Oh?" Tankerton was a shade easier. "That might turn out a bit of a problem, murder of a man they never found the body of and who didn't, so you say, exist in the first place."

"Sid, you've got me wrong again."

"No, I haven't. That five hundred in your pants pocket got you thinking if Mr. P. will cough up on that scale just for keeping a mouth shut about Glover being at a party, what won't he pay for a bit of quiet, too, on the subject of Samuel Wetherfield."

154

"You don't have to worry about *that*."

"But I do. I worry about how Mr. P. isn't going to like what you are, Johnny, and that's a bloody blackmailer. We can be—"

"—very, very mean. Sid, you won't let me explain. Of *course*, neither he nor anybody's going to be in trouble over the Porth Cove thing." He hurried on, saying that at worst it couldn't come to more than causing a public mischief, which was what people were charged with who wasted policemen's precious time, rot them, and who'd bother to blackmail a man in Mr. Parthessen's position over such a minor misdemeanor even if there was proof of it, which Sid knew as well if not better than anybody there wasn't?

"That's right." The unwavering knife continued to point at John's stomach across a gap of somewhat less than a yard. "That's right, Johnny. So for the last time, what the hell *are* you talking about?"

"I said it, plain."

"You said 'murder.' "

"Yes, Sid, I said 'murder' but I never said it was *you* gave Glover the pills. It's obvious, drunk though he was, he still wouldn't—*Sid*, don't look at me like that—Glover wouldn't take a whole lot of pink pills from someone he didn't know, and a servant at that, just because the chap told him they'd cancel out the booze so his girl friend wouldn't notice. *But he'd take them from your Mr. P.* Oh, I'm not saying you didn't do your bit, like finding his body and lending a hand with it on the Epping Forest trip. You might even have been the one with the bright idea to leave a tablet in his pocket, to show it was suicide. The same kind of thinking as the empty dinghy off Porth Cove."

Five seconds' silence seemed an hour. Tankerton spoke in a flat voice.

"You and your madam have done a good deal of hard digging together. It's a shame you hadn't the guts to stay with her. I'm not saying she'd have got away with it, if a bit knocked about. But now you've put her in a very nasty position. And me. I don't mean because I was seen coming up here. I wasn't. So as it's natural to think of oneself first, this means doing something Mr. P. mayn't approve of, although he'll be grateful for it later, maybe. The cops won't need to look for a motive *why* she carved you up before she took off, because the knife will be right there on the sofa beside you and who else could have done it?"

155

"Do you think the porter didn't see me come up just a minute ago? Two hours after she'd left for the continent? Even your Mr. P. would have to alibi her, little as he'd want to."

John would never know, of course, whether Tankerton could have brought himself to use the knife but it wasn't a moment to wait to find out.

He reached out for Tankerton's wrist and pulled it—and his knife hand—in the one direction the man wasn't expecting: toward himself, and with force. At the same time he slid sideways off the end of the sofa and was on his feet behind it as Tankerton lurched forward, unable to prevent the knife blade's slashing the upholstery of the back cushion.

John shook his head at him.

"Sid, you talk too much. I don't suppose that kind of kill comes off unless you go through with it before the target even realizes you have a weapon."

Tankerton came around the sofa, perhaps to have a try of his own volition, and again John did the unexpected thing. Instead of evading him, he jumped *at* him, wrapped arms around him, smothering the knife, and as suddenly threw him away, not caring much where he ended up. As it happened, it was slap into Ted Harris, just entering the living room, on his way to the rescue, who said, "Thank you all the same, John, but I didn't like him either."

But he caught Tankerton awkwardly, with the result that the knife snicked the edge of his left hand. However, he tossed the man right back. John side-stepped and Tankerton banged into the secretaire, rocking it and slamming its doors on falling glassware.

John was aware of a disgraceful satisfaction. He had enjoyed this deplorable outburst of violence and did not like himself for it. He downed the rest of his whisky too quickly and coughed painfully.

Harris sucked at his hand, took out a small camera, clicked off three rapid shots of Tankerton trying dizzily to get up but sinking to his knees because his legs wouldn't support him. The knife lay on the white carpet close to him and would show in the pictures.

Harris put away the camera, saying, "I'm only showing off. But you never know, the judge may just for once overrule the defense and say they're admissible evidence."

Tankerton was dazed but hearing every word. John picked up the knife. "But he'll admit a tape recording?"

"Oh yes, I should think so."

156

"Assuming we decide to bring charges against poor Sid."

"Let off a murderer? You're crazy!"

"I told poor Sid," John helped the man to his feet, "I don't believe Glover would have taken the Soneryl from anybody but Parthessen, but that won't be Parthessen's story when it comes to the crunch."

Ted Harris agreed. "But killing doesn't bother Sid, from what I heard on the monitor just now. Sid isn't averse to murder. In fact, my impression of it was strong enough to send me galloping in. Maybe I was mistaken?"

"You can listen to it again," John said, "on the tape."

"So I can."

"Tape . . . ?" Tankerton's fingers twitched.

Ted Harris realized what John wanted.

"Like this," he said and held up the cigarette pack. He slid the front away with his thumb, revealing two miniature spools that were revolving slowly. He took the matchbox from the ash tray and held it toward Tankerton. "Normal speech level at ten feet, if you've any more to say. Counting this session and the one at Haycott Close, we've still another five minutes left before it needs a fresh tape."

Tankerton looked at John and then at Harris.

"Who . . . are you?"

"This is Edward Harris," John told him, "security officer at Hammond and Morgan."

The dark, expressionless eyes remained fixed on John. "And you're no bloody chauffeur."

Harris sucked his cut hand. "But Mr. Addis put up a fair imitation, you'll agree? Mr. Addis is a private investigator. In the meantime, Sid, he's saying the big boy will sit back and let the hired hand carry the can."

"Having hired him," John took it up, "for peanuts. The other thing in my mind, I wonder how much poor Sid saw of his Mr. P.'s half-million steal? . . . Sid, take hold of yourself —here, sit down. You need that drink you never got to."

The man sat down in the nearest chair and John handed him his whisky.

He swallowed some and talked to himself. "So that's what it's all been about. Half a bloody million. It had to be big . . . a man like him—" Tankerton drained his glass, held it out to be replenished. "But I tell you, God's truth, Mr. Addis, I had nothing to do with any pills. You know me. I'm not that kind of a fool, not with Mr. P. as a witness. Any more'n he'd be if I was one."

157

"But you helped him with the Epping Forest thing."

"What would *you* do? I go into the garden for a last smoke, like I always do, and find a dead man on my favorite seat, a guest I'd seen—Johnny, I *saw* you help him into the car. You drove off with him there in the back!"

"You didn't hear us come back when we found he really was 'in no condition'?"

"No."

"All right, you discovered him on your bench."

"So I hurry into the house and tell Mr. P. and he says damnation this could be a nuisance when I'm busy with the biggest thing in my life, and anyway we don't want to involve that dishy Miss Norton, do we, so it's up to us to hand it on to somebody else, anybody else. That's all there was to it. The other thing was just a business angle."

"Whose idea, to put a tablet in Glover's pocket to make them think he'd poisoned himself?"

Tankerton's knuckles showed white bone as he clasped the tumbler. "If there was a tablet, Mr. P. planted it when I wasn't looking. It would have been easy. I had to get the station wagon out of the garage while he fetched a topcoat for himself and a rug to put over the body. Johnny—Mr. Addis, I swear it."

"What did you mean about a business angle?"

"The action at Porth Cove you were talking about, in that attic place. Mr. P. was helping out a friend. The bloke's brother had gone off years ago and had not been seen again, and it seemed easier to have the chap seem to drown himself for all to see than hang around for months for a court order giving 'presumption of death.' "

"And how did Mr. P. sell you that?"

"He said it was to do with an inheritance. All I did was help him help out his friend."

"The 'friend' being Owen Wetherfield."

"That's right. I went along with it. I was a new boy then, anyway."

"How did you and Mr. P. come to meet?" Harris asked, which was a question John had been about to put.

"Through the P.R.V.S. Where else would he pick up someone with my know-how?"

"Prisoners' Rehabilitation Voluntary Service? I thought so. And what was there in it for you?" Harris wanted to know.

"A couple of yards and a permanent job. With him. I was bloody lucky!"

Yards? Crook for "hundreds"? John remembered the five yards in his hip pocket. He pulled it out and dropped it at Tankerton's feet. He stared down at it.

"I can't take it back to him. God knows what he'll do, me letting him down."

"Isn't it a case of who has let down whom? Where's the permanent job now? And did it include being accessory to murder when called upon?"

"I told you! I knew nothing of that!" He continued to look down at the money. "What do I do with it, Johnny?"

"You'll have to earn it," John told him.

Tankerton waited, an often-broken man if ever there was one, who is suddenly shown a new survival.

"Is Parthessen going to contact you before he returns from this trip?"

The valet shook his head.

"Won't he want to know if you successfully nobbled Miss Norton's chauffeur?"

The man shook his head again. "It wasn't in his mind I'd have any trouble."

"All right. We reverse the proposition. *You* go away and stay away. The only difference, I shall want to know where you are."

"You *can't* let him go," Ted Harris said, unable to contain his uneasiness.

"Why not, Ted?"

Tankerton didn't want to hear why not. He said, "You keep out of this, I'm dealing with Mr. Addis." He turned to John. "Is this on the level?"

"You'll have to decide that."

After a moment Tankerton moved to pick up the money.

"My turn," John stopped him, "to say there's just one more thing."

"Ah—" a deflated sound.

"In this instance it really is a little thing. I want to know where your Mr. P. has gone."

Tankerton looked relieved. "Switzerland, of course."

"Where exactly in Switzerland?"

Tankerton did not know.

"You can't afford to kid me any more, Sid."

But Sid was cringingly anxious to be believed. That was all he knew, honest. Mr. P. had said Switzerland, until Wednesday late or Thursday morning. Nothing more. As to just *where* he'd be at any one time, maybe nobody knew except perhaps his office could say. On these short business trips he moved around most of the time.

"*Business* trip?"

"Oh, he's traveling his entertainment along with him instead of picking it up as he goes along. It's happened before, but it's always business before pleasure. He's doing some deal or other, you could tell. The Norton girl's on the side."

"The keys," John said.

Tankerton looked blank, then remembered. He produced them. 'Sorry, Johnny. I'm a bit confused. I really didn't mean—"

John believed him. He put the keys in his own pocket. "Don't forget to let us know where you are, will you, Sid? Send your address to Mr. Harris, at Number One. Confidentially, of course."

Ted Harris interposed, did John really think the little villain would do that?

John asked, "How else can we send him his retainer fee? He'd be a fool to pass up twenty-five a week."

Sid's jaw dropped.

John told him to get on with it—pick up the money. "You're working with us now, Sid."

Sid picked it up and went, a little unsteadily. Things had gone so much better for him than he'd dared hope.

Ted Harris looked unhappy. "He's not to be trusted. He's a both-ends-against-the-middle type of villain."

"But I don't think he'll go near Parthessen. He can't before Parthessen gets back in any case, and if he ever does he'll wait until he sees a safe opportunity. With Parthessen, 'safe' isn't an easy word."

"That's not the point."

"It is for me, Ted."

"He's a witness in the Glover death."

"Let's tidy up while I put you in the picture."

John put him in the picture, more or less, but dwelt with emphasis on Borrowdale's most unwelcome intervention.

"The Norton's *husband?*"

"No less."

"Apart from which you sent him to Chexbres."

"At the worst possible moment, because Owen Wetherfield is the other half of the fraud and even more so because I'm guessing Parthessen will go to see him in connection with this deal he has on. Borrowdale showing up even in a half-baked sniffing around would alert them."

160

Ted Harris wanted to know what the deal might be, but John shrugged his shoulders. "Some sort of international investment scheme."

"For the company?"

"I daresay." John didn't propose to elaborate. It was an area in this already complicated situation where Sir John Hammond was too prominent for "John Addis's" peace of mind if he was to see this thing through without the magic wand of the Hammond name and power.

"So?" Ted Harris asked.

The answer to what came next? There were two parts to it, John said; the first, to prevent Borrowdale throwing a God almighty spanner in the works; the second, somehow to wake up Victoria from her fantasy of believing she could use sex and blackmail to make Parthessen provide her with a life of ease.

"It has happened before, a million times," Ted Harris commented. "He doesn't know she's married?"

John shook his head. "It's the last thing she'd tell him. There must be no obstacle to Parthessen making her his, unless she puts it there herself in the course of getting the best terms out of him."

"Basic. And he'll spot with eyes and ears shut."

"She hasn't a clue about him. When I realized what had happened to Glover, I tried to make her see what the man can do when he is pushed."

"But she didn't want to know?"

"She did not. That's the trouble. It's one thing for me to use her to get close to Parthessen as part of finding a chink in his armor, but something else to let her risk her life at it, even if she *is* chasing her own rainbow."

Ted Harris looked narrowly at him. "You really are worried."

"I am."

"So?" he asked again.

"While I am trying to think up how to handle part two—how to get her out of it—do you think you could deal with part one? Go to Chexbres and put a snaffle on Borrowdale?"

"Only too pleased. When?"

"Now. I'll drive you to the airport. There'll be night flights. You shouldn't have to hang around for long. You can pick up Swiss francs there, or wait until you land at Geneva."

Ted Harris rubbed his face, squashing his squashed nose with large fingers. "You get to the point, don't you, John?"

John said there was another point, where to find Borrow-dale. "All I have for you, he's staying at a Hotel du Lac, the *lac* being Lake Geneva, and there'll be a dozen Hotels du Lac in the towns and villages scattered about its shores."

"But it will be near Chexbres."

"I should think so."

Ted Harris asked should he use Hammond and Morgan money for the expenses.

"No."

Ted Harris's eyes opened at the sight of the sheaf of notes from which John subtracted several, and remarked that the chairman's reputation as a close man with a buck obviously wasn't true.

John picked up the briefcase and checked the contents: half a dozen of the wide computer sheets, each covered with columns of figures. He didn't doubt they were those he had seen Victoria put into it originally. "I'll look after these if you'll keep the tapes in a safe place."

Ted Harris said he could put them in the security strong room, if John would take him to Number One before going on to the airport. In any case, his passport was there.

"You'll make this all right with the captain? My detachment to work with you is a bit vague."

"Of course. Tomorrow morning."

Ted Harris still seemed a shade uncertain, but the stimulus of a sudden assignment abroad would overcome any misgivings in an office-bound young man, something John could understand and rely on.

17

John's exhaustion was such that he slept without stirring until nine-thirty, and then awoke gradually. Reality hung in scattered threads in his mind and did not come together until after he was shaved, bathed and dressed.

He called Mr. Brown at Brook Street. Should Miss Stewart arrive before he could get there, would he please stall on her service contract and ask her to wait. He wanted a further talk with her before she finally decided to take the job.

"I expect she'll take it."

"She won't if she's wise."

"All the same . . ."

"What does that mean?"

Mr. Brown said it meant that most young women would jump at a chance to work with him.

"With John Hammond?"

"But she only knows you as Addis." Mr. Brown had reason to be puzzled.

"That's one trouble," John said, "apart from others she also doesn't yet know about."

"I'm sure everything will turn out well," said Mr. Brown, groping.

John envied his optimism.

He fetched the Bentley and drove to White House, reaching it at ten-fifteen with a feeling of time wasted, if unavoidably. It made him sharper with MacGregor than he meant to be. "No, Mac, I've no time for breakfast. Please just answer the question. Has there been a call from Miss Norton?"

There had not. Hope that she had had second thoughts about going away with Parthessen, small as it had been, fell away.

He asked about Acantha. Yes, Mrs. Morgan had got off safely yesterday evening on a BOAC flight due to arrive in Quebec just about now. There she would take an intercity flight to Montreal and be met by Mrs. Parthessen, to whom she had cabled. Ross had taken her in the Rolls to the airport and reported that she had seemed, in *his* words, "halfway to the post before the starter had the gate up."

"On second thoughts I *could* eat some breakfast. Can I have it in the library? Thank you, Mac." He smiled apologetically. And would he please ask Ross to give the Bentley a quick servicing.

MacGregor went away, mollified, and John in the library got out the Bentley's documents, and his passport. By employing a firmer tone on the telephone than he would have been capable of in other circumstances, he persuaded the clerk doing this Saturday's duty stint at the insurance brokers to arrange for an international insurance certificate for the car, to be delivered to him care of St. Justin's Bank, 169 Brook Street, within the hour. Or else.

Booking the Bentley on a Lydd-Le Touquet aircraft leaving at two-forty-five was easier.

He sought out MacGregor to help him bring the three deed boxes downstairs, to be loaded in the Bentley when Fred Ross had finished with it.

Fred, straw in mouth and hissing loudly, was sorry about having left his gray cap lying around in the car. "I could've sworn I hung it up on the peg."

John assured him that it hadn't embarrassed him in the least, and asked, "You have a passport, Fred?"

"Of course, Mr. John." He removed the straw.

"Would you like to put it in your pocket and pack pajamas and toothbrush?"

"I would, sir, and thank you." His eyes shone like two small bright stars. John then explained a proviso: he was using the name "John Addis" for all purposes and with all people during the trip to Switzerland. Did Fred think he could remember that? Fred thought he shouldn't have any trouble. As a matter of habit already, when he wasn't addressing him as "sir," it was as "Mr. John." He'd never gotten used, had he, to Mr. John inheriting the title?

"A pleasure trip, sir?" He knew it wasn't. Too many unusual things were happening in and around White House just now for this to be anything but one of them.

"No, Fred." Also it was right that Fred should know he was being asked to go into possible danger. "No, Fred, it's not a pleasure trip. We are involving ourselves in grand larceny, maybe murder, and the destruction of the family firm."

Fred Ross said, "My gawd!" and asked quite open-mindedly, on which side? For or against?

"Against, Fred, and for your very private information the gentleman who is 'for' these things is Mr. Gordon Parthessen."

"Him?" Fred thought a moment and nodded. "Oh, yes." As though he should have realized sooner that it couldn't be anyone else. "I'll be with you in a moment, Mr. John." He turned and ran up to his rooms and was back in a very short moment indeed with a shopping bag by way of luggage.

Fred helped him carry the deed boxes in to Mr. Brown, to whom John gave their keys and an invitation to discover from them as much as a banker should know about a customer's financial position, which would be everything. Mr. Brown looked a little awed but rubbed his hands in anticipation.

Miss Stewart, he said, was here, and looking over the build-

164

ing. She had been a bit put out at not being able to conclude a service agreement straightaway.

Mr. Brown led the way upstairs by the side door. She was in a soft blue frock and had a wary expression for Mr. Addis. To Mr. Brown she said, "That fig tree down there—" she turned to the window—"isn't it rather remarkable? A few yards from Bond Street . . ."

"London comes up with that sort of thing," Mr. Brown pointed out, "in case people think it can't be anything but a swinging city."

"Mr. Addis"—she gave him a grave smile—"I think you can't do better than this room for yourself. It's quite the nicest."

Indeed it was. Pine-paneled, a ceiling decorated with shallow, Adamesque garlands, its period only a little later than the Founders' Room at Number One. It had been tenanted by a lawyer, Mr. Brown explained, whose lease had of course come to an end with the others and who wanted to sell the furniture. Carpet, desk, glazed book shelves, etcetera. There were two other rooms on this same floor, also well furnished . . . a most agreeable suite of offices if Mr. Addis . . .

But they must excuse him; he would be down in his office where they would find him if they needed him. He went quickly, a man glad to escape. John envied him as Rosemary Stewart left the window and came across the room to look at him very seriously and searchingly.

"Mr. Addis, what has happened to change things?"

"My job has changed, the priorities are different."

"Overnight?"

"Overnight," he agreed.

"Overnight you've decided that I'd be no good as a p.a.?"

"Of course not." He wished she wouldn't stand so close to him. "I can't explain—you'll have to accept the fact that you can't join me."

"I can't?"

"No."

"I don't understand. We were—" She paused, miserable and defeated. "The Founders' declaration of intent . . . that's finished?"

"It's nothing to do with it."

"Then what is?"

"For heaven's sake don't take it so hard . . ." He stopped. Her expression had suddenly lightened.

"You're afraid for me," she said with the confidence of sure instinct.

"No—"

She shook her head. "Yes, you are. Please tell me what has happened."

"We'll compromise." Why hadn't he thought of this before? "You take a temporary job somewhere and if things work out all right with me, then we'll be able to talk about it again. Or if you prefer a retainer until—"

"I should prefer," she said, "to keep to the arrangement we made yesterday. It's a p.a.'s first function to be able to adjust herself to unexpected changes."

"Not this kind," he retorted, realizing he should stop this conversation here and now.

"Is it," she asked, "that you can't afford a p.a.?"

He should have said, "Yes, I'm afraid you've hit the nail on the head," but he didn't think of it soon enough.

"Then if it isn't that," she said, "you have to tell me the reason."

This was too direct, and he could take advantage of it. "You've realized by now," he said, "that my job is fundamentally a security one. There are things I can't tell anyone."

"Except your p.a."

"You're not my—"

"—who in the very nature of the relationship is utterly trustworthy." She held up a small but firm hand against his further protest. "I think I know what has happened."

He felt safer. She couldn't know. But in the next breath she dumfounded him by saying with some positiveness, "It's Gordon Parthessen. And that means I'm right. You *are* afraid for me."

He began to protest again, but she was watching his eyes. She said, "He has found out what you're doing."

"Please God he hasn't. . . ."

"Ah, so it *is* him."

"Not in the way you—I mean it's nothing to do with what we were talking about, a possible realignment of company policy—"

She interrupted again. Of course Parthessen wouldn't want a policy change of that kind at this moment when everybody knew he was planning an even tighter grip on the company, probably some sort of reorganization. This angle had come up last night when she was talking to Lord Ashworth.

"But it isn't directly that either, is it, Mr. Addis? It's the

166

effect of it on him you're worried about? Because he's a really very dangerous man?"

John didn't remember going to the ex-tenant's desk and sitting himself down in the comfortable leather chair but he found himself there and trying to get a final grip on the situation.

"You know he's dangerous?"

"I know he's the sort of man who reacts with real wickedness if he can't get what he wants by conventional means. And he's grudge-bearing, vengeful. There was a girl—" She interrupted herself this time. "But that's only relevant as an example."

"What girl?" he demanded. His change of subject brought surprise to her large eyes.

"My predecessor in the secretariat. He broke up her marriage because she changed her mind about sleeping with him. But this is quite different, and anyway I'm not afraid of him if you aren't." And to throw her out like this after making her so happy—it wasn't fair. It was to have been *the* job where she could be really *useful* in a *cause* she believed in. "Mr. Addis, you can't be so unjust."

He was near loss of temper with her obstinacy. "Oh yes I can! I'm throwing you out!"

"It's too late."

"Too late to change the fact that Gordon Parthessen is a bloody thief and murderer! I will *not* take the responsibility of having you anywhere near this thing the way it is now."

"*Murderer*, you said?"

Instead of putting her hand to her mouth in horror and alarm and running out of the room, she sat down in what had been the client's chair and said, "Please could you begin at the beginning?"

He said very firmly that he wouldn't begin anywhere. Parthessen crossed in getting his own way was bad enough; Parthessen in danger of utter ruin to say nothing of prison up to and including the term of his natural life was something from which . . .

"Mr. Addis. You can't frighten me."

"Leave me out of it. Parthessen—"

"And Parthessen can't either. You're a very old-fashioned person. You don't seem to know anything about women."

He scowled at her, but she was past taking notice of what she seemed to regard as mere petulance.

"Well?" she said, putting her left knee over her right.

167

She had asked for it and he gave it her, straight and stark, including the probable cause of Glover's dying but not the true place of it. He was sorry and glad to see her shocked expression. There was a swallowing within the slender throat, a visible movement, and a silence. Then she nodded to herself.

"And this Victoria Norton knew about Glover . . . and still went away with Parthessen?"

"She knew everything, and because she knew everything—particularly about his primary role in the fraud—she went with him."

Rosemary was shaking her head. "Is she such a fool, without a smidgen of intuition?"

"I can't say I've noticed much."

She said she thought she had seen the woman around.

"In fact I'm sure I have. One couldn't help it. Lovely. But she didn't look as though she had a scrap of ordinary feeling. Men are for what they've got for her; things like gratitude wouldn't be in her. She used the fact that you're attracted to make you do an awful lot for her."

"I had to let her think I was."

"Yes, of course," she said perfunctorily. "She was a lead to the fraud—Lencorp Fording, did you say? I don't remember ever hearing the name."

"I don't imagine it was allowed to be heard outside the investment committee."

"But H.H. somehow found out about it."

He didn't contradict her. This was the other thing neither she nor anyone else had to know: Bertie's total ignorance of the fraud.

He was glad now that she had forced him to tell the story; it had given her a feeling of participation without the actuality, and himself a chance to be honest with somebody for a change. "So you see how things are at the moment. But I promise, as soon as I think it's safe, to get in touch. We'll make a fresh start. Yes?"

He left the desk to escort her downstairs for Mr. Brown to complete the formalities of temporary parting. But she made no move except to cross her knees the other way.

"I suppose your next step," she said shrewdly, "will be to let Parthessen know that *you* know he has taken this Victoria Norton with him?"

Her accuracy of forecast took him aback, and before he had time to think, he said, "That's the general idea."

168

"I suppose by walking in on them?"

Could she read his mind, for heaven's sake?

"I have to find them—"

"And confront him? You're crazy!" She apologized for the overemphasis with a flutter of her hand. "Mr. Addis, there must be a less dangerous way."

"Not as convincing"—he had thought about this—"nor a better way to keep him unsuspicious about the fraud investigation. I will have a purely personal motive, a straightforward story. I am clearly infatuated with Victoria. I have come chasing after them to break it up. I am at once a witness to his having her with him. She might even use the incident to demonstrate how completely she's on his side by bawling me out again. Double insurance for her safety."

"It would still be dangerous!"

He couldn't tell Rosemary Stewart, or again anybody, that Parthessen was unlikely to do grievous bodily harm to someone on whose goodwill he was depending for the acquisition of a large block of Hammond and Morgan shares.

She began to talk quickly. With respect, his plan was foolish because even if it came off, he might so easily and unnecessarily show something of his hand to Parthessen. His job was to catch the man over the fraud, put an end to his buccaneering in the company, and help H.H. bring back the Founders' charter. "On the other hand, when we've found them, why shouldn't I, for instance, telephone this Norton woman as an old school friend of hers who'd seen her—"

He opened the door. "Mr. Brown is waiting for you."

"—seen her with *such* a good-looking man and couldn't we meet for lunch and talk? *That* would work—"

"It wouldn't, and anyway I haven't found them yet."

"But that shouldn't be difficult. You know he has gone to Switzerland. Isn't he very likely to see this man he did the fraud with, to bring him into this new thing?"

Having really to fight her now, he told her truthfully he had already thought of this, as was surely evident in his having sent Ted Harris to stop Borrowdale.

"All right," she objected, "if you won't let me help you in your drama over this Norton— Why do we call her Norton when she's really Mrs. Borrowdale?"

"Habit."

"You still need a p.a., Mr. Addis, for all the other things." She developed the theme. Did he think, for instance, he could go to an airport and step into the first plane he saw, and say

169

Switzerland, please, like a taxi? Who but she would remind him he had to take his passport? Also there was his attitude toward money, which seemed to be careless if not downright profligate. Somebody had to look after that. . . .

He took his passport from his pocket and held it up. "And I have a booking on the two-forty-five flight from Lydd to Le Touquet."

"That's for cars," she said a little desperately.

"The car is outside, waiting."

"You need an international—"

"—insurance certificate? It is being delivered here by twelve o'clock." He ticked off on his fingers the things he still had to do before leaving: collect foreign currency from Mr. Brown; go to Number One to tie up loose ends with Randall. He could assure her he hadn't forgotten anything.

The mention of the security chief reminded her of Harris.

"Harris—" She was clutching at straws. "I didn't raise the point when you were telling me about it all, but you recruited Harris for this business, even when you'd had that brawl with him in the secretariat?"

"That was nothing."

"Well, it looked quite something to the secretariat. My point is, how can you *trust* the man after a thing like that? He'd need watching, and you, Mr. Addis, won't have the time for it." And apart from that, Mr. Addis might easily find he had to have outside assistance when he was in Switzerland. Did he have the Hammond and Morgan confidential directory, which included all the foreign agencies that represented the company? No. But she had. As his p.a. presumptive she had pinched a copy yesterday, knowing it might be necessary to his work. . . .

"Oh, damn you, Mr. Addis!" Tears were in her eyes and she was appalled that he should see them. She jumped out of the chair with sudden and furious energy and dashed past him out of the room toward the stairs.

He caught up with her just before she reached them and flattened her against the wall to be immediately terrified by her smallness and fragility. But this was to an extent put right by the savagery with which she kicked him, feeding his anger.

"You've got the job!" he said between teeth gritted against the pain in his shinbone.

"I d-don't want it be-because I cried like a baby for it!"

"Who cares why you cry? After you've talked with Brown go straight out to the car, a gray Bentley, and tell Fred to

170

take you to wherever you live, to wait while you pack a bag and to get you back here by twelve-thirty. And don't *you* forget you'll need a passport!"

He slammed down the stairs, out of the side door and into the bank by the main door. Mr. Brown took the news calmly that Miss Stewart would be down in a minute or so to fix her service contract. "A charming and competent young woman. It would have been a pity to lose her."

"Also impossible. Don't stand any nonsense from her."

"I won't, Mr. Hammond."

"Addis!"

"With Miss Stewart and everyone else"—Mr. Brown was a little hurt—"of course it's 'Mr. Addis.' "

A pity to lose her? He wasn't committing himself yet. But her idea to telephone Victoria was a valuable and a practical one. Parthessen would already be conditioned to expect and accept that kind of fortuitous mischance.

He went out to the car, told Fred to put himself at Miss Stewart's disposal, and ran after an unoccupied cab slowed down by the traffic. Fred at least hadn't argued with him, wanting to know what was this with Miss Stewart. He'd soon find out, though. His obviously self-immolating Mr. John had taken a viper into the nest.

The loose ends did not take long.

Randall looked scarcely less worn than last evening. He accepted with fortitude that his Ted Harris had been shot off to Switzerland in the middle of the night, although he had to say he hoped Addis knew what he was doing as far as H.H. was concerned. "Don't let him catch you out on a limb. He'll chop it off soon as look at you. Sooner. And I don't want to be out there with you."

What was new on Glover? Nothing yet. The brass was quiet, preparing its attitudes for after the weekend. The chairman's reaction? Unsurprised. Glover, H.H. felt, had always seemed an "unfortunate" type, although first-class, of course, in his job. "Not a hint," Randall added, "suggesting the man's suicide might be connected with the Fording Lencorp business. But of course H.H. wouldn't—to me."

"He doesn't know Glover was involved." "Doesn't know" was his ever-louder litany around Bertie; John realized he couldn't hope to continue it much longer. Randall was already bothered by the vagueness of John Addis's terms of reference and would probably be the first to demand clarification of them.

The captain was distracted for the moment, however, by Glover's death, and John occupied his mind further by asking him to hold a watching brief on his behalf here at Number One while he followed Harris to Switzerland to take a look at Owen Wetherfield. Also would the captain make himself responsible for collecting the Lencorp files from Secretarial Services, 9:00 A.M. Monday?

"Personally? Just as you wish." The files themselves to go to Parthessen's p.a. without comment; the photostat copies into the strong room.

"You think he wants them back to destroy? It still beats me why he kept any of the stuff in the first place. What's left doesn't amount to a public prosecutor's definition of evidence, but it's still sufficient for strong presumption of conduct unfitting in a Hammond and Morgan director—or any other company director."

"Yes," John agreed.

"Must be some sense somewhere, but I can't say I see it."

John, on the other hand, thought *he* could, but didn't say so.

Returning to Brook Street he remembered Rosemary Stewart's saying something that had been irrelevant to their argument. Fully engaged trying to make her see reason, it had slipped his mind. But he wouldn't forget it again. No hurry, though. Ignore the whole involved, troublesome business for a little while in the interests of peace and amity.

Also conducive to this ideal was the rhythm of the Bentley's seventy miles an hour through the green Kentish countryside. It was now after one o'clock, and he was able, for instance, to occupy himself with the mundane problem of lunch. He himself wasn't hungry after MacGregor's whopping great breakfast, and Fred, knowing that they would be on the road during lunch time, would have arranged his own commissariat.

But what about the p.a.? Whose responsibility was she? There should be a convention to cover it, but he didn't know what it was. She was riding in the back; he glanced in the rear-view mirror. She didn't *look* hungry, and with her littleness still fresh in his physical impression of her, he couldn't believe she ate more than once a week. This should solve the difficulty—except that today might be her eating day.

Would Fred perhaps know the convention? He asked him about it in a low voice. Should they stop at the next town, Maidstone?

"No need, sir. She had a thought to stop off at a delicatessen on our way back to Brook Street, so there's a picnic lunch in the trunk." He dropped his voice further and left out the "sir" of social inequality. "You've picked a good one there. Small, but she'll take any fence you put her at, not to say run till she drops for you. All heart, she is. I keep thinking I've seen her before, but of course I haven't. It's me seeing something on its way before it gets here, so that it's kind of familiar when it does come. My mother was like that, as you know, but worse."

"If it's convenient," said Rosemary from behind them, "could we eat now? I'm terribly hungry."

Three meat pies, bread and cheese, a bottle of lager for Mr. Addis, one bottle of beer she would share with Fred. (He'd said he didn't like to drink when driving.)

"Cheaper than three of us in a restaurant," she pointed out virtuously. Yes indeed, thought Mr. Addis, regretful that he hadn't had the same idea in Jermyn Street, when the taxi was passing the rear entrance of Fortnum and Mason . . . salmon mousse in there, and salad and peaches and cream and a bottle of hock . . .

Not only had he gotten himself a p.a. but a parsimonious one as well. Efficient as hell, too, remembering they'd have to eat en route to catch the plane. He let himself drift off into a dream of when this Hammond and Morgan thing was behind him, and there she'd be, still his p.a. because he couldn't think how to get rid of her, sitting in on preparations for his Nuristan project. In no time at all she'd be the only person who knew which mule pack the flea powder was in and, furthermore, her charm would prove particularly effective in apologizing to Afghan officialdom for being on the wrong side of the Basgul Mountains without a permit because Afghan officialdom, properly suspicious of strangers wandering about in the eastern provinces, wouldn't have given you one if you'd applied for it.

The daydream was so vivid and lingering that while they watched Fred drive the Bentley up the ramp into the aircraft at Lydd, he asked her, "How are your Afghan languages?"

"Did you say *Afghan?*"

Very silly. "Please take no notice. A complete non sequitur in any context."

She went up the gangway ahead of him and took the inside place on a double seat. As he sat down beside her, she confounded him by saying, "West of the Helmud River they

173

speak Turki. I'd be lost with that, but east of it, where it's mostly Pushtu, which has Arabic and Persian roots like Urdu, I think I should manage. My Urdu is still quite good."

It would be. To daydream anywhere near her was clearly a dangerous habit.

"You've been investigating me, Mr. Addis? Another reason for recruiting me, that your next assignment is in Afghanistan?"

"Good heavens, no!" he said in alarm, "and I certainly didn't investigate you." He gathered that she felt he should have done so, his work being what it was, and he listened with gloomy foreboding while she told him she had been born in Quetta when her father was serving in the seventh Gurkhas and stationed in North-West Frontier Province. So naturally she'd had an Indian ayah and just as naturally had spoken Urdu better than English almost into her teens. She still spoke it at home sometimes for the colonel's sake, in case the British raj returned to save a politically and economically bankrupt India. "Some hope, poor man."

Some hope, too, for a traveler choosing Nuristan as the place to convince himself that he was independent.

Then he remembered her blind harpsichord maker. She wouldn't absent herself for any length of time, since Charles's objections to marrying her might harden still further. A girl so full of heart, as even Fred had noticed she was, would never let career ambition take precedence over that of love. It would be all right. Nuristan, here I come.

"So it didn't mean anything," she asked, "about speaking Turki or Pushtu?"

"Not a thing."

She shook her head. "I didn't think you were a non sequitur kind of man, Mr. Addis."

He said he was afraid he was all kinds of a man, mostly devious and deceitful and—as she knew—unjust.

"Poor Mr. Addis," she comforted him, "I'm sure it's only when you have to be."

Poor Mr. Addis thought how right you are and took this excellent opportunity to change the subject by asking the so far unasked question: "What was that you said this morning about Lord Ashworth? Who is he and where does he come in?"

"I rather dragged him in. I delegated some of the responsibility. He is senior partner in Harbord Associates, where Hammond and Morgan hold a quarter interest, and they have a nonvoting seat on the H and M board. They're the only out-side group that has."

"Lord Ashworth is one of our directors?" he asked in surprise.

The "our" was a slip, but she didn't notice it.

"No. Their second man, Stanley Ledger, represents them. It's because of that I thought of Lord Ashworth for this. He's a sort of friend of the family—he was in the war with my father. In fact it was through him I got my job with H and M."

"Thought of him for what?" He was still in the dark.

"It's common knowledge he doesn't hit it off with H.H. and Mr. Parthessen."

"Ah, I see." That is, he hoped in time he would see. "So you dragged him in. Tell me more."

She told him, slightly stunning him in the process. When she had got to thinking about how to go to work spreading the rumor of pending policy change, she had remembered she had an "in" with a key figure in the Hammond and Morgan scene. This wouldn't mean she'd neglect the lower echelons, but this seemed a fast and certain way of getting the thing moving.

"So I called him and told him I had heard something I felt I shouldn't keep to myself, and could I see him at once, and he cut a banquet and gave me dinner at his club instead, the ladies' dining room—rather awesome, the whole thing—I couldn't come out with it until I'd two glasses of hock in me. You know what he said? He said, 'I hope to God it's true.' "

John stared sideways at her. Her quiet voice went on against the drone of aircraft engines. "Of course I didn't reveal my source and he didn't expect me to. But I knew he was assuming, because I was in the secretariat, that it must be the chairman himself, and I let him. You see you aren't the only deceitful one."

She underwrote this recital of unauthorized initiative by tacking on a "sir" and added, "I know I should have had a word with you first, and would have if I could have reached you. But I knew it was a good idea. Years ago he was very close to Sir John Hammond. He was made a life peer the other day."

Although jolted by hearing his own name on her lips, John realized she was talking about his father. And then a bell rang. "What was his name before he became a lord?"

"Channing."

Boyhood memories again. George Channing, his father's

particular friend. Inevitably, also, the club would be the Malvern, which meant that last night while he was downstairs listening to Parthessen's plans for stealing Hammond and Morgan, his clever little p.a. was upstairs in the ladies' dining room arranging that it shouldn't be worth anybody's while.

Good old circumstance, at it again.

Aided by Michelin he got his own back for the meat pies. Keeping east of Paris and avoiding the heavy traffic of its environs, they took N 37 for the southeast and Switzerland but debouched at Soissons or Épernay via Reims, reaching its three-red-forks-one-star restaurant at an appropriate time for dinner: *Oeufs pochés vignerons, brochet à l'ardennais,* and *poulet sauté au champagne,* suitably accompanied by another *spécialité,* a black-grape white wine, the *vin nature* from which champagne is made.

By this time John was sure of the convention that a personal assistant should eat with the boss when they were traveling alone. Just as a chauffeur even of Fred Ross's superiority was more comfortable on his own in the *brasserie,* where he ate as heartily if differently, and drank familiar beer.

On this occasion the p.a. enjoyed the food and ambience with unaffected pleasure but at moments was uneasy, feeling they shouldn't be in a place where the *patron* suggested your menu instead of allowing you to see one and make gastronomic mistakes in terms of his chef's view of what you should eat on this particular evening. She guessed this would mean both parties to the transaction were being completely disinterested in its ultimate cost in money.

She guessed right, and was further frustrated when John in paying, after a secretive glance inside the folded bill, did not let her see the denomination of the travelers' check. She couldn't know, however, that this also enabled him to conceal the name he had to sign on it.

In the car again, she thanked him very nicely for one of the best meals she'd ever had in her life, but a few moments later said, "You know, Mr. Addis, one of the chores a p.a. should concern herself with is looking after cash disbursements during business trips and so on. Otherwise the expense sheet can get out of hand and cause difficulty when submitted for payment."

"I'll remember," he said.

She had to make do with this but before relinquishing the subject emphasized its importance to the profitability of their assignment. The H and M internal-accounts department penny-watched with the eyes of mean-minded hawks, and Mr. Addis might easily end up losing on the swing what he was paid on the roundabout.

She was afraid her metaphors were in a terrible muddle . . . and oh dear, how sleepy she was . . .

Fred stopped the car without waiting for orders, got out a rug and tucked her up with a soft hissing sound, in which was a clue, perhaps: a small-boned, stouthearted creature deserved the best possible care against the time she might be called upon to run for Mr. John until she dropped.

She was asleep before the car was moving again.

Pontarlier, at the frontier, was a long drive, and there'd still be forty-odd miles to go before they reached Lausanne, but you'd feel you had arrived when you crossed into Switzerland. John continued to spell Fred Ross at the wheel. The Bentley, with personality so often met in great cars, responded happily to the arrow-straight traffic-free *routes nationales* after the frustrations of short scrappy journeys around a city.

The night was dark, the headlights carving out the way through it. Now and again a white wall in a village would throw back their light so that John could see the sleeping girl in the driving mirror, tilted a little to avoid the glare of cars he had overtaken.

It was inevitable that at one of these moments he should suddenly and unpleasantly remember that Boyle Glover had been the previous and most recent occupant of the rear seat. Equally unavoidable was the persistence of this visual memory as the kilometers sped past, humming motor and singing tires adding hypnosis to the belief that if the car hadn't been haunted before, it was now.

18

"Why here?" Rosemary asked, waking up.

He explained that it was only seventy kilometers from Chexbres. "Also it's where—"

"I mean this *hotel?*" she interrupted, looking out of the car window at the Beau-Rivage. It rose from its gardens with imposing grandeur against the pale sky of pre-dawn.

"—also it's where Harris is staying."

"Then he shouldn't be, Mr. Addis. I've heard of the place. It's where kings and queens and Texans stay."

It was also where Hammonds sometimes stayed. He had suggested it to Harris because it was the only hotel of which he knew the name, here at Ouchy, the lakeside of Lausanne. He told her they would move somewhere else if they had to stay longer than a night. "Or what's left of it."

"Perhaps they won't let us in at this hour in the morning."

"You wait in the car while I find out. Let me have your passport. And yours, Fred."

Rosemary rubbed the sleep from her brown eyes.

"It's my job—"

"Wait in the car."

The night-duty reception clerk glanced at the passports, accepted instantly the fact that Sir John Hammond was traveling incognito as Mr. Addis, and was presently ushering them into a suite of three rooms.

"You say this is the smallest suite?" she asked.

"Yes, Madam." The clerk hoped this particular millionaire realized his good luck.

John let her salve her p.a. conscience by asking her to make sure herself that Fred had a comfortable room in the servants' annex. "And please arrange for me to be called at ten to eight. I'll have breakfast up here at a quarter past. Grapefruit, kedgeree, hot rolls and honey."

"Yes, Mr. Addis. Crystallized or runny?"

"What?"

"Honey."

"Crystallized."

He went into the larger of the two large bedrooms and shut the door. An occasional jump through a hoop to make her feel better was one thing, but to prevent her slightly having him on in revenge was another.

"No, Mr. Addis," said the reception clerk on the telephone at six minutes to eight. "We haven't a Mr. Edward Harris on the guest list. I've checked again."

Puzzled and a little alarmed, he was about to hang up when the clerk said, "One moment, Mr. Addis . . . you're Mr. Harris, sir? Mr. Addis is asking for you. Would you take it over there in number three, please."

"Ted? I was worried. They say you aren't staying in the hotel?"

178

"No"—Harris was out of breath—"I was able to cut a few corners at the airport by telephoning around hotels du Lac and found Borrowdale. Point is, could you catch a plane and get down here fast?"

"Ted—"

"So far I've only made telephone contact with him. He just wouldn't give me the time of day, said he'd never heard of Hammond and Morgan and I believe him, the ignorant bastard. He's convinced you're a crook and me another. I've a feeling I shan't do any better face to face with him on my own. *Can* you make it?"

"Try me, or rather try Suite G, third floor."

"What?"

"Come on up."

"Come . . . ? Oh, trust *you*." Harris laughed with relief and rang off.

John read the legend over the buttons on the base of the telephone and pressed one.

"Good morning, Mr. Addis."

"Good morning, Rosemary. Ted Harris will be breakfasting with us."

"I will speak to service." Her voice was the summer morning, cool and fresh. He caught himself thinking what an awful shame to have to waste it because of a man like Gordon Parthessen. The summer morning, he meant.

He tried to recapture a fugitive idea that had come from sleep to the moment of waking. Something to do with the Bentley. He went to the window and pulled the curtain cord. The lake glittered under the misty pall of dark mountains that separated it from a translucent sky. Damn Parthessen, yes.

Harris's sense of hurry had eased on the way up to the suite. "Golly, I'm glad you've come out. But why?"

"A hunch Parthessen will be seeing Owen Wetherfield today, Sunday, when it's not practical to visit gnomes in Zürich and such places. They're old friends. Victoria is with him. We daren't underestimate his ruthlessness, *their* ruthlessness. She must be got out of their hands."

"I see . . . yes. Well, there are plenty of craggy precipices to drop a girl off up there behind Wetherfield's palazzo. Quite apart from Borrowdale to complicate things and make them extra jittery." Ted Harris tactfully forbore to remind him how Borrowdale had come to be here to complicate things.

"You said 'palazzo,' Ted?"

179

"Local showpiece, seven kilometers off the Chexbres-Forel road." He took a color postcard from his pocket. "Some natives call it a castle."

It stood atop a minor mountain. There was a tower at one end, making it castlelike, but pale stone walls, flattish red pantile roofs, a second floor set back behind an arched loggia, and chimney pots wearing tile hats gave it an Italianate look, its great size justifying "palazzo" as opposed to "villa." A forest sea of pine and larch around the hill sent blue-green waves up the steep slopes to the ground floor windows. A narrow road curved from the foreground across stony scrubland into the woods, to vanish in their deeps. Increasingly sharp gradients would force it into hairpin zigzags in order to climb to the top.

"You could hazard a guess," Ted Harris remarked, "that the Fording Lencorp fairy tale helped to pay for it." He added that he had a map back in his room at Vevey showing the surrounding terrain was comparatively unpopulated. "And all ups and downs at that."

Rosemary came into the room by the communicating door and said, "Good morning, Mr. Harris. I am Mr. Addis's p.a."

She was wearing a pale-yellow cotton frock and her hair was in a pony tail. She looked about fifteen, if well developed, and not at all like anybody's p.a.; the stenographer's notebook in her hand merely added to the barefaced lie.

"Good thing, I'm sure." Harris managed to close his jaw without having to use his hand. "Very kind of the chairman to let us have—"

"Mr. Addis recruited me himself."

Harris recovered sufficiently to remark that this was yet another instance of John Addis playing a card close to his chest, and even faster than usual.

"Yes?" she said in a tone to indicate that Mr. Addis's chest was no concern of hers, nor his speed.

Harris didn't do himself any good with her either when he surveyed the laden trolly wheeled in by two waiters and cried, "Now that *is* a breakfast! I shall be happy to join you."

Her look accused him of being too ready for fleshpots on the expense account.

It was here that John caught up with his waking thought. He excused himself for a moment—Rosemary would preside over the breakfast—and went to the telephone in his bedroom, closing the door against her sharp ears.

But no need to explain to Fred. To take against a car for

no reason, as he had done in the case of the E-type a little while ago, was characteristic of a car maniac. It seemed ungrateful after enjoying the Bentley's faithful and impeccable performance, but if Borrowdale was allowed to set eyes on it, revelation would threaten the secret area of the story.

Fred repeated the instruction: "Something fast, and big enough to carry six people in comfort? Does it *have* to be black, sir?"

"Black for top executives like Mr. Harris and me. Why not?"

"My black cap is back home, and you said just pajamas and toothbrush. I didn't bring my dark suit."

"We're only hiring the car, Fred."

Fred relaxed. "In that case, sir, it won't matter so much."

Just as well the p.a. hadn't heard the conversation; it would have started her off again. Even hiring the thing was going to upset her. But he had averted a real danger, and, hallelujah, put an end to driving around with a ghost on the rear seat.

Breakfast had begun. If there'd been a hatchet between his p.a. and Ted Harris, they had buried it, and from the way they stopped talking the moment he opened the door, he guessed they were approaching an alliance that would add to his difficulties in the mystique of leadership. He could see that when it came to having more than just the one subordinate you put yourself even more on show, with your uncertainties more noticeable.

And you must play a definite act of knowing all the answers. However, there was refuge in asking questions yourself, and don't reveal how your mind is working by putting them in logical sequence. Dart around a bit. Thus:

So Ted had installed himself at Vevey?

Yes, the town on the lake; six kilometers from Chexbres, which was in effect an outlying suburb. He had gone straight there from the airport after tracing Borrowdale to that particular Hotel du Lac, and had found himself a room at Le Trianon, a smaller hotel across the street.

How far had he got in assessing Borrowdale?

Some progress. The man's appearance, that of a badly articulated stork, had made inquiries easy. A waiter, for instance, in the Hotel du Lac bar, which Borrowdale spent his time propping up, had been quite ready to play a guessing game about who and what the man was. Certainly he wasn't as energetic as a tourist, which he claimed to be. His explorations of Switzerland had taken him no further than the telephone booths in the foyer, and then never longer than for a minute or so, which suggested that he was having little joy in his efforts to contact Owen Wetherfield. The number he was calling could be checked because the foyer lines went through the hotel switchboard, where the operator would keep a record.

This, Harris said, he was proposing to do as soon as he got back to Vevey.

The next question should have been: and what, Ted, were you planning to do after that? But instead John asked Rosemary if she could describe a typical Hammond and Morgan board meeting.

The digression confused her a little, but she went ahead and gave a detailed account of the proceedings.

"Thank you. So you've actually been at a board meeting."

"Once, when Miss Maple was sick, to take notes for Mr. Hammond. The minutes are the company secretary's job."

"Call Ted's hotel at Vevey and book rooms for us. That includes a sitting room, as usual."

"We openly join forces, then?" Ted Harris asked.

"Are you sure we need—" Rosemary began, but John was absorbed with the picture postcard.

"Ted, we want to know more about this place. I suggest you take a close look at it without drawing attention to your interest in it. What transport are you using?"

"Public, so far."

"If we're joining forces," Rosemary said, "Fred could take him there in the Bentley."

"Ted, get hold of a car. Fred Ross—he's our driver—can help you. The concierge here will find him for you."

"Right."

John was aware again of the creases between his p.a.'s delicate eyebrows that were appearing too often. It wasn't entirely his fault she was here, but he hoped he wouldn't be responsible for the two small lines becoming permanent.

She wanted to say something.

"Yes, Rosemary?"

"Mr. Addis"—she made it businesslike—"what do we gain by Mr. Harris's looking more closely at that house? Isn't it still sacrificing the substance for the shadow? We're investigating what these two men have done to Hammond and Morgan in the past and are trying to do to it in the future. Shouldn't we be concentrating on Borrowdale, to stop him from warning them there *is* an investigation? Isn't that the substance?"

"And the shadow"—Harris was with her—"means trying to get Victoria Norton off the hook."

"When she doesn't wish to be taken off it. Mr. Addis, can't you see we're right?"

"Maybe he doesn't want to," Harris muttered into his cup.

Rosemary would have agreed audibly if the telephone hadn't rung. She went to it. "Fred?"

She listened a moment and glanced across with a puzzled expression.

"Fred says he has found a 'Merce'—whatever that is—and will it do?"

"Mercedes?" Harris translated.

"Tell him yes, and be ready to take us to Vevey in about half an hour."

"Mercedes? That makes three cars! You're determined to go on throwing it away?" But John showing no interest in her distress, she had to relay his message to Fred.

"Just what's the plan?" Harris asked.

"Borrowdale is Victoria's husband."

"Yes indeed. You have an angle?"

Another mystique: "Never Explain." It worked. After a moment of silence Harris said, "Ah yes . . . I see," but he didn't, and his expression seemed respectful as he left to consult Fred about a car for himself.

Rosemary, on the other hand, veiled her face with a look of sheeplike dumbness that didn't suit her at all and strolled to the window where she stood gazing out, a now familiar ploy heralding a change of tactics.

This time, however, she began to talk about what she was seeing: the lake with the sun on it and the backdrop of mountains. "It's wonderful in a stagey kind of way. I don't suppose you've had time to look at it."

She didn't include a "sir" or even a "Mr. Addis," and he didn't say, "As a matter of fact it was the first thing I did." But he joined her at the window. She said, "Parthessen is a plain nuisance, spoiling a day like this," stealing his thought as she had done before.

She turned her head and looked at him, *up* at him, which was still a novel experience for him. Her brown eyes were candid and she was smiling apologetically. "I want you to forgive me, amongst other things, for going on at you for being extravagant."

"You explained why. Forget it."

"It's odd, though. Spendthrifts generally know they are, and are defensive about it. You don't give it a thought one way or the other, as though you really feel it *is* 'only money.' "

"Hammond and Morgan money—"

"Don't be silly!"

"What's silly about it?"

"You're not dishonest. You wouldn't run up bigger expenses than you have to. This is no kind of conversation to be having with my boss."

"I hope," he said, "you'll never forget to be a human being. I'm sure I won't."

"I'll try not to." As though to make the promise meaningful she moved closer to him but without apparently taking the smallest pace.

Her attraction for him was suddenly personal and considerable. In fact she would do well to step back. He would have stepped back himself if there'd been room to, but he was awkwardly placed between her and the window.

Suddenly he found himself kissing her, without holding her, however, without contact other than his lips on hers.

It was the shortest but sweetest kiss. She said, "This won't do at all. . . ."

He kissed her again, this time putting his arms around her so that she couldn't avoid it. She didn't exactly resist but she drew away and shook her head.

"It's in all of you—the knight errant ready to waste his sweetness on the first scheming woman he falls for."

She turned and went quickly to her room.

The penny dropped. It would have dropped earlier if for a moment he had forgotten her blind harpsichord maker.

His p.a. had almost—not quite—dangled herself in front of him in the way of duty. His p.a. had been checking on the extent of the damage. But his p.a. had decided that he was so hungry for Victoria that he'd take a bite at the nearest apple, just to take the edge off.

In fact, who was leading whom?

Lest there be any doubt about it he went to her door and knocked sharply on it. "Come out here, please."

She came out and he kissed her a third time, firmly and with intent. When she had got her breath she used it to say that that was absolutely and for ever the last of *that*. . . .

"Of course. You've found out what you wanted to know

184

and so have I—that any kind of sex, even the slightest, should be avoided between p.a. and boss."

"Yes," she said. "Oh yes, Mr. Addis."

19

Harris's hotel, Le Trianon, was small but comfortable and, as he had said, across the street from the Hotel du Lac. Standing on his bedroom balcony John could just see the windows of Borrowdale's room; the angle was sharp but not enough to prevent your making out whether the curtains were open or drawn. At eleven-fifteen this Sunday morning they were still drawn.

This could be diagnosed as a combination of a habitual Sunday lie-in, too much drink last night and sheer laziness. But you couldn't say whether it also meant that Borrowdale had nothing to leave his bed for, that he had at last fixed an appointment with Owen Wetherfield. Ted Harris *thought* he hadn't yet succeeded in that direction. But suppose that he in fact had? And that because it was fixed for later in the day or perhaps even tomorrow he could afford to relax?

John, however, could not. A move must be made, a crucial one, and no more delay; he daren't wait, for instance, for Ted Harris to return from reconnaissance.

He left the balcony and went into the suite's sitting room. Rosemary heard him and came from her room wearing her business face. He wondered if she had been practicing it in the looking glass.

"Borrowdale seems to be still asleep, but we have to assume he'll be up and about any moment. I'd be glad if you'd get over there and keep him occupied."

She was startled but did not lose her detached expression. "You want me to pick him up?"

"And charm him. You should have no difficulty."

She knew what he meant. She had recently demonstrated her skill.

"You want him kept busy, Mr. Addis?"

"I want the edge taken off his efforts to embroil himself in this."

"For how long?"

185

"As long as possible. I'll tell you when you can let him loose."

"Thank you, Mr. Addis."

"But first—" He handed her the slip of paper on which Ted Harris had written the La Rouette telephone number.

"The original plan? Letting them know that somebody knows she's there? No walking in?" She couldn't hide her relief.

"Try to give the impression that you're a French operator on the international exchange asking if Monsieur Gordon Parthessen will take a personal call from London."

She took the paper and said she thought she could do it speaking French, and then English with a French accent to make the "London" part of it sound right. She hesitated. "But it's still a local call."

"Ask the hotel operator to put you on the line immediately the ringing tone begins. Then yours will be the only voice."

She was still puzzled, and made an impatient gesture. "But if there's to be any talking it should be *me*, asking to speak to *her*. I know I can't play the old school friend thing. I just ring off. They'll realize it's known she's there."

"Let's not confuse the issue. You will say the call is for Parthessen."

"Suppose he won't have anything to do with it?"

"Give the caller's name as 'Hammond.' "

"What?" Her business face forgotten in her anxiety to protect him from foolhardiness, she held on to verbal formality.

"I'm sorry, Mr. Addis, but I must ask if you feel this will be all right with the chairman? There could be repercussions, using his name fraudulently for your . . ."

"Can you think of a better one to bring Parthessen to the phone?"

She gave up. She went hesitantly to the telphone on the side table. Her performance, however, was firm and convincing. She even spoke away from the mouthpiece to give the impression that several connecting links in the line were reducing transmission power.

Someone answered at La Rouette to whom she announced dispassionately in French that she had a person-to-person call from M'sieur 'Ammond for M'sieur Part'essen.

She covered the mouthpiece and whispered, "A manservant, I think. He merely said, *'Un moment,'* didn't seem surprised or taken aback. Parthessen *is* there."

"Good."

She kept the receiver to her ear and eyed him surreptitiously, worried that he should deny her his full confidence but blaming herself for being unable to fill in the gaps with her own intuition.

He did his best not to be sorry for her.

She stiffened slightly to a sound in the earpiece.

"M'sieur Part'essen? I 'ave a call for you from London—a M'sieur 'Ammond. You wish to take it, pliz . . . *merci. Un moment, s'il vous plaît.*"

John took the receiver from her and nodded at the door. She went quickly to it and out of the room without a backward glance; he was along with the telephone and his crucial move. He used her trick of keeping the mouthpiece at a distance.

"Mr. Parthessen?"

"Is that you, H.H.?" The voice was puzzled and careful.

John had to fake a double impression to include his established Woosterism and an uncertain maturity born of sudden and unaccustomed responsibility.

"Who—what? Oh, sir, not *Bertie.* This is John. Can you hear me?"

Parthessen, surprised but easier, said that he could hear him. And how the devil had John, my boy, known where to reach him. And what could he do for him?

"I know it's an intrusion but I *had* to talk to you. Not just a bone to pick, although it wasn't very nice, was it—with respect—your saying why didn't I have a go now I was free of the John Addis nonsense, when you—when all the time you were all set to dash off to Switzerland with her practically that very minute!"

"Oh that—" Parthessen sounded relieved. "All's fair, my boy. But how the hell—?"

"No secret at Grosvenor Towers, where she was off to, but nobody there knew who with. On the other hand a description of the chap . . ."

There was a pause, then—you could imagine Parthessen's man-of-the-world expression. "I thought I'd get clean away with it." He chuckled fatly. "But it seems I didn't. Suppose we go on from there?"

"Well, you know how it is. Damn sore and damn-all I could do. But no, of course you don't. Then yesterday there were developments and it seemed absolutely necessary to contact you. Bertie had said something vague about where you'd be 'covering the ground,' so I—

"H.H. knows why you've been trying to find me?"

"Good God, would I mix him up in this? That puritan!"

Parthessen grunted and came to the crux of it. Even H.H. hadn't known exactly where he was heading. Uneasy again, he had to ask it: how had John traced him here?

"I'm afraid, sir"—apologetic, and fingers crossed—"I talked to one of your domestic staff."

"But dammit, I didn't tell them."

"—as I soon discovered. But after a lot of trouble I did at last get a name connected with Switzerland—a personal friend. I thought he just might know . . ."

Was the grunt an imprecation? *Blank* that *blank* Tankerton . . . ?

John plunged on. "I felt justified. I *had* to reach you. There couldn't be so many Wetherfields in Switzerland that the telephone people couldn't find him. Anyway I thought he could even happen to be one of the chaps you were planning to see about this what's-it consortium thing and I said to myself, John, I said, suppose . . . but now I'm beginning to waffle. Look, sir, I have to tell you—by the way, you're alone? She isn't in the room with you?"

Another perceptible pause told of Parthessen's indecision. Then, "Hold on a minute, I'll close the door."

The worst was over.

Probably the door was already closed but Parthessen wanted a moment to assess the situation.

When his voice came back John could hear his thought: don't flap, this is no more than an adolescent simpleton, full of guff and calf love, on his own and out of his depth.

"All right, John my boy. What's on your mind?"

John gulped audibly enough for the line to pick it up. "I—I hate this like hell but she—well sir—she could be—be *dangerous!*"

"That's a strong word."

"I know, but it's the only one for it."

Parthessen urged him on. "Well?"

"It's Glover—Mr. Glover. You don't know—who'd have told you? She was *his* girl friend."

"Was she, by God!" Nicely done. Convincing surprise.

"Ah, I was sure you didn't know."

"As a rule they don't chatter about their past loves. Not to me."

"Past love. That's truer than you know—you haven't heard

188

yet about Mr. Glover. It didn't come through until after you'd left."

"Glover has turned up?" Alert and interested, but detached.

"This'll be a shock. He's dead, sir."

"Good God! I'm sorry . . . how very sad."

"Suicide."

"Oh dear me . . . these poor wretched fellows *will* drive themselves . . ."

"Trouble is, our security section—" John hesitated.

The first sharpness since the original surprise touched Parthessen's voice. "What about the security section?"

"They found out about him and her. There's every chance his suicide will turn out to be directly attributed . . . you see what I'm getting at?"

"I think so."

"Your position . . ." John's tone lacked nothing in respect. "And particularly at the moment . . ."

"You don't have to stress it. This is extremely awkward."

John produced a soothing point to give his next its full impact. "Mr. Glover didn't actually leave a note bringing her into it."

Parthessen agreed that that was something, but all the same . . .

"You're right to be uneasy"—now for a solid chunk of reality in a house of cards—"I don't see how the implication is to be avoided when it comes out she had a husband in the background, making trouble."

He heard the breath go out of Parthessen. *"Husband . . ."*

"Yes, sir. Apparently it doesn't show in her personnel file, but Glover would have been in a position to find out, wouldn't he?"

"You're quite sure of this?" High marks for a steady voice.

"There's no doubt of it. I could ask Captain Randall to call you and confirm it."

Parthessen said thank you, there was no need. "It's obviously true. She's the type, if you stop to look at it. I'm grateful to you, even if you have given me a bellyful to think about. So now what?"

"You mean how to ditch her?"

"She's not the ditchable sort."

"Oh dear. What—er—was the plan if this hadn't come up?"

"Bern tomorrow, then on to Zurich."

189

"Quite a honeymoon."

"All's fair, John, as I said before. So let's be adult."

"I told you, sir, I can't help feeling sore. I'd set my mind on it."

"But not your heart."

"That would be going a bit far. . . ." Softly, softly, the monkey was coming around the next corner. It was here.

"In that case, my boy, perhaps you'd take her off my hands?"

"What!"

"Too sophisticated for you as a solution?"

John said "um" and "ah" but obviously must not seem to be anything but sophisticated, which also he should overplay.

"Tell you what, I'll buy her from you."

Parthessen laughed. "What's your offer? No, my boy, you're welcome to her. But what about *your* reputation?"

John's turn to laugh. "Who cares what I get up to? I'm not a respectable big businessman responsible for other people's money." He asked how they were to set up this mutual good turn.

Parthessen said it would take some figuring—let him think a moment. One thing was out. She'd kick like the devil if he tried to send her home halfway through the trip.

"You could insist."

"You don't know her."

Again John's turn to laugh. "Here's hoping." He added eagerly, "It looks as though I should come and fetch her, doesn't it?"

"You'd do that?"

"Why not? I could appear . . . very romantic—the fairy prince a-rescuing her from the wicked ogre."

"Thank you."

"Just a figure of speech."

Parthessen was briefly silent. Then: when could John get here? John, feeling overrich in cunning, asked, Where exactly was "here"?

Parthessen hesitated again but told him. "And when could you make it?"

"Soonest. And you wouldn't have to wait for me to arrive. A bit embarrassing, your being there. Anyway, shouldn't you shake loose at once? This call could be about your business trip. You could say you have to get going at once. Don't give her time to argue, eh?"

"You're using your head."

"Blondes seem to stimulate the old gray matter. Your Mr. Wetherfield won't mind if you leave her with him for a few hours?"

"He won't mind."

"That's the kind of friend to have. You will tell him I'm turning up?"

"Of course."

John allowed a doubt to appear: "What about *her*, though? She'll be properly mad at being fobbed off with me."

Parthessen said nonsense, John underestimated his attractions.

"All the same—"

"I promise you she'll be expecting you with all her heart."

Parthessen rang off, leaving John with a feeling of success marred by a faint, underlying uneasiness. Had it been too simple? Could you imagine Victoria letting Gordon Parthessen go off without a fight? And then sit with folded hands in breathless anticipation of John Addis's arrival, John Addis whom she had thrown out with last week's trash?

Hadn't the man had every kind of opportunity to find out what made the girl tick? And yet he hadn't revealed a shadow of uncertainty that he would be able to leave her behind.

John left a note for Ted Harris with the concierge and went to look for Fred, whom he found drinking a bock in the café belonging to the Trianon. Fred had a strong survival instinct; somehow, somewhere, a Sunday notwithstanding, he had acquired not only a black suit to wear with the Mercedes but a chauffeur's cap, black too, of course, with the Mercedes three-pointed star above its peak.

John let him finish the beer before taking him into the hotel to consult the local map on the wall by the reception desk. He showed him the road junction that a car coming from La Rouette must use to reach the Bern road by way of Forel. They would go to it, leave the Mercedes somewhere out of sight—perhaps in the entrance to that track there—see it? And walk back to the junction, where with luck they should find cover from which they could recognize the occupants of any car that came into it from La Rouette. It was likely to be the first and only one to appear, although just when he couldn't say. But probably inside two hours, not longer.

"We will see Mr. Parthessen?"

"We hope so, Fred."

"And Miss Norton?"

"We hope he will leave her behind."

Fred looked at him with undisguised if possessive admiration.

They hadn't gone a hundred yards when Fred spotted the Mini and sounded his horn; Ted Harris saw them. He parked the Mini and joined them in the Mercedes.

He seemed a little depressed and gave his report in the form of questions:

"Tell me, why a twelve-foot link fence with barbed wire at the top that I daresay is electrified, why double gates of the same, why a rifle so handy leaning against the wall by the door of a lodge that looks more like a blockhouse? Incidentally the barbed wire angles outward, the only indication that the place isn't a concentration camp to keep the inmates inside."

No, he hadn't seen anybody, although obviously there was someone in the lodge, the door being open and that damned rifle close to it.

John agreed that these things sounded discouraging for uninvited callers. But they didn't have to be more significant than that the area was as remote as the map indicated, and the owner a rich man.

As for the rifle, under the Swiss military service system, every army reservist, which meant every able-bodied male between twenty-one and forty-five, kept weapons and equipment at home instead of drawing them from the quartermasters and armorers on call-up or for annual training.

Ted had read about that somewhere. But surely the usual place for the reservist's rifle was in the chimney corner wrapped in oily rags?

The general topography of the Wetherfield estate?

The small mountain was larger than you expected. The nearest high ground—no more than a hillock—was where the picture postcard had been taken, and even with binoculars to compensate photographic perspective, you couldn't see through the treetops that hid the lower half of the house. The windows of the upper floors were smallish, and although some of them were open, you couldn't see into them.

"It's a hell of a big place."

John asked him if he had his Hammond and Morgan identification with him. He took out a small leather folder. "It was to use it on Borrowdale, remember? But a fat lot of weight it carries in these parts."

"You may find it useful."

Ted Harris opened it and gazed gloomily at the passport-sized photograph of himself. "It looks like bloody anybody." He put it back in his pocket.

They lay, Ted Harris and himself, on the stony hillside above the road junction, sharing the concealment of the same boulder.

The La Rouette turning came down the opposite slope, a narrow dusty lane that straightened out for a hundred yards directly facing them before it dropped down for the final fifty or so to its meeting with the Forel road.

It was a good vantage point. The car would be in view for half a minute, during which they should be able to get, for at least a few seconds, a sustained glimpse of its interior.

If it came at all. They had been there a full hour. In that time Fred in the Mercedes had passed and repassed the junction a dozen times, the alternative to hiding the car where the map had suggested. On the ground the track had turned out to be nothing of the kind, but in fact a swift brook flowing from the hills into a stream that accompanied the road down the valley toward the lake.

Ted Harris looked at his watch. "Maybe he left before we got here?"

"Twenty-five minutes? He had to pack his bag, excuse his sudden departure to Wetherfield and have a scene with Victoria about leaving her behind. And there wasn't all that hurry. He thought I was calling him from London and wouldn't get here for several hours. But in any case I'm taking a back seat."

"What's that?"

"Ted, you're a bit older and a lot bigger than I am and you are a Hammond and Morgan security officer. Wetherfield will listen to you."

"Oh, will he . . . when I'm not even clear what we want from him?"

"Evidence to help Hammond and Morgan institute criminal proceedings against the perpetrators of the Fording Lencorp fraud."

"Good God, he was one of them!"

"You mean his late brother was."

"But he didn't have a brother—John, you *can't* rely on his believing we don't know that."

"What else?"

193

"You mean what *next*. I'll tell you. Mr. Wetherfield will out with his little handgun and pop-pop, farewell Johnny and Teddy, the boy investigators."

"Don't let that rifle prejudice you."

"It gives me a picture—"

Ted Harris raised the binoculars to stare at the empty lane. The sun was hot on the shoulders and back of the neck. Fred's Mercedes came into sight at the Chexbres end of the section, passed the junction below and disappeared in the Forel direction and the place where Fred could turn for the reverse run. The scent of pine and resinous larch mingled with the no less pervasive herb smells. In front of them the mountain seemed to fill the sky.

John felt Ted Harris's uncertainty like a physical contagion. Where was leadership?

"Ted, I believe that once we're past that fence it won't be so difficult."

"Give me one reason."

John gave him two. He gave them at length, and because he believed they were valid he spoke convincingly. But he realized with some desperation that he wasn't getting through.

Ted Harris stared at the opposite slope through the binoculars; there was nothing to see but rocks and bushes and higher up the trees of the forest's outskirts.

The second reason was so particularly pertinent that John went over it again.

"Think, Ted. You took an interest in the Fording Lencorp files in the first place because they were sent to security in a hole-and-corner way. You looked them over and found up to half the material missing—or so it seemed—and Randall, and later myself, agreed with you."

"That's right."

"So, why didn't Parthessen destroy the lot while he was at it?"

"I told you. It didn't occur to me. Paper work isn't my cup of tea."

"But security is. You're trained to recognize a lack of it in other people. Parthessen wouldn't be what he is if he couldn't think in terms of his own security."

"Then why—"

"I think he didn't destroy the rest because he hadn't got it. He and Owen Wetherfield arranged what in effect was a joint insurance policy of mutal blackmail. They divided the written evidence between them in such a way that neither set of papers was sufficient proof of their fraud without the other."

Ted Harris lowered the binoculars, and John explained his reasoning based on the way Parthessen had preserved his share of the material without having it in his physical possession. He had buried it where it couldn't be safer from the chance eyes of accountants and company law experts, yet he could recover it any moment he might need it in the event of a run-in with his partner in crime.

Parthessen had made one mistake, however. He should have been just a little bolder. If he had taken the small risk of sending the files to security under his own name, as director of the investment division, to Randall personally as the security chief, no one would have dreamed of looking at them before locking them away.

"Doesn't it all make sense? *Sense*, Ted?"

There was movement in the shimmering air of the opposite hill, a small dust cloud swirling, becoming larger . . .

Ted lifted the binoculars.

It was a wide, green Cadillac, and since it was another product of goldfish-bowl culture, John without binoculars could be as sure as Ted Harris was with them that there were two people in the car and only two. The driver, a Swiss blond young man without hat or cap; and in the rear seat, in a cream suit making him larger than his large life-size, Parthessen reclined, solitary but not lonely, supported as he was by his usual state of full self-confidence. This was as clear to see as the cigar in his mouth and the blueness of his tie.

They could look deeper into the car when it came to the dip in the road. No one was crouching in it. . . .

It paused at the junction, waited for two cars to pass, one in each direction, and moved into it, turning toward Forel.

John found he had been holding his breath. "He seems to be doing what he said he'd do."

"Unless he'd no option."

"I meant that he has left her behind."

"So did I. But couldn't take her with him because she's full to the neck with sleeping pills or dropped down a hole in the mountain."

"No, Ted."

"Then before she is, let's look for a place to go through the fence."

"Only by the gates and with Mr. Owen Wetherfield's knowledge and permission."

"For God's sake, you've come all this way to save the bloody girl! All the rest is fiddling guesswork!"

John began making his way down the slope with Ted Harris just behind him. The Mercedes reappeared and instead of continuing as before toward Chexbres, stopped at the road junction below them, confirmation that Fred Ross, now getting out of the car to wait for them, also had seen Parthessen. When they reached him he opened the rear door, touching his cap.

John smiled at him. "That's right, Fred. We're now in the executive class."

"In that case, Mr. John . . ." Fred pressed a button to raise a glass partition that converted the car into a limousine; he got behind the wheel again.

Frowning, Ted Harris climbed into the rear seat and John followed him. The big motor hissed softly and they turned off the main road into the lane. They sat in silence while the car climbed the hill toward the forest. John asked where the fence was.

"After the second hairpin bend once we're in the woods. I feel lousy about this thing."

That was obvious. But why, after dong so well? What was the trouble?

"I'm out of my class here."

"Wetherfield is only another crook. If necessary you can buy him the way we did Sid Tankerton."

"Pah!" said Ted Harris, and waved his hand to embrace the forest, the villa, the vastness of Wetherfield's estate.

"You can tell him Hammond and Morgan will pay fifty thousand dollars for that evidence."

"Fifty thousand dollars!" Ted stared sideways at him.

"Or the equivalent in whatever currency he fancies."

"This makes less sense than ever. It's bloody cockeyed!"

"The company's only concern is to demonstrate that no one can get away with cheating it."

"Money no object? Throw good after bad?"

"If necessary."

"The chairman," said Ted Harris slowly, "really has given you a free hand. Eh?"

As usual John knew better than to start discussing what the chairman had or hadn't done. He kept quiet and let Ted Harris mull it over. The result, an unhappy resentful mutter, was barely audible and discouraging.

The Mercedes came to a halt.

"Christ, the gates!"

"They're where you said they'd be," John remarked.

Ted Harris stared at them and the lodge beyond and noticed that anyway the rifle had gone, which was something.

But not enough?

The gatekeeper, middle-aged but tough-looking, appeared. He carried a small clip board, and wore an expression of doubt. He reached the gates but did not unlock them, waiting for one of them to get out of the car and come to him, to state their business.

Ted Harris took out his leather folder. "Shall I talk to him?" A question he shouldn't have had to ask. Either he went without comment to beard the man or he sent Fred—a more executivelike ploy. But he did neither, a state of indecision that wouldn't be lost on the gatekeeper.

So John took the folder from him—he made no demur—and got out of the car himself. He talked with the gatekeeper in French. They were representatives of an important international company who had come for consultation with M'sieur Wetherfield. John held the identification folder open between the links of the gate. He would be obliged, therefore, if the villa could be telephoned and their arrival announced.

The man looked from the folder to the clip board and back again. He shook his head. The name "Harris" was not on it. No one was admitted without an appointment. . . . He paused, frowning, ah! perhaps he had misheard M'sieur André, the secretary. Could it be that "Addis" should be "'Arris"? But no, that couldn't be, because in either case M'sieur Addis or 'Arris was not expected until this evening, perhaps late.

"*Montrez-moi, s'il vous plaît,*" said John firmly.

The gatekeeper hesitated but held up th clip board. It said:

Borrowdale—1400 heures
Addis—ce soir

John was very tempted to say, Yes, *M'sieur le portier*, that's the explanation, you have the name down wrong; it should be "Harris," and we have managed to get here sooner than we expected.

They would be past these gates and in Wetherfield's presence as fast as the Mercedes could reach the mountaintop.

But "Addis" couldn't be both the lovesick playboy *and* "Harris" the security officer, not without confusing Wetherfield into dangerous suspicion that would send him straight to Parthessen for explanation and protection.

No, *M'sieur le portier,* you have not made a mistake. Will you therefore call the villa to inform your master that two representatives of *la compagnie* Hammond and Morgan have arrived to consult with him. "In fact I will speak to M'sieur myself, to make sure he understands there is urgency."

The gatekeeper rejected this attempt to usurp his function. *"Je lui dirai moi-même."*

"Then, take this"—John pushed the folder through the wire —"and be very sure you read out the name of our company so that he cannot be in doubt of it. We do not threaten— we advise—that the job of anyone who prevents or even delays our consultation could be lost to him."

The gatekeeper turned and went into the lodge; he didn't hurry but on the other hand he didn't dawdle.

Nearly one o'clock. John had had personal experience of Rosemary's ability to occupy a man's senses, but where she might for a while have distracted Borrowdale from continuing his attempts to fix an appointment with Wetherfield, she wouldn't be able to stop his keeping one he had already succeeded in arranging. No one could.

So there was now only an hour, less than an hour, in which to do what they had come to do.

Time dragged on. Everyone had plenty of it except himself. Wetherfield was up there guessing possible significances; the gatekeeper was waiting for him to speak, minutes or hours being all the same to a porter whose trade was waiting on other people's comings and goings; and as for Ted Harris, he would be grateful for delay in a situation he did not understand any more and somewhat distrusted.

Looking around for something to occupy his mind, John bypassed the Mercedes and Ted Harris's worried face, and as with sheep for insomnia, he began to count tree trunks on the other side of the track. Methodically he started from the first one visible on his right and worked back toward the gates.

He reached thirty-two and stopped, he hoped not too suddenly, and turned his back on them.

The rifle had gone from where Ted had first seen it beside the door of the lodge, but it hadn't gone far. It was now being nursed in the arm of a man leaning against the trunk of a larch tree some twenty or thirty yards from the gates, a suitable range at which to command them. He was dressed in

198

clothes so nearly the color of the forest shadows that he was all but invisible.

At this moment of discovery the gatekeeper came out of the lodge. In place of the clip board he carried a key dangling from an iron ring. He unlocked the gates, pushed them wide, and handed John the identification folder. *"Merci, M'sieur."*

"All right, Fred. On we go." John got back into the car.

He didn't mention the rifle to Ted Harris; he might feel the urge to settle his disquiet with the panacea of direct action, like stalking the rifleman and disarming him.

The hairpin turns were more frequent, and the forest became thicker and darker, the trees meeting overhead. John could think of nothing better to say than, "Oh, come on, Ted. It's only stage fright. You'll be all right."

Then it came out. Ted must have been bottling it up for some time. It was this: no one could work for six years at Number One, at his kind of job, without getting a pretty accurate picture of the man at the top.

"John, you make him out to be a one-man band, a chap who knows his mind, decisive, a power in his own right. Which he could be, but isn't. He's a committee man—chairman of committee, if you like—but still only a figurehead. In fact—and to hell with my pension—he's a bloody cipher. He'd never stick his neck out against Parthessen. And certainly not to the extent of throwing money around the way you're doing. It's all wrong. Doesn't ring true!"

Having startled himself by what he had said, he added that this was a crazy way to talk. "I'm calling you a phony. Which you're not."

"Could be, Ted."

"Balls!" Ted Harris was torn by contradictions. "You wouldn't have an honest little man like Fred Ross working for you if you were. Or a Rosemary Stewart falling for you, a girl who'd see a phony through a brick wall with her eyes shut. I'm so mixed up I don't know where the hell I stand!" An appeal for reassurance he had every right to ask for.

Two words would give it to him, instant and complete. But say them, and all that "John Addis" had done for John Hammond would go for nothing. The alternative? Get on with the job himself, stick to the brief he had given himself at the beginning—to go through with it unaided by the leverages of his birthright. Ted Harris was doing him great service by forcing him to finish this business alone.

Finish? Not quite yet, but nearing it. There was likely to be nothing more after this that would demand more of his will and competence.

"Ted, you don't have to stay with this. You can turn around now and go straight back to Vevey, and Fred can come back for me. But first let me have the equipment and show me how to work the tape."

Several seconds felt like an hour while Ted adjusted himself to sudden release from direct responsibility. He unstrapped his wrist watch. "Take off yours and put on this one. Less noticeable than toying with the matchbox. I'd like to stay outside in the car with the cigarette pack."

John smiled and thanked him for this—yes, still valuable support.

Ted took out the cigarette pack. In these open conditions it would be sensitive up to half a mile from the wrist-watch microphone. "For instance, you could drop me off here. I could sit behind a tree, nicely out of sight."

"I'm afraid we have to assume that the gatekeeper has told Wetherfield how many we are. It means you will at least have to be seen in the car."

There was also, if it came to inexplicably sitting behind the trees, the matter of the man with the rifle. But it was still sensible not to mention him.

Ted Harris said, sure, he'd stay in the car.

"My God, just look at it!"

"It" was the villa La Rouette.

They had emerged abruptly from the forest, coming out of the trees as though through a gap in a wall, and drove onto a plateau of gardens, huge lawns, shrubberies of flowering bushes and marble—a lot of marble in statuary, pergolas, fountains, archways and other landscaping objects.

The stone façade of the huge three-story house stretched a hundred feet in each direction from a tall, semicircular portico rising above a flight of shallow steps. Smaller buildings of brick and stucco clustered together like a small village beyond the right-hand wing.

"He's either so rich or so broke," said Ted Harris in an awed voice, "that fifty thousand dollars won't mean a thing to him. He'll have to have another reason for selling Parthessen down the river." What had seemed an open-and-shut case against Owen Wetherfield from behind a desk in Number One looked like whistling in the dark when faced with the reality of the man's background.

"Two hundred and twenty thousand pounds," John said, "will buy a lot of background." Then he remembered that La Rouette had been Wetherfield's address at the time of the "Samuel" inquest.

But he hadn't had to say *how long* he had lived there; since the "suicide" had been set up several weeks after the fraud had paid off, he could have bought the property in the interval, having already had his eye on it.

It might even have been his motive for going in with Parthessen. After self-preservation, territorial acquisition was man's strongest instinct, with sex trailing after it. There was a lot to be said, too, for such grandeur for a financial con man's shop window.

Ted Harris held up crossed fingers for good luck. "And keep your left hand at a distance when you're talking or you'll blast the microphone."

John looked at the watch and saw the tiny grilles on each side of the winder button. He also saw that it kept accurate time. One-fifteen. Three-quarters of an hour before Borrowdale would arrive. He opened the car door.

Ted Harris had an afterthought. "What if the Norton girl sees you, for God's sake?"

"I don't think she will." He stepped out onto the gravel. He meant he was gambling on Wetherfield's being uneasy enough about this visitation out of the blue to make him want to receive it in private.

The place should be large enough for this to present little difficulty.

As he began to walk to the steps his sympathy for Ted Harris suddenly became wholehearted. He now knew how Ted felt about this, how failure of self-confidence set up misgivings not only about his own capacity but, as in this instance, about the role and authority of the man to whom he had committed himself.

He—the man concerned—felt the same disbelief in himself, a helplessness, a hanging by a thread, a consequent panic or whatever this hot-and-cold, knee-weak sensation should be called.

20

A large manservant in black with shining whiter-than-white cotton gloves opened the giant front door in response to pressure on a small bell push. He glanced down the steps at the Mercedes, registered the fact that John alone wished to see M'sieur Wetherfield, and led the way through a carved-pine archway immediately to the right of the entrance lobby.

John had only a fleeting view of the hall beyond a wider archway of the same kind; it seemed to have the dimensions of a medium-sized church. He didn't think there was anybody sitting in the numerous easy chairs and sofas grouped here and there on a marble-paved floor, its starkness relieved by scatter rugs any one of which would be too big for the average living room.

Nor could he see anyone on the open wooden stairway that curved gracefully up to a wide but equally deserted gallery at the far end.

He followed the manservant for some thirty yards down a broad corridor past tall windows looking out on the front. A left turn brought a staircase to the floor above, another corridor, another turn, more doors, until at last one that the man tapped on and opened for him.

John would have said he hadn't an idea what Owen Wetherfield would look like, but he was startled, as though finding that a familiar photograph had been mistakenly captioned.

He realized what had happened: associating Wetherfield with Parthessen as two of a kind, his imagination had endowed the former, whom he hadn't met, with the physical attributes of the latter, whom he knew.

The gray-haired man in a white-silk suit who stood with his back to the ornate black-stone chimney piece was clearly, by his cocked head and air of command, Owen Wetherfield. But he had none of Parthessen's florid, elephantine magnificence. He was a little man. His head was small, his appearance neat, the narrow wings of his gray-and-white spotted bow tie were level with each other. His coloring was neutral, a grayish white, his forehead like wrinkled parchment, and by contrast with Parthessen's large sparrow-egg eyes of bulging honesty, these were dark, deep-set and secretive behind a narrow, high-bridged nose.

Wetherfield spoke across the room to him.

"I thought there were two of you." His voice was thin and peevish; John couldn't imagine it in conversation with Parthessen's plummy tones of manufactured good humor.

Unexpectedly a tall, bronze-haired woman in her late twenties rose from an armchair that had its back to the doorway.

Since clearly she intended to leave the room, John waited until she had done so before answering Wetherfield. She passed close to him as he held the door open for her. The red lights in her hair were natural; she wore a green frock of soft jersey, announcing that her breasts owed nothing to uplifting or padded bra. She also wore a platinum wedding band, held down by a very large ruby ring, and a scent that he couldn't identify beyond placing it—as he had done in the case of Victoria's—in the top cost bracket. Her expression of haughty superiority was as inborn and unconscious as Victoria's was deliberate and practiced.

She was also as obviously Wetherfield's wife as she was twenty years his junior, and it seemed quite inconceivable that she loved him or would have joined her life to his except in marriage. But this was guessing. If you were interested in examples of incongruity, study women's taste in men.

Her eyes, wide, greenish, full of light, moved briefly over him as she passed him, but without the faintest curiosity.

Wetherfield called after her that he wouldn't be more than a few minutes but to start luncheon if the others were around.

She nodded without looking back. John closed the door.

"Yes, sir, there are two of us, but as this is a delicate business we thought you'd prefer . . ."

"*Delicate?*" Wetherfield snapped.

"And also, I'm afraid, painful in some aspects."

As John moved into the room he began to feel almost at ease, with a comfortable warmth that tempted him to be kinder than he had intended. He knew why. There wasn't an inch either way in their comparative heights.

Fortunately Wetherfield's unpleasant voice put a stop to undesirable softening.

"I'd like you to understand—Mr. Harris, is it?—that if it hadn't been for the name of the firm you represent and for which as a banker I have some respect, I shouldn't have dreamed of seeing you without an appointment based on precise terms of reference."

"I quite understand, sir. We are extremely sorry."

Wetherfield had taken out a pair of huge spectacles with a clear plastic frame. He lodged them on his sharp nose and stared. "You are somewhat young, I think, to represent anybody. What *is* this?"

John finished his apology. But, with great respect, Mr. Wetherfield had precipitated things by neglecting his own rule never to see anyone without first knowing what precisely he wanted.

"You are giving an interview to a Mr. Borrowdale without knowing the precise terms of reference. We know this is so because he doesn't know them either. We learned of the appointment only very recently. We had no time for telephone calls. He is due here in thirty-six minutes."

Wetherfield removed the spectacles and put them on again, as though the sudden contrast in focus would help him see John more clearly.

"And there is quite a lot," John added, "to explain before he gets here."

"Continue, Mr. Harris."

"He has probably convinced you he had information for you that he can't put on paper or talk about on the telephone. This means he wants to watch the effect on you of preliminary hints about what it is. A way of assessing how much you'll pay to stop him going elsewhere with it."

Wetherfield was silent, rocking gently on his heels.

"Sit down, Mr. Harris."

This wasn't politeness, of course, but a behavior syndrome that couldn't have had a more sympathetic witness than John himself. An adversary must be seated in case superior height should give him psychological advantages.

The conversation began in the only way it could begin. Wetherfield was grateful, of course, to Hammond and Morgan for sending someone all this way to warn him about this, but why should they take the trouble?

John shook his head regretfully. "A security leak at our end. That's all I can tell you, sir."

Wetherfield took off his spectacles and polished them with a gray silk handkerchief that matched his tie. "A recent one?"

"Why do you ask that, sir?"

"It so happens that I have had a very recent contact with a Hammond and Morgan director."

John shook his head again. "This goes back quite a while, and I should say at once, sir, it only concerns you indirectly—" John hesitated. "I did mention that this might be painful . . ."

Wetherfield was looking at him again through the gleaming picture windows on either side of his high nose.

"Painful, not recent?"

"Your late brother Samuel had dealings with my company shortly before his death. These are now being looked into in circumstances of extreme secrecy."

Wetherfield predictably said "Good God!" with appropriate horror and incredulity.

John nodded to himself, as though confirmed in a long-held belief. "You couldn't know about it, of course. You had little or nothing to do with your brother for many years, I believe."

"These dealings, as you call them, were not—aboveboard?"

"I realize this is a great shock, sir: they were fraudulent."

Sadly Wetherfield confessed he had on several occasions doubted his brother's moral fiber. . . . "And now suddenly this . . . from the grave. You'd better tell me about it."

"We wanted you to know that Borrowdale knows absolutely nothing about the details, including those of your brother's involvement."

"That's something, I suppose."

"We're also asking that you should regard this information as confidential—about the investigation."

Wetherfield nodded but couldn't leave it there.

"Certainly, but why?"

"I'm afraid the swindle was instigated by a person high in the company's trust. Inquiries have reached a critical stage, and although there's nothing this man can do to escape the results, it would be inconvenient if he got wind of them."

Wetherfield frowned. "A man *inside* Hammond and Morgan? That's difficult to believe. But be that as it may, I am disturbed by something—"

"Sir?"

"How did this Borrowdale discover that I am Samuel's brother?"

Of course, Borrowdale hadn't discovered it. But on the false assumption that he had, John had two answers ready.

He kept one in reserve, used the other: "For a moment two years ago it was publicly known." Meaning at the inquest.

It was a good answer. Wetherfield pondered it and John was happy that he should. It explained how Borrowdale could

205

have found him, and better still it also reminded him that the existence of a younger brother had been substantiated by a due process of law: an inquest culminating in a coroner's death certificate.

In this fact was Wetherfield's bolt hole, and the essence of John's strategy was to make him believe in it as an unassailable position from which he could cut loose from Parthessen.

Now was the tactically right moment to appear to have finished what he had come to say. He stood up. "Thank you, sir. That's about all."

Wetherfield was engrossed in his own thoughts.

"You would prefer, of course, that I shouldn't meet Borrowdale?"

"That's up to you. You *now* know his game is ninety-nine per cent bluff." John moved toward the door but paused, saying apologetically he didn't think he'd be able to find his own way out.

Wetherfield wasn't listening. He said, "Of course I shan't see him."

"He'll be here in ten minutes. *He* mustn't see *me*."

"He won't get farther than the gate. . . . Mr. Harris, wait —come back and sit down. What would you like to drink?"

"I've already kept you from your lunch."

Wetherfield came to him and, about to lead him back to the sofa, realized for the first time that here was someone who did not qualify under the "you sit down I prefer to stand" rule.

He stood in front of John, eye to eye as it were. "There's another thing troubling me."

"Anything I can do?"

But Wetherfield hesitated. He didn't want to come to it. He had to, of course. John had left him no option.

"I wish you'd change your mind about a drink." He looked down at the carpet. "I mentioned that I'm in contact with one of your directors."

John helped him along. "Yes, sir, you did, but I don't suppose—" He stopped himself abruptly. "I'm afraid, sir, that policy—the high-finance stuff, international bank business and so on—doesn't reach down to the security section. I wouldn't know a thing about it." He began to make for the door again.

Wetherfield said, "Wait," and caught him up. "I have to know—" His hand was under John's elbow but John kept moving so that Wetherfield had either to let go or come with him. He came with him.

"I'll show you the way. . . . I can't ask you to divulge—" He stalled again, then found an indirect approach.

"Harris, I think you were at the point of telling me the man you suspect high up in Hammond and Morgan may also be the same I'm having talks with?"

John showed reluctance to admit it. This was dangerous ground. But it was on the way to driving Wetherfield into the bolt hole and keeping him stewing there for the next few days. John was betting that Parthessen had told his partner about Glover's death but not *all* about it; frankness to that extent would have been injudicious.

John said, "I really can't talk about it, Mr. Wetherfield. There's been a complication. A minor character who might have helped us has just removed himself from the scene in a positive and final sense—" He paused. "Or been removed."

Wetherfield took a second too long in getting out a passably astonished, "Good heavens! I can see that would add considerably to your difficulties."

"Or possibly has simplified them."

"How could that be?"

"I left before the details came in, but if the man's suicide does turn out to have been something else, it means our suspect has made a terminal mistake." John was pleased with the professional-sounding phrase. He hoped Wetherfield wasn't. They were now at the top of the stairs; departure was only seconds away.

John stopped in mid-stride to emphasize the importance of a striking thought.

Wetherfield also stopped, anxious and watchful. "What is it?"

Now for the reserve answer to "how did Borrowdale know": "I missed something. It is more than likely that *his wife* told him Samuel had a brother, and where to find you, sir."

"Borrowdale's wife?" Wetherfield was thoroughly confused.

"They're estranged but could still be in business together. Blackmail business. And she has been in a position to pick up useful information for him."

"Borrowdale's wife—" Wetherfield repeated.

"And this is also where our security leak could have come from. Of course! Why didn't we see it!" John was nicely chagrined.

"There—there is a connection?"

"I should say. He's running around with Mrs. Borrowdale, and Mrs. Borrowdale is an employee."

"And that means—"

"Yes. I'm afraid it does. Gordon Parthessen, as one of the few people in this thing who knew your brother—" John pulled himself up, a man who was talking too much. "Forget, please, sir, that I mentioned his name."

"Of course," Wetherfield said half to himself. "Tell me, this Mrs. Borrowdale. Is she good-looking, a blonde?"

"A blonde of blondes."

"Goddamn the fellow." Wetherfield was scowling but, safe in his bolt hole labeled "Samuel's brother," saw a further claim to noninvolvement.

"Harris, I'd be obliged if you would come in here a moment." He turned back and went to the top of the stairs and opened a door. John hesitated. The last thing he dared risk was a face-to-face meeting with Victoria. But coming to the landing he saw only an empty gallery beyond the doorway. He followed Wetherfield into it. One wall was hung with pictures, the other was a row of high windows shaded by venetian blinds against the midday sun.

Wetherfield went to the nearest and parted the slats.

"Do you recognize anyone?"

John stood by his side and looked down on a wide terrace. Four people, the sexes evenly divided, were at lunch at a long glass table. A servant waited on them.

"Well?" Wetherfield snapped.

"Yes, sir." John stepped back from the window.

"That's her?"

John nodded. "She uses the name Victoria Norton."

"The bastard," Wetherfield said.

"It doesn't mean he would necessarily know about the blackmail."

"That's neither here nor there. He shouldn't have brought her here in the first place!" He led the way out of the picture gallery. "Nor left her here in the second! Went off at short notice half an hour ago. Said someone would come for her later. But how do I know if that's true? He could have left her here so that there'd be two of them to work on me! She and her husband!"

"Your talks with him were as recent as this?"

"Damn the talks! They were nothing more than a proposal that I should make an investment if a future situation eventuates, dependent on this and that contingency. An

208

attractive investment. It may come off—if he can side-step this awkward business you're talking about." He drew in his thin lips. "A case of wait and see. But all I'm interested in now is that woman down there. I want her out of my house. At once!"

"If she's being collected anyway?"

"I told you it's not necessarily true. Look, I'm having trouble with my wife. She says the woman is making a play for me or some such nonsense!"

"Your wife may be right."

"Whatever she's up to, goddammit, it's for you to take her away. She's part of the Borrowdale situation you came to clear up."

John said he wished it was as simple as that. "She's not just Mrs. Borrowdale. She's Mr. Parthessen's mistress. That crosses wires for us. Captain Randall wouldn't buy it."

Wetherfield demanded, who was Captain Randall?

"Our chief of security."

"Surely it can be managed somehow? *Think*, Harris."

John prolonged uncertainty by letting the seconds go by before he said, "Mechanically it might be worked, perhaps, but the security risk . . . I wonder though. I'd be covered if you could give me another quid pro quo, your first one having turned out to be a dud, sir, so to speak—" He grinned in a manner he hoped was ingenuous.

"I don't bargain." It sounded grand but he added, "What do you suggest?"

"Well, I'm thinking how hot the captain is for concrete evidence. He hasn't as much yet as he'd like. So if in recognition of services rendered in the Borrowdale problem you'd help us to fill in the gaps?"

"Me? How the devil should I be able to do that?" Wetherfield was wonderfully astonished.

"I'm talking off the cuff, of course, but you might be able to say if your brother left any papers, business documents, letters, or such, that seem to connect up with the company? I mean if there are any, and you could put us on to them?"

Wetherfield was silent a moment looking at him. "I'd have to think. There *was* a box of odds and ends some friend of his sent from Paris. I think one of my lawyers looked through it. But I'm sure there's nothing there. . . . Meantime it's nearly two." He went out of the picture gallery rather quickly, his small feet pattering on the marble floor, and hurried back to the living room.

A white telephone with a number of gold push buttons in its rectangular base stood on a side table. Wetherfield pressed one of them and asked in a French with strong Anglo-Saxon accents if M'sieur Borrowdale had arrived. *"Pas encore? Alors, écoutez. Je ne suis pas chez moi. J'ai dû partir pour Genève ce matin. Vous n'avez aucune idée quand je reviendrai—"*

"Hold it, sir," John interrupted. "If that's the gatekeeper, don't let him tell Borrowdale anything. Just ask him to wait. Not to open the gates except for us when we come out."

Wetherfield, puzzled, changed the instruction. He asked John, what about the woman? He had a thought how to fix it? Wetherfield stabbed another button on the telephone. "What do you want my secretary to tell her? . . . André, hold on a minute. Well, Harris? Shall he tell her that whoever was to fetch her has arrived earlier than was expected?"

It was pleasant to hear Wetherfield producing the plan as though it was his own.

"It will have to be convincing. Does your secretary happen to know the name of the 'whoever' Parthessen said would fetch her?"

"André is a very competent young man." Wetherfield relayed the question to the secretary, listened, told him what to tell the lady and turned to John. "Somebody called Addis." He added caustically that he hoped the name didn't set up further security problems.

"Addis? No, I don't think so."

"I'm so glad. You get out to your car—take the stairs, turn right at the bottom, then left and right again. She'll be with you in ten minutes or so. Give me a call and let me know what happened."

"I'll look in tomorrow morning. Would ten o'clock be all right?"

"I meant telephone."

"I'd rather come in person, sir."

"Your pound of flesh?"

"You may be glad, sir, to shed it," John said. "A man in your position wouldn't want to stand in the way of a wrong being righted. Even if it involved a relative."

Wetherfield pursed his thin white lips. "You say you think he was 'persuaded'?"

"Well, sir, you know Mr. Parthessen."

"Very slightly."

"That would be enough, with your experience of men, sir."

Wetherfield nodded. "Samuel wouldn't have stood a chance. . . . I may have a moral responsibility. Nothing more."

"Financial?" John laughed at the very idea that one could be held liable for a brother's torts. "These days one need scarcely be liable for one's own—if one's lawyer knows his job."

Wetherfield observed that for a young man he showed shrewdness. "I hope it's appreciated at Hammond and Morgan."

John sighed. "It's a very large company."

Wetherfield said he would show him the way to the stairs.

"Thank you, sir. Would you regard it as impertinent—" John paused. "If I asked you to be careful in your contacts with Mr. Parthessen during the next week or so, that you don't—er—"

"—indicate by so much as a lifted eyebrow that he may be for the high jump? Harris, I'm not a fool. Also I haven't an idea where he is or is likely to be for the next week. When a man is setting up an if-and-when deal, the first rule is to name no names of prospective partners as he makes his rounds."

"I guessed it might be like that."

"I thought just then you were about to ask me for a job."

John said respectfully that he wouldn't be so casual in his approach to such a notion.

At the top of the stairs Wetherfield shook hands with him. "If it should occur to you, don't frig around worrying too much about how to ask. I like the way you handle things."

"Thank you, sir."

As long as Wetherfield didn't realize that the handling had included him. He had an uneasy feeling that the interview had gone too well.

Two minutes later he was at the open rear window of the Mercedes. Ted Harris held up the cigarette pack. "Very nice indeed."

"Don't put it away yet."

"She may have something interesting to say? I'll put in a fresh spool."

John gave him back the wrist watch, which he strapped on, and asked, "Is she likely to recognize you from Number One?"

Ted thought the chances were even. She regarded all men as less than the dust etcetera, but you never knew when that sort might be looking over the chariot's side. "But she'll certainly know *you*, if it matters."

"It matters." John opened the driver's door. "Fred—"

"Sir?"

"I'll take it. You get in the back, on one of the folding seats. You are Mr. Harris's assistant."

"Yes, sir."

"The only *not* very nice thing," said Ted Harris, "was my name being taken in vain in there."

"I'm sorry. But I had to go along with the name on the identification." He got it out and handed it back to Ted Harris, who still disapproved of a professional's allowing a personal interest to take precedence over his assignment. He seemed not to have noticed John had also tried, if not very conclusively, to do what he could for the assignment.

John found the switch for the partition and lowered it. "Your cap, please, Fred."

He put it on. They endorsed the successful effect—provided, Ted Harris qualified, he kept his eyes to the front and the woman didn't know him so well that she'd recognize him by the back of his neck.

"It's a risk I'll have to take."

It was one he was practiced in taking, and with built-in odds still in his favor: she herself had been the first to point out that a chauffeur was part of the furniture.

They discussed further details of the immediate arrangements. Ted was interested in a particular factor. "What's going to happen if the Borrowdales see each other?"

"Not if," John replied. "When."

Ted Harris laughed. "The balloon really will go up. I think you mean it to."

John pressed the control button and raised the partition again, stopping it within four inches of the roof; he wanted to be able to hear what went on in the back.

Victoria, chic in a pale-gray silk suit, a pale-gray chiffon scarf tied loosely over her gleaming hair against the rigors of motoring, emerged from the house; she was also cheerful almost to the point of forgetting to be regal in her thanks to the handsome young secretary who escorted her, with two white-gloved manservants carrying her suitcases and a hat box down the portico steps to the Mercedes.

"Thank you, André. I've had a wonderful time!"

John was puzzled by her cheerfulness, but he couldn't have said just what he had expected her mood to be. Reserved?

Watchful? Relieved? Certainly nothing so extrovert as this. . . .

Fred performed his duties as planned. He stood aside while the secretary helped her into the car, superintended the luggage-stowing in the trunk, and sat himself in the left-hand occasional seat. The secretary shut the car door and bowed to Victoria's smiling loveliness, and John, who had the motor running, turned the Mercedes toward the exit road as Ted Harris began his speech about Mr. Addis's suggestions for Miss Norton's immediate future.

She interrupted him with a light, confident little laugh. "Mr. Addis will know what is best for me. For instance, he is quite right to take me away from those dreadful people, and of course in the circumstances I shouldn't expect him to come out to fetch me home himself. Discretion is all. I really do understand."

"I'm glad to hear it, miss."

As for John, anger drove the blood singing to his head. Parthessen! He should have known the bastard would use the one sure bait to hold her at La Rouette, a bait strong enough to persuade her to let Parthessen go in favor of a bigger fish. He had merely told her who her devoted, lovelorn John Addis really was. . . .

Obvious, obvious.

As the trees closed in on the road and threw back an uneven whoosh of whirring tires, he had to strain his ears to hear the conversation behind him.

She had recognized Ted Harris and he was taking advantage of it in terms of the assignment as he understood it. "So knowing who I am, Miss Norton, it will occur to you we want to know just what your connection is with these dreadful people?"

"Oh, you do, do you?"

"Yes, Miss Norton. You're an employee of the company."

He had startled her but she was keeping her head. "You have the nerve to tell me that I must account for how I spend my spare time? To somebody like *you*, Mr. Harris?" Ice in her voice to chill him dead. "Don't you care for your job at all?"

"There are times when it's less attractive than others," he said with heavy meaning. John listened but without pleasure. Ted sounded like an old-fashioned plain-clothes policeman, but it was keeping her attention from the back of the chauffeur's neck.

"You, Harris," she continued from above the snow line, "must be unusually stupid. Or do you really *not* know what's behind this? It's possible, I suppose, and in your ignorance you have to dress it up in your tiny mind with complicated security flimflam."

"The flimflam is good enough for me."

"You wait!" she said vengefully.

In his mind's ear John could hear a future dialogue: "John darling, something's worrying me——" He could also feel cold but sensual fingers caressing the back of his neck, a neck so fortunately at this moment unrecognized. "John darling, there's a man in the security section . . ."

". . . persecuting *you*, sweetheart? He wouldn't dare. . . ."

". . . Johnny, you keep forgetting who you are, saying you can't do anything about it. . . ."

Ted Harris chop-chop, just as she'd promised.

The gates came into sight. They were closed. Slowing the car, John could see a vehicle beyond them, and a tall, thin figure standing by it.

John touched the horn to call the gatekeeper and stopped the car as near the gates as he could get and yet leave room for them to be opened.

The gatekeeper came out of the lodge with his key. Frank Borrowdale left the vehicle—a taxi, its driver sitting at the wheel—and walked up to the gates, seeing this as an opportunity to persuade the gatekeeper to let him in.

John edged the car forward as the gates began to open. The moment there was space enough he drove through the gap, and stopped again immediately he was clear of it.

This placed Borrowdale, who had had to step aside, level with the rear window and looking straight into his wife's face.

Victoria gave a short, sharp scream, and Ted Harris spoke his prearranged line: "Ah, there you are, Mr. Borrowdale. Your wife's going to the airport. You'll be able to travel home with her."

While Ted was saying it Fred Ross opened the rear door and got out. At the same moment John took off the cap, dropped it on the seat, and slipped out of the driver's door, leaving it ajar.

He heard Borrowdale shout an obscenity and Ted Harris say, "Get in, Borrowdale. You can discuss it on the way," and then Borrowdale's retort that he'd be glad to, although "discuss" was a mild word for what he'd do with the cheating bitch—thinking she could trump his ace or whatever she'd done.

John didn't wait to hear more. The Borrowdales were in a state of mutual shock, each aware of nothing but the hated other.

He went not too quickly to the far side of the taxi, which was parked off the roadway. He kept in its cover, telling the driver he would be taking over as passenger back to Vevey but please to wait for the Mercedes to go ahead. "They have a plane to catch."

Borrowdale was settling himself in the rear seat between Ted Harris and Victoria; Ted pulled the door shut. Fred was already behind the wheel with the cap back on his head. At the sound of the rear door closing he drove off down the lane's tunnel through the forest.

Neither of the Borrowdales had noticed the switch of chauffeurs.

But someone else had, someone John had forgotten until, as he was getting into the taxi, a grating voice behind him barked, *"Alt!"* He turned slowly. The man with the rifle stood there, the weapon trained on him. The gatekeeper, who was about to lock his precious gates, paused.

"Qu'est-ce-que-ce passe, alors?"

Nothing, John told the rifleman, that he should or need be concerned about.

"Au contraire! Ne bougez pas!"

No braver than anybody else with a firearm trained on his stomach, John had no intention of budging. But suddenly the taxi driver gave him a chance to, by letting out a bellow of Schweizer-Deutsch—a language John prided himself on not knowing—in complaint that seemed not so much against this display of armed force in principle as its practical effect on ultimate payment of his fare from Vevey and back.

The rifle didn't move but the man's eyes shifted from John to the source of the shouting three feet away. John made a left-swerving lunge forward and slapped the rifle to the right. It went off with a blast of cordite gas to warm both his cheek and his anger. Although he realized that probably the jerk on the man's trigger finger rather than his intention had fired it, the shot was an affront. Adrenalin gushed.

Since his momentum was taking him past his opponent, the only strike available to him was a karate knife-hand blow on the left side of the man's neck.

He went down and stayed down, with perhaps three minutes' unconsciousness ahead of him. John picked up the rifle and walked toward the gatekeeper, who decided it would be safer to stand still with arms raised than to make a dash for the shelter of his lodge.

John pushed the gates ajar, handed him the rifle and told him to wrap it in oily rags and put it in the chimney corner. He returned to the taxi.

Anger was appeased but he was left with a trembling so pronounced that he had trouble with fumbling fingers to get a hundred-franc note out of his wallet and tuck it in the unconscious man's breast pocket.

The taxi driver was somewhat dazed. But he was able to ask if *mein Herr* had gone out of his mind. Giving money to *dem mörderischen Schweinhund!*

"Hotel Trianon, please . . ." He got into the cab, breathing ridiculously fast. He lay back and tried to relax. But there were nots in his stomach and his hands were so clenched that his nails bit into the palms.

21

"It went wrong?"

Rosemary Stewart stood looking at him as he leaned against the door. His stomach was still knotted and he couldn't unfist his hands.

"What happened?" She moved toward him.

He shook his head.

"You're hurt!"

He shook his head again.

"Mr. Addis"—she was trying to be objective—"I think you should sit down."

The words unlocked frozen leg muscles and got him to the chair.

He said, "When shall I grow up?"

She had taken one of his hands and was opening it, uncurling the fingers one by one and flexing them.

"I'm sick or something," he explained.

"I'll take your temperature in a moment." No limit to the functions of a p.a. She put a hand on his forehead. "I couldn't hold Borrowdale. He took me to the bar and bought drinks.

Three minutes later he got up and walked away as if I didn't exist. I didn't, of course. Even if I'd had knock-out drops to put in his gin, he didn't drink more than two sips of it." She was telling it in detail, not to excuse her failure or fill him in on something he should know, but in the hope that talking would unclench his mind as her fingers had done for his hands.

He realized this and thought once again how remarkable she was. He also felt a greater need to explain himself to her. He began at random. "I had only to wait. The gatekeeper had a telephone. He would have used it to call for a word that would have put it right. But oh no, I had to tell myself a Black Beld has a status to maintain. How old-hat can you get! Judo, karate, private-eye stuff—dodo dead if anything ever was. The bullet tried to get into my ear." Now he sounded lightheaded.

"Someone *shot* at you?" This time she gathered up both his hands at once and held them to her breast.

"No, no, he'd never have pulled the trigger if I hadn't helped him."

She shouldn't be holding his hands again, now they were all right. And certainly not like this. . . .

"And I may have failed with Wetherfield," he said.

Her large eyes were warm and comforting. "It didn't go well?"

"On the surface, better than I expected."

"There's a 'but'?"

"Not one I can put my finger on. It's there though."

He began to tremble again.

She said, "I think this is a bigger job than any you've done before. A lot bigger?"

"Yes."

"And quite different, with people involved in it of a sort you haven't tangled with before?" She looked at him closely a moment. "Can you afford to take it at less pressure for a little while? A few hours?"

"I have nothing until tomorrow morning at ten. W-Wetherfield at ten. Perhaps he *is* cracking . . . enough to part with his sh-share of the files."

She wasn't listening. "This is simply nervous exhaustion."

"Yes, doctor. I need a drink."

"You go to bed, Mr. Addis." She released his hands. They missed the softness under them.

"I can't go to bed in the middle of the afternoon."

217

"Try." She crossed to the telephone and asked for service.

The shaking wouldn't stop. Perhaps she was right. He went into his bedroom, took off his clothes, put on a silk robe and compromised by lying down on the bed instead of in it.

She knocked and came in, gave him another clinical look-over, arranged the eiderdown over him and, on her way out, closed the curtains to make a restful twilight. He mentally addressed his toes, telling them they were gradually losing sensation, gradually up his shins to his knees, and sleep would creep . . . sleep would creep higher and higher until it took over his whole body. He had known it to work, once, but this wasn't to be the second time. Even his toes took no notice. Perhaps they'd been helped the first time by being worn out with fatigue, helping him claw a way up the north face of the Eiger. In summer. He was no hero. . . .

Rosemary returned after a few minutes with a bottle of champagne wrapped in a napkin on a small tray. She must be weakening. Also there were two glasses. Thoughtful. Drinking alone would be too blatantly medicinal.

She explained apologetically that she wasn't in a much better state herself. "Not knowing what was happening."

There she went again, the p.a.'s obsessive identification with the boss. She poured the champagne and had to hold his glass carefully while he drank in case it broke against his chattering teeth.

She asked, "Where is she?"

"Who?"

She frowned. "Victoria. You can't have failed *there*?"

He laughed after a fashion. "No, Miss Stewart. I know why I'm like this. It's not because I've lost her"—for a moment the stammer was easier to control—"I didn't lose her, I put her back in the bosom of her family. An asp for it, maybe, but that's where she is. Ted is seeing off the ever-loving couple at Geneva airport."

She refilled his glass. He didn't need help with it now. "I know where this virus comes from."

Alarm filled her eyes. She put cool fingers on his forehead.

"Nothing like that, doctor. It builds up in me, comes to a s-sort of crisis"—the stammer was back—"hanging around this morning, probably that's what d-did it, and trying to m-make Ted t-take it on, and he getting c-cold feet and suddenly it was up t-to me after all."

She said, "Please don't talk, it's making you worse."

"I *have* to tell you. You're the p.a. You're there to suffer.

218

You'll have to get used to my p-panics and the childish bad temper in reaction afterward. It's when I'm faced—*think* I'm going to be faced—with a big situation that I can't imagine I shall be any good in *because I'm so bloody little!*"

She nodded slowly. "I thought that's what you were going to say."

He jerked himself into a sitting position and stared at her. "*How* could you know?"

"Napoleon and so many others not as tall as the rest—"

"Don't dress it up. You mean I'm *shorter* than everybody else. For miles around."

"Don't get angry with *me*."

"Why not? You're the p.a. You—"

"Where's your anklebone?"

He asked her what in God's name had his anklebone to do with it?

She said she'd show him if he'd put himself flatter. He did so. She got on to the bed and lay alongside him with her ankle touching his.

"You see?"

"See *what*?" Now the shakes were fearful and continuous. "Where my head comes to?"

It came to his shoulder, the brown hair smelled delicious.

"Well?" she asked from somewhere around the upper part of his arm.

He told her where her head came to.

"So how do you think *I* feel when I realize I'm smaller than everybody else for *more* miles around?"

"You're a woman."

"Nobody would think so—or are you too occupied with your own troubles?"

"This—this—is impossible!" he said. "You don't have to prove something to me that I've known all along."

She asked what that might be.

"Victoria—"

"Yes. Tell me."

"She attracted me about as much as—as—" He had put himself in need of a simile and could think of nothing better than, "As a glass of iced water appeals to a man with toothache. And in any case, what about Charles?"

"Who?"

"A blind harpsichord maker you want to marry."

"Ah, yes. I remember. It's the 'blind' that stops them," she said, "or at least it works with Anglo-Saxons, their sense of fair play being so strong. The French and Italians"—he felt her small shoulders shrug—"with them it's a matter of being able to run faster."

"You were establishing a position?"

She said that that had been the idea.

"You felt I was someone who needed it spelled out to him?"

"Oh, no. You looked most proper and well behaved."

"I tried to give that impression."

"It's pretty clear now"—her voice was muffled—"that I was spelling it out for myself, knowing you would only have to lift a finger. Like kissing me as you did this morning."

Just who had started *that* he still wasn't sure, but he ventured to say, "You were trying to find out if Victoria was more important to me than my job."

"An excuse to account for a great wave of affection for you, from absolutely nowhere, at nine o'clock in the morning!"

"You'd better resign."

"Oh, yes, I resign, I resign! You accept my resignation?"

"With all my heart."

"Not with *all* your heart. Not with *any* of your heart. So I will now get up off this bed and order some food for you. There was very good cold chicken pie for lunch—"

But she didn't get back to the subject of chicken pie for at least an hour.

And before she did, the telephone rang. John took up the receiver. Ted Harris was calling from the airport. He had found seats for the Borrowdales on a plane leaving in thirty-five minutes, "And if I may keep it aeronautical, the balloon is still very much up."

John gathered his somnolent wits. "But neither objects to leaving?"

"She can't wait to get home, thinking her John Addis is waiting for her with open arms."

"And Borrowdale?"

"Is a hundred per cent sure she's got a big racket going and wants in."

"How does she react to that?"

"When she's not biting his ear off she is thinking up how to give him the slip, which he is well aware of and determined to prevent."

"Who would you bet on?"

"Her."

220

"Ted, is there a third seat available that you could use?"

"Meaning she mustn't be allowed to shake him?"

"He's the handiest preoccupation we can provide her with."

"To keep her out of your hair. It struck me too. So I had them hold a third seat for me. You'll pay my bill and collect my stuff? Fred is already fixed to do the same for Borrowdale at the Hotel du Lac."

John thanked him and reminded him to give Fred the keys of the Mini so that it could be returned to the people it had been rented from. Ted Harris wished him luck with Wetherfield at tomorrow's further meeting. "You'll start for home after it?"

"I'll call you at Number One."

"See you."

Rosemary, who hadn't had to move an inch to have her ear as near the receiver as John's, commented that Ted Harris had sounded almost eager to be in the third seat.

John also had noticed it but without surprise, having already accepted Ted's homesickness born of uncertainty.

"Although," she added, "I should have thought he would want to see things through with you here." She made a small noise like a chuckle. "But I'm prejudiced. And shameless. Do you think there was ever a more immoral listening-in to a business conversation?"

He didn't answer because he was occupied with the future which was darkening this happy present. Fantasy seemed to offer the only escape.

He asked her if she had done any rock climbing when she lived in northern India.

"Your contradictory genius for the non sequitur is one of the things that sets up these waves of affection. Before another swamps me I am going to order the chicken pie. Two portions. I am hungry. Of course I climbed rocks. There wasn't any other way of getting about. Why?"

"We'll spend a couple of days, checking. Bernese Oberland. Meiringen, for instance. Best rocks in the world—we'll go there in the morning."

"But you're to see Wetherfield—"

"He'll keep. *This* is important."

"Rock climbing?"

"Practice."

"An excuse," she said laughing.

He said it was nothing of the kind. "I said 'important.' "

"Ah, but why?"

221

"Nuristan."

"Oh," she said, and again. "Oh—our next assigment, the one you said didn't exist? Where my Urdu would be useful?"

"That's it."

But it still didn't exist except in the fantasy, and Thursday would see the end of it—if he could hold out that long against the accumulating guilts of his conscience. And they'd accumulate, God knew, what with these waves . . .

"When do we go to Nuristan?"

"The moment this job is finished. Maybe Friday."

"And the job there?"

"To find out what life was like before the telephone. We may have to go east, though, into Bhutan. There isn't a single one there, not in all sixteen thousand square miles of it."

"I should think," she said slowly, "we'll find out what life is like, John Addis, wherever we are. Or we would—"

"What does that mean?"

"We would if it could be real."

It hadn't occurred to him that for reasons other than his own she also might realize this was a dream. Some of the sharpness went out of his guilt.

After the chicken pie he called Wetherfield to say he was sorry but he would have to ask to postpone tomorrow's appointment. Wetherfield replied that "cancel" would suit him better. There was really nothing left for them to talk about.

"Your brother's papers, sir—"

"I have checked with the lawyers, Harris. There's nothing there, nothing. Good day to you." Wetherfield rang off. Checked with lawyers? On a Sunday?

John looked blankly at the silent receiver, knowing that Wetherfield's shrewdness had penetrated the web of fact and fiction. Or had he been in contact with Parthessen, who would have told him everything was under control and to keep his mouth shut?

Perhaps he had been warned by the rifle incident at the lodge that there was enough iron fist inside "Harris's" velvet glove of deferential respect that he should steer well clear of it from now on?

On the other hand he could have simply decided he had no need to rush into cooperation; he would sit still in his bolt hole and wait for Hammond and Morgan to make a more prestigious move than sending a security officer to try to negotiate with him.

John found his mind refusing to accept that it mattered one way or the other. Since the love-making he could think and feel only that tomorrow's day was full of promise, human and tangible, to be grasped in the brief interlude between gloomy realities. He wanted the sun on his face, high clean air in his lungs and this girl's small hand in his.

22

A fair morning upheld the promise, but John had to contain his impatience until he had made four telephone calls to London, of which three must of necessity wait until the office day began.

Rosemary, for the moment a p.a. again, wanted to help him with them but he sent her to shop for an outfit in which she could climb rocks; the stretch pants she had brought with her were quite unsuitable.

She protested that they would do perfectly well.

"They'll rip to shreds. Rocks have sharp edges."

"I haven't forgotten that nor how to avoid them."

"What did you wear in those days?"

"Well, not very much."

"Now you're older you'll have to wear more than that. Also you'll need a warm polo neck. Wool."

"It's all a waste of money."

"Go waste it, please."

The first call to MacGregor. MacGregor had two pieces of news for him. The "Miss Norton" whose possible telephone call had been anticipated had in fact made it half an hour ago. But contrary to expectation she had asked to speak not to "Mr. Addis" but to Sir John Hammond. "I was somewhat perplexed," MacGregor explained. "It suggested that the lady's—er—status had undergone a change, sir, since you gave me your instructions. But lacking others, I ventured nothing except that Sir John was not at home and I could not for certain say when he would be, but she might like to leave a message." She had declined this and said she would telephone again.

"Tell her I shall be abroad until the end of the week. If

she asks where, you can say 'Switzerland,' and should she want a more exact address, I haven't one."

"Very good, Sir John. The second matter is a cable from Madam in Montreal, which I took the liberty of opening since it was addressed to me. I say liberty, Sir John, because the contents are for you."

"Read it out."

Acantha had done it. A photostat copy of the option was following by wire, the air-mailed original should reach London on Wednesday or Thursday and she herself would be staying on for two weeks with Martha "to hold hand and protect against feared repercussions which trust you to obviate at your end good luck darling aren't I a clever one."

She was indeed.

The second call was to Ted Harris. Ted had had a rough journey, but the Borrowdales had had a rougher since their storms were directed at one another, while he suffered only by reason of his proximity. "Anyway, she didn't escape although she tried twice."

"He is still in touch with her?"

"As far as I know. I couldn't do much about them after we landed. Both wanted to see the last of me soonest. A couple of sharpies if ever there was. She's the worst because her camouflage is better."

John changed the subject, saying that at the moment his chief worry was Sid Tankerton. "I know we think he's safely bought, but there's time between now and Wednesday night, or whenever his Mr. P. gets back, for him to start thinking he can sell the news of our investigation to him."

Ted had to admit agreement. "Short of knocking out his brains, how do you stop a man's thinking?"

"Perhaps it's a question of putting him where it won't matter."

"A deep cellar and lose the key?"

"Or a Hebridean island—anywhere far from the madding crowd. But where we can reach him and Mr. P. cannot."

"I see—" Ted paused. "All right. But it will cost. Do I use company money?"

No. Such money as might be needed would be suppled by Mr. Brown. "I'll call him now to tell him about it."

This seemed to shake Ted Harris. He asked who and where was this accommodating Mr. Brown? John had forgotten Ted didn't know. "He's at 169 Brook Street, ground floor. He looks after things for me. It's a bank," he added.

Ted said cautiously it wouldn't be one very long if Mr. Brown made a habit of handing out money to total strangers on a customer's say-so on the telephone.

And, continued John, would Ted please deliver to Mr. Brown the photostat copies of the Fording Lencorp files marked "for Mr. Brinkley's immediate attention." "You've collected them from Secretarial Services?"

The captain had, and the originals were on the way back to where they came from, as per requisition. "Let me write down that name—'Brinkley.' Who's he?"

John explained that the sooner an expert accountant got to work on them the better.

"And the tapes?" Ted wanted to know.

"Not the tapes. I shall need those later."

"Okay." But John could still hear an undercurrent of the same doubt that had clouded Ted Harris's earlier enthusiasm.

Both the remaining calls, to Tom Brinkley and Mr. Brown, took longer to put through.

Tom Brinkley, expecting to hear that he could start work, was quick to absorb John's request, which he repeated to confirm he understood it.

"In three and a half days' time you want from me a short preliminary report, based on three incomplete files and a set of computerized accounts, on what happened to four hundred and twenty-six thousand that seems to have gone missing two years ago. How it went, and where. Contact Mr. Brown at 169 Brook Street—isn't that a St. Just's branch?"

"It used to be—may still be for the moment, I mean—but don't let it bother you."

"I won't. Mr. Brown has this source material for me?"

"And rooms upstairs where you can work in peace. If you need help, hire it. If you need anything, in fact, get it and tell me afterward. Mr. Brown will provide."

Mr. Brown took even less time to get the gist of what "Mr. Addis" was telephoning to say: a Mr. Harris was bringing documents that were to be handed over to a Mr. Brinkley, who would also be arriving and should be installed upstairs and given all facilities he might ask for, including cash— which Mr. Harris should also be given on request. Mr. Brown, determined not to turn a hair and succeeding, said, "Of course," and added that during the weekend he had given much thought to the situation vis-à-vis his head office and would prefer, if Mr. Addis didn't think it unethical, to say nothing to them about the "new customer." Let them continue with their plan to shut down the 169 Brook Street branch —and accept his, Thomas Brown's, resignation.

John couldn't see that ethics were involved. If the frontage of 169 had been a foot or so wider he wouldn't have gone into the place. In fact St. Just's had thwarted his intention to become a St. Just's customer by turning against the branch because it wasn't *fifty* feet wider. As for his personally conceived notion to buy the building himself and ask Mr. Brown to look after his money there, what had the head office to do with *that?* "It might be that I shouldn't be using their strong room as temporary storage for a couple of packages. Buy a safe or something for upstairs and shove them in it."

"Ah . . ."

"That solves your problem?"

"It does. I like your simple approach to things."

"Simple?" John said, thinking that ethics were funny things. "I wish it were."

Although these calls had occupied nearly an hour, he was mildly surprised Rosemary wasn't still busy at Les Sports Alpines, but more surprised to hear that she had been and gone. *Oui, M'sieur.* A message for him as to where? *Non.*

"Les deux messieurs," explained the larger of the two large Swiss lady assistants, had come into the shop not five minutes ago, and one of them spoke to Mademoiselle in English. Mademoiselle had put down *le pull* she was considering and gone straight out with them.

The elation that had carried John on air down the street from the hotel had lost its buoyancy long seconds ago. Alarm now rushed with heart-stopping suddenness into the vacuum it had left.

It was well the glass door of the shop was open: he'd never have seen it as he swung around and ran out into the street. The sun that should have graced the first day of freedom after so many months and years, a day of happiness and loving, mocked and blinded him as he looked for her up and down the busy street.

But five minutes, even if the assistant had overestimated it by half, was still long enough for them to have taken her out of sight.

He didn't mean to hurt the large Swiss girl as he caught her by the arm. His own voice was unrecognizably thick but its stammering familiar.

"She went—went w-willingly?"

But yes. In fact she went ahead of them out of the shop and had glanced back impatiently as though they did not appreciate she was in a hurry. "It was clearly an emergency, m'sieur." The girl rubbed her arm, her doll's eyes curious and excited. The dark man had sat in the back with the lady, while the other drove the car.

"Car, what kind of car—and the dark man? *"D-décrivez-le mois s'il vous plaît—si v-vous le pouvez."*

She described a man who could have been the secretary, André; John's certainty made up for the description's inadequacy. He didn't wait to hear what the driver looked like, or the make or color of the car. He couldn't hope to catch up with it before it arrived where he had to believe it was going but he would be close behind.

There was a burning sensation inside the back of his skull. It made orderly thinking difficult but was a stimulus to the emotions and their physical requirements.

He ran back to the Trianon, a hundred yards or so, in twelve seconds, spent twenty in finding Fred Ross, a further half-minute getting Fred into the Mercedes passenger seat and himself behind its wheel. The car was pointing the wrong way for La Rouette and he had to wait a minute for the traffic to let him make a U turn. The burning sensation continued. He now knew what caused it: undiluted rage.

"Sir"—Fred was hissing badly—"sir, beg pardon, but what's happened?"

John told him, snarling it in the same thick voice. Fred's comments were in language no self-respecting man should use in front of his employer, but then he had lost respect for himself. In some convoluted way he blamed himself for this. He should have been watching over her. . . .

"But she'll keep her head, Mr. John. She won't let them scare her. . . . Have you figured *why*, sir?"

"Could be several reasons. Maybe the bastard is trying to take out an insurance policy. I don't *know* . . . so shuddup, would you, Fred."

"Yessir." Mr. John was quite right. It wasn't safe to talk at this sort of speed.

They came to the La Rouette turning, swung into it on two screaming wheels, and went up it with John's foot flattening the accelerator into the lush carpet.

The big car rocked and swayed but clung to the loose surface with assurance. No traffic now, and John eased his concentration. "Is that dust ahead?" he asked aloud.

"Could be, sir."

"Or mist. Cool air from the forest coming out into the sun."

"We must be pretty close, sir."

"A seven-minute start in ten miles, Fred? If they averaged even as high as sixty, I'd have to stay up in the top eighties to gain—how much? A minute? They're home by now, home and bloody dry."

This was the intolerable thought. That she was in the hands of a man—of two men if Wetherfield had been able to contact Parthessen—with the world to lose. "Goddamn them, Fred."

Fred saw the wisdom of returning to a shut mouth. But he couldn't stop himself saying, "Mr. John, the *gates!*"

Mr. John seemed unaware of them. The needle was on the hundred-and-five-kilometer mark and moving up. The gates, of course, were closed. A man stepped from the trees and stood a yard out on the track. Fred shouted, "Look at him! That's a *gun!*"

"Rifle, Fred. Get your head down and hang onto something."

23

The man began to raise the rifle but incredulity and self-preservation arrested the movement. He jumped aside and for the second time in two days pulled the trigger without meaning to. The bullet drilled a clean, starred hole through the screen in line with where Fred's head had been a half-second ago. The crack and the duller sound of its exit somewhere above the rear seat merged with the crash with which John drove the car through the closed gates.

He braked at the moment of hitting them, skidding the car to a stop where it would be a shield against the rifle. He leaped out before the debris had settled and plunged inside the lodge. As he expected, he found the gatekeeper lifting the receiver from the wall telephone. He grabbed it from him, ripped it off and in case the man or his mate was engineer enough to reconnect it, gripped the instrument in both hands, jerked it bodily from the wall and smashed it down on the floor.

He went out as fast as he had gone in and came face to face with the rifle but again not unexpectedly, which enabled him to continue his momentum in a dive for the man's knees and bring him down, the weapon clattering on the stony ground. He rolled over and picked it up as he came to his feet. This time he wasn't returning it to any chimney corners.

He pulled back its bolt, ejecting the cartridge in the chamber, since it would be dangerous if left there while he was holding the barrel and bashing the stock against a handy rock. It splintered and broke off. Another slap and the firing mechanism disintegrated. The magazine sailed ten feet in the air and landed somewhere to the left. He flung the barrel in the opposite direction, hooked the rifleman accurately to the jaw, put two hundred francs in his breast pocket to find when he woke up, and turned to assess Fred's degree of survival after being tossed around by the collision with the gates.

He seemed to be in good order. He was standing there with an uncertain grin on his face and a very large automatic pistol in his hand. It was trained on the unconscious man, which was a likely explanation why the rifle hadn't for once gone off on purpose. "I'd have used it, Mr. John," he said with false conviction, "if he'd tried anything."

He asked Fred where the hell he'd got hold of the thing.

"I had it in the Bentley's tool box. I transferred it to the Merce."

"Where'd it come from in the first place?"

"Your father, Mr. John. He took it from Mr. Goering's adjutant—I think he was—and gave it to me. 'Fred,' he said, 'you shoot the bugger if he tries anything.' Best moment of the war, it was. I kept it for a souvenir."

"Is it loaded?"

"Yes, sir."

"Put the damned thing away. If anybody has to be killed, I'll do it. Let's get this car working."

The Mercedes was crumpled here and there about its front. Fred pulled a strut from the wrecked gates with which to prize the tip of a fender clear of the tire, while John went to the Jeep standing where he'd seen it yesterday, in the open shed by the side of the lodge.

He removed the rotor arm from its distributor. A three-foot woodsman's ax among the tools clipped to the wall caught his eye

He appropriated it and put it in the Mercedes.

The car worked. Apart from undignified rattles from loose

229

metal, it went up the mountain road as though nothing had happened. But again the speed called for all his attention and he had to ask Fred to keep his eyes open for telephone poles. "I think I noticed somewhere the road zigzags up the steepest part. We want an accessible one." He meant accessible from the road.

Fred found him an ideal one on the narrow verge at the apex of a hairpin bend that perched it over the precipice. Rather than try to back the big car down the twenty yards or so by which he had overshot it, he got out and went back to it on foot. Fred wanted to be allowed at least to carry the ax but John told him he was already sufficiently accessory before and after. "Who would drive for Mrs. Morgan while you rot in a Swiss jail?"

Fred was more interested in the three sets of wires carried by the pole. He diagnosed the lower as those linking villa to lodge—"small insulators." The middle set was the main telephone, and the top, power lines. "Very doubtful practice," he said, "having *them* on the same poles."

"But natural. There'd be difficulty enough getting one lot of poles up this kind of hill."

John had come to look back somewhat ashamedly on his various obsessions with body-building, adolescent attempts to compensate for his shortness. But tree-felling in the Selkon woods had done more than put breadth and muscle on his shoulders; it had taught him to fell trees.

What was a telephone pole but a nine-inch trunk already conveniently stripped of blade-cloying bark?

It spoke well for Fred's nerve that he didn't utter a syllable while he watched.

But it wasn't as dangerous as it would have been on level ground. Gravity and the load of its head swung the pole outward, away from the road and the mountainside. As it twisted the power lines crossed and blue flame cracked and flashed explosively, melting several feet of them, releasing the pole to fall with a twanging crash against the rocky face of the slope below.

"For a while," Fred observed with admiration, "nobody is going to talk to nobody on *that* blower. I do hope, too, they've got plenty of candles."

John led the way back up the road to the car. Violence at the gate and ax work on the pole should have taken some of the steam out of his rage, but it hadn't. It demanded further and instant expression. With an effort he persuaded it to let

230

him stop the car again at the entrance to the plateau, a few yards short of the gap in the forest.

He arranged for Fred to drive on through at his signal, and went forward on foot to where he could see the villa and its gardens.

Peace and tranquility reigned. The only living thing in sight was a solitary gardener at work amongst rose bushes far away in a corner; but for glimpses of a floppy straw hat and the muted clink of his hoe, you wouldn't know he was there. The cluster of buildings to the left of the house were curiously quiet. No children's voices or dog's bark, and blank windows, many shuttered. The branch road leading there was weed-grown, and four cars were standing in an open garage that could have taken a dozen—everything suggested this was an almost deserted place.

His impression of yesterday, that Owen Wetherfield kept a household smaller than his grand home was accustomed to, was stronger than ever. A man by nature too big for his boots seemed to have overdone compensatory attempts to find a larger size.

He raised his hand to Fred to bring the Mercedes to the gap; he climbed in. "Drive straight into that garage. Top gear as soon as you can to keep it quiet."

Fred proved the motor's flexibility by starting in third and moving into top almost at once. They covered the distance, nearly a hundred yards, two-thirds of it roadway, the rest open gravel, with a noiseless engine; the gentle speed on a smooth surface silenced the injured bodywork's previous rattles of complaint.

Four cars. One of them, a big Renault, was hot to the touch. John opened the rear door, hoping to find evidence of Rosemary's recent journey in it—a handkerchief or some other identifying object she might have left tucked down behind or beside the seat when she realized she had been tricked. But there was nothing.

In fact if the lie or excuse André used had been good enough to get her into the car, it would stand up as long as she was in it. She wouldn't discover the falsehood until she was actually in the villa.

As he was shutting the door her perfume touched his nostrils. It was very faint. He sniffed deeply, thought he detected it again, but in the next moment doubted it. Sense of loss together with fuming anger could set up any delusion.

He found the hood release, removed the rotor arm and

231

moved to a station wagon on which he performed the same immobilizing operation.

Fred dealt in a similar way with the remaining two cars, making a total bag of four rotor arms. John lifted one end of a covering plank over an inspection pit and dropped them into its darkness.

Fred backed the Mercedes from the garage and they drove toward the villa's portico. Fred's remark that it had been a piece of cake so far could be taken to mean they'd had a good deal of luck up to now but shouldn't count on its continuing. "I'd like to stay with you, Mr. John."

"You're more valuable sitting where you are with the motor running, ready to move if we come out in a hurry."

"Mightn't be a hurry if the two of us go in."

"I'm grateful, Fred, but no."

"You're in a bit of a state, Mr. John, and likely to—"

"I *know* I'm angry—"

"—with reason, sir."

"—and knowing it, I shan't be so likely to lose my head. I'm going to try talking. To start with." He stretched an arm over the seat for the ax.

"With respect, sir"—Fred stopped the car at the steps—"they'd be inclined to watch their p's and q's if you told them straight off who you are."

"Don't you believe it." John got out holding the ax behind him and looked up at the massive door. Fred mumbled something as he watched him go up the steps.

All the same Fred's effort to stop his being unnecessarily impetuous may have had an effect. When he had pressed the bell a second time with no result he paused just long enough, before taking the ax to the problem, to realize that the bright-blue flash halfway up the mountain would have included the bell in its withdrawl of electricity from the villa's amenities.

So he used the blunt end of the ax as a door knocker and after a moment heard a sound in the lock. He put the tool, handily but out of sight, in the corner on the hinge side of the door.

White Gloves opened it, the same manservant who had been on duty yesterday.

Eyebrows rose in surprise. M'sieur wished to see M'sieur Wetherfield? Regrettably M'sieur Wetherfield was not at home, and in any event visitors were not expected. It would be interesting to know—the question was a silent one—how

232

the visitor had managed to get past the gate. If John hadn't been blocking the view of the Mercedes' front fenders the man might have answered it himself.

"I had an appointment with M'sieur Wetherfield."

"I think not, m'sieur." The door began to close but stopped because John's foot was in the way. White Gloves pushed hard but John pushed harder and more suddenly, and the man stumbled backward. John went after him, kicking the door shut. He got a grip on his wrist, an advantageous starting point for immediate and over-all control of the rest of the body, and suggested if he didn't wish to suffer a broken arm, he should become instantly quiet and attentive.

"You will take me to Mr. Wetherfield without further discussion."

The manservant grunted and tried to pull away, an effort that pain speedily inhibited.

"This is an outrage—the police—"

"I quite agree, the police should be sent for. But that's for M'sieur Wetherfield to say. Not you, *mon ami. Peut-être*," John accused him, *"vous êtes l'auteur de cet enlèvement?"*

The man became still. *"Enlèvement?"* he repeated as though the word touched an existing thought.

"That's right," John said in English, "a kidnapper!" and added for good measure because German was the language for bullying, *"Ja! Ein Menschen-räuber!"*

On an impulse he dropped his demand to be taken to Wetherfield. *"Alors, M'sieur Wetherfield n'est pas chez lui?* I will talk to Madame Wetherfield. *Allons-y!"* He propelled his victim ahead of him into the hall.

Owen Wetherfield might be either formally or literally "not at home," but for some reason—perhaps he feared her less—this change of plan seemed more to the man's taste. It was certainly more to his own, if his sudden instinct was reliable. The man said, *"Ça va, ça va!* But you must permit me to announce you in a dignified manner, m'sieur."

24

It was a small, vaulted room, the arched ceiling a dull gold, the walls white, the furniture ancient, square, making a suitable background, if austere, for this woman's personality. She wore the same green frock as yesterday and she sat in a high yellow-velvet chair in the window bay, working on embroidery stretched on a dark-oak frame, with the sun in her bronze hair. A medieval picture. A medieval situation, if you looked for analogies: a robber baron had stolen an innocent maiden—a more or less innocent maiden—and carried her off to his mountain fastness. And here was John, the knight errant, overcoming all obstacles in riding to her rescue. But he couldn't see himself in the role. His motives weren't that simple, and anyway a knight who knew his job would never leave his battle-ax on the porch, apart from which there wasn't going to be much gentle *parfait* knight in his dealings with the robber baron's lady.

Needle poised, she looked at him, surprised and affronted by the intrusion. She spoke to the manservant in French. "Don't go, Jules."

"Words out of my mouth." John used English. "I don't want him running around loose just at the moment. Mrs. Wetherfield, your husband is in trouble. I've come straight to you as the best person to get him out of it."

"Really?" Word and tone came direct from the English shires via Benenden and a debutante season—albeit ten or so years ago—to congeal them beyond all unscrambling.

"Yes, Mrs. Wetherfield. Bad trouble." Calmness at all costs.

"I saw you yesterday. You were the man who came to take away that woman?"

"Among other things. And now your husband has repaid me with a very dirty trick." He couldn't keep his voice down.

"I am in complete ignorance about my husband's business affairs and always have been. I don't wish it to be otherwise"—the needle pierced the embroidery with unwavering precision—"and incidentally, my name is Lady Mary Wetherfield."

The Lady Mary? This was laying on the medieval a trifle thick, but it made her the daughter of an earl, or better.

Better than he'd hoped, although this was the direction in which his lunch had led him.

"In that case, Lady Mary, you know how socially undesirable it is that he should be allowed to pick up young women in Vevey and bring them up here by force."

She was looking at him carefully; she had forgotten about the needle, waiting to be pulled through from underneath to complete the stitch.

"You're out of your mind." She didn't believe this but she wanted less to believe the alternative.

"In this instance she's not just any young woman," John said. "She happens to belong to me. And the kind of trouble I'm going to make will knock Mr. Owen Wetherfield off his mountaintop and his Lady Mary with him for good and all."

"Don't shout at me." She finished the neglected stitch while he begged her pardon, between his teeth.

"A young woman. When was this supposed to have happened?"

"Fifteen or twenty minutes ago. In broad daylight, in a shop in Vevey."

"A *shopgirl?*" She gave a superior laugh but there was a shrill note in it. "I happen to know my husband hasn't left the house. I—"

"Megalomania is persuasive, I understand. He seems to have got lickspittles such as André believing in his divine right to do as he likes without regard for any kind of law. He sent André to kidnap Miss Stewart."

"You," she said, "are the one in bad trouble. This is quite unbelievable except as an attempt at extortion or something. My husband is a wealthy, influential—"

"Nobody doubts that, Lady Mary." He had let himself go too far; however angry he was, he mustn't close Wetherfield's bolt hole.

"Well?" she demanded but didn't pause in reaching for the receiver of the internal telephone on a table by her side. She pressed a button, then another.

"I don't think it's working," John said. She frowned at the receiver and replaced it.

He said, "Your husband is being driven by fear for his dead brother's honor"—this sounded like a speech from a Victorian novel—"into indefensible conduct. He seems to have completely lost his head."

"His dead brother's honor?" She was nicely taken aback. He was getting through to her now.

"Yesterday I had to tell him that two years ago his brother Samuel took part in a fraud that netted him the equivalent of two-and-a-quarter million Swiss francs."

"Samuel?"

"Samuel."

She looked across at the manservant, who hadn't understood more than a word here and there, and told him in

235

French to find Mr. Wetherfield and ask him to come here, please, at once.

"Jules," John said, *"ne bougez pas."* Jules budged not. She stood up straight-backed and poker-faced, and looked at John closely. "And you think my husband has taken this—this step as part of persuading you to help him save his late brother's reputation?"

"It's the only explanation."

She now asked a question that told him he was coming into the straight and well out in front.

"Is a man called Gordon Parthessen involved in this?"

She knew he was. John only had to say, "A corrupt man. He was the other partner in the fraud—" to gain her slight nod of comprehension. He added that the firm concerned knew it couldn't do much about the dead partner but it was going to have the survivor's hide.

She said carefully. "You came here yesterday to ask for Owen's help but he refused it. Because of his brother's good name?"

"Samuel's good name."

"Samuel," she said again. A slow flush spread and spoiled her features' perfection. "Owen is making a mistake. I'll talk to him for you."

"Talk?" He roughened his voice. "Don't you understand? I came to you as a quicker means of finding her than beating him up and tearing the place to pieces. You can talk to him as much as you like *after* he frees Miss Stewart, which he must do *now*."

"What can I do except make him see reason?"

"Could you, though? In a situation as bad as this, when he's fighting with such desperation?"

She didn't answer. Her color was still high.

He asked, "Does he value you?"

She stared at him. "That's near-insolence."

"Believe me, I can get nearer and be damned to you, Lady Mary."

"Do you think," she stormed suddenly, "I'd be here if he didn't *value* me as you call it?"

"No," he agreed, "and it would have to be above rubies, wouldn't it?"

She almost smiled with certainty, pride and perhaps the defiance of a woman who has made a good marriage without looking as closely as she should at the meaning of "good," and told him that the next card would fall right for him.

236

"You will do it like this," he ordered her. "You will send Jules to your husband to tell him that I have taken you with me. That if he wants you back he must release Miss Stewart at once. We will wait in the car where the forest begins, for ten minutes. He must send Miss Stewart there on foot and alone."

"And if he doesn't"—there was some scorn in her tone but less than there might have been—"you'll lose your head completely, take me away, using violence?"

"There are other ways of taking a wife away from a husband."

"Oh?" Scorn was no longer in question. "I suppose you will make me fall instantly in love with you?"

He shook his head regretfully. "It would do my ego a world of good. No, Lady Mary. I'll just use a short conversation. If he hasn't sent her out to me by the end of the ten minutes I shall start talking. Make sure Jules tells him that."

She gave this several moments' thought, her eyes on his face; she saw nothing to make her doubt him but she had to put it in words. "After the short conversation with you I shan't *want* to go back to him?"

"The little time I've had to get to know you I'd say there's a good chance of it, depending on whether you could still believe the rubies you've been valued above are genuine." He turned to the perplexed manservant. *"Jules, Madame demande que vous apportiez un message d'urgence à Monsieur toute de suite."*

Jules, experiencing the most puzzling day of his life, was doing what he could to keep up with its twists and turns. He looked from John to his mistress.

She asked him, was it true that M'sieur André had fetched a young woman from Vevey this morning?

Jules's reluctant nod was all the confirmation anybody should need.

She was in the house? Where in the house?

John said sharply, "Let's not mess about. Just give him the message." He stepped up to her to take her arm and set her moving, but she gestured that she would come with him. She gave Jules the message, went out of the room, the man opening the door for her, with John at her heels.

Her eyes opened wide when she saw him take the ax from the corner by the front door but she said nothing. He doubted if she appreciated its battle-ax connotation.

His hostage, the Lady Mary, sat placidly in the rear seat. Fred beside him at the wheel waiting, and no doubt trying to guess what all this was about, seemed as stolid as a block of wood, a sign that he was as tense as John himself.

The Mercedes was positioned inside the forest but with the distant portico well in view. John kept one eye on it, the other on his watch.

Seven minutes, seven minutes fifty . . .

"I wonder, Lady Mary, if your husband is relying on you not to believe what he knows I can tell you?"

Eight minutes . . .

"He has a sister," she said apparently at a tangent.

"Yes?"

"But no brother. He never had a brother."

"No Samuel?"

"No Samuel."

"Which is causing you to think."

"To think that you don't invent a brother unless for good reasons."

"Or bad."

"That's what I said."

Fred let out a sharp hiss. "She's coming, sir."

At the same moment John saw Rosemary at the top of the portico steps. But relief was swamped by his always lurking anger. She was not alone. But it was not some kind of trick. Alone she couldn't have kept her feet.

André was helping her. He had her arm over his shoulder, holding the wrist, his other hand was round her waist. Her legs were moving but they weren't strong enough to take her weight. Her head lolled.

For a terrible moment John thought they had hurt her and he was out of the car with murder in his heart and mind. He checked himself.

Her injury was no more than sleepiness. But realizing they had given her something would still be sufficient to make self-control a problem when André came within the reach of his hands. He gave them something else to do by grasping the edge of the door; the inch of lowered window protruding from it was sharp and welcome under his palm. The Lady Mary looked at him, trying to hide alarm.

"Fred," he said, "go help the bastard."

He shut his eyes, closing out the sight of the small rag-doll figure the man was half-carrying, half-dragging toward the car.

He would have liked to continue to hang on to the door while Rosemary was being helped into the car, and until André and the woman had gone, but the secretary himself made it impossible. Instead of going away quietly with the Lady Mary when the exchange operation was completed, he had to say his piece.

"I am instructed to tell you, M'sieur Harris," he said in French, "that you will not get far. That you have Mr. Wetherfield's promise on that. *Son jurement bien sérieux.*"

John still held the door with both hands but he felt his grip loosening. He tried to establish it again. And not to look at Rosemary now lying in a corner of the rear seat, her eyes closed, her head slack.

"What"—his voice wouldn't work properly—"what have you given her?"

"It will pass," said the secretary behind him.

John knew what was going to happen. He would let go the door. His right hand would close in a fist with the first two fingers folded so that their middle joints protruded; then pivoting on his toes he would sink this armed fist in André's solar plexus without caring whether it killed.

With enormous effort and still without looking around, John gave the man a second chance: "What have you given her?"

Did the secretary sense momentary reprieve from death? He answered at once: "Pentothal."

"Why?"

"M'sieur Wetherfield wanted to get the truth from her about the blackmail. She being one of you."

"Who is 'you'?"

"You and the Borrowdales. I thought it unlikely myself. After we had heard what happened at the lodge."

The secretary didn't know he was saving himself. John's short laugh told him nothing of what had so nearly happened to him.

"You thought it unlikely she'd talk because a so-called truth drug isn't yet discovered that will make a person say anything he is beforehand determined *not* to say?"

"No. Because I couldn't believe in such subtlety. To use the Borrowdales as a feint? Deliberately to expend them in order to pose as a security agent working against them to gain the confidence of M'sieur Wetherfield? *Non m'sieur, pas pour moi.* . . . I injected a very mild dose. She will be herself in an hour."

239

"You know why Wetherfield is afraid of blackmail?"

"No, m'sieur."

"Do you doubt he has reason to be?"

"Clearly. His reaction is that of fear."

John finally turned, his right fist at his side, and let it loosen as he realized what he was seeing. He laughed again, but silently, and under his breath said, *"Cicisbeo,"* because the Lady Mary wasn't halfway back to the house and her husband's frightened bosom, but was standing with her arm linked in the secretary's, her expression protective and full of love. They made a handsome couple.

"André was acting under his orders," she said defensively. "You know that."

"The old excuse that didn't save them at Nüremberg."

They did not know how close it had been. While he went on saying what he could now say, he was resolving with all his being that never again would he close his fist in the *kazumi* position, never again use his *yudansha's* skill against a man except in self-defense.

André repeated what John told them, to make sure he·understood. John went over it again in English in case the Lady Mary had missed the point: that should there be a dearth of the rubies she was accustomed to being valued above, Hammond and Morgan would pay fifty thousand dollars, call it forty thousand francs, for a collection of papers in Owen Wetherfield's possession, identifiable wherever there occurred, in addition to the company's name, those of Fording Lencorp; "Samuel Wetherfield"; "Dr. Charles Bowen"; "Boyle Glover"; and possibly "Gordon Parthessen," although this one wasn't likely to appear.

The Lady Mary's fine eyes were bright with comprehension. She asked a most promising question: "If we find these papers," she said, "whom do we negotiate with . . . at Hammond and Morgan? You, Mr. Harris?"

He told her it would be more *convenable* to approach the chief of security, Captain Randall.

They watched him get into the back of the car. The secretary was frowning. "M'sieur Wetherfield is resourceful. He has power with the authorities. He means what he says: you won't get far. What then?"

John said they could but try. "Let's get moving, Fred."

If the couple didn't mind putting their affection on show, neither did he. He had an arm around Rosemary and her sleeping head on his shoulder before Fred had the car in gear.

240

"How is she, sir?"

"All right, I think. Breathing normally."

"The *sods*, sir."

Fred took the "let's get moving" as an exhortation to be urgent about it. John had to tell him to take it easier. They didn't want to get down the mountain except by the road.

Fred braked slightly. "That fella was right. Maybe Mr. Wetherfield hasn't transport or telephone for the moment but he's not just going to sit there looking silly."

"It's a long enough moment to give us reasonable time to pick up our things at the hotel, transfer to the Mini in some quiet spot and drive on to Lausanne and the Bentley."

Fred said approvingly that that would be the ticket, but what about the messed-up state of the Mercedes—and how would they get through the frontier?

John thought neither problem insurmountable. The car-hire firm could be compensated in due course by Hammond and Morgan's Zürich agents, and as for the frontier, hadn't the real Mr. Harris left the country yesterday?

"Of course!" Fred's doubts vanished. "So it turns out okay and she didn't tell 'em."

John was thinking about the minor problem of replacing the Bernese Oberland as a rock-climbing practice area. The French Alps? Chamonix?

"Tell them what, Fred?"

"Who you were, sir."

John sat up, almost forgetting what was on his shoulder. She murmured at the sudden movement. He tightened his arm around her.

"Didn't tell them who I am? What the hell are you saying? She doesn't *know."*

Fred took a moment or so to gather his courage in the face of that forceful tone again.

"I think she does, Mr. John."

"You *think?"*

"This morning, sir, when you were telephoning London and she was going off to the shops I began to talk to her some more about my having recognized her ahead like . . ."

John told him to get on with it.

". . . and she suddenly looked at me and her face went sort of strange and she said she thought in this instance it wasn't a case of second sight, that she'd just that minute remembered how she'd seen me before—and I must have seen her. It was one time last year when she came to White House

241

to collect a letter Madam had forgotten to put in the post to Mr. Herbert Hammond. She—Miss Rosemary—being one of his secretaries, you see, he'd sent her for it, and of course I had my cap on, she said."

Fred added in a subdued voice that he'd then remembered the incident. He'd been waiting in the Daimler to take Mrs. Morgan to the zoo—a new young walrus—when Miss Rosemary had arrived in a taxi. "So she was right, Mr. John. It hadn't been a case of me knowing something ahead. . . ."

Mr. John didn't speak. Fred was glad to be able to concentrate on the hairpin bends that were at their worst just here. Anyway, there was nothing to say that wasn't obvious: everybody knew White House was Sir John's town residence—when he was around. Miss Rosemary wouldn't have had much guessing to do, once she recognized Fred Ross. Wonder was she hadn't done so earlier. Although, of course, like with Mrs. Borrowdale yesterday. Who took all that notice of a chauffeur?

Between one hairpin and the next he ventured to ask, since there was no panic to get out of Switzerland, would Mr. John perhaps go on with the program he had been planning? To Meiringen?

"No"—a flat voice over bitterness—"to Geneva. The airport. Miss Stewart and I have to get home as soon as possible."

And Fred would have to bring the Bentley home by road, or if he preferred, by car-ferry service, for which there was a terminal at Lyss, a two-hour drive from Geneva.

John's apology for having to leave him to follow on alone was delayed. Two figures came in sight, toiling up the road toward the villa. They saw the car coming and flattened themselves hurriedly against the rock face to let it pass.

Fred remarked that the gatekeepers seemed to have caught on at last, and by the fact they were going up instead of down it looked like they'd decided to find out what the score was before yelling for outside help. "A bloke like that Wetherfield, you'd never feel easy in your mind, working for him."

And as for the Bentley, yes, he'd like to use the car-ferry service. "You're going to be busy, sir, I daresay, so you'll need me."

"I'll be busy. I've landed other people with more responsibility than they should take alone. And thank you, Fred. I will need you."

Fred felt warm and cozy and pitied the gatekeeper and his assistant with the rifle. Ex-rifle.

John, on the other hand, felt cold and pitied only himself.

She stirred and moved her head, opened her eyes and saw him. She spoke a word softly but quite clearly.

But before she closed them again he saw how cloudy they were, opaque in semiconsciousness, and knew she wasn't able yet to relate the present to the past. Whatever she said when she finally opened them with the drug slept out of her, it would not again be "darling."

Nor would she ever again put a groping hand inside his jacket and under his shirt to rest it for reassurance on his chest. Her sleeping touch thrust him into a remorse near to self-hatred. At a time and moment when he should have ended all deception he had let her go on thinking he was John Addis. Her only possible conclusion: that for John Hammond she was no more than something she wouldn't knowingly be to any man, a casual love. Even now he was stealing her affection when her back was turned.

But it was typical of her essential niceness that when the showdown came she should try to hide the extent to which he had hurt her.

Memory began to come back to her in the Bentley somewhere between Lausanne and Geneva. By then he had reluctantly given up his role as a tender prop and put her away from him in the corner of the rear seat. Her eyes were open and aware when Fred brought the car to the airport's reception hall. John knew her memory had returned because although still sufficiently shaky to have taken his arm from the car to a chair near the reception desk, she would not do so. She did not stress her refusal. "It will wake me up to make it by myself."

Her only blank, in fact, would be the period she had been under the hypodermic's effect. He wondered when or if she would refer to it. In the meantime she found something to take her mind from the pain and humiliation he had inflicted. He wasn't prepared for it; she did it when he was at the desk talking to one of the uniformed girls about available seats and flight times and not liking what she had to tell him.

"Nothing before that?"

"No, m'sieur." She put on the impersonally patient expression, always recognizable, for dealing with the impatient traveler. She didn't know how unusually impatient this one was.

"Forty-five minutes?" he asked incredulously. "To whom do I talk about chartering a plane?"

Penciled eyebrows were raised at him—was she *trying* to irritate him? But before he could say, yes, that's what I said, charter a plane, a voice beside him asked, "Can I help?"

He realized that it was his erstwhile p.a., forcing herself back on to the job in a wholly understandable, gallant and pathetic attempt to recover her poise long enough to get herself home without breaking down. After that she would never have to set eyes on him again.

The least help he could give her was the bullet of opposition to bite on.

"I can't hang around for forty-five minutes," he said obstinately. She turned momentarily from the desk.

"Are we in a hurry to go," she asked, "or to arrive?"

"Arrive."

This filled in one detail on her memory blank: they weren't running away from anyone.

He said with finality that if somebody would tell him where to find a charter company's representative he could get on with it. "We're wasting time."

Rosemary smiled at the clerk as one girl to another in conspiracy against a fractious male, and asked what *type* of plane was the regular flight?

"Jet."

"Can we charter a jet?" She knew it was unlikely and the girl behind the desk confirmed it. Turbo-prop at best. The two of them worked out with swift efficiency that a chartered turbo-prop might be in the air twenty minutes ahead of the airliner but with its slower rate of knots would lose those minutes and maybe ten more between here and London.

That fixed that. Then Rosemary took the most difficult hurdle obliquely but in her stride. She said, "Sir John will decide, I think, to take the two seats on the regular flight, please." Her voice was stronger. "Sir John"—she addressed him directly but without looking at him—"you might like to lunch before we leave. If you'll find a table in the dining room, I'll deal with the tickets—and if I could have your passport."

The passport he'd had to be so careful not to let her see.

When she joined him it was with a litttle color in her cheeks, but he saw a heart-rending weariness of spirit in the way she stared at the menu and said she wasn't hungry. He ordered smoked salmon, chicken salad and a white wine from Crépy.

She scarcely spoke again until they had been airborne for nearly half an hour.

"I want to thank you," she said formally, "for getting me away from La Rouette."

"I should have foreseen Wetherfield would have second thoughts and get difficult."

"Was it—difficult?"

He saw that there might be an edge for him if he could keep her worrying about the gap in her memory. "Difficult?" He shrugged his shoulders. "Not really."

Her face was away from him but at last it dawned on him that her self-respect, demanding that she should owe him as little as possible, had put her under a compulsion to find out how he had rescued her.

"I had a vague feeling," she continued hopefully, "they were uncertain about what they were doing. I'm sure the youngish dark one was. He's the secretary?"

"Yes."

"He told me you'd gone to La Rouette at short notice and wanted me to join you. Looking back on it, he wasn't very convincing."

"But you went."

"I wasn't thinking clearly."

"By then," John said, "you had recognized Fred Ross." Another ray of hope shone. "You went with them because you thought I needed you."

Her face was still averted. "The boss has sent for me, I have to go—that sort of reflex."

"But you still went shopping after you'd talked with Fred."

"I had already started out. By the time I got to the shop I'd decided, of course, that I wouldn't buy anything."

Of course. The ray went out, leaving him in darkness—comparative darkness if there was still a glimmer of light in the fact that he had balked her effort to get to him to talk about what had happened at the villa and she would have to try again.

To keep the glimmer alive he used silence as the best insurance against being trapped into telling her. If *she* began a conversation—well, she would have to bring it around to the subject without his noticing. Too difficult for her in her mixed-up state?

France slipped away below; gray-blue water like a sheet of

245

galvanized metal took its place, but in minutes was itself gone to reveal the patchwork of the southern counties.

Rosemary's silence had become as preoccupied as his own, but he hung on to his faith in her compulsion, and sensed—or perhaps kidded himself that he sensed—her losing struggle against it. She had to know the extent of her debt to him.

She left it too late. The last moment came before she could find the right words to ask with. In fairness to her skill it was his contriving that brought on the last moment sooner than she expected it.

Because White House was Sir John Hammond's home and, coming from the airport, farther to go than Kensington, where she lived, she had given the cab driver her own address as his first objective. The gentleman would take the taxi on, she had explained. But in King's Road, when there were still many minutes left in which she would have found her courage and her tongue, John tapped on the partition and asked the driver to take the approaching left turn into Haycott Avenue, and to stop at the entrance to the Close a few yards up it.

Rosemary, startled, said, "But—"

"I'm living here at the moment," he said. Within seconds the taxi had drawn in to the curb and he was getting out. He took his suitcase from the front and with cunning asked her if she had sufficient English money to pay off the cab. "And don't forget to charge it to your expense account. See you at Brook Street in the morning. Nine-thirty? There's a hell of a lot to do before Thursday afternoon."

She had put herself back on the job at Geneva and now he was brutally taking her at her word.

She was looking him full in the face for the first time, her beautiful lips parted but silent. If giving a right arm for something had ever been practicable, he would have given his to kiss them.

He picked up the suitcase and walked into Haycott Close, searching his pockets for the front-door key. He knew the cab was still there and she watching him, reasonably expecting that all this was a trick, another deception. Was she relieved when she realized he must have a key, to be able to go straight in like this? Relieved? That presupposed a degree of caring on her part, which on his was whistling in the wind.

None of it was a trick, of course. He had to keep away from White House because Victoria would have it under seige, and in any case this secret attic was the place for solitude and sorely needed stocktaking.

He didn't get it. He had scarcely unpacked his toilet things when a casual glance dragged him straight back to the beginning, to the evening he had looked out of the dormer window for the first time.

There she was, hair shining in its usual spun-gold way, caught by the late afternoon sun as she stood at her bureau, telephoning.

But there were differences, the most noticeable, perhaps, that she was wearing a lot more, conspicuously more—indeed was fully dressed in a dark, high-necked frock. Also she had company. Just behind her Frank Borrowdale lounged in an easy chair, a leg hooked over its arm. He was holding what looked like a horsewhip.

John couldn't for the moment believe the whip, an illusion produced perhaps by window reflection, but it became real when the object began moving. Borrowdale tapped Victoria's left shoulder with it twice, not harder than to make her wince slightly and remember he was there and in control. The whip hand, it could be called.

If not incredulous, John remained astonished. But it was Borrowdale in character, Borrowdale still forcing himself into what he believed would be a profitable partnership, the whip his power to do so.

John felt a strong impulse to go over there and break his arm as a practical way of reducing that power, but while he was wrestling with himself Victoria put down the receiver and turned to look at her husband with an expression of hatred almost beyond reason.

John wasn't sorry for the man but it seemed no longer necessary to be sorry for Victoria.

Suddenly she ran past the poised whip into the bedroom, slamming and locking the door. John watched her lean against it for a moment with a hand holding her shoulder. Then she went to the dressing table, where she sat and stared at herself in the mirror. He didn't think she was looking for unlikely flaws in her beautiful face but most probably for a ploy by which to ditch her Frank. She should soon find one and be re-established at Grosvenor Towers by the time she would be needed again. He admired her forethought in using the Haycott Close flat as a safe house.

But it was a nuisance to have to leave Haycott Close himself in case one or the other Borrowdale should accidentally catch sight of him. He put his toilet bag back in his suitcase and went to Claridge's, where they gave him a quiet, even peaceful room, although it hadn't the attic's anonymity.

But against that he was now only a few doors from 169 and the next three days of horrible paper work. And a p.a. to whom he could no longer look for support except of a strictly technical sort. But strictly.

25

However, John did not go to 169 Brook Street straightaway that Tuesday morning. Instead he went to Number One, where Randall's manner endorsed the good sense of obeying an instinct to see the security chief before doing anything else.

Randall said, "Ah," at the sight of him, a relief tempered with a look of "now for it." He flicked over his intercom and said, "Harris, he's here. Come in, would you," and to John: "I was giving you until ten to show up."

"And if I hadn't?"

"I'd have gone ahead notwithstanding. I can't hold this any longer."

"Hold what?"

"Harris will be here in a moment."

John settled himself in the chair; this might take a little while. Harris arrived, also relieved but looking as though he hadn't slept.

"Ted," Randall said, "has played me these tapes you made between you. I have asked the chairman to see me. I'm carrying too much responsibility without a shred of authority, without a word on paper in the way of a directive."

"The responsibility is mine. Entirely mine."

"So you say, but I want our chairman to say so too—on paper. A thing as big as this, and apparently already coming rapidly to an explosive head, isn't a matter for the old-boy network. This isn't personal, Addis. You understand that. I can't carry you any longer."

"You're not carrying me. Officially you know nothing about all this." He heard himself becoming defensive.

"I attached Harris to you. Detaching him now, as I've done, doesn't cancel what I've already involved him in—and ipso facto, myself and my department."

248

Ted Harris was very unhappy. "John, it began to go off the rails with your sticking your neck out for the Norton woman."

Randall made the short comment, it had never been on any rails. And as for sticking out his neck, John Addis had done nothing but, from the start. "Taking mine with it."

Ted Harris muttered that things had built up in a way nobody could have foreseen.

Randall said, "All right, Ted. I'll deal with this."

"You listened to the Tankerton conversations?" John asked.

"It's one of the reasons I'm getting this business on a proper basis as fast as I can. There's no legal evidence worth a damn in that stuff. Parthessen feeding Glover the Soneryl is pure speculation."

"Have they done the autopsy?"

"Yesterday." Randall said he was waiting for a word from his police contact, but how much or little Soneryl Glover had in him wouldn't prove he didn't take it himself and voluntarily on account of Victoria Norton or any reason you liked, and again there was no clear evidence he had been in on the fraud—if there'd ever been a fraud. "You're after Parthessen. Maybe you're right about him in every respect, but —Oh, for God's sake, Addis, you aren't a fool. You know the position you've put me in. If the thing blows up in your face, you say sorry, and walk away. But it will be in my face too, and I'll be out. And not just this job but every other of its kind. Industrial security is a tight little shop."

John couldn't give up yet. "It's possible that in the near future Owen Wetherfield's wife will get in touch with you. She may be prepared to sell the other half of the Lencorp files for fifty thousand dollars."

Ted Harris stared at him.

Randall remarked, that sounded fine—if it happened—but spending money on that scale put the affair beyond his function, let alone his competence. "I have an appointment with H.H. at ten." He glanced at his watch. "Thirteen minutes. I am quite willing you should come with me."

John spoke slowly. "I don't want Herbert Hammond brought into this, into any part or aspect of it, until I'm ready. He is wholly Parthessen's dupe. He knows nothing of all this."

There was a silence in which they looked at him; Randall with a frown of perplexity—a man who had made himself

249

very clear but without effect; Harris, wild-eyed, was looking for an explanation where he knew none could possibly exist.

Randall shook his head. "You'll have to do better than that."

John sighed. This was defeat, long escaped but always inevitable. "You've heard of John Hammond."

"He's dead," Ted Harris said. "Died ten, fifteen years ago."

"Nearer twenty," Randall corrected him.

"I'm talking about his son. He has a middle name."

They were still watching him, now with similar expressions easily translated as "so what?"

But after a moment Randall's face changed in that it became blank, as though he didn't want his thoughts to be seen. He dialed a three-digit number on the house telephone and kept his eyes on his blotting pad while he waited for the connection. Ted Harris tried to look as though he knew what was going on.

"Blanes? Randall here. A private question for you. You're an authority on the company's history and so on. . . . Sir John Hammond had a son, as we all know, of course, and inherited . . . yes, also called John in the family tradition . . ."

Blanes, whoever he was, unasked must have added the middle name. Randall said, "That's what I wanted. Thank you." He put down the receiver, still looking at the blotter.

By then John was on his feet, feeling a little sick. "I am extremely sorry. It began more or less by accident. I wasn't down there in the computer room looking for anything. I was just there, trying to be . . . Anyway, it dropped into my lap. Victoria Norton dropped it. But for her I'd never have got on to it. A reason for pulling her out of the Chexbres situation. Couldn't let her risk . . ."

"What the hell—" Ted Harris began loudly.

"So"—John went doggedly on—"I pulled a fast one on you, a succession of fast ones, using my personal relationship with the chairman to let you jump to a totally wrong conclusion."

"We wanted to jump to it," Randall said. "We couldn't wait."

"Captain," Ted Harris appealed, *"what is this?"*

"From where I sit," Randall told him slowly, "it looks like the beginning of a revolution."

"I hadn't thought of it as that," John said, "but I see what

250

you mean." After defeat, retreat: he was already near the door.

"Revolution?" Ted Harris rubbed his unshapely nose in a harassed way. "I'm lost, captain, I'm going around in circles."

"Call it a palace revolution." Randall began to grin and went on grinning. "Ted, call Miss Maple and say I shan't be bothering the chairman after all."

"Somebody lend me a compass . . ."

"Shall I explain to Ted? Nobody else, unless or until you say?"

"Please." John opened the door. "I'll be back, of course. But I hope I can have Ted's help a few days longer?"

Randall unhesitatingly agreed. In that case, could Ted bring the tapes and photostats of the Lencorp files to him at 169 Brook Street.

"Who should he ask for?"

"Me," John said and got out quickly before he realized he hadn't specified which "me." But at 169 they knew both of him.

He was still a little shaken when the lift stopped at the ground floor. A thought came as a batch of people began to enter the lift, their expressions appropriate to being a few minutes late for work in a place where the passing seconds were valued as jewels. He earned black looks for pressing the subbasement button before anybody could reach the control panel, and four of them glanced meaningfully at their watches during the descent.

He wanted badly to shout at them that he was John Hammond the Seventh and everybody in the lift could take a week's holiday with pay as from *now*.

He wasn't surprised to see a pale young man at his old desk in the glass box. Nervous eyes looked up at him.

"Research?" John asked.

"N-no. I'm computers. Deputy third assistant, in a manner of speaking. You wanted Mr. Addis? He has left the company."

"I wish to God he had." John saw that the wall behind the desk was bare. "I came to take down the map of Nuristan."

"The maps—oh, yes, those. The chap from office management took them away. I could give him a ring for you."

"On no account," John said, and tried to look friendly and reassuring. "You don't mind being in this cellar?"

"Cellar?" Another week or so and the youth would have acquired sufficient self-confidence to be affronted. As it was he said on the contrary he considered himself very lucky. "You don't realize what it is, to be in Hammond and Morgan."

"I'm beginning to find out."

John left him. It had been a depressingly symbolic moment.

He called MacGregor from a coin box in the main hall.

Not only had Miss Norton telephoned twice yesterday but had finally appeared in person at White House late in the evening, with a gentleman. In MacGregor's view, a somewhat curious visit.

"I am mistaken, of course, Sir John, in having an impression of veiled threat behind it. But if I am wrong in that, there's no question of the lady's anxiety to see you. Life or death, she seemed to be saying, and finally, she, ah—offered me an inducement to facilitate a meeting with you at the earliest possible moment and gave me a number for me to telephone. I was in some difficulty . . ."

"But realizing I was busy stalling her, you accepted the inducement and sent her away happy."

"I shouldn't say happy, Sir John. I gather, sir, you are back in this country?"

John admitted it but didn't elaborate. He asked please that Fred, who would be home sometime today, should report at his convenience with the car at 169 Brook Street.

"And about Miss Norton? Do I telephone her as she asked, sir?"

John arranged to call back in a few minutes with a precise time when he should be able to meet Miss Norton at 27 Savile Row tomorrow, Wednesday, afternoon.

"At your tailor's, Sir John?"

John let this error go by as a happenstance he would be ungrateful to reject. MacGregor would now almost certainly identify 27 Savile Row as Sir John's tailor, with words to the effect that he couldn't say why Sir John should have asked Madam to meet him at his tailor's unless being a very busy man he was sometimes forced to do two things at the same time.

But whatever passed, Victoria would keep the appointment. He hadn't lately been able to feel so sure of anything.

In the orderly manner proper to an executive, he dealt with fixing other appointments before getting on with the rest of the day's work. The first he arranged himself then and there, the next he turned over to his p.a., walking in on her at 169

Brook Street with a brisk "Good morning, Rosemary," and bridged the personal gulf between them by going on in the same breath, "I'd be glad if you would ask Lord Ashworth to lunch with us tomorrow. Claridge's, or anywhere he chooses. We may want to come back here to continue our talk."

"With 'us'?"

"You recruited him into this and should be there to umpire our talk and to hear what we have to say."

"It will be rather short notice for him."

"You don't have to be told that's one of a p.a.'s natural hazards."

"Yes, Sir John."

He repressed an impulse to demonstrate another; he couldn't believe she *meant* to look so extraordinarily attractive this particular morning, but there was no questioning it. He felt a new anger beginning to simmer. All right! He had grossly deceived her. But it didn't entitle her to hold it against him forever, an intention she subtly but unmistakably expressed in an undeviating remoteness that never for a moment made her less than pleasant and amiable. John couldn't remember a more irritating thing to have to go along with.

She went into her room to call Lord Ashworth and he went upstairs to join Tom Brinkley and the paper work in which that *genuinely* pleasant and amiable man was deeply concentrated. He had found himself an assistant, unexpectedly a middle-aged lady who looked like a slightly scatty duchess— not that you could have defined the type if asked to—whom Tom Brinkley introduced as "Mrs. Shaw, one of those mathematical geniuses who would put the computer-makers out of business if there were more of her."

She held out a hand. "Most pleased, Sir John, to work with you."

He nearly kissed the hand, which would have been his mistake, not hers, and liked "work with" as being the way he wanted them to regard it. If he must have a staff, please God they should help him be as unaware of it as possible.

Mrs. Shaw knew and had used his real name. This meant that only Rosemary could have taken the initiative in deciding there was no need for its concealment within the closed circle at 169. Hating him apparently did not prevent her understanding his discomforts, sailing under false colors being not the least of them.

Work had already begun on the account sheets from Victoria's briefcase, now spread out on a large table. Mr. Brown, interpreting Sir John's wishes, had suggested they should try to trace a figure of four hundred and twenty-six thousand pounds through a maze of double entry and cross-accountancy in order to find the exact point at which it disappeared without affecting the balance of last year's final accounts in relation to the previous year's.

"We think we're on to the method used." Tom Brinkley was frowning but confident. "And that's half the battle."

The lunch with Lord Ashworth went well; it reached John's objective in nearly all respects. Again he could thank Rosemary, not only for her unobtrusive contributions to the talk but for her earlier description of the man and his instinctive attitude toward Parthessen. John found himself ready for the resistance he came up against in Ashworth's reaction to what he wanted him to do, but it was Rosemary who spotted the reason for it; one-time friendship with John's father and a present enmity toward Gordon Parthessen were not the kind of influences a man of objective judgment cared to be under. She smiled at his lordship and told him that no one should think badly of himself for giving in occasionally, even in very serious issues, to emotional prejudice. "Like Sir John here, who seems none the worse for it, would you say?"

Ashworth laughed and let himself become emotionally prejudiced, while John felt momentarily confused. Was she double-talking?

This working lunch took until just after three, but the top of Savile Row was near enough Brook Street to walk to in ten minutes, and John reached it in plenty of time to stand at the corner of Burlington Street opposite Number 27 and wait for Victoria's arrival there.

It was one of those instances when you *knew* that a particular taxi you could see all the way as it came along the street held the person you were expecting.

Or persons?

His hunch didn't include knowing whether Victoria had succeeded or failed in shedding her Frank at some moment during the previous forty-odd hours. He might have checked, of course, by calling Grosvenor Towers. If she was there, she had succeeded. But it hadn't seemed to matter one way or the other.

As the cab began to slow up, moving in to the curb, John began to cross the roadway and was within a couple of yards of it when the door opened and Victoria got out, noticeably

254

well groomed for a momentous meeting, and was too occupied with paying the fare to see him there.

His thought that she had after all escaped her husband did not last. Borrowdale was also paying a fare, that of a second cab which had drawn up ten yards or so behind hers. He looked, if anything, scruffier than ever: hatless, his hair long and stringy, his tie loose, creaseless trousers drooping over dirty shoes, he achieved the widest imaginable contrast between himself and his beautiful wife.

But there was striking similarity in their expressions, first Victoria's since she was the nearer, and then Borrowdale's a moment later as each realized that above the doorway of the squat gray building where the street number might have been was a rectangular box sign. It was made of glass and lit up from within at night to show the place was open for business every hour of the twenty-four, Sundays and public holidays included. POLICE, it said, with neat unpretentious brevity in white lettering on a blue ground.

Borrowdale's narrow eyes left it and found John Addis at the bottom of the six steps that led up to the swinging doors. Nervous, cunning eyes with a quick, foolish brain behind them.

Victoria's glance also came down from the word and rested on Sir John Hammond. A wide-eyed glance; comprehending, astute, and only a little anxious, revealing a cool, clever mind.

Borrowdale said, "Treacherous cow!" turned quickly, pulled open the door of Victoria's late cab as it was beginning to move away, tumbled awkwardly inside, dragged the door shut, and was never seen again.

Victoria took one of her deep suggestive breaths. "Johnny, you've done a lot for me, oh, such a lot, but that was the best, I think. You knew I couldn't get rid of him, so you thought of the one really effective certain-sure way. You knew Frank had been in trouble before?"

"It was a reasonable guess." He hadn't really thought about it because he hadn't lately thought about Frank.

She put an arm through his and said so much, oh so much had happened but they could go home now, at last, "to that lovely flat you found for me."

Never mind the original reason he'd found it. Who finds a lovely flat for a woman who hasn't love in his mind and is assured it's in hers too?

Her arm being in his, he didn't have to take hold of her to prevent her doing a Borrowdale. He merely tightened the

255

muscles of his own arm, gluing her to his side. He began to march her up the six steps and she cried, *"Johnny!"* in very real alarm. He told her to be quiet. "This is where you cut your losses." He had to take all her weight to get her through the swinging doors.

A very young constable on duty in the foyer looked expectantly at them.

"We have a three-thirty appointment with Mr. Smith."

"If you'd please tell the duty sergeant at the desk, sir." The policeman indicated the public hall to the right. The various businesses of several people at the long counter were being dealt with by a sergeant and two constables, giving Victoria a brief opportunity for further violently felt but muted protests. "I won't *do* this, whatever it is!"

"No option."

"What are you going to do? This Smith, who is he?

"Tell him the lot."

"No."

"—with you nodding your head at suitable moments."

"It's crazy!"

"The alternative would be crazier."

"Johnny, don't *do* this to me. You love me!" She pulled out her ace in desperation. "You can't! *I know too much!*"

He shook his head. "You did for a little while. But we're going to put that right. Now. You don't have to panic like this. Just hang on. If you're not in jail—and that goes for me too—you'll be out of this damnable business for good and all. You'll still have the penthouse. In a place like that there'll be at least two millionaires between roof and street level, so you won't even need an umbrella—"

"Johnny darling—"

"No," he said. "You're not getting *this* one. He has seen the wheels going around. No bliss without ignorance. In any case, you're too tall and raving beautiful for a small plain chap like me."

The small plain chap resisted her sudden jerk to break his hold and she gasped with pain. It must have felt like trying to get her arm out of hard-set concrete.

He moved her up to the counter, where an avuncular sergeant glanced at their affectionate contact, smiled, and said he was sorry but marrying the customers was about the only thing he couldn't do for them, so what should it be?

"Mr. Smith, please, sergeant. Three-thirty appointment."

The sergeant looked down at his clip board and stopped smiling.

"Sir John Hammond? That's right, sir." He pressed a button on an intercom and said, "C.I.D.? Visitors for the Chief Inspector are here."

"Chief Inspector . . ." Victoria's alarm was not diminished.

Between then and the moment when a plain-clothes man escorted them to the office of Detective Chief Inspector Christopher Smith, John was able to finish bringing her into the state of cooperation needed to save her from herself. To have done so sooner or in any other way would have given her time to think up some overcunning and therefore ultimately unsuccessful play to avoid it.

"Ten thousand," he said, "is only a twentieth, I know, of what you set out after. But with that and the penthouse—"

"Ten thousand?" It sounded like money, even enough money to distract her for a second from her fear of what he had trapped her into.

"Share of the Hammond and Morgan reward for bringing down Parthessen. You've all but done it. This is where you simply nod your head from time to time to confirm what I'm telling Christopher Smith—let me finish. Ten thousand and the penthouse. As good a starter as a girl could ask for? Worth a little risk, Victoria?"

"*Little* risk."

"Or," he went on, recognizing it as the tail end of her objections, "you could mark time for a while. Stay on with the computer, get your breath back. The company might even throw in a brand-new up-to-date one, no bigger than a typewriter, along with the ten thousand. Ten thousand, Victoria." Bribery, but no corruption. She was already corrupt.

"Sir John Hammond, sir." The C.I.D. man opened a door and they were inside, face to face with the law in its most dangerous form, and no less so because this particular detective chief inspector stood up behind his desk and said in a most friendly voice, "Nice to see you, John. And this is Miss Norton? Sit down and tell me what I can do for you. Does Miss Norton know you once tried to join the force? An inch and a half below minimum height. But they've brought it down one inch since then, and if you're patient I daresay they'll get rid of the remaining half."

"I'd need more than patience now."

"So it has caught up with you?"

"Hammond and Morgan has caught up with me." John

defined it for Victoria's benefit. He was wary, on all his toes, but had a brief thought why Captain Randall had reminded him of someone. Christopher Smith had something of the same bony features and eyes that nothing could be hidden from.

John wasn't going to try to hide anything but it was permissible to say, "It's a biggish thing, this. There's likely to be a point early on when you will want to stop me and remind me of my right to have my lawyer present and warn me that anything I say may be taken down and used in evidence. I will then have to shut up. I shan't want to and you won't want me to."

"You can't make a deal, John."

"I shouldn't think of it," he said ingenuously.

The chief inspector thought for a moment. "You've broken the law?"

"We" John changed the pronoun—"broke two ordinances applicable to a sudden death."

Victoria made a sound in her throat. Smith gave her a quick all-seeing glance.

"You thought you were, shall we say, morally entitled to break them in view of a pertinent situation at the time?"

"Your finger is on it," John said, "as usual."

"A big situation?"

"As big as a half-million-pound swindle, as big as causing an inquest to be held on a nonexistent suicide, as big as murder or what seems to be murder. I think if murder is finally proved it will be only and solely because we broke the ordinances."

Smith looked speculative. "Last time you seemed to know what you were talking about. If this is more than guesswork it will involve Scotland Yard homicide boys, and if the swindle took place in the city . . ."

"Yes. The City Police fraud squad. It will."

"But not my central division."

"You're a top C.I.D. officer. You'll be able to judge its worth and how it should be coordinated."

"So presumably you have evidence?"

"Documentary for the fraud in quantity but a bit sketchy. I hope this is improving. Then there are these—"

John brought out the small tape reels and put them on the desk. "I expect your technical people will have the necessary apparatus to play them back."

Smith eyed them.

"Tape isn't admissible evidence."

"I expect it has been used once or twice to suggest where to look for the sort that is."

"Once or twice," Smith admitted, going along with euphemy. He looked at the wall clock. "This will probably take quite a time?"

"With questions to clarify, quite a time."

"I suggest then—"

"No," John said sharply. "Now."

His tone added "or never." But he let his eyes flicker in Victoria's direction and again Smith was aware. He couldn't know just how very tricky she could be, but he was ready to take John's silent word for it.

"All right," he said. He instructed somebody on the intercom to see that no calls were put through until he lifted the ban, no interruptions of any kind.

There were none, and none from Smith himself even at the point John had asked him to watch out for. Now and again Victoria nodded her lovely head, a self-incrimination perhaps, but made easier by Mr. Smith's kind manner, as though he was a man who appreciated how terribly difficult the world could be for a beautiful woman. Her story of how she had let Gordon Parthessen seduce her in the cause of justice was enough to make such a nice policeman cry.

However, he managed not to, John noticed, and such tears as were shed came ultimately from Victoria. John was responsible for them. He wanted to clear up a question he had been too busy to raise earlier with her.

Was it normal for someone other than a member of the computer staff to use the office next to hers?

No.

Or for a new employee in another division to be put there so that she could keep a critical eye on him?

No.

Had Glover expected her to report adversely on John Addis?

"Expected, Johnny?"

"You know what I mean."

She didn't like this. But she admitted Glover had hinted he would be relieved to have confirmation of his own views as to John Addis's aptitude for desk work, for office routine.

"Adverse views?"

"Johnny, I didn't know who John Addis . . . I don't think

259

Boyle did either. He wouldn't have dared even for Parthessen."

"Exactly."

Smith asked John what he was getting at.

John said as he saw it, whoever had had the original thought to ease him out—cousin Herbert or Parthessen—each had a motive. They were the only people at Number One who knew who "John Addis" was and why he was there. Glover was in a key place to get him out in a way nobody would recognize as deliberate. "But also he was Parthessen's man, and the incident looks like another circumstantial proof of it."

"You call it an incident?" But "circumstantial" suited Smith. "In a case of this kind, if it *is* a case, the evidence will largely be that."

John became aware of rapidly thawing ice in Victoria's azure eyes, and was surprised. "You have nothing to weep at. Self-interest? Isn't it always? For your own reasons you did what Glover wanted, and just as blindly. As for now, Christopher Smith doesn't appear anxious to throw you into jail nor to let anyone else. We're what they call 'informants.' We can expect protection for our own crimes in helping to bring home larger ones."

But Victoria seemed uncomforted. She asked the chief inspector if she could go now please. Yes. Of course she would be available to make statements or do anything required of her in preparing a case against her seducer. She departed with eyes shielded with a wisp of lacy cambric in character with her taste in underclothes, as John remembered them, and no less deceitful.

Smith said he thought she might be weeping about something else.

"Yes?"

"Such as having you under her nose from the beginning and not seeing you."

It could be. John found himself hoping the setback wouldn't seriously inhibit her return to active ambition.

Was it his imagination or a fact that today's being the day of a Full Board meeting caused a difference from other days in the atmosphere of Number One? He felt it, or thought he did, as they came into the main hall by the front entrance from City Wall. Was Rosemary aware of it? Since her withdrawal her thoughts and feelings had been less visible to him than through a glass, darkly. They were totally obscured. Even though she seemed to be walking by his side she contrived to keep a half pace to the rear, as if to show that although she was accompanying him she was not, so to speak, with him.

Also the briefcase she carried was her own, with her initials on it, to give independence within the framework of protocol's dependence. Had he possessed a briefcase himself, he felt she would somehow have prevented his using it.

But when in response to a childish thought he led her toward the private lift she let him press the summoning button, and even watched the door open upon its pink elegance, before she suddenly balked. He said, "Go on in. You might like to see Miss Maple's expression. So should I, for that matter."

"No," she said and backed away.

"You're right, of course." He wondered why she shot him such a quick and penetrating glance. Then she was the p.a. again, although for a yard or so as she moved toward the main elevators she forgot to give him the half-pace precedence. But reaching them she was well behind him, making him go ahead of her into the next one about to ascend and already nearly full.

This time he would have had nothing to gain by trying to get closer to her. Nothing.

26

John had left telephoning Bertie until the last possible minute in order to give the request an appearance of a casual whim and no time for Bertie to find convincing excuses to refuse it.

He had listened in when Rosemary instituted the call; she correctly expected it to be filtered through Miss Maple.

"I'm speaking for Mr. Addis. Mr. Addis would like to speak to Mr. Hammond for a moment, please."

Miss Maple immediately regretted without a trace of regret in her tone that Mr. Hammond was not available to speak on the telephone.

"It really is only for a moment, Miss Maple."

"I know your voice—" Miss Maple briefly forgot to be impersonal. "Rosemary Stewart, isn't it?"

"If you'd be good enough to tell Mr. Hammond—"

"Let me remind you there's a meeting of the Full Board in half an hour. *You* should know the chairman is up to his eyes at such times. It's quite impossible. And undesirable."

Rosemary asked her tartly if she'd forgotten what had happened last time Mr. Addis was denied access to the chairman. "And this is only for two words on the telephone."

Miss Maple snorted fire but thought again.

"Attend the meeting?" Bertie repeated doubtfully when John asked permission.

"Is there anything in the constitution against it? All kinds of odds and sods will be there, won't they?"

"I don't see what conceivable interest—"

"Wouldn't it please the old girl if I can tell her I put on striped pants and did a couple of hours' stint as a businessman? I mean, if there's no chance of my being on a board or anything until Parthessen's take-over . . ."

"Shut up!" Bertie had said in a low urgent voice and total lapse of dignity.

"Sorry, old man. Hush-hush even on the blower? So you won't mind if I drift in, sit at the back with nobody knowing —or caring? You won't forget to tell the man on the gate? See you."

And now here he was, his p.a. beside him, in adjoining straight-backed but still white-leather-upholstered chairs at the back of the big conference chamber. This was as far as he could be from the great horseshoe table, where Bertie was enthroned in the high chair with Parthessen on his right and the other Hammond and Morgan directors spread out fanwise on either side in diminishing status toward the two ends. Mrs. Crayton (social services division) at one; Anderson (research division) at the other. Thereafter, at extension tables continuing down both sides, came the chairmen and directors of the subsidiary and associated organizations that made up this group. Each, like the Hammond and Morgan directors, had assistants and advisers sitting behind him so that his importance should not be in doubt; he might even need to consult them. Each was a large frog in his own, if smaller, puddle.

Rosemary, identifying them for John, had to stand up to see over the heads of the audience, itself composed of people of consequence in the Hammond and Morgan empire. The head and deputy head of every division and department in

Number One were present, and such privileged staff as might be earmarked for promotion to brassier jobs, who should benefit—indeed be uplifted—by an afternoon's foretaste of glorious responsibility to come.

Whatever difference in rank and divergence in function, everyone in the assembly had eyes and attention only for the center of the horseshoe as the source of being. John felt cozily unnoticed. And safely detached. What his p.a. felt was, of course, a secret, but he didn't think she could avoid identifying herself with his reason for being here. This, whether or not she liked it, brought her closer for the moment.

When she had described one of these occasions that time at breakfast in Lausanne, she hadn't needed to draw his attention to the flaw in the meaning of "Full Board" and the pomp and circumstance it called forth. It hid from all but the cynical—and, of course, from bystanders like herself whose little axes were too insignificant to sharpen on such a powerful grindstone—that in spite of its title, suggesting a vigorous nod in the direction of the democratic principle and majority rule, the Full Board had no more control over events, including its own decisions, than the board of Hammond and Morgan cared to allow it.

In short, this assembly could deliberate until the cows came home; it could recommend, it could pass resolutions as unanimous as the movements of a flock of birds, but it couldn't effect the buying of a postage stamp if the board didn't feel like it. Hammond and Morgan was not a public corporation answerable to public investment. Hammond and Morgan was a private company and could tell everybody to go to hell, and that included its dependencies in the group, which similarly were also private companies, every single one of them.

The chairman didn't have to bang a gavel. He simply got slowly to his feet and instantly you wished you had a pin handy to see if it was true that there really were moments when you could hear one drop.

The ladies and gentlemen were greeted with a graceful "Good afternoon" and asked to welcome, if only for this one occasion, a new face on the board, that of Lord Ashworth, who as everyone knew was senior partner in Harbord Associates. He was here in place of Mr. Stanley Ledger, who was indisposed—nothing serious, all would be happy to know.

Bertie was wrong about that. It was the most serious indisposition; not for Stanley Ledger, of course, but for Bertie himself and the board and all.

The smile with which Lord Ashworth rose and acknowledged the chairman's announcement was the smile, John confidently hoped, of a tiger, although it was difficult to see one inside the rather tubby figure in its neat dark business suit and rounded, cheerful, innocent features.

Lord Ashworth sat down and began to light a large cigar with the air of a man who had all afternoon free to enjoy it. John was reassured. His lordship was overplaying, a sign that he was properly keyed up.

The chairman declared the meeting open, asked the secretary to read the minutes of the previous one, and sat down. He rested his cheek on an elegant hand, ready to be absorbed in the proceedings—or bored, John would have liked to believe but couldn't.

Mr. Secretary, on Bertie's left, got obediently to his feet and galloped through the minutes at a good pace; even so, it took him nearly a quarter of an hour. Every paragraph began with variations on the same theme: "It was resolved that . . ." "It was decided to suggest . . ." "Mr. so-and-so drew the board's attention . . ." "It was unanimously recommended that . . ." All phrases to introduce a series of complex tangles of verbiage delivered six months ago and now fairly safe from challenge as not being a true record.

When the chairman asked formally if it was agreed that it was such, and in consequence, also the meeting wish he should sign the minutes as read, he was already putting his name to them in the large, vellum-bound book Mr. Secretary had placed in front of him.

He coughed slightly and reminded the assembly that it was his custom to reserve his chairman speech until the close, although they might feel it would be a superfluity when facts and figures spoke so eloquently for themselves. These were the subject of the next item on the agenda, to which he would now pass. Copies of the Consolidated Accounts for the year ending the fifth of April had been sent out for scrutiny at leisure—a rustle of paper swept softly through the conference chamber—and he hoped it would be the meeting's pleasure to recommend the board to pass them. But in the meantime he would ask our chief accountant, Mr. Thomson, to come forward, prepared to elucidate—through the chair of course—such points as anybody might wish to raise.

The blue-covered chunk of Consolidated Accounts held in both hands, Mr. Thomson came forward from behind, where he had been sitting at Parthessen's elbow, and found a place to stand between Parthessen's right-hand neighbor, Colonel Gregory, and the man on his left, George Fanshawe, both voting directors, Rosemary whispered. But John knew this and was more interested at the moment in noticing that Mr. Thomson, cadaverous as a bean pole, could have been given space immediately next to Parthessen without crowding even that large-built body. But he hadn't. If one regarded the two of them as closely related in the everyday affairs of the company, the visual effect was disassociative.

The chief accountant seemed to have been type-cast. Meticulous, a Scot in every bone, he looked nervous; you could have seen a guilty soul in him and been wrong. He was merely uncomfortable as the focus of attention from so many people even in this familiar ritual, always as brief as it was silent. His eyes took refuge in the nearest chandelier while he waited for the chairman to release him with the usual "Thank you, Mr. Thomson."

He missed, therefore, the warning belch of cannon, the blue cloud of cigar smoke from Lord Ashworth's mouth, through which a question shot out like a shell. Its explosion was dampened somewhat by the voice's detachment, with the result that although Mr. Thomson heard it he didn't immediately understand what it meant.

"I should like, Mr. Chairman," his lordship said, "to inquire of our chief accountant—I hope he will forgive my lack of comprehension—inquire where we should look—in which section of Statement Three on pages twelve through fourteen—should we look for the figure of four hundred and twenty-six thousand that first appears in Section Two-A of the corresponding statement for the previous year and seems nowhere accounted for?"

His lordship waved away the smoke and was seen to be holding his cigar in the other hand, inspecting it to assure himself it was burning evenly. "Anyway," he remarked conversationally, "that's what our IBM thing at Harbord Associates tells us. It had the advantage of being programmed with all three sets of accounts."

John was watching Parthessen, lolling at ease, large head against the back of the chair, eyes half-closed, hands clasped across his comfortable stomach.

You hadn't expected him to jump out of his skin, but there might have been physical evidence of shock, some sign at least of having heard and understood Lord Ashworth's little speech. For a moment his stillness was disappointing, bringing sudden doubt—the man had no reason for alarm? Then it became as significant as the most startled movement, because he was the only person in the room who had not reacted in this way or that: a jerk of head; a shift from one buttock to the other; a hand taken out of a pocket; a cough, a sigh; a craning of neck to improve a view of the board table and Lord Ashworth in particular. Even the chairman leaned forward, frowning in an effort to force the questions into perspective. He failed, and for a second or so, his distinguished features seemed blurred. He turned, as from long habit, to Parthessen next to him and said something. Parthessen came to life, but in a deliberate fashion, as though finding himself physically on uneven ground that called for care in placing his feet.

By now Mr. Thomson had automatically opened his mouth to reply and discovered he hadn't an answer. Should he have anticipated a question that related last year's accounts to *the year before that?* He stood petrified in helplessness, staring at his lordship.

The room's restlessness of the moment before had become a deep, tense silence. They saw the chairman incline his head to bring his ear closer to Parthessen, who was talking into it with emphasis but at too low a pitch for them to hear. John stole a glance at Tom Brinkley, sitting in the middle of the room, where he had been placed to be able to sense the general mood. Tom was straining his ears as hard as anyone to catch Parthessen's whispered words.

Bertie listened and nodded agreement. John did not expect Bertie to go to the extreme of saying, "Thank you, Lord Ashworth. Next item on the agenda, Mr. Secretary, please." He was smoother than that. But he nearly pulled it off. He shared, he said, Lord Ashworth's disquiet that there should be a technical error in the accounts. As regrettable as it was unfortunate. However, he was sure Lord Ashworth must agree it would save the Full Board's valuable time—there was an amount of business to get through—if the point could be referred back to the Hammond and Morgan directors; the matter came under the heading of Primary Investment, in any case.

But Lord Ashworth begged to differ. He felt the group should know what the IBM's conclusion was. A basic principle of ethics might be involved. . . .

"In effect, sir, that an investment by Hammond and Morgan of four hundred and twenty-six thousand in a firm called

266

Fording Lencorp Corporation has been written off. And the fact not mentioned. Ever or anywhere."

Bertie began to rise up in wrath, but Parthessen caught his arm, pulled him down into his chair, and whispered again, rapidly and forcefully. Bertie listened again, now scowling and tapping the table with impatient fingers. He seemed to give in. Without getting up, he cleared his throat to address the room.

"Obviously, as I said, there is some simple explanation. It certainly cannot be what he—what his lordship—the Harbord Associates' representative director—seems to be hinting—"

"Hinting?" his lordship interrupted. "How plainer do you want me to call a spade a bloody shovel?"

Bertie looked stunned; Parthessen's readily bulging eyes bulged.

"You didn't catch on, Mr. Chairman"—Lord Ashworth took in and slowly expelled a lungful of Havana to give his next words due weight—"or perhaps I expressed myself too loosely when I said *three* sets of accounts. I was talking about those of the previous year and the *two* for the year under review, particularly the first edition of them. Not this *second* edition, the one now in the hands of the meeting, the one we received at Harbord Associates. Eyewash!" He pushed aside the bound copy with contempt and slapped his hand on a less tidy collection of account sheets held together by a mere paper fastener.

"But for my money this *first* edition, predating the second by a few weeks but *not* issued, is what we should take as the true statement of the financial position. It is marked 'Draft Only' with a red rubber stamp, but I like it better than *that* thing"—he gave the bound copy a further push away from him—"because the four hundred and twenty-six thousand is here, large as life, but the grand total of funds invested is strangely short by exactly the same amount—" His lordship stopped and suggested that the chairman give the chief accountant permission to sit down before he fell down.

This drew everyone's attention not only to Mr. Thomson's swaying stance but also—as was Lord Ashworth's purpose—to the intensity and direction of his gaze. Parthessen was oblivious of it, but no one doubted to whom the draft of the accounts had been sent for clearance before issue.

Mr. Thomson stumbled back to his seat without waiting any longer for the chairman's thank you. As the scuffle of his flight died away, Parthessen's whisper reached the farthest end of the chamber. "Close it down, H.H. Close it down. *Now!*"

Again before H.H. could open his mouth Lord Ashworth was off again. He realized, ladies and gentlemen—through the chair—he begged the chairman's pardon—through the chair he wanted to say he realized the gravity of his allegation, and in tabling this first version of the Consolidated Accounts as a basis for investigation it behooved him to put a motion to the meeting, asking for a resolution to this effect, a thorough—

John saw Bertie at his best now. His voice cut off Lord Ashworth's peroration like a knife. "You are out of order, sir. But be that as it may, the group can rest assured that we do not require a resolution to urge us to do something we shall and must do in any event. A technical error. . . . Next item of business."

"Out of order?" cried his lordship plaintively. "But you yourself suggested we should ask—"

His protest was drowned in a loud murmur from the assembly that seemed to be an encouragement to his view that he couldn't be out of order in raising a point of the sort the chairman had asked should be put by anybody who felt the need. Anybody meant anybody, and that surely included Hammond and Morgan directors, even if it looked like dog eating dog.

John clearly heard Parthessen repeat his demand that H.H. should close the meeting forthwith. No one would ever know whether Bertie misheard or deliberately misunderstood. He got up, bringing silence as before by doing so, and announced that this matter was in essence and nature outside the competence of the group board to determine a proper course of action. It might be that the meeting would be asked to resume —there was a great deal of business still on the agenda—after an interval in which refreshments would be served in the adjoining room of the secretariat, while in the meantime the Hammond and Morgan board would go into closed session to discuss the situation.

Parthessen was angrily shaking his head. "Closed," not "closed session." But the mistake had gone past his or anyone's ability to recall. The Hammond and Morgan directors began to leave the table and move toward the door of the Founders' Room as the main body of the meeting, buzzing like a very disturbed hive, broke up into a collection of individuals. Each had been thrown into his own particular pother and now started to circulate in search of friends and associates with whom to discuss the drama, speculate about its results and find comfort in mutual anxiety.

The effort was general but subdued tumult. Tumult, nevertheless, John was satisfied to regard it as.

He was nearer the discreet white door of the holy of holies —and by several yards—than the foremost of those coming toward it. He was able to enter it first, his p.a. close behind him, and make for a spot as far from it as he could get, between the fireplace and the corner itself, and put himself with his back to the glazed bookcase on that side, a position from which his ejection would be difficult except by prolonged force. Who should be called upon to exert it would again be a problem for anybody proposing it. Captain Randall and his merry men, for instance, were much too busy just now.

"So far it seems to be going according to plan," he said.

"Oh yes!" Rosemary's vibrant excitement made him glance sharply at her, but of course a good p.a.'s identification with her boss's interests etcetera, which had explained away similar outbreaks, was at work in her.

"Try not to look so *pretty*," he told her. "It draws attention."

27

Miss Maple, very properly the vanguard, came through the doorway and loudly exclaimed in horror and indignation at seeing him there.

"No!" she said. "This is a *closed meeting of the board*. You will please leave immediately, Mr. Addis!"

"Sorry," John said, "I have to be here."

"The chairman's reluctance to allow you to attend the group meeting—"

"The hell with that," Rosemary interrupted, all decorum dreadfully in abeyance. "Before you sound off any more, take a look."

John was as surprised as Miss Maple was puzzled. Rosemary was pointing at an upward angle across John's chest toward the portrait above the chimney piece. Her small forefinger moved downward and, still pointing, stopped an inch or so from his left cheek.

"See, Miss Maple?"

"See what?"

But Miss Maple was staring from one face to the other and back again, from the painted to the living. She swallowed, her Adam's apple protruding with her upward glance, and an "oh" of recognition came from her open mouth.

Then Parthessen came striding in with Bertie after him, the others at his heels, Lord Ashworth bringing up the rear. The room was full. People began settling in scattered chairs or pulled up to the big writing table. Parthessen had gone straight to the chair behind it and plumped himself down.

If he saw John, his presence didn't bother him. He had other things on his mind. He launched immediately into a commanding opening.

"H.H. has been considerably shocked by Ashworth's indiscretion in raising the matter with the group board and feels he should be spared the formalities of clearing this ridiculous business out of the way. This is where I can help as deputy chairman. I'll take this meeting, H.H., but you'll have to sit in at it, I'm afraid, in case it comes to a vote."

Bertie waved a hand to indicate it was his duty to see the terrible situation through to its end, even if he didn't feel up to the strain of conducting the proceedings himself.

"Very grateful, Gordon. Please carry on." He went to his chair at the window. He had registered John's intrusion and could now deal with him as some contribution to easing his colleague's burden. " 'Closed session' means what it says, John. You must excuse us."

But John was dense. "That's all right. I expect I can stick it out."

"That isn't what I meant."

"Oh, you want me to shove off? Just when I am getting interested?" He hesitated. "Wouldn't Acantha rather hold it against us?"

Not a pair of eyes in the room but was on him, giving him a first taste of the stage fright even the least public of men must presumably have to learn early to get over.

He crossed a Rubicon by stepping a pace forward from the bookcase and said mendaciously he'd do his best not to be in the way.

In the brief silence Miss Maple saw an opportunity to trim her sails to the wind coming from a new quarter. She suggested audibly to the chairman that perhaps some of the directors didn't know, didn't realize *who* . . .

Bertie introduced him, stiffly, with uncharacteristic absence of "image" graciousness, as though a seldom-heard instinct warned him of a sudden viper in the nest.

Lord Ashworth led the handshaking, saying, well, he'd never—his old friend Johnny's boy—but of course he'd have known him anywhere. Surprising if he hadn't, after lunching, dining and talking for hours with him only yesterday. The others were more cautious about releasing affability in the playboy's direction. In short, he saw the same wariness in their faces that came over those of nine people in ten whom he met and whose lives might be affected by his mere existence. His discomfort in consequence was also familiar but easier to bear this time because he had something other than himself to think about and he was able to hold on to his main intention.

George Fanshawe, Colonel Gregory, Richard Horton, Loanis-Andrews, and so on—they had nothing to worry about, but he couldn't tell them so.

Lord Ashworth appeared to catch sight of Rosemary for the first time. "Seen you before, m'dear," he said with equal truth and mendacity. "Jock Stewart's daughter, I believe. How is the old devil? And now you're lending Sir John a hand, I suppose. Showing him his way around, eh?"

Rosemary smiled at his lordship with the falsest modesty. John hadn't ceased covertly to watch Parthessen, who had neither time nor attention to waste on this social interlude. He drew in his paunch to open the middle drawer of the writing table. The mere fact that he was sitting at it was an affront to decency—an interloper, the sneak thief in your room, turning over your things.

He found what he was looking for in the drawer, an ivory gavel, yellowish with the patina of the years. Affront became insult, and commensurate anger mounted. Stage fright faded, vanished.

The gavel hit the polished walnut.

"Have you lost all sense of proportion, gentlemen? Let's get on with it! John, I don't want to be discourteous, but this is no place for you and you're delaying us. I happen to know what's behind all this and you have my sympathy—" The cold, golden shade of Victoria Norton hovered between them.

John hesitated. "Sorry, Mr. Parthessen." He moved through an embarrassed silence toward the door. Lord Ashworth, who might have been expected to intervene, did not. John was grateful. These details hadn't been rehearsed, but his lordship realized he was building up a shock impact for the attack. But Rosemary? He hoped she wasn't thinking this apparent retreat was a last-moment loss of courage. He could feel her following behind him. He turned at the door. Her expression was confident although her fingers were crossed and held furtively against her thigh. He looked past her to Parthessen, who stared steadily at him, waiting for him to be gone. John counted three and spoke.

"It might come to a vote?"

Parthessen continued to stare at him. "This board has seldom in practice voted on any resolution. Every decision is unanimous."

"Because the distribution of shares is so weighted against the minority holders that they keep their mouths shut or fall off the band wagon."

"Somewhat crudely put."

"I'm sorry. I'm new to all this. But in a few minutes a resolution will come up that's rather different from the usual—"

"It will not come up. Good day, John."

"The boy has a point," said Lord Ashworth.

"The boy can mind his own business!"

"Isn't that precisely what he's doing?"

Parthessen swung round on him. "You've done enough damage! What would happen if we went back to those cretins out there and told them *independent* investigation had even been mooted?"

"Alarm and confusion on a national scale."

"Which is why nobody is going to propose a bloody crazy thing like an independent investigation into a trifling cock-up in accountancy that we are quite capable of sorting out for ourselves!"

John raised his voice slightly. "When Lord Ashworth puts the resolution I want to vote for it."

"You want—" Parthessen's eyes were leaving their sockets again. "You have no more right than Lord Ashworth—"

"I would have, if I were a director."

"You're not one, and in any case H.H. has your proxy."

"Who gave it him?"

Bertie lifted a hand for attention and on account of long habit got it. "Acantha Morgan, as your trustee—"

"I thought she'd stopped being my trustee?"

"We arranged—but in any case, John, you're out of line. You don't understand these things. We—"

Parthessen banged the gavel. "The meeting will come to

272

order. The board is now in session. John, the chair formally instructs you to withdraw and take the young woman with you."

Lord Ashworth didn't wait this time. "What are we thinking of? Here's a *John Hammond* with all the qualifications he needs. Does that mean nothing to you?" He looked from one to another as though he couldn't imagine what was the matter with them. "In fact, it gives me great pleasure to propose Sir John Hammond's election to this board."

"I second that motion," said Loanis-Andrews, a small man perhaps with sympathy for fellow small men but looking for reward. He got it, a quick nod from his lordship, promising great favors to come, that wasn't lost on the others. There was a chorus of "ayes" before Parthessen could ask for a show of hands. No one seeing his present expression would think of him as dear old Gordon.

"Elected unanimously," Lord Ashworth said heartily, and at once apologized to the chair. "It comes of always being in the chair myself. Thirty-two companies. I must be out of my mind. Come and sit down, John. And Miss Stewart. She'll want to take notes for you. Miss Maple will show you how, I'm sure."

Miss Maple, mindful of her new course, looked as though she'd be almost glad to engage herself in the superfluous tutelage.

"All right, all right," said Parthessen grimly. "We'll now lay this stupid business on the table. Of course I'll look into it— it's an investment-division pigeon—but I'll say straightaway if there *has* been a bad error, we've got to be extremely careful about what action we take. It would be better to lose the money and forget it than drag—"

"Good God, yes," said George Fanshawe fervently. John had so far known him only as a name. It was presumptuous in somebody like himself, half the man's age, to see him as a fool.

"In any event," Parthessen went on, "we have to be practical. Does anyone believe for a moment if there was some kind of hanky-panky innocently involving Hammond and Morgan that there's a shred of evidence still lying around after all this time?"

While they were contemplating this reasonable thought, circumstance played one of its last cards, a lovely big ace.

Bertie's communication unit emitted a tuneful but restrained buzz. Bertie frowned at it, Miss Maple gave it an annoyed

"Tch!" and picked up one of its five receivers. "I gave instructions—Oh, I see. Yes, he's here. . . . It's for you, Sir John."

John went over to her. She handed him the receiver with a reproving smile; he would have to be told, oh very tactfully, that no incoming calls except of great urgency were put through during board meetings.

Captain Randall came at once to the point. "She's here, and the secretary chap. They've brought the stuff with them."

"Is it right?"

"Seems to fit in with what we have. But I'm not qualified—"

"Get Brinkley to look at it. Call me back."

"She's asking to be paid."

"When Brinkley's satisfied, take the matter to Mr. Luke in Room One Hundred. I've already spoken to him. Fifty thousand dollars or its equivalent was the agreed price."

He put down the receiver. "Sorry about that."

In a sense he was, too. He thought of saying, "I'll never learn," to indicate a costly pay-off for another folly, but Parthessen's suspicious stare as he sat down again confirmed that the playboy act was getting rapidly out of date.

Parthessen began to say he wanted a motion passed, therefore, giving him a free hand to deal with this thing as he saw fit. John interrupted him. "Isn't there something wrong here?"

"The chair is speaking!" Parthessen snapped. "I was about to add—" And he warned the board that his ultimate view might be that, although the loss of four hundred odd thousand was something even Hammond and Morgan should not regard lightly, it could be a cheap price to avoid the destructive scandal of a public revelation of irregularity. "But I stress again, *if* there is proof of such, *this*, gentlemen, is the only sane and reasonable approach. I know H.H. and the rest of you can support it."

"May I now clear up a misunderstanding?" John asked.

"Of course," Lord Ashworth said simultaneously with Parthessen's saying, "Not yet."

John chose to hear the former. "I wasn't referring to what the chair was trying to say but to Bertie's mistaken notion that its present occupant is eligible to take it."

Of the several hushed moments of the afternoon these twenty-five words produced the most astonished silence. John dropped another rock into it before somebody spoiled the effect with an irrelevancy. "Either now or in the future," he said.

"What!" Parthessen shouted. "I don't care who you are, you—"

"Not care?" asked Lord Ashworth softly.

Bertie climbed out of his chair and made himself a tall figure of authority against the sky-filled window, prepared for one of his finest hours. He began a slow speech of devastating reproof. "John, this is an intolerable situation that even your youthful ignorance cannot condone. You will apologize immed—"

"For what?" John cut in. "*I* didn't make the board rules. *I* didn't set up the constitution that says the chairman of the voting board must be a stockholding director or represent by proxy a stockholder or stockholders who don't necessarily have to be members of the board themselves."

"The child," Parthessen remarked with a yawn, "has been doing his homework."

"Not more than I had to, I admit. But enough."

"Then know that the conditions are in order and shut up! Let your elders and betters get on with their business."

"You're a proxy holder?" John asked, looking down at the edge of the writing table.

Parthessen slapped down the gavel with a crash and called John a puppy. John said, "I move that the proxy papers under which nonstockholding directors present can vote should be tabled forthwith."

"Seconded," said Lord Ashworth with his usual promptness.

"This is sheer obstructionism for the sake of showing off!"

John shook his head. "You've put someone in the chair who isn't legally entitled to be in it."

"Gordon holds his wife's proxy and—"

"Where is it?"

"—just as apart from my own shares, I hold Acantha Morgan's proxy for hers."

"Where are they?"

"This is outrageous! Where are *what*?"

"Proxies. According to the Companies Act, section whatever it is, paragraph so-and-so, they must be in writing on forms like this—" John took the form handed to him by his p.a.—perfectly on cue—and slid it across the writing table to Lord Ashworth. "Proxy for six of my shares, sir, to put you in the voting class."

"Thank you, John."

Parthessen said loudly that this was carrying formality to

ridiculous and unnecessary lengths. As for his proxy right, it had never been questioned before.

"Well, it seems to be now," Lord Ashworth remarked. "And in your case as deputy chairman," he added mildly, "it's rather important, don't you think, to establish a firm claim to eligibility?"

"This is bloody nonsense! I've held my wife's proxy for the last ten years—"

"Fine. Just put it on the table."

Parthessen swore under his breath. "This is a snide trick to get me out of the chair! You know my wife's abroad and likely as not omitted to sign a proxy form before she left!"

Bertie came ingeniously to his rescue. "Miss Maple, find me a proxy form, please. This is quite simple. I will assign Mr. Parthessen *my* vote on fifteen shares." He sat down and while he waited for Miss Maple to produce the form, he got back to his finest hour with oil of charm to pour on the troubled waters. "I ask you, Gordon—gentlemen, all of you—to overlook John's gaucherie. He will learn, if his patience equals his zeal and allows him to remain one of us— Thank you, Miss Maple—" He signed his name. "Will learn that we are a small but close-knit group of—we have to face it—powerful men, who in the very nature of their power, must take each other on trust and—"

"—and so let nearly half a million pounds fall illicitly into the pockets of the trustworthy," Lord Ashworth commented. "However, where's Acantha Morgan's proxy?"

Bertie raised an eyebrow at his p.a.

"It wasn't in the mail this morning, sir, as I was expecting it to be."

"You sent it for signature as usual?"

"Of course, Mr. Hammond. Last week." Miss Maple was in torture.

He supposed she had a good reason for not mentioning this slip-up?

Miss Maple went red. It hadn't seemed important. It had happened before and no one had worried. A formality . . .

Bertie frowned. The whole afternoon was being wasted. "Miss Maple, get me Mrs. Morgan on the phone. I presume her oral proxy will suffice?" He looked down his fine nose at Lord Ashworth: disagreement would be *lèse majesté*.

Miss Maple was addressing the blunt end of a pencil to a telephone dial before John decided that Bertie's peremptory

276

refusal to listen to him wasn't her fault. "Mrs. Morgan is away from home," he said.

Parthessen wanted to know how the devil he knew that, to which John replied it would be a bit odd if he didn't, since it was his home too.

Bertie gestured to Miss Maple to carry through his instructions. She spoke to MacGregor briefly, put down the receiver and achieved a minor bombshell all her own. "Mrs. Morgan is in Canada, sir."

"*Canada?*" Parthessen's voice struck an octave higher than his normal, mellifluous baritone. "My wife also is in Canada. . . . I smell conspiracy. . . . Get me Montreal, Miss Maple. The Regius Hotel. Priority person-to-person, either or both ladies, preferably both."

Miss Maple raised her eyebrows at this direct order from someone other than her principal, but John saw Bertie's slight nod to her. He left his window chair and came to the table saying, "Gordon, I think I should take an active part in these proceedings after all, but you keep the chair, of course. I'll sit here."

How true, it struck John later, that small events can change the course of a man's life as profoundly as any of the large. If at that juncture Bertie had asked Rosemary for her chair in another way—a gesture of request in an outward turn of his white hand, for instance, or a smile saying, you don't mind?— John might have kept to the decision made earlier with Lord Ashworth to save Bertie's face as best they could.

But Bertie chose merely to snap his fingers at her.

She gave him her chair and stood behind John, who was counting ten to himself, slowly. By the time he'd done this, Bertie had drawn the chair up to the table next to John himself—as though to control him?—and was authoritatively suggesting that while they waited for disposal of this hairsplitting proxy question, the board should take the item on the agenda it would have come to first, if attention to the agenda hadn't been frivolously diverted. "Formal ratification and signing of the Conway Plastics contracts and agreements. Eh, Mr. Chairman?"

"Yes indeed, H.H."

Lord Ashworth's oar was ready for putting in again. "Disagree. Ratification of a major deal is as much a matter for a formal vote as the question of whether or not to have an independent investigation into a barefaced, impudent fraud."

"Oh yes?" Parthessen snarled. "And in my view his lordship

277

should try a little simple arithmetic in the matter of a board vote on *anything* and ask himself how does his suddenly acquired six-share vote plus what is left of John Hammond's thirty per cent—assuming he's in your pocket—stand up to the votes of the rest of the board, representing the balance of the hundred per cent of stock, who aren't such fools as to vote for motions that will either discredit them or deny them the profits of their industry?"

The communications unit buzzed once in its quiet, superior way and put the period mark to Gordon Parthessen's last speech as deputy chairman of Hammond and Morgan.

"That will be Montreal," he said violently and viciously. "This will settle it!"

It wasn't Montreal but it did settle it.

"For you again, Sir John—" Miss Maple held out a coral-red receiver.

John glanced over his shoulder to his p.a. "Would you take it, please?"

"Oh for God's sake!" Parthessen exploded. "This is a farce!"

No one else seemed to think so; they didn't watch Rosemary cross to the telephone but they knew they had to listen. There wasn't much to hear. "P.a. to Sir John Hammond . . ." She paused. "Thank you." She returned to her place. "I'm asked to tell you, Sir John, it's all right and they're going ahead."

Parthessen sighed elaborately. "How nice. Now perhaps Miss Maple can hurry up that call."

John said, "You won't reach them."

"Oh no?"

"They checked out of the Regius on Monday afternoon."

"Oh yes?"

"They've gone on a trip."

"They have? Since you seem to be this afternoon's prize bloody know-all"—Parthessen's sneers were revealing—"you can tell us, I daresay, just why my wife should choose to go off on a trip without letting *me* know?"

"Perhaps to get away from the telephone."

"Go on, please."

John put out his hand for a second document from his p.a.'s briefcase. She gave it to him.

"It may be Mrs. Parthessen didn't want to have to go into explanations about *this*, feeling it's an explanation in itself." He laid the paper in front of Bertie and added that it was a

278

wire-service copy of the original, which was on its way by express airmail.

"Let me see that!" Parthessen reached across the table for it but Bertie picked it up in order to finish reading it.

His comment was less than understatement. "Dear me," he said, and gave it to Parthessen, who read it and sat very still under a battering of breathless curiosity.

"No . . . she can't do this . . . it's illegal!"

"Do what?" somebody asked.

"Sold her shares to *him!*" He glared at John.

Bertie, shaken under his calm, was perhaps beginning to realize he might have to look for a new right-hand man. He pushed the receipt across. "I think, Gordon, the fifty thousand dollars was for something else."

"Yes," John said, "something else. I'd like to explain."

"Save your breath!" Parthessen cut him short with the gavel. "I ask the board to vote on the two motions, the first that we hand over the Consolidated Accounts mix-up to independent investigation; the alternative, that it be left to me to sort out. But I'll remind you all that the controlling vote position is unchanged. In exerting it we shall be acting, as always, for the best."

"Whose best?" Lord Ashworth was drawing a fresh brown cigar from black crocodile trimmed with gold.

"No more"—Parthessen rounded on him—"from *you!* Or would *you* like to indulge bad taste further by continuing to challenge H.H.'s proxies on a technical formality?"

"If I did"—the cigar was minutely inspected—"I'd say H.H. has become so accustomed to regarding Mrs. Morgan's twenty-three per cent, and through her Hammond trusteeship a further thirty, as his own, that he has forgotten the true state of representation. Otherwise, how did he come to sign a proxy in your favor a moment ago for one more share than he *possesses?*"

Parthessen said "Ha!" and looked grimly around the table. "Just so. Roughshod over the way we conduct our great business while he fools with a damned cigar! Very well! You know what I'm going to do? This meeting stands adjourned until such time as the formal proxies can be tabled! And they will be! We shall contact my wife and Mrs. Morgan and put this noble lord and his vassal, this ignorant young—" He stopped, the hypnotizer hypnotized for once by the deliberate way the ignorant young whatever took the final paper from his p.a. and again put it in front of Bertie, who picked it up

279

and scanned it anxiously, the rank and file watching him, trying to read through his eyes.

"Christ!" Bertie's voice came through a throat closed by shock. He dropped the paper; Parthessen lunged across the table and grabbed it.

John didn't wait for him to digest it. He said briskly that when the board had been properly reconstituted to exclude the nonstockholder at present in the chair, he would second Lord Ashworth's motion for an independent inquiry.

"Backed by a vote," his lordship murmured to his cigar, "of fifty-nine per cent of the stock without calling on any other board member for support."

"Deed of gift!" Parthessen shouted and flung the document from him. "I don't believe a word of it! H.H., you won't let her get away with this! D'you hear me? You'll sue the bitch from here to doomsday!"

"Doomsday," John said, "is about it."

"So it is," Lord Ashworth agreed. "The boy's on the ball, you know. Fifty thousand dollars for the rest of the documentary evidence—cheap, I'd call it. I gather, John, you are advised that it fills the gaps?"

"It fills the gaps. Mary Wetherfield kept her side of the bargain."

Several pennies dropped simultaneously in Parthessen's brain, causing him to stand up so suddenly that his chair fell over. He strode around the writing table and stood behind John, a towering volcano of vengeful rage.

"I'll get you for this!" he shouted. "I'll get you!"

John sank his head protectively between his shoulders as though lumps of rock were about to fall on him. Confused sounds of voices clamoring for peace and order made him raise his own to be sure Parthessen heard it.

"Get me, sir? But how? Send Tankerton after me with a knife again? He's not available. Slip me a handful of Soneryls? Have you any left after feeding Boyle Glover with them when he was drunk?"

John chanced an upward glance at the huge Nemesis, and was startled, thinking he must have overdone the shock treatment.

The crimson moonface had a purple tinge; an opening barrage of obscenities stopped abruptly in a choking sound and the great body slid to the floor, its hands fluttering like white moths at its own throat.

280

Someone—it sounded like Colonel Gregory—roared "Give up, give up!"

But surely Parthessen had given up? Then John realized what the Colonel meant. Rosemary had her heel in the small of Parthessen's back, the ends of his silver-gray tie were in her small fists and she was pulling on them with all her strength.

John shouted to her to stop it! Perhaps she recognized the voice of the master. She dropped the tie ends and Parthessen was saved from a terminal throttling.

The room now seemed crowded to bursting. Apart from Randall and Ted together lugging Parthessen to his feet like a half-empty sack, Christopher Smith was there and the two other plain-clothes policemen: Superintendent Fuller, the city fraud-squad man, and Scotland Yard's detective chief inspector Carling.

"*Out!*" Lord Ashworth was urging. "Everybody *out!*"

He also told the faces clustering in the doorway that the meeting of the Full Board would be resumed as soon as this tiresome disturbance had been resolved, if they'd please go back to their seats. "Mr. Harris, these are your matches, I believe."

At last the door was closed and John sat down at the table again for as long as was necessary to suggest that the board's best hope for cushioning the aftereffects of the crisis would be to accept Lord Ashworth's generous offer to take over chairmanship of Hammond and Morgan.

The board was no longer able to register shock. It listened in numbed paralysis while he explained that in every sane view, Lord Ashworth was the greatest expert in the country on company reorganization. In this instance he might advise forming a publicly owned corporation or alternatively restoring autonomy to the subsidiaries, a course that appealed to him personally.

The position of the present chairman was difficult, they would all agree, if only because he had been extremely unfortunate in his choice of his second in command. However, in resigning he would not necessarily cease to be a member of the board, if he felt he could still serve the company usefully. . . .

John heard himself droning on as pompously as any of them, and stopped. He had said everything there was to say

281

and since no one was prepared to dispute the common sense concealed in it—or rather the might of his overwhelming vote —he got up and asked Miss Maple for the key of the flat glass case on the wall that held the Founders' Declaration.

Miss Maple, in no better condition than anybody else, was near the end of her tether. She did not burst into tears but she was gulping.

The glass case hadn't a key, she explained, because it was hermetically sealed against dust and insects and whatever else might be deleterious to an ancient piece of paper.

"But not against neglect," John said. He took the gavel he had picked up from the floor and smashed the glass. He detached the paper from the mount to which it was attached behind its corners, and handed it to his p.a.

She put the declaration tenderly in her briefcase. Bertie, still dazed, his long-enjoyed reign at an end, was able to react automatically in its lost manner; he wanted to know what John thought he was doing.

John didn't answer. He left the room with his p.a. and as he shut the door heard Lord Ashworth answer for him. "I rather think he's going to start a merchant bank."

In the next moment John found himself giving another indication of that intention. Philip Conway was standing there with a most anxious expression, a man whose future had been put in greater jeopardy by the events of the afternoon than any in the huge room, waiting on tenterhooks for the outcome.

He looked dumbly at John, and John nodded and asked if tomorrow morning, ten o'clock at 169 Brook Street, would be convenient for a further talk along the lines of that last Friday. "Three hundred thousand, a straight loan at seven and a half, no share issue, no strings?"

"Oh my God, yes," Conway said under his breath.

Aware of what felt like a thousand eyes fixed on him, John shied away, a reaction his p.a. noticed and took steps about. She made a sign and he followed her quickly to the mural-painted wall on the right, where she pressed the lower button of an eighteenth-century blue waistcoat worn by an early client of the company; the gentleman next to him slid away into the wall to reveal the quilted white interior of the chairman's private elevator.

The next moment they were inside it and the door slid shut as she touched the button marked G. His stomach told him they were in a downward movement but his more subtle senses were in greater discomfort because she was inescapable so near him. To cover having to be severe with them he was severe with her.

"You nearly killed him."

"And you"—she retorted—"you just sat there like a dummy! You bang people about when you don't have to and then when it's really necessary you act as if you didn't know how. He could have killed you!"

His heart jumped a little. This wasn't the way a p.a. should talk to her master.

"Before we get any angrier," he said, "I want you to know how sorry I am."

She looked down and said nothing, by which he knew she understood he wasn't being sorry for having left it to her to nearly kill Parthessen, but because he should have told her he was John Hammond before or at least immediately after they . . .

"The truth is, I was a coward. I dared not."

This could also have applied to his not turning violently on Parthessen, but again she understood. Her face remained averted.

"Ninety-nine times out of a hundred," he said, "when people discovered who I am they look at me as though I'm either a dehumanized freak or the national gold reserve."

"You thought I was like one of those—" Her head came up and the fire of scorn flashed in her eyes.

"No, *no!*" he said loudly. "I didn't think anything of the kind. It was automatic cowardice *from fear of losing you!*"

"Oh," she said, and nodded. "That did occur to me."

"And it also occurred to you that you knew perfectly well who I was before Fred Ross let it out how you were at White House—"

"I almost guessed the day you recited the Founders' piece. You looked like somebody I knew, but things happened rather fast and I didn't catch up with myself over it until today, when you were sitting there under the portrait."

"You very nearly walked out on me."

"I stayed because I believed what I wanted to believe," she said.

"Which was?"

"That you hadn't told me because, as you've just said, you were afraid . . ."

"As I still am."

"Is it a very strong feeling?"

283

He looked at her, and she asked how long did he think it would last?

"How do I know?" he said almost irritably. "I've never had it before."

She said, "Oh," again, this time as the most noncommittal sound he'd ever heard.

"But I'm aware," he told her stiffly, "that it's a feeling with signs of permanency. I won't ask you to marry me because you'd refuse because your father has properly brought you up to believe inherited money is the cursingest of all evils."

She nodded. "So he did. And one way or another you've been acting all along as though you believed it too. So we're square on that, anyway. You mean," she added conversationally, "you're asking me to be your mistress?" Her large brown eyes regarded him thoughtfully and he persuaded himself they were no less warm than usual.

At this obviously crucial moment she suddenly realized that although the elevator had started down to the ground floor appreciable minutes ago, it hadn't yet arrived there.

"Did you press the red button?" she asked in a controlled voice.

"The red button?" He sounded as innocent as he knew how.

"It's not the 'stop' button, if that's what you thought."

"No?"

"It's the 'emergency' one." She glanced at the indicator panel. "You've stopped us between floors all right, but you've also set off the security alarm bell in Captain Randall's office, to say nothing of those in the foyers of twenty-one floors. And of course in the basement and subbasements."

"What happens next?"

"Everything else stops too. Everything." Except the guards on street level, who would rush to close and lock all doors so that nobody could get out or into the building.

It was his turn to say, "Oh," but they laughed together at the same and precise moment. "And what happens to us?" he asked.

"We wait patiently until somebody—" A muffled telephone bell began to ring, muffled yet seeming only inches from them. "Whatever is that?"

"Something about this place you don't know?" He traced the sound to a small panel in the quilting and opened it on a white telephone. He handed her the receiver.

"P.a. to Sir John Hammond . . . yes, Ted. . . . No, nothing like that. Inadvertently Sir John pressed—yes, the red one . . . thank you, but I promise you nothing's wrong, nothing at all . . . you'll *what?* Sorry, I didn't get the word 'activate.' Thank you."

She put back the receiver. "They're going to 'activate the release,' which means we can press the ground-floor button as if nothing had happened."

"But it has, hasn't it?"

She agreed softly that it had.

"In that case which floor is office management?"

She told him the twelfth, but why?

"They've appropriated a map of mine."

"Are you going somewhere?"

"We are going somewhere Monday afternoon, if not sooner."

"Sooner would be better." She smiled at him with all her heart in her eyes. "What about 169 Brook Street and the new merchant bank?"

"Later, later. Conway Plastics will be enough for the moment. You wouldn't want us to run before we can walk."

"I don't know that climbing is the answer."

"I think you and I between us are beginning to know some of the answers."

Months later Ted Harris nearly found himself in bad odor with the boss as being suspected of starting the rumor about Acantha N. Hammond having been conceived in the chairman's private elevator at Number One City Wall. Ted was quite sure he had never actually put the thought into words.

He would have been wrong anyway. A clue to the real story could have been found in the child's middle name, Nuristan, which mayn't have been a girl's name in the first place but certainly sounded like one.

285

Clip and Mail This Special Shipping Label and...

Let these Get-Ahead books help you write better, read faster, speak more effectively!

Here's an unusual opportunity for everyone who is determined to get ahead in business, socially or at school. Just print your name and address on the special shipping label printed on the opposite page. Clip it out and mail it together with the coupon below. We will paste your label on a package containing six valuable get-ahead books jam-packed with the powerful ideas, practical helps and short-cut steps you need for improving your writing, reading and speaking skills right now. These books cost $26.30 in their original hard-covers. Now, they're yours for only $3.95 in practical paperbacks. Here's a brief glimpse of what you get:

(1) Better Writing
Shows how to get your thoughts on paper easily, quickly, more clearly and forcefully.

(2) Faster Reading
Proven-successful ways to increase your reading speed and help you understand and remember more.

(3) Speaking Effectively
Tested ways to improve your English, sharpen your speaking skills, sway an audience, add power to talks.

(4) Synonyms & Antonyms Dictionary
Provides exact words you need to express your written and spoken thoughts. Easy to use.

(5) Increase Your Vocabulary
How to expand your vocabulary quickly. 30-day new-word-mastery technique.

(6) Desk Dictionary
632 pages of clear, complete, up-to-date definitions, pronunciations, usages, origins of words. Illustrated.

MAIL THIS COUPON WITH SHIPPING LABEL NOW

FREE TRIAL OFFER

Popular Library, 445-01345-075
355 Lexington Avenue,
New York, N.Y. 10017

Send me postpaid, all six get-ahead books, in handy desk-top slip case. I'm enclosing $3.95 and, if not fully satisfied, I may return the books in good condition within 10 days for a full refund.

Name_____

Address_____

City_____

State_____ Zip_____

Be sure to enclose shipping label with coupon